# TRUST IN∞MINE

## PART I - PART II - PART III

# SAN LURO

*For Joe -*
*your 19th century entrepreneurial*
*spirit continues to live on*

# CONTENTS

## PART I

## PART II

# PART III

# PART I

# PROLOGUE

*1839 Newport Rising, Wales*

Panicked men bore down on him, their screams soaring over his head and dissipating into the darkening night. He barrelled through the surging press of bodies, stumbled on, staring into the shadows when he could.

*Is that her? Not her. Is that my wife? Not her, not her. Move on. Move.*

A razor-sharp sting peeled open his scalp, his vision blurred. He swiped his eyes and blood poured into his mouth, coppery and hot. He spat at the mob, spat to breathe. His son—where's Jac? Twisting to look behind, he bellowed as the mob pummelled into him, throwing savage blows. 'Jac.'

'Here, Da,' a shrill voice called. A small, stripling body bumped alongside, grabbed his shirt and held on. His boy, Jac, dark haired like he was, had wide blue eyes like his mother. His boy, safe with him.

'*Lilpah.*'

'Here, Da, behind ye,' she shouted. Lilpah with her pale ginger hair, her blue eyes, bright and burning. She was gangly, lean from hunger.

Ishmael Owen reached around as he lumbered over the cobblestones. A cold, damp hand thrust into his grip. His girl was safe, with him.

'We'll find Mam,' the boy yelled and jumped, ducked around a stranger's flailing arm. Another big body lurched towards him. He sidestepped, light and nimble as a dancer, and the man stumbled past him.

Ishmael tugged Lilpah. Jac kept apace, surging ahead, and shouting at the top of his lungs until he pitched over a solid sack in the middle of the street. Squawking a yelp he fell, all four limbs splayed.

Howls erupted. Running men tripped and staggered around the boy who tried desperately to scramble up. Ishmael ploughed into his son, down onto his knees. Lilpah reeled wildly over them, tumbling raggedly, and her breath grunted out of her. '*Da.*'

Blood still blurred his sight. Hunched over, his head bent, Ishmael thrust out an arm to fend away more flailing bodies. The mob parted around his family, a crumpled island in its wake. He squinted, wiped his eyes. Blinked, and found horror on Jac's face, fear and revulsion as the lad stared at the sack beneath him. In the fading light of the dying torches, the boy clung to him in terror.

Ishmael gut clenched cold. He knew what he would see. He knew. He looked down. Silence filled him. Silence, as if he were deaf. As if the world had lost all sound.

*Yellow hair. No face.*

Wynny. His Wynny. Her face. His Wynny's face was gone.

Lil's thin voice keened, a worm that wended into his head. Then from deep within him, a wounded bullock roared. Pain crushed his chest. He stared down at what had been his wife then swung away from her battered body.

Lilpah crawled in the bloodied puddle, edging her way to her mother's body. Gore and mud mingled on her threadbare shift and her bare legs. Her knees scraped over the cobblestones. She reached out and snatched at her mother's neck, came away with a bloody string and a dangle of wood. Her mother's love spoon, carved for her by Ishmael as he courted her, a companion of the one he carried around his neck. She heard Ishmael's breath shorten. He hawked, and his eyes glazed red like those of a cornered fox.

Lilpah saw a terrible madness in him and shrieked, 'Jac, get Da's spoon.'

Jac leapt. Ishmael felt a stinging snap as something jerked from around his neck. He flung around and tossed the boy aside like a handful of hay. His stomach surged up, spewed out its meagre contents and black lung gobs came with it, splattering in the blood leaking all around him.

He staggered to his feet, knees shaking and as he stepped over Wynny, Lil's keening wail began again. She was on her knees over her mother, holding her belly, her anguish. He pushed past his daughter and looked about.

*There.* Against that ragged brick doorway, not ten yards from Wynny, two government men cowered. Above them, the flame from a scrap of tallow stuffed into a hollow, shed low light. They crouched, watching the stampede of fools and cowards, and others of their own.

Ishmael lumbered towards them.

One man's stare filled with fear. 'You're a mad man,' he shouted, and waved the useless gun by the barrel, its bloody butt glistening.

*The cringing bastard is afraid.*

*My Wynny.*

The roaring bullock filled his head again. Ishmael Owen charged, his life damned forever after.

*

'Who speaks for this man?' Magistrate Wortley said and looked up a moment towards the dock. He was a grey complexioned, hollow-cheeked Englishman whose stately robes, once well-fitted, now slid loosely on his shoulders. Interested in the dirt he'd picked out of his nostril, he studied it, then flicked it off his fingers. He sniffed. 'Well?'

'Alun Brice.' Standing nervously behind the rail, the thickset man held his cap in hand. His face and neck had been wiped clean, but a stripe of grime ringed his collar. He was thumped in the shoulder from behind. 'Your Worship.'

The gallery snickered.

'Alun Brice. So, you'd speak for the prisoner?' A hand waved towards the man barely upright between his captors. His face was streaked with soot and dried blood, and his hands and feet were shackled. Ragged clothes hung from his frame. 'The prisoner who crushed to death not one but two of the Queen's own men. How is it any God-fearing man would speak for such an animal?'

Alun bared his teeth. 'He weren't no animal before they stomped on 'is wife's face, clobbered her with the butt of a rifle and murdered her.'

The press of bodies surged forward, and the ancient timbers of the benches and rails creaked and squealed. Officers of the court manhandled the throng back to order.

'Murdered her, eh?' Wortley smiled, his mouth missing teeth. 'You are accusing someone, Alun Brice?'

Alun lost some of his ire at that. He took his time as he stared from face to face around the room. Bodies jostled. Some to get a better look at him, and others perhaps to hide. 'Too dark to see.' He fidgeted under the gaze of the gallery.

'Of course. We wouldn't want you falsely accusing anyone.' The magistrate swept his glance over his comrades alongside. 'I think we should move—'

'He are a God-fearin' man.' Alun raised his voice, the shake in it strong and urgent. 'He were quiet, hardworkin', never missed a day down the mines. He helped any poor body needin' it. He worked more shifts than others to help a sickly one—'

'Oh. A real saint by the sounds.' With a sweep of Wortley's hand at a court officer, Alun Brice was shoved from the dock. 'Moving on.'

Alun braced himself. 'He got children,' he called stoutly.

The magistrate's eyes popped. 'He's got children, is it? Didn't think about them when he bashed … what was his name again?' He leaned down to his bailiff. '… Dunstan, did he? Or what was the other …?' He leaned over again and when his bailiff whispered, he shrugged, '…the other poor fellow.'

Ishmael caught Alun's look, then his own gaze darted around until it settled on a sturdy post holding up the gallery floor. There was young Jac, and Lilpah. The girl's stare was first on the magistrate and then on the others. The black-haired boy clung to his sister, his luminous blue eyes wet, his face contorted with silent weeping. The boy would not dare weep aloud.

The magistrate conferred with a gentleman on his right, the exchange inaudible over the murmuring, shuffling crowd. Wortley looked up once or twice as if to check his courtroom. Then he straightened in his seat. 'Alun Brice. Stand back in the dock.'

All heads turned in Alun's direction. A hush descended. He stood back in the dock, taller. He set his mouth, trying to be brave but fear was trickling down his spine.

'Where are these children?'

Alun blinked. His eyes met those of the magistrate who raised his eyebrows and tilted his head in a query. The man alongside Wortley sat up, his interest awakened.

'Well?' Wortley motioned to a bailiff who stood alongside Ishmael.

Ishmael froze. He could feel Alun's torment. Did his gut creep and his bowels loosen? Alun was only hoping for mercy for Ishmael's children—

'I am here,' a thin girlish voice rang out through the courtroom.

'No,' Alun breathed, not looking at Lilpah. He stared back at the magistrate, a look of horror on his face. Then another voice was heard, a voice that gave way to a squeak.

'And I am 'ere.'

Ishmael grunted in the dock.

Bodies bumped and huddled, trying to hide the children, herding them back into the crowd until Lilpah thrust out, her pale wide-eyed stare on the magistrate, only a fleeting glance towards the man alongside Wortley. Her brother inched after her.

Ishmael sagged. Defeat was stark in his reddened eyes.

Wortley shuffled on his buttocks and sat back in his seat. 'Look what's come forward. I am astonished. But you must wonder at the intelligence of these pitiful folk. One would think their offspring to be wilier, to have scurried off. Would you look at these scrawny Welsh puppets, Sir Hugh? Just offering themselves up, trusting in our young Queen's justice system.'

'Indeed.' Sir Hugh Rigg, seated beside the magistrate, leaned forward. Some would say he was a handsome man, tall at five-foot-ten, well fed, but not fat. Strong tapered fingers tapped the bench top, and there was a breadth to his chest under the waistcoat and cravat. His intense brown eyes narrowed on his prey, his gaze falling on the young girl. His mouth took a cruel twist. Some said that it was just his natural look. Today it was pronounced, turning his features from handsome to ugly.

The magistrate addressed Ishmael Owen. 'I have the perfect punishment for the murderer of two of the Queen's men,' he began. 'And it is this.' He waited for the gallery's murmurs to subside. He glanced a moment at Sir Hugh, who nodded. 'Your children, your innocent babes in this pathetic, ridiculous skirmish intended to usurp authority, will be taken to Sir Hugh's house, Rigg Manor, at Rogerstone.'

A cry went up, torn from the collective at the horror of the children's fate. No child came out of the terrible Rigg house alive. The crowd heaved towards the bench but the line of officers, struggling at the rails, held it back. The magistrate's men grabbed the children and bustled them out a heavy door behind the Sirs.

Jac's yells echoed beyond the room. '*Da! Da! Da!*'

Ishmael's torment caught in his throat, and the suffering wrenched his mouth until his lips bled again. His body hung between his captors; his legs wouldn't hold him. The agony in his heart tore his voice away. He barely heard the magistrate.

'And on the morrow, you will be hanged until dead.'

# CHAPTER ONE

*Rigg Manor, Wales*

Lilpah grabbed hold of Jac and tugged hard. His skinny body slithered the rest of the way through the hole in the crumbled, damp-ridden stone wall.

He was soaked through. It was raining again, and he'd had to crawl through a puddle. Grunting a little—he knew not to cry out—he plopped to the dank ground inside their cell. Besides, his lips were too sore and split with the cold to make a noise. Better to keep his mouth closed.

'Did you get some?' Lil held her breath.

He opened his fist. A tiny ball of twine slowly unfurled, as if glad to be freed from the grimy palm.

Lilpah squeezed his shoulder. 'Good lad.' She peered at it in the dim light then she turned and pushed the loose rocks back into the hole in the wall. Dusting her hands off, she ignored the smarting scrapes on her knuckles. 'Can you stand yet?'

Jac nodded and swiped a forearm over his face. He pressed up to his knees, and then got to his feet.

'Good.'

As he watched her, Lil lifted the hem of his shirt and eased out the wooden spoon he'd snatched from Da's neck. 'Stand still a moment while I fix this.' She took the twine and knotted it at one end. Then she poked the other end through the open circlet of the carved spoon. The rest of the new twine she plaited with the two remaining original strands. When done, she secured the end with another knot, dragging it tightly with her teeth to make sure it was fastened.

'There. These spoons are all we have left of Mam and Da,' she whispered.

'I know.' Just for a moment Jac's throat tightened but he didn't want to cry, knew he shouldn't for fear his jailers would hear. He sucked in a breath to hold it back.

Lil pressed his hand, then tapped his forearm twice, lightly, a soothing signal he trusted. 'Feel the spoons, Jac, they're part of our custom. A man, our pa, gives to his woman, our mam. He made them for her long before we came.'

Jac nodded, reached out and stroked his spoon, only as big as his hand. Intricately carved with meticulous care, he imagined their father transforming the sturdy twigs into his declaration of love. Both spoons were fine and smooth to the touch, made from a sycamore tree, he'd been told. An eyelet for string to go through to hang the spoon around a neck, or for a nail to attach a carving to a wall. Their father had fashioned a lock in one, a key in the other. The timber had been carefully chipped and notched and smoothed to resemble wooden twine that wound around both shanks and down to the bowl of the spoon, which was as deep as the tip of Jac's little finger. It signalled abundance.

Lil held the spoon for a second longer then tucked it back

inside his short hem. Retying the string holding the ragged pieces together, she said, 'Soon we'll have to find more twine, so I can fashion a weave into these fraying pieces to keep the spoon safe.' She tugged gently on the hem of his shirt, pulled it lower. 'This thing won't cover yer knobbly knees. Even with the poorest of vittles, yer growin', and yer shirt canna keep up.'

Jac shouldn't steal another shirt. Too dangerous. He'd be thrashed to death for much less, for as sure as he breathed, it would be noticed in an instant.

'What about your spoon?' he whispered.

'Mine's all right.' She hugged him to her and withdrew her own carving, the one she'd grabbed from her dead mother's neck. 'See?'

Together they peered at the tightly plaited woollen yarn attached to the wooden carving.

Lilpah tucked it back under her shirt. She slipped it further down into a slim pocket she'd secured inside her own shirt hem. Jac knew it never came off. Even when they took her away and—

Heavy footsteps sounded. 'They're coming again.' Jac's whisper was hushed and fearful.

Muffled voices and laughter came ahead of them of the footfalls, winding eerily down the long hallway to float above their cell.

'It's not my turn today.' Lilpah hugged him tighter. 'Let's get into our little ball and they'll go right past.'

Jac tucked himself deeper into her embrace and the little warmth between them gave him hope. 'We will not be without hope,' Lil had said when they first came here, 'even when they separate us.'

Even when he believed he could hear her screaming for him. *Even when—*

Jac held his breath. Lil was there but he was still scared.

'Sweet Jesus,' she whispered, and gripped him tightly. 'They're not moving past the door.'

His stomach curled, and his fear was great, but he had to be brave, like Lil.

The turnkey grated loudly in the silence and the door swung open. 'You two.'

Jac stared at the hulking figure stooped in the doorway. The light behind only showed a hooded thing; it was Hogsbreath, he could tell because of his crackly voice. This one was named for his stench.

Jac was in Lil's fierce grasp, but his skinny arms came out and held her tight. 'I don't wanna go, Lil. It hurts too much.'

'I know but be strong to stay alive,' she breathed, tapping his arm, halting his wail.

'Get up where I can see yer.'

They struggled to their feet, clutched together. 'It's not our turn,' Jac whimpered.

His desperate cry was barely a gasp against her cheek. Lil tapped him again for silence and they shuffled to the foot of the step.

Hogsbreath stood upright, hands on hips. 'Good to see yer got on yer Sundee best. Yer both to git up to the kitchen with me.'

The blast of death-breath hit Jac squarely in the face and he edged away, clinging to Lil's side.

'Git.' Hogsbreath shoved them ahead of him through the doorway and into the long corridor.

Many times before now they'd trodden the cold stone floor to the kitchen. Many times before now the promise of hot soup or warmed bread enticed them to move a little faster. Each time only led to another type of hell. They trudged, resigned, fearful.

Hogsbreath prodded them once or twice as they snaked along the corridor. He was so huge that his stinky breath fell over them from behind. Jac wondered if he ate rotted things then he shied away from that thought. Many others had not returned from this walk—never seen again by the inmates in the cells. They knew all too well what could happen after they arrived in the kitchen. So far, Jac and his sister had always been returned.

Today—was it still day?—the walls were more foreboding; the cold and damp of the bitter winter had penetrated deeper into the granite. The silence seemed heavier. Lil's grip tightened. Jac glanced her way, barely moving his head for fear of being thumped behind his ear. He returned the pressure. She too must feel something was different.

'Git on wi' yer. Haven't got all feckin' day.'

Whatever lay in wait for them in the kitchen, Hogsbreath was almost genial. It had taken them a long time to distinguish his moods. The expectation of something far worse ahead was upon Jac, and the tang of fresh sweat that dampened Lil's armpits was sharp in his nostrils.

'Now don't neither of yer piss yerselves this time. Don't forget yer in yer Sundee best.' The chortle blasted out and an odorous cloud of decay enveloped them.

Terror escaped Jac in a sudden rush of urine, drenching the front of his thin breeches. His only sound was soft fearful dismay, a sob so quiet only his sister heard.

Lil brushed his forearm. '*Dim ots.* No matter, Jac,' she murmured. '*Daliwch ati.* Keep going.'

Warm piss soon turned cold against Jac's skin. He reached down and felt for the spoon tucked into the hem of his shirt. It helped, knowing it was there.

They took the last turn in the corridor. Jac imagined he could feel the heat of the kitchen fires. The sturdy old cast-iron stoves would be chugging out warmth and the smells of its meagre output reached them. The aroma of soup teased him. Lil's face came up as she too was drawn to the waft. And that other smell—bread? *Bread!* His mouth watered. He felt a little spittle hit his arm and sucked on his chapped lips to hold it in.

Stopping at the huge entrance, they hung back as Hogsbreath

pounded on the heavy door. Just as it swung open, he thrust his face close to the children. 'When you come back, I'll find out which one of ye couldn't hold yer piss.' He pushed past them.

Jac stared straight ahead, ignoring Hogsbreath. A great delight was in front of him. His sore mouth fell open as he gazed at the loaded timber table. Food. Steaming heaps of food. *Vegetables.* Potatoes, perhaps turnips, and the orange colour must mean pumpkin. He started forward, but Lil gripped him with steely fingers.

A young woman stepped into their line of sight. 'Take your leave, Tucker. Your stench is worse than theirs, man.'

'An' good day to ye, Miss Emily.'

'Don't lip me, man, or the master will be down to clear you out.'

Hogsbreath turned, muttering and nudged Lil a little as he retreated into the hellhole. The stinking beast would await their return, and they'd both pay a price.

Jac gazed at the woman, Emily. A right lady she looked, though Hogsbreath would never have spoken like he had if she really was one. She must be a maid or something from Downstairs. Her cap was starched, and not a wisp of hair fell on her face. She was neither slim nor stout, but she was strong looking. Perhaps a little taller than Lil but not by much. Her black brows were dense over dark eyes. The bones in her cheeks stood out like she had foreigner's blood in her veins, and her beaky nose attested a gypsy or another heathen tribe from distant shores he'd heard about. But her voice and her language were pure homeland, country of his birth.

He was desperate to get to the plates on the table. Lil tapped him again. He stood stock-still, met the woman's stare, and saw her nose twitch.

*It's just too bad that we stink, and no fault of our own,* Lil would say to him when they huddled on the damp floor of their cell. They picked nits off each other. They scraped out hollows in the dirt to sleep. They had to relieve themselves in the same place they lived.

He dared then to check the rest of the kitchen for other occupants. No one else but this woman. His mouth was filling with saliva and his guts felt queasy.

There in the corner alongside the wood stack was a deep copper tub. Steam from it drifted up towards the crucifix behind on the wall. Lil turned her face away, disgusted. She'd told him often that 'their god couldna be bothered with us'.

'You are to disrobe and get into the tub,' Miss Emily said.

Jac's eyes darted to her and back to the vegetables on the table. 'What?'

'We are to get out of our clothes, Jac.'

'You will wash yourselves off. Then you will be scrubbed down properly once you are clean enough to get near.'

'All our clothes?' Jac was distracted. He wasn't asking it of the woman. If they took off their clothes, what would it mean for their spoons? Lil had made it clear to Jac that nothing, and nobody, would come between them and the spoons. They were all they had to connect them to their parents.

'Yes,' the woman hissed and stalked behind them to close the heavy door to the corridor. She shoved the door closed, threw the bolt, and turned her back on it. 'I will sit here until you have done what you're told.' She perched on a stool opposite the stove, and waved Lilpah towards the tub.

'You first, Jac. I'll help you.' Lil shuffled him over to the bath. 'Tear open the seam,' she whispered hoarsely, 'but not enough to drop the spoon.' Her eyes were bright, intense.

He fumbled a little.

Lil turned to Miss Emily. 'He's a bit frightened. He doesn't like to have a bath.'

The woman wrinkled her nose. 'But he will. And when you've got him in, put those clothes in the stove. Then you're for the bath, too.'

'Yes'm,' she said. She felt Jac's spoon slip into her hand. 'Jac, I'll have to get me own spoon out quick.' She slid his spoon out of sight along the rounded end of the tin bath.

He turned his face away, shucked his breeches and pulled the threadbare shirt over his head.

'You're a skinny sight, lad,' Miss Emily said. 'Why is it your bony knees don't knock together?'

Jac clambered into the bath, no answer for her.

'It's hard to tell if you have bruises, or whether you're just filthy. Is that blood on yer arse? Clean yeself up.'

Jac didn't need help settling in the tub, but Lil pressed close to him, shielding her free hand. He watched as she scratched at the sturdy knot securing the spoon in her own hem. For the first time she looked as if she'd cry aloud—this time she needed the knot and the twine to be feeble, and it wasn't.

Jac dropped lower into the water. Surprised that the water wasn't as frightening as he imagined, he felt something akin to glee. He loved the warmth on his skin—

Lil frowned. Still picking at the stitches with one hand, she used her other to scoop water over him. He dropped his smile and put on an appropriate scowl.

'Get that rotting pile of his clothes into the fire.'

Lilpah gathered Jac's clothes and crept towards the stove. He busied himself, splashing and scooping water like Lil had done and watched as she gripped the tamp with a rag close by. She poked his lousy shirt and trousers into the flames inside. Even from where he was, he could see insects leapt about until they fried in the heat. They had been company of sorts, a constant, and only a small discomfort compared to the rest.

'Hurry up. Now you,' Miss Emily said to Lil and gestured with her thumb.

Lilpah returned to the bath, wrenched open the tight seam on her shift that she'd sewn over and over again. It wouldn't matter if the woman heard; the clothes were so ragged and frayed a tear would be natural. She caught the spoon before it could clatter to the floor, thrust it with Jac's spoon, and pushed them both out of sight.

Then she tugged off her thin dress and was about to climb into the tub when the woman snapped at her. 'Get that lot into the fire, too.'

Naked now, Lil gathered her ragged chemise, stained with dried blood, and filth from their cell, and trudged it to its fate. At least the chimney still worked here; the room hadn't filled with acrid smoke. Returning to the tub, she stepped in.

'It's nice and warm, Lil,' Jac said and saw her smile a little in surprise.

'No talking,' the sharp command rang.

Rarely ever had they ever been in warm water. 'But is *y Diafol*, the devil, gonna take our souls, Lil, because we're bathin' in our nakedness?' Jac asked despite Miss Emily.

'Nay, Jac. The devil dinna care for us either.' Lil set about scrubbing off the dirt. Jac mimicked her not sure what else was required of him.

A door on the far side of the room creaked open and a stocky girl emerged. She was dressed like Miss Emily, but a smaller version. Her hair was dark gold, the colour of ripe wheat before it dries and her brows were thick. She had chubby, red cheeks that made her look as if she laughed often. Jac liked her instantly his gaze met hers.

She carried linens, and folded clothes. On top, a large pale bar of something sat on a small plate. The girl placed everything down on a stool near the bath.

'Need new water, miss?' she asked, her voice clipped, as she surveyed what was before her.

'We will need that other tub after all. This water's not fit enough for pigs, now.'

Jac splashed a little until Lilpah elbowed him. He watched the grime float off them and cling to the rim of the tub. He wondered what all this burning of clothes meant. He glanced at Lil. Her eyes were squinty, watching everything. That alarmed him. Maybe they were for the gallows, too, like their da. Maybe you had to be washed and clean before you met your Maker, even though He couldna be bothered with them.

The new tub appeared, and great buckets of steaming water were lugged in by a couple of young men. Jac saw that Lil shrank in the water as their gaze flicked to her but when Miss Emily stamped her foot, their eyes dropped to their task. Heaving the buckets and dumping water into the clean tub, they retreated silently the way they'd come.

'Miss Emily, I'm to stay and wash 'em,' the stocky young woman said, her eyes flickering over Jac and Lil.

'The boy first, Tippy.'

'I'll give you the sign,' Lil whispered to Jac.

The girl beckoned Jac out of the dirty water into the clean and with only one look over his shoulder at Lil, he gladly leapt from the cooling tub into the hot water. He gave a yowl at first and then settled in. Tippy leaned over and dunked his head under. He came up spitting. 'My head,' he screamed as she dug in her fingers with a rough block of soap—did it have flint mixed in with it?

'Yes, ye dirty little drammer, we even wash yer head. Only once a year, mind, less'n yer need it more oft. But don't worry, yer brains won't fall out like you think.'

'I didn't push no coal carts so I ain't no drammer. I was a door-keeper,' Jac said, his head gripped in her hands. He didn't like her so much, now.

The Tippy woman rolled her eyes. 'That's so grand.' Her strong fingers kept up with the scrubbing.

Jac could see Lil, wide-eyed and watching Tippy work the soap over him. She tucked up her knees. He glanced at the first bath, saw that the spoons remained hidden. Lil would have to come up with something quick. She'd have to wait for a moment to grab them and hide them properly somewhere.

'He's still filthy.'

Miss Emily frowned. 'Then get the men to bring more water, Tippy. If they're not cleaned proper, it'll be me an' you for the lash.' She turned to Lil. 'Come along, you. Out.'

Lilpah stepped out of the tepid, filthy water and Tippy peered into the dirty tub. 'There's fleas in there, swimmin'.'

Ordered to stand and wait until the new bath was filled, Lil edged close to the spoons. Dripping and shivering, she flicked a foot at them. They slid into the wood stack and nestled under a bowed log alongside the great cast-iron stove.

'In here, girl,' Tippy said to her. Turning to Jac, she said, 'You, boy. Dry your head then wrap up in this and sit there.' She handed him a linen and pointed him to a stool by the stove.

Lil settled into the new bath and suffered a long scrubbing from Tippy's firm hand as Jac had done. The hard fingers were in her hair and on her scalp, pushing roughly over her body. She stared at Jac, no alarm on her face. She'd been hurt far worse than a good scrubbin'. He wasn't sure why, but times when she'd return to their cell, she could barely walk, and blood would be drying on her thighs.

'Out you get.'

Lil stepped out on the side of the bath closest to the spoons.

'Here.' A linen was thrown at her. 'If you still got nits after that, I'll shave your head.'

Lilpah clutched at the linen but gave no sound.

*Shave her head.* Joe was horrified. Shocked, his sister put a hand to the long, scraggly, wet mass that was her hair.

Then Tippy whispered kindly, '*Cymerwch ofal, ysgafn.* Take a care, lass.'

*Wait*—was that *Cymraeg*, his own language, that he'd just heard from the woman? His ears were dreaming. Rattled by it, he barely heard Miss Emily tell Tippy to stuff the filthy clothes further into the oven.

'But they're so loaded down with dirt they're choking off the flame.' Tippy removed the tamp and shoved the poker hard into the oven. Smoke billowed out.

Lilpah sneezed. It was their signal—Jac went into a frenzy and jumped and ran and screamed around the kitchen.

Miss Emily tried to catch him. Tippy dropped the poker with a clang and howled as hot coals from the fire leapt after it. She dashed them back under the stove, her feet too quick for a flame to catch.

When Jac came to a complete stop, his breath ragged, snot running down his face, he darted a glance at his sister. She nodded; she'd done it. He didn't know where they were, but the spoons had been safely hidden. How or when he'd ever see them again, he wouldn't know.

Jac had been given old clean clothes, musty smelling, but not rags. Lil, too. A long-sleeved chemise each, britches for him and an over-skirt for her, and soft slippers on their feet.

'Where are we going?' Lilpah asked.

'To see the master,' Miss Emily replied and kept her nose in the air. She stepped ahead of them, her nose twitching.

Tippy brought up the rear with a torch. 'New blood.'

Jac glanced at Lilpah. *Blood?*

'Foolish talk, Tippy,' Miss Emily called over her shoulder and moved swiftly ahead.

Tippy moved up to Lilpah. 'Though dunno why he wants ye brother. The master only wants to get a look at you again, you're the right age an' all, and here under his nose,' she said, then whispered, 'Miss Emily there won't 'elp ye none, but I will.'

Lilpah clutched Jac's hand.

'Move,' Miss Emily snapped.

They were hurried along the short corridor. The door ahead loomed large. Miss Emily rapped hard on it, and then hammered it, as if enraged that it was closed. The massive door absorbed the rage, and she sagged until it swung open. She straightened and glared over her shoulder. 'Get in here.'

Jac clung to Lilpah as they crept up to the doorway.

Tippy grabbed Joe's arm and pulled him out of Lil's hold. He yelped and lunged for Lil, but Tippy pulled him against her.

'You won't want to go in there with Sir Hugh,' she snapped, her voice tight between her lips.

Jac lunged for Lil again and Tippy swung him away. He let out another yell, struggling wildly.

'Get out of it, Tippy.' Miss Emily took two strides and shoved the woman.

Tippy threw her arms high in the air, as if in surrender.

A voice boomed from the doorway. 'Stop the squabbling. Emily, what's got into you?'

Miss Emily spun around.

Tippy darted to Lil. 'Don't do any talkin'.'

Jac shot to Lil's other side. He swiped a hand over his dribbling snot, then wiped it on his new clothes.

They stood and stared at the man in the doorway. Sir Hugh Rigg, Tippy had said. Jac had never seen him up this close. He was the man beside the magistrate the day their father had been sentenced to hang, but he hadn't remembered him looking as grand as this. It didn't make Jac feel good at all. Lil didn't look as if she was feeling good either.

A head of dark sandy hair swept back from his face. His eyes were blue, but their look reminded him of the poisonous toadstools that sprang up in the fields at home, small and mean. They were intense eyes under sparse eyebrows that met in the middle. He was square jawed and thin necked. His lips were lean, and blue-ish too, as if he was always just in from the cold. A snarl curled on them.

*Cunning, like a rat, he was.* Jac watched the man eye Lil, just like the old miller used to do when he'd come to deliver Ma her flour.

Ma had refused to see him in the house without Pa around. She'd thrown his coin out the door at other times.

When the man's glance swept to him, Jac shrank against his sister, his guts shrivelled. The stare darted back to Lilpah and an eyelid flickered.

Miss Emily's mouth was sour. 'Just a scuffle, sir. Feet clumsy in the cold.'

'Is that right?' He eyed her until she bobbed again, lowered her eyes. He said, 'And what of the—'

'I'm tryin' to tell her ladyship here,' Tippy said and pushed forward, her hand once again on Jac's arm. 'That this 'un has a pox. I saw it meself when he was in the tub—'

Jac squawked. Lilpah froze.

'—and weren't be no good to take him, sir.' She held Jac fast.

Jac took in the leer on Sir Hugh's face. The twitch in his eyelid and the flexing of his hands and fingers. Miss Emily's glances darted about. Tippy's hand still clutched Jac's arm, squeezing hard. Sir Hugh's repulsion seemed to hit Jac fair in his chest.

Miss Emily lifted her chin. 'I was about to report that, sir. He—'

'I don't want the boy. I told you that. What's he doing here? He's to be saved for—'

Jac didn't hear any more. He shut his ears, squirmed afresh but Lilpah stilled him with her hand on his other arm. '*Byddwch in dal i, Jac. Byddwch yn arbed hwn,*' she whispered. 'Be still, Jac. You'll be spared.'

He gaped. 'I won't be sent away from you, Lil, it's us two, together.'

Sir Hugh pointed a finger. 'That bloody heathen language will not be spoken in my house,' he snapped.

Tippy jumped. 'Aye, sir, heathen it is, but they said naught. Somethin' about how kind you look, sir, after that two-headed stinkpot in the workhouse.'

Sir Hugh advanced into the hallway. The siblings steadied.

'I said, I don't want the boy. I don't care about the filthy little bastard. Take him back to where he was. I said only the girl.' He glared at Miss Emily who ducked her head. 'You test my patience, Emily.'

Tippy tugged Jac. 'Come on, lad,' she urged softly.

He resisted, a silent pleading on his lips. Lil gave him another small shake of her head. When Sir Hugh pushed Emily aside and reached down to lift the hem of Lil's chemise, Jac stood stock-still.

Sir Hugh inspected Lil from the front, leaning back to take in the view. 'Turn around,' he barked. He kept hold of the chemise.

Lil let her bladder go and urine splashed at her feet.

Sir Hugh jumped back. 'Dirty piece of baggage.' He flicked a wrist at Miss Emily. 'Get her cleaned up before you bring her back. And do it without the boy,' he shouted, turning on his heels and stalking back inside his chamber.

'Tippy, take the boy. He's too big and too old for the chimneys. It's the mine for him, where he belongs.' Emily turned and beckoned Lil to follow her.

Lilpah held her chemise away from herself and stepped out of the sodden slippers.

Jac struggled in Tippy's grip. 'Lilpah!'

She turned, her eyes dull. 'Go,' she said *y Gymraeg*. 'Do what they say.'

'Lil.' Jac felt the snivel coming fast. His heartbeat was wild, pumping hard.

Tippy had him about the chest with both arms. 'You keep this up,' she said in his ear, his own language soft on her tongue, 'and the master will come out and beat you, throw you both back to those English guards. Come on, lad. You have a chance. Better off down the mine than with them animals here.'

Jac thrashed, held fast by Tippy. 'I don't want to leave you, Lil.'

Lil flew back to Jac. A fierce heat burned in his sister's eyes.

'You look after yourself,' she seethed at him and pinched both his ears. 'Burn with hate for the Englishman, Jac Owen, d'you hear me? Do it for Da and Ma. Look after yourself. For *me*. Do you hear me?'

He stared at her. 'We can run, Lil.'

'Nay, we canna run.' Still he struggled in Tippy's steely grip and Lil dropped her hands, squeezing his shoulders. 'Go on,' she whispered in their home language. 'You know where the spoons are. Go find them, leave mine and take yours. Look after it.' Then she pushed away.

Tippy heard every word. 'What spoons?' she asked in Jac's ear, *y Gymraeg*.

'Goodbyes are over,' Miss Emily snapped and wrenched Lilpah by the arm. 'Don't keep me waiting.'

# CHAPTER TWO

Lil edged along the huge granite wall of the manor house and peered around the corner. Rainwater still dripped from the roof, but a new downpour hadn't followed. No one was around; she'd be able to make a run for it without being seen and get across to the front gardens.

The most bountiful patch of parsley grew among the hibiscus and the fig and holly. Why the head gardener hadn't ripped it out was beyond her. When his head garden boy had sepsis of the foot, she'd been ordered to replace him because no other healthy boys had been available. They'd all been sent away for the mine work.

Lil could see the fine carriages arriving and hear the chattering of the gentlewomen and the maddening empty hilarity and greetings of the gentlemen. They alighted the front steps with a pomp that was laughable, except that Lil dared not laugh. Her face hurt. Her sore lip throbbed, stung with every breath and when touching it with her tongue, a ferrous taste alerted her; it was bleeding again. She pressed her forearm over it, hoping to stop fresh spots of blood dropping onto her clean apron.

For weeks, Downstairs had been preparing for the great dinner tonight. The house had been scrubbed, walls and floors and ceilings, and then scrubbed all the way back again. The silver- and glass-ware polished, furniture oiled and rubbed. Bed linens washed and aired. Drapes and curtains taken down, and the dust pounded off with brooms. The fire pits scoured, and the hearths buffed.

All chimneys had been swept and cleaned, and the household had only lost one climbing boy this time. The child perished when he got stuck halfway up the flue. The waistband on his trousers had rolled, wedging him tight. They'd put a fire under him to move him along, but he died. Suffocated, they said.

Downstairs had been subdued about losing the boy. He'd always been a cheeky little bugger who'd brightened the day. It was no doubt why Mrs Hopwood, the cook—who'd happily gone against the orders of half rations for the chimney sweeps and fed him an extra morsel—was bereft for days; blamed herself because perhaps he'd gotten fat and therefore stuck in the flue. The men had to shove a long poker down from the top to dislodge him. Lil had been there when they removed his blackened and battered little body from the fireplace.

Sir Hugh had stood and watched as Lil gathered up the poor wee boy's tattered clothing.

'I hope that stink will be gone by tonight's dinner, girl. There's only two hours till guests arrive. Be sure to have the place well cleaned of it.'

Lil staggered to her feet barely able to hold down her bile. She'd watched as one man silently gathered the boy's remains in his arms and, with tears streaming on his face, trudged out of the room.

She knew better than to answer back. She knew better than to make eye contact with the master. She knew better than to stand tall and proud. But she did. Her parents were gone, Jac was gone… anything else she held dear in her life was gone. Nothing mattered.

She looked him in the eye. 'The stink will never leave this place.'

Sir Hugh's eyes bulged, darted a glance about him. Too many other servants had heard her, evident in their hesitation before they scurried away.

Clutching the boy's rotting clothes, Lil walked past him to the door alongside the fireplace. She turned to close the door but Sir Hugh had borne down on her.

'You had better ensure it does for tonight, girl.' And then he backhanded her.

Her lip split on her teeth and she tasted blood and soot as she'd dropped to the floor, still clutching the chimney sweep's clothes.

'I'm not finished with you.' He stepped over her and stalked off. His particular brand of punishment would come later.

Tippy, who'd been shoved into a doorway on the other side of the room before she could intervene, hurried over and helped her stand. 'C'mon, lovey. We need to get them tatters in the fire and your face cleaned up. Too much to do before the big pig feed at the trough tonight. *Dewch ymlaen, nawr.* Come on, now.'

'*Rwy'n anghofio eich bod chi'n Gymry.* I forgot you are Welsh,' Lil whispered back, remembering she'd heard Tippy speak before.

'I was once.'

'We are always,' Lil returned, as fierce as her low voice would allow.

In the big kitchen, Mrs Hopwood ordered Lil's blood-spattered apron off. She supplied another but only after Lil had wiped her face and had stopped the blood seeping from her torn lip.

'Ye keep gettin' thrashed, girl. Sometimes I wonder why God only sends me fools,' Mrs Hopwood muttered and crossed herself, ending with a touch to a tiny crucifix around her neck.

Tippy was standing beside one of the stoves where pots of boiling water bubbled away on top of them. 'It's because He likes to see ye among yer own.'

Mrs Hopwood reddened. 'Mind your manners, Tippy Bowman. No tea for you.'

Tippy ignored her. Her head bowed a moment over the chimney-sweep's clothes in her arms before she shoved them into the fire.

Mrs Hopwood huffed and ordered Lil to the herb garden. 'The best parsley, you.'

Lil knew the best parsley wasn't in the herb garden.

Now from her vantage, she saw the last footman turn his back for indoors. The final carriage drove by her, heading for the stables. She darted across the concourse and disappeared into the maze of garden, unerringly headed for her clump of parsley. Bending, she brushed the lush, dark green, tightly bunched leaves and they tickled her palms. She loathed to pull the plant. Its life was healthy, and to pull it up would surely kill it, but at least it would be useful at its end. She tugged and up it came.

'I trust you are not stealing a delectable bunch of herbs.'

Fright sent her on her backside but she scrambled and twisted around on her knees. The man was dressed in dull trousers, a waist-coat over a loose-fitting shirt and a wide rimmed flat top hat sat on his head. The shadow on his chin made his face appear swarthy, but he didn't look unkind.

'No, sir. 'Tis for the kitchen. It's the best of our parsley, hidden here in these well-tended beds.'

'Hmm.' He glanced at the bunch in her hand. 'It's been many a day since I've seen food so fresh as I am seeing here.'

Unsure of her situation, she darted a glance through the hedges.

'You're quite safe. I don't believe anyone else saw you,' he said, his hands behind his back.

Fear darted in her gut.

'I was taking some air. There seems little inside the great house.

36

So close and dark, isn't it?'

She remained crouched, still clutching the parsley, careful not to drag it in the dirt. 'Not mine to say, sir.'

Continuing to stand with his hands behind his back, he was talking as if he were on a pleasant day's outing. He smiled. 'Me, I'm more used to the ocean. Though sometimes a ship's hold can be as ugly as the inside of this place.' He looked back over the hedge towards the house.

Lil blinked. She crabbed a little further back until she felt a hedge behind her. *Trapped.*

'What's your name?'

'Lilpah Owen.'

He gave her a mock bow. 'My name is *Veniamin* Polites, Mistress Owen, although in English it is pronounced Benjamin.' He frowned. 'I mean to do you no harm and that might come as a surprise, I know.' He looked about him again. 'If you go now, no one will see.' He stood out of her way. 'But go straight back to the kitchen with your prize,' he said. 'There would be unsavoury types about today.' He looked as if she should know what he was talking about.

Clambering to her feet she took off down the row, and squeezed into a narrow opening in the hedge to check her path was clear. She dashed across the concourse to the house, sprinted along the side and past the outbuildings. Around the back was the enclosed little yard. Under the doorway porch and puffing for breath, she didn't notice anyone else. After wiping her feet vigorously on an old flour bag, she pushed open the door to the kitchen.

Mrs Hopwood held out her hand. 'And just in time. Give it here.'

Lil dropped the bunch into the large, scarred hand and glanced at Mrs Hopwood's face. But the cook's eyes were not on her. They were on something behind her and had widened in surprise.

'What have we here, Mrs Hopwood?'

*Oh no.* Lil spun around.

It was not the master, but another man who must have followed her into the kitchen. His face was pockmarked under a sparse and wiry black beard. His enormous hooked nose hovered like a bird of prey over a wide leer, showcasing a mouth missing some teeth.

'Oh, Captain Zephinia.' Mrs Hopwood gave something of a curtsy. 'We weren't expecting you downstairs, sir.'

''Course you weren't, but how could I miss coming to visit when I know what delights you harbor down here. I see you've been hiding this little morsel. Just caught a glimpse of him darting back inside here, thought I'd come see for myself. But ahh, I see I've made a mistake. It's not a young lad, but a skinny maid.'

Lil dared a glance at the cook who didn't look back at her.

''Course, sir.'

'I might just have some of that tea you're brewing, too, Mrs Hopwood.' He took a seat by the fire and continued his scrutiny.

Lil backed around the table to where Mrs Hopwood had been chopping vegetables.

'Now, don't flee before I've had a good look at you, girl.' He cocked his head side to side. 'You might be useful at market. Fetch a good price for those interested in cunny.'

Lil felt the slide of repulsion creep into her throat. Mrs Hopwood pressed her fingers around the cross she wore, a look if horror on her face. What god would send men such as these to good people?

'Come around here,' he said.

Tippy burst in the back door and glared at Lil. 'There you are. I've been looking for you everywhere. The master wants his—' She spotted the captain. 'Oh, Captain Zephinia, sir.' She curtsied too and kept talking. 'Sir, but the master wants this 'un to tend him.'

'Timely.' Zephinia waved a big hand, fingers large and covered with black hair between the knuckles. 'What's your name?' He studied a ring on his forefinger.

'Tippy Bowman, sir.'

'Not you, I know you. I meant her.'

'She's Lilpah Owen. She don't speak much English, sir. She's a native.'

'Native, like you,' he scoffed. 'You all speak English.'

'The master wants—'

'Go then. Make haste.' His mug of tea was put before him. 'I'll speak to Rigg myself about the chit.'

Tippy pulled Lil out of the kitchen and into the yard. 'Get. Run and hide.'

'But the master—'

'He doesna ask for ye. But even he's better than that monster.' Tippy pushed her again. 'He takes boys apart, but girls he leaves for—'

Benjamin Polites stood between them and the yard.

Lil's breath caught in her throat, fearful, but he simply inclined his head and stepped out of their way. They ran past him to the edge of the courtyard, ducked around the wall and out of sight from the kitchen.

Tippy let out a breath. 'I saw that Zephinia follow you in. He's bad, that one. God knows what he'll get up to tonight after a bellyful of grog. Him and the lot of them.' She stood with her hands on her hips. 'Go. I'll come for you when he's gone.'

Lil was changing her bed straw. The old crawly batch had been swept out into the hall waiting for her to carry it back out to the garden.

It wasn't Tippy who'd come for her. Miss Emily pushed into Lil's sleeping closet, which was along the dank hallway of downstairs. 'You are to come with me,' she said.

Lil eyed her a moment. It seemed Miss Emily had been where Lil now found herself. Difference was Miss Emily had enjoyed her previous station. 'What for?'

'Master sent me. You are to be bathed and dressed.'

Lil's heart sank. She had hoped the grand dinner event would distract Sir Hugh.

Miss Emily led Lil to the bath in the kitchen to supervise the ablutions. No one took any notice of them; they had a corner to themselves and easy access to the hot water. At least she'd had plenty of time over the last months to find a safe place to hide her mother's spoon. Under her bed straw, she had scraped away a little hollow and tucked it in there.

Jac had been distraught when he couldn't find the spoons, believing they were missing. He'd sobbed and snivelled his outrage to Tippy. She'd found both spoons while cleaning the kitchen and produced them triumphantly from her chemise pocket. Somehow, the boy had got under her skin, and so she secured Jac's on new twine and it hung around his neck. It hid under his shirt as he waited in the dungeon to be taken to the mines. She'd brought Lil's to her that same day.

Tippy had handled the spoon in a caress. 'I don't remember me da's spoon to me ma. I barely even remember me da and ma. I'm glad to help ye keep these safe.'

Lil had snatched it from her.

In the tub under Emily's beady eye, Lil washed her hair again. It got washed so often, at least once every week, that she was fearful of it falling out. Thankfully, that hadn't happened yet, and it seemed whatever soap she used kept the nits away a little longer, too. The master hated nits.

On Miss Emily's order, she stepped out of the bath, dried herself off, dressed in a clean chemise and followed her out the door. In the distance, behind the big old door that she and Jac had come through all those months ago, she heard indignant yells. She hesitated. It would be a lad, she reckoned. The voice, changing as it matured from boy to man broke in fury and in its outrage scraped and squeaked. Squealed in agony. Hogsbreath must have got hold of him, would have him up against a wall. She tried to shut her ears, sickened. Still she was only glad it couldn't have been Jac's voice. He'd be down the mines by now. This voice belonged to some other poor child.

'Hurry up,' Miss Emily said and pushed Lil through the opposite kitchen door.

They scampered light on their feet into the chamber adjoining Sir Hugh's room. Inside Lil spied a gown draped over the bed that she sometimes occupied. Miss Emily took her arm and propelled her towards it.

'There. This is what you will wear for this evening. I'm to accompany you, and we will sit at the maid's table.'

'The maid's table, why?' Wary, Lil stood her ground.

Miss Emily reached for the gown, a plain green, the colour of clover. She tugged it over Lil's head, ignoring her query.

The dress was old, Lil could tell, and by the look of the scuffed hem it had been worn many times before. But it was clean, soft on her skin and, as she brushed it down, the fabric was smooth under her palms.

'Was this yours?' Lil said, staring.

Eyes on her task, Miss Emily did not stare back. 'At one time.'

'So, tell me why I'm to sit at the maid's table.' Lil felt a flutter in her chest. Miss Emily kept her mouth closed, her lips tight. 'Only those who are to be sold off sit there,' Lil pressed, fear dancing in her stomach. She would be sitting at a table behind the main, against the wall, and facing all of Sir Hugh's guests. On show. The servants would serve dinner to the gentry first and afterwards, those on the maid's table would be 'selected'. She was afraid of life here at Sir Hugh's residence, but she was more afraid of the unknown.

'Nonsense. You'll be observed. Nothing more.'

'I won't go.'

Miss Emily pushed a pair of soft slippers at Lil's feet. 'You will, and don't use that stubborn tone of voice with me. Put these on.'

Lil did not move.

Miss Emily straightened. 'You will go, brat. I'm told the master has a nice surprise for you.'

Lil blinked and swayed a little in shock. The master's surprises were not something to look forward to.

Miss Emily continued, her hands on her hips. 'Slippers on, and a brush through that raggedy thatch of yours.' She scowled as Lil still hesitated. 'I'll wait until you do,' she said between clenched teeth. 'Your life is not worth the thrashing I'll get if you don't.'

Lil stepped into the slippers, not because she might get a back-hand from Miss Emily, or because of the veiled threat, but because surviving was her only option. To live another day was the only thing Lil dared dream.

That, and perhaps one day, away from this horrible place, she would find her little brother Jac alive and well.

The big hall was loud with booming laughter and, every so often, a tinkling of fairer tones. Heavy perfumes of citrus, musk and rose hung in the air, but nothing could disguise the sweat of unwashed bodies and clothes from the nose of freshly bathed Lilpah Owen.

She wondered why she needed to be so bathed when clearly the gentry, who filled the room, by and large were not.

It wasn't the stinking body odours and perfumes which commanded Lil's attention as much as the aroma of the dinner. While she, Miss Emily and Tippy Bowman sat at the maid's table, platters and boards piled high with meats and pies, and jellied this and that were being delivered to the guests. Her stomach growled. When a plate of food was dumped on their table, her stomach cramped painfully. It looked nothing like the feast before the master but that didn't matter. It was food.

Tippy barely waited a moment after the plate had dropped in front of her before her hands were on a dried-out leg of a game bird. It looked to Lil as if it had been forgotten in the ovens and, as such, could not be presented to the guests, or even to the Downstairs. Tippy almost sucked it down. Lil snatched a morsel dropped from Tippy's handful, and swallowed it, hardly chewing. It could have been boot leather for all she cared. Her stomach roiled. It had been so long since she'd had meat it might not stay down.

Carrots and turnips lay in a bowl, still steaming from the pot, not yet dried beyond recognition. She slid her plate under and tipped some on to it, careful to leave a few bites for the others. Fingers smarted on the hot morsels. Blowing a cooling breath she pushed them into her mouth, chewed quickly and gulped, then wiped her hands on the underside of the table.

She looked up to meet Captain Zephinia's gaze, which slid to Miss Emily and back again. He tilted his head towards a table of other men, some of whom shovelled in the dinner even while their gaze was on the maid's table.

Her food suddenly lost its appeal.

Sir Hugh stood, pushing away his chair and it seemed to Lil that everyone froze at that moment. He wobbled just a little as he banged his fist on the table, and shouted, 'Now, sirs and ladies, I have been remiss. Might I introduce an esteemed gentleman, Mr Crawford, who is a landowner, and new among us.'

Lil glanced at this Mr Crawford. A slim man, pale, with a shining bald head and wide eyes, kept his chin down but his gaze on Sir Hugh.

'Forgive my manners, Mr Crawford,' Sir Hugh bawled on, 'but we others are so much kith and kin here that I hope you will allow me some latitude.' Murmurs and laughs all around as Mr Crawford politely acknowledged the apology with a nod. 'And so that we don't send everyone to sleep with long boring speeches, wasting good eating and drinking time, I give you Captain Pero Zephinia, a great seafaring man who's also in our midst. His ship, *Revival*, is about to embark on another journey—shipping coal, doncha know.' He tapped the side of his nose and slumped to his seat.

Captain Zephinia rose to address the guests. 'Thank you, Sir Hugh. And shipping coal it is.' He winked at a line of bewigged gentlemen down the table. 'Of course, shipping to faraway places, such as China, via Bengal.'

A moment's silence and then one of them said, 'Ahh yes. Of course. Coal to China.'

Others looked askance until fellow guests whispered in their ears. The news was passed around the table and more snickers were heard. *Opium trade. Slaves.*

'So, I beg of you good folk, indulge our hard and dangerous journey by underwriting the many arduous legs of the voyage.' More vigorous nods and nudges.

Lil noticed there were some folk whose chins had dropped a little, with a look much like Mr Crawford's.

'And to those of you who sign up to assist, we can guarantee the best of returns on your investment.'

Amid hearty slaps on backs of camaraderie, Sir Hugh staggered to his feet again. 'We mustn't insult the ladies by presuming to conduct business in their presence. So, my dear gracious gentlewomen, madeira and sago pudding is to be served for you in our drawing room, if you would, while these ruffians partake of cigars and port with me.' He bowed low over the table.

Zephinia grabbed Hugh's coattails before he landed headfirst in the duck dish.

Chatter died away as the ladies filed out. At the brief silence that followed, Tippy shifted in her seat. Lil rose quickly but Miss Emily snatched her wrist and pulled her down. 'We stay.'

'And so, gentlemen,' Sir Hugh began. 'We come to the trading part of the evening.' He waved at the maid's table.

Lil looked about. There were nine men, including Benjamin Polites, the man in the hedge earlier today, Sir Hugh, plus Captain Zephinia.

'Rigg, I know this is not all that's on offer,' Zephinia complained with a drunken leer and gestured to the closed door.

'No, Captain. It's not all.' Sir Hugh waved a hand at the same door. 'We have another delicious morsel to tempt some of our investors.'

Suddenly sickened and fearful, Lil stared. There were too many men, too many leers in her direction. Tonight would be a night of horror and—

'Captain.'

Zephinia turned to the man who'd approached. 'Mr Polites?'

'Sir, if I may, I don't believe—'

'Keep your beliefs to yourself, man,' the captain snapped, leaning over. 'You are my navigator, not my moral compass. We have fresh meat to deliver.' Zephinia waved to the under-butler who flung open the side door. Two men in livery dragged three boys into the room.

*

Jac, gripped under the arms and not able to stand on his own, squinted into the light of the room, darted a glance around before it caught his sister. Her eyes said everything, but he didn't utter a sound. Instead, struggled silently against the hold of his captor, his gaze only on Lil. His belly felt like it would go to water, but he had nothing in his guts to let go. He'd purged everything two nights ago after the hard, brutal rod between the man's legs had shoved into him. The boys beside him were cowed, whimpering in the grasp of two uniformed men.

Lil pushed out of her seat. So did Miss Emily and Tippy. This was bad again; terrible, menacing. Jac heard his breath jag in his throat. Lil grabbed the back of the chair as if to stop from falling over.

Sir Hugh laughed. 'Our little game.' He turned to Lilpah. 'You see, your precious brother is still with us. And he is destined for great things, is he not, Captain Zephinia? Not for the mines after all. We'll patch him up, good as new, for you, Pero.'

Zephinia turned his attention from Jac to Lil. 'Ah yes, family. I wonder, it might prove an interesting combination.'

A dark-haired, gypsy looking man stepped forward. 'Captain, we could use this boy. He'd be a fine apprentice for—'

'Which boy, Mr Polites? That one?' Zephinia pointed to Jac. Then he looked at Lil. 'He is marked for me but I'll take them both,' he said, expansively and jiggled a bag of coin.

Sir Hugh said, 'Nay, Pero. The girl stays here.'

Zephinia narrowed his gaze at Rigg. 'I might remind you, I take who I choose.'

Sir Hugh wobbled a little more and then sat heavily at his table. 'Don't bring that up again.'

Zephinia smirked. 'Well, there's no need to bring it up. The chattels promised didn't die under *my* care.' He nodded around the table. 'You were lucky I paid your bail.'

'A debt paid in full.'

'We want no more mistakes of that nature, though, do we? Trade in flesh is becoming expensive. Black market stuff.'

A man, his glistening bald head shining in the low light, came up halfway out of his chair.

'Sit down, Mr Crawford,' Sir Hugh ordered. 'Zephinia finds my discomfort a source of hilarity.'

Jac stared hard at Lil. He'd only really understood a few words. *Die?* He didn't want to die, no matter what. Lil gave a short shake of her head, then she put two fingers on her own arm, tapped it. Jac saw but it didn't help.

Sir Hugh, distracted by Jac's struggle, said, 'Stop the fuss, boy, or I'll hand you over now.'

A hand slapped over Jac's mouth before he could let out a fearful yell.

Zephinia laughed. 'He's trapped, and he knows it. And what a honeyed trap it is.' He leaned forward, eyes on the boy.

Jac locked eyes with Lil. Danger and dread prickled his skin.

He wanted to run to her, have her snatch him up, but he couldn't move.

'So, what say you, Mistress Lilpah?' Rigg drawled. 'Should he have a short life in the coal mines, sure of black lung? Or should he enjoy what you enjoy?'

Captain Zephinia raised his eyebrows. 'Though not here in this delightful palace, this sparkling abode which belongs to Sir Hugh, my fine hospitable friend.' He barked a laugh, leaning toward Rigg. 'You have plenty of money, Sir Hugh. Try spending some of it instead of hoarding it.' He pursed his lips and looked back at the swarthy looking man. 'No, not to enjoy hospitality here but on the high seas, with us, eh, Mr Polites? Serving as my cabin boy. Apprentice, did you say?'

Jac saw Lil's face go white, heard her gasp, watched as Tippy grabbed her arm. *Oh no, this must be badder than even the other night* ... His backside sorely pained him but he squirmed, he twisted and writhed until he was knocked to his knees with a punch to the back of the head. He fell to the floor and lay still, and the light around him snapped into darkness.

*

Lil dared not even gasp. She covered her mouth, her split lip opening again. Her eyes smarted with tears she dared not shed.

Zephinia cried, 'Good God. Not dead, I hope, Baskins, you're too heavy handed.'

Nervous laughter erupted from the men who'd remained in the room. Mr Polites elbowed his way between those standing over Jac and scooped the boy up in his arms. 'Not dead, Captain.'

'Good man. See to his removal to the ship.'

Mr Polites barely gave Lil a glance before he hurried out the main door. She watched, helpless, as the door was shut behind them. Tippy's arm, shoved under hers, was the only thing stopping her from sliding to the floor.

Mr Crawford stood and with a curt bow began to excuse himself. 'If you please Sir Hugh, I will take my leave.'

'Oh ho—what say you, Mr Crawford?' Zephinia boomed. 'Scuttling away?'

Red-faced, Crawford marched out of the room.

'Oh, there he goes,' Zephinia said. 'Short in the cock department, is he?'

Sir Hugh let out a breath. 'His absence doesn't do our coffers any good but he'll redeem himself at some later point, I know. He's very adept with numbers.' He leaned back in his seat. 'That Polites man. He's a foreigner.' He signalled for more rum.

Miss Emily pushed Lil hard and thrust a pitcher of rum into her hands. 'Go,' she ordered, roughly.

'Greek, they say. Good sailor. Works hard.' Captain Zephinia also held his cup aloft for a refill. 'Says his life is on the seas like other poor bastards.'

'That so?' Sir Hugh asked, watching Lil move to fill Zephinia's cup.

She side-stepped the groping hand of another, trying desperately not to spill anything but her hands shook as if the devil had hold of her.

'There's no life after sailing the seas, they don't live that long. Is only fun for a while then scurvy gets 'em, or a plague, or if they're unlucky,' he said, and laughed, 'the cat o' nine. We don't pay 'em.' He slugged back his rum and held fast to Lil's wrist for another. 'So sharing the spoils of a good transport of opium gives them high ideas. He'll be off first grab at the winnings, making a run for land. That is, if I don't wager it back off him first. He's a sharp throw of a dice.'

Lil shook as she poured again and rum spilled over Zephinia's sleeve.

He still held her, her wrist burning in his grip. ''Tis a good thing I'm in a fine mood, slut.' As Mr Polites stepped back into the room, Zephinia thrust Lil away. Addressing Sir Hugh, he said, 'We sail day after tomorrow.' His gaze swept the room once more. 'So, good gentlemen. Your promissory notes, if you please, and Mr Polites will supply a nib pen and an inkpot.'

'Captain, I carried no writing implements and have no knowledge of this house where pen and ink might be. Perhaps the girl?' Ben Polites pointed to Lil.

Sir Hugh pointed. 'You, Lilpah. Fetch the pen and ink for Mr Polites.'

Lil remembered to bob before she banged the rum pitcher on the table and scurried out, Mr Polites behind her. In the great ante-room beyond, the house was eerily quiet.

'Wait.' Mr Polites caught up with her. 'I'll be quick. The boy, he's your brother?'

Lil nodded, her mouth open, but her voice stuck in her throat.

'It's a grim one, this ship of Zephinia's, but I'll tell the captain he ran off, and if I can hide your brother, I might be able to save him.'

Suspicion was ahead of any manners she might have had left. 'Why would you do that?'

Mr Polites snorted at her derision. 'A good question. The best answer is that I had someone look out for me twenty years ago, on a boat engaged in battle at Navarino Bay.' He shrugged. 'I see the name means little to you, but I'll do the same for your brother as was done for me.' He gave a little laugh. 'The god of my homeland might then smile on me.'

'Where is that?'

'An unsettled country to the east, Greece by name, ruled by a catholic Bavarian king and his regents. It's poor, revolutionary, but the air is warm. I might be able to get your brother there.'

Lil's eyes went wide, and her breath was short. 'Take me, too.'

'Nay, lass. It's bad enough for a boy on these ships. But if they find they carry a young girl … No.' Polites held up a finger. 'Now, the ink. Be quick.'

Lil ran to the desk in the corner. She took out the tray on which stood a small oft-used well and some assorted feather quills and nib pens. She carried them back to Benjamin Polites. 'I want to be with my brother,' she pleaded.

'You'll see your brother again someday.' He took the tray from her and started back to the great room. 'Pray for it.'

Lil knew it was futile to argue. 'I'll see him again, but it's not prayer to any god that will bring him.'

Polites looked over his shoulder. 'It matters not the god, but the prayer itself. Remember that.'

Lilpah followed as he pushed through the part open doors and set down the ink well and quills on Sir Hugh's table.

# CHAPTER THREE

*1841 Aboard the East
Indiaman ship, Revival*

J ac didn't like it at all when Ben left him in the cabin for
hours at a time. He was scared. Always scared. The Englishmen could find him any time if he wasn't quiet, and patient.
Jac hated Englishmen. They'd done horrible things and now
it was hard closing his eyes to sleep because he knew that
nightmares would plague him. His screams in the night were worse
when he thought that Zephinia would find him. No one took
notice of his screams; they just joined the screams of others suffering at the captain's hands. Ben would soothe him with whispered
words, hold him close, a little help, not much. Jac's guts churned,
but he didn't want the shit to escape his bowels again so he turned
his thoughts from the monster who commanded the ship.

Ben had told him earlier today that they were going to get off
the ship soon, but something had taken him on deck and he'd been

gone a while. Their cabin felt strange; all the noises from outside had stopped. Even the waves seemed to have stopped. Maybe they were becalmed; Ben said that could sometimes happen.

Then Jac heard a man's bellow, thudding feet, and mad yells. Agonised screams went on and on. A long count droned over the slap of a whip on flesh and Jac knew it was the lash ripping a man's skin from his back. He scrambled up to the hammock to put his ear to the cabin ceiling to hear more clearly. It wasn't the first time that sort of punishment had been metered out and he was now scared again.

Where was Ben? What had happened? What would happen to him if Ben didn't return? Ben had looked after him when he took him from that awful house. He'd tended him, found ointment for Jac to use on his sore arse, had even cradled him when Jac had cried. What should he do, now—stay quiet and patient, still? He wished he wasn't always scared when he was on his own.

He was never scared when Ben whispered tales of his homeland where there'd been mighty gods and big armies. Where there was food aplenty, and sunshine. White sand and sparkling blue seas. And people sang and danced, Ben said.

It sounded like a happy place there, but Ben always looked a bit sad when he talked of Greece. He said he'd had to leave because of trouble there. Trouble must be everywhere in the world, even in a place with white sand and sparkling blue seas.

In the quiet, now, Jac noticed that the ship rolled a little more than before. He looked out of the porthole. Dark clouds billowed in the distance, and the horizon was tilting.

*

Ben Polites steeled himself. He should keep quiet and just go down with the doomed ship. *A coward's way out.* Instead he risked a flogging by embarrassing this fiend, or worse, being tossed into the sea anyway before the storm got them. Bringing Zephinia's inadequacies to his own attention was dangerous.

Zephinia waved off the mate who had tried to forestall Ben's approach. 'And what the bloody hell could you want, Polites?'

'Not sure you want to hear it, Captain.'

'Agreed. Not a lot that you have to say would be of interest. Since you neglected to deliver my prize before boarding this ship, I doubt anything—'

'Nevertheless,' Ben insisted between his teeth, head down, voice measured and calm. 'We've strayed off course, we've sailed far from Shanghai.' He had hoped to jump ship with Jac there. 'And by my calculations, we are now in the north of the East China Sea.' Ben waited for the punch to his head for insubordination. None came. He'd glanced at Zephinia who glared at him. Any fool would've known of it had he been sober enough to read the stars or check the charts himself. Ben could see it dawn on Zephinia.

The captain's face mottled in a rage. He roared for the sextant. He pored over the charts, his rum breath fetid, the stench of hell itself, and his bloodshot eyes had the look of a demon. An unhappy truth had been thrust upon Zephinia and his ignorance was in full view of his men.

Retribution was swift and savage. The navigator who'd replaced Ben was strung up by his wrists on the top deck, his back shredded by a cruel lash, his head hanging. After fifty cracks with the captain's big cat o' nine, a whip of its type abandoned on civilized ships, the man was most likely dead. Better off that way. Long ago under another ship's master, Ben had earned ten of the best for speaking his mind. He smarted at the memory. The old ropey scars on his back were still taut.

The new navigator's drunken night, a shaky hand on the sextant, the bleary eyes and the terrible hangover could now prove fatal for all of them.

'Mr Polites,' the captain said, his rage gone, the eerie calm in its place, sinister. He looked up from the barometer and lifted his chin westward, over the rails. 'Look yonder.'

Ben Polites was steady despite the ever-increasing roll of the ship. The captain had called him back to the helm after his bellowing rage earlier had subsided. Zephinia needed him again, but his tone hid a menace.

Just prior to boarding weeks ago, Ben had been stood down as ship's navigator because he'd confessed that the boy, Jac, had escaped him while the ship was still docked.

A lie: at night Jac slept in a hammock rigged above Ben's cot. A smallish lad who didn't know how old he was—Ben estimated that he was about nine or ten years of age—managed well in the tight space.

Despite the captain's snarling disdain and a brutal backhand at the time, Ben's swift demotion had been a suspiciously mild punishment.

Zephinia, it seemed, had been preoccupied; there'd been other boys to satisfy him, yet they too had mysteriously disappeared before the ship had sailed. He constantly checked over his shoulder, gaze shifting, darting. Once underway, his caution dissipated.

The roll of the ship had picked up; the sea already knew that a monster storm was coming, The men could do little to prepare. The sails were furled, yet the ship hosted a sudden whoosh of wind where hardly a wisp had been moments before. Deck timbers protested with long creaking groans. A colossal whorl of storm bore down, the air dense with humidity. The sour and pungent sweat of terror dripped from the clammy skin of every man on board.

Ben said, 'Looks a big typhoon. Nearing the end of the season, it's unusual.' He studied the boiling mass in the air, the whipping sting of salt spray, the waves angrier under the tossing ship, and with heart pounding, he stared death in the face. It would be a killer. Today Zephinia's luck would run out.

The captain snorted, glaring at the billowing clouds. 'Opium trade sends British ships mad for company profit at all costs. A little war with the Chinese government won't stop the trade, so why should a typhoon, eh?'

The man was mad.

His forehead and neck glistened and drops of moisture ran under his loose shirt. No naval dress today. He grunted. 'God-forsaken corner of the earth.' He gripped a swinging boom and shouted to a sailor. 'Tie it down, you stupid bastard.' Tossing the boom towards the waiting seaman, he wiped a forearm over his mouth. 'We can't outrun it.' Zephinia's gaze was still on the band of charcoal sky. Another grunt. 'We should turn back out to sea.'

That could be as fatal as not. Ben shrugged a little, remained silent. The captain well knew it; he had no reason to ask for an opinion.

Zephinia swung around, steadying against the deck rails. 'Then again, Mr Polites, how long to land fall?' He stared at the far away shore.

Ben didn't need to consult the charts. 'If we turn into the reach, stay ahead of it we'll pick up the—'

'Yes, yes, how long?'

Another line of sweat dribbled down the side of his captain's face despite the whipping wind. Zephinia faced plenty of storms at sea and had never shown dread. He'd lost men—*tossed* men overboard, lost cargo. But never the ship. Never his life. This time he was afraid.

Ben waited a beat, his gaze on the dense, bulging cloud mass in the distance. 'The tide, this wind will take us in. Maybe an hour.' He wasn't sure they'd risk it.

'Not enough time, Mr Polites.'

Around him, seamen had come to a standstill, staring at the destruction heading their way. Ben heard the ship's mate roar a command and bodies scuttled into action. A warm breeze surged over him, and the captain's shirttails flapped.

'Captain, we need—'

'Mr Polites, I will mind the needs of the ship.' Zephinia turned sharply and took Ben by his shirt, shoved him, short and hard. 'Presume nothing about me,' he said, and spat to the side.

Ben stood as still as he could against the increasing roll of the ship. 'Sir.'

'Aye.' Zephinia glared at him. '*Sir.*' His nose almost touched Ben's and the rum on his breath flew into Ben's mouth. 'I had a use for your little cabin mate. If you recall that night at Rigg Manor, he was to have been *my* cabin boy. I would've made shark meat of you both, today. I was looking forward to it. Instead …' He flicked a hand at the lifeless body still tied to a mast, shreds hanging, the blood had stopped running. 'I had to forego for this,' he said and turned to the storm. 'My entertainment must wait.'

The hot damp wind surged, and the swell had grown. Ben staggered on his feet, the ship's sway and roll was deeper, longer. Zephinia could not believe he'd outlive this storm; his bravado was absurd, insanity.

'Aye, Polites, hold your tongue about your young friend.' His smirk, the mania, cut a swathe between them. 'I'd a mind to let you watch me have my fill, then I'd have tossed you into the sea while I kept the boy. But all hands-on-deck for this is far more pragmatic.' His scorn was cold. 'There are some on board I own for all eternity, Polites, and one of them sold you out. Only just this morning, imagine that. What timing. I wonder who else will give up secrets, eh?' The pitch of the boat thrust him sideways.

*Lecherous mongrels.*

The *Revival* was an older ship with many nooks and crannies; a small boy could easily scoot away unnoticed by most on board if he was sharp—if Ben was sharp. A few trusted crew but someone had informed Zephinia. So, which of them?

Rage swelled. He spun; he'd know the guilty degenerates—

they'd shy from his glare. Blood boiled. No one stared back, too busy. No one could be grabbed by the throat and swung overboard.

The captain took Ben's shoulder at his neck in a vice-like grip and shook him. 'Get ye prepared for this.' He pointed at the storm. 'And pray to your Greek gods I don't survive if you do.'

Shoved away, Ben spun and bellowed orders to ready the storms'ls, but he knew the jibs would be next to useless; let the ship aim for shore, ride the tide to the coast and hope they could outrun what was brewing behind them. He cracked out more commands and took note of those whose gaze slid from his. Today the storm would exact the only deaths on this destined-for-hell ship.

Hurling himself below deck, he wove like a drunk to his cabin, a tiny hole between the men's quarters and the rum store. Jac had been safe here; there was scarce room for anything but one body in the cot, which was where Jac had lain day in day out. No one should have suspected another to be inside, but they had.

*

Jac heard Ben's signal knock. It was quiet, urgent, then Ben slipped inside the cabin. 'You feel the ship?'

Jac gripped Ben's cot against the pitching and rolling. 'What is it?'

'A storm. A big one.' Ben took Jac's shoulders. 'We won't outrun it, but we'll head for land, there's a better chance of surviving than turning back out to sea. There are no rocks here, no cliffs.'

'I canna swim.'

'That won't matter. If the ship breaks up, or you get cast off, go with the water, lad, don't fight it. Do you understand?'

Jac gave him a quick nod, then a shake of his head.

Ben's voice was low, urgent. 'The surge of the tide and the wind will take you to shore and dump you safe.' He needn't tell him anything else.

'I'm scared. What else? What else will happen?'

'I'm scared, too, lad, and it'll help keep us alive.' Ben gripped Jac by the scruff, pulled him to the porthole. He pressed the boy's face to the salt-scathed glass. 'You see that line there on the horizon?'

'Land.' The line bobbed and swayed, dipped below sea level now.

'If you get tossed off the ship, boy, the water will take you there.'

Jac didn't believe it. 'There are monsters in the ocean, and a body could fall off the edge of the sea. Neptune will take me down to a deep cold grave where things will eat me alive. I heard the men talkin' in the next cabin.'

Ben shook him. 'There's a much more fearful monster on board the ship.'

If Zephinia was anywhere near Jac, his bowels came loose and his piss came quick. He tried not to think of that because Ben would have to clean him up again.

'Do you have a god, Jac?' Ben asked.

Jac bit his lip, and tasted blood over his teeth. 'No.'

'Then trust in mine, lad.'

Jac clutched the spoon that dangled from his neck and pressed it to his lips. 'This is all I trust in. It's done me good this far.'

'Well, if that's so, lad, hold it tight.' He squeezed the boy's neck again and then fell away as the ship pitched. He clambered up and lurched out of the cabin, shoving the door shut.

Jac turned back to look out the porthole. He was gonna puke up his guts if the ship kept rolling around. He heard sailors' bare feet slapping the deck. Some shouts, and thumps as bodies fell to the deck. He imagined each man above him was desperate for a rope, or something to grab hold of. Salt spray snatched at the porthole and already he could see the deadly rigging cords, loose from their sheets, whip viciously into the air past his little window.

*

Ben climbed up from below, fighting the wind as it funnelled over him. He put Jac out of his head. He'd given the boy false hope, but better that than none.

*Trust in mine,* he'd said to him.

He didn't have a god any longer, but today he thought he might have need of one.

# CHAPTER FOUR

*Quelpaert Island (Cheju), off the coast of Korea*

**W**et, soaked through. Me pants are wet. Damn me if I haven't pissed myself and fallen at the tavern. Head's burning. Mouth's cracked. I'm eating sawdust. Not sawdust... Sand.

A strange creature tiptoed past him. Six legs—eight? Scurrying by, a shell on its back, its dainty feet hardly leaving a trace in the—

*A crab.*

Grit against his cheek. Salt stinging his tongue and the open wounds on his face. Damp seeping up his leg again. Lapping waves. The sand drew back under his knees and his feet, returned, and indeed his pants were wet once again.

*Alive.*

Heaving, his gut twisting, he spewed sea water. It streamed out of his nose, made little runnels in the sand before it slipped between the grains. Snorting sand, choking spasms that gradually slowed, he spluttered a name. 'Jac.' His tongue was fat in his sore mouth, clumsy, sticky. *Blood.*

He turned his face, hadn't the energy to lift his head, and saw the flattest, leathery-skinned foot sink into the sand. Then another foot landed, and his face submerged a little. He heard a string of sounds ... Might have been language, musical, lilting, a question in the tone. Female voices. He grunted, and more sea water dribbled out. Then a whacking on his back, and more water snotted out of him. Strong hands tipped him on his side and more broad brown feet appeared.

*This must be heaven and they are angels. So, I found a god and I am dead.*

'Ben.' A voice reached him. 'Ben.' A vigorous shake on his shoulder and then a pale face appeared over him. The boy's hair was tacked with strands of green seaweed. A cheek had been scraped bloody. A strong lean little hand gripped Ben by his chin.

'You're alive,' Ben rasped, his brain spinning. 'And I'm not dead.'

'*You're* alive.' The boy turned and bellowed at his companions. 'Help him, help him, help him.'

'Jac,' Ben croaked, beckoning. When Jac knelt beside him, he grated, 'They're foreign, lad, not deaf.' And a merciful darkness settled on him.

Ben opened one eye. Nothing hurt. Not badly. An ache in his side. A dull pound in his head. He expected worse, to be delirious, maddened by ingesting seawater, crazed by hours in the sun, skin bleaching and peeling in the tropical heat. Yet, he was cool. He was clean. There was a cloth over his hips.

The boy slept on a mat across the small hut, his sunburned arm flung over his head and his mouth open. Salve of some sort had been smeared all over his reddened body. A fabric swathe wrapped the boy's hips like a babe's swaddle.

The ship had hurtled towards the shore, sailors screaming as a monster wave heaved the ship skywards. Screeching winds whipped away their voices and their bodies; they'd bounced and slid, broken, powerless. The navigator's torn body had flung past him into the thrashing sea. Ben's arms wrenched from sockets as he'd clung—

Then the shore, the warm, wet sand. He closed his eyes to think. *East China Sea.* Far from Shanghai. That's where he suspected they'd been when the storm hit. Uncharted waters for him. Uncharted waters for Zephinia. He tried to recall a map. Somewhere near Korea, maybe? If so, they'd been a lot further off course than he'd thought. Had they been blown from the north?

Had Zephinia survived, or others of the crew?

Cool, he felt cool. He lifted an arm and saw that he had the same salve as Jac. Soothing ointment. Blisters here and there, but not bad, not painful. Not yet.

He ran his tongue around his teeth. All there that he could tell. Maybe a shaky one in front.

The hut was thatched, rough posts held up a roof. Earthen floor. He could see clear sky through a missing thatch and wondered if the storm had torn it off. A water bowl sat on the dirt between him and Jac and he licked his lips anticipating a drink. He couldn't lift his shoulders. So he stayed calm and quiet. *Alive.* He listened to voices outside. Men and women, children. No one came. Voices drifted. Sleep came.

Chatter at his shoulder. A tap-tap on his forehead. He opened an eye and a small brown-faced man smiled at him, eyes crinkling. Still the chatter, and a hand indicating Ben should eat.

Pushing up on his elbows, the aroma teased, Ben's belly growled. The chatter turned into a laugh. A bowl was thrust under his nose and fragrant soup loosened his saliva. Beckoned to drink from the bowl, Ben let the man's lean, strong hand guide his head. Warm broth slid into his mouth and down to his stomach, and he slurped more as it was offered. He wanted more when it was withdrawn.

Jac had gone. He reared back from the concerned brown man who still held his soup. 'Jac,' he croaked, though he'd tried to yell.

The man nodded. 'Jac.'

'Aye, Jac. Where's the boy?' Ben lifted his hand to indicate Jac's height and pointed around the man to the boy's mat on the dirt floor.

'Ah. *Geu sonyeon.*' The man put down the soup, sprang to his feet and padded to the doorway of the hut. A few called words, waved a hand and Jac appeared.

The boy's face split with a grin. 'You're still breathin',' he said, as the old man left the hut.

'Happily,' Ben croaked again. He blinked. Jac's skin was peeling all over, but he seemed fine. Ben fell back on his mat. 'You all right, lad?'

'All right. Stings a bit, me skin.' Jac knelt by him and took up the bowl. 'We found other men, but they died on the sand. Found bodies. Some only half bodies, looked like they been teared apart.'

Ben only raised his eyebrows. Sharks.

'And some, only an arm or leg come ashore.' Jac put his hand behind Ben's head, helped him up again and put the bowl close. 'Been days now,' he said. 'No Englishmen made it alive.'

*Days.*

'Found nothing more on the beach so far today. We went out in the fishing rafts, pulled up broke up kegs, some other timber, but nothing else.'

Ben squeezed his eyes shut. Opened them. 'Drift might have taken things off, who knows where. Was one of the bodies Zephinia?'

Jac flattened his lips and shrugged.

Ben cursed under his breath. 'They bury the bodies?'

'Don't know. They were took off the beach. After that ...' Jac shrugged again. Then his face lit up as he poured more soup into Ben. 'This is a real good place, Ben. At first, I was scared, but not now.'

'Oh, how so?' The soup was more than good, and the bowl was nearly empty. Jac kept tipping it towards his mouth.

'Food, Ben. There's food. And we catch it, and then we cook it, and then we eat it. I get to eat.'

Ben agreed. 'Truly a heaven.' The last of the soup went down his throat.

'And then the women-folk dive under the water, Ben. They stay down there for hours and hours.'

Ben made a face. 'I doubt it's hours.'

'The longest time, Ben, and they come up then suck in the air, and whistle, and hold up a bag of strange looking creatures. Then we eat them. We could stay here forever.'

Ben lay back and closed his eyes. A possibility, but it didn't depend on him. It depended on the generosity of these coastal folk. 'Have they told you where we are, lad?'

'I dunno, maybe they did, hard to understand. I told them I come from *Tỷ du*, Rogerstone.'

Ben popped open an eye. 'How'd you manage that?'

The boy stood. 'I went like this,' he said, and slapped his bony chest. 'And said, "Jac", then I tapped the ground and waved my hand away, way away, and said *Tỷ du*.' He seemed happy with himself. 'Then they're all nodding their heads and waving their hands in the same direction and saying *Tỷ du*, but it sounded a bit funny. Then they're tapping their middles, and the ground, saying, "Chay-choo" or summat.'

'Ah.' Ben knew it from the charts. Cheju was the old name for Quelpaert Island in the Korean Strait. Some said it was named for the Dutch ship that passed by centuries ago, others that it was a bastardised version of the French word for 'somewhere', *quelque part*.

They were indeed clearly far from Shanghai. They'd need to get to the Chinese mainland, or to Formosa, the old Dutch outpost now back in Chinese hands. They needed to get on a ship sailing south.

65

'But the best thing,' Jac said, and held up his amulet. 'I kept me da's spoon. I took it off me neck before the storm and wrapped the strap around and around me arm, here—' he pointed at his wrist, '—and held it in me fist the whole time I were bounced in the water. It weren't so bad.'

Ben could hardly believe it but there it was, large as life. Maybe it had kept him safe, like the boy believed.

'The missus here, she made me a new twine for it. Look, it's even stronger than the one you made me. Wraps around me arm the same, and goes tight, too. I ain't ever gonna lose it, ever.' Jac's eyes were shining. 'An' I can put it in her treasures box if I want to, she says. Or I think that's what she says.'

How the hell the boy had gleaned all of that, Ben had no idea. It didn't matter. 'That's grand, lad, grand.' He closed his eyes as relief caught him, and sleep brought oblivion.

Ben could've been out to it just overnight, or days and nights. He didn't know. Aware of loud voices outside, he rolled off the sleeping mat to his knees. He steadied with one hand on the floor while the other gripped the cloth around his hips. Waiting until his brain stopped sloshing around, he tried to stand. His bones shook, and he dropped to the ground, a retch in his throat.

Sucking in the air, he waited some more. The giddiness fell away, and carefully, he clambered upright, tested a step or two and staggered to the hut's doorway. The chatter outside halted abruptly. Jac was sitting away from the group and his dark head bobbed up at the silence.

Brown-skinned people squatted in a circle. A sinewy man, barefoot, dressed in a raggedy long-sleeved tunic shirt over loose trousers, stood. He beckoned, confidently.

Ben weaved a little until, after the tittering of the locals, he stood at the edge of their circle. As soon as the lean man indicated that he should sit, Ben dropped to the ground and sat cross-legged, dragging the sheet to try and cover his privates. Laughter burst from some on the other side of the circle. The elder frowned and it subsided.

A woman jumped to her feet and left, returning moments later with a tunic shirt, which she thrust at Ben. He shrugged into it aware that the scrutiny was curiosity, open, and forthright. The lean man reached over and waved in front of his face, fingers moving rapidly as he asked a question. Ben shook his head that he didn't understand. The man tapped his own chest. 'Kim Tae-yong.' He tapped again. 'Tae-yong.'

Ben tested the name on his tongue. '*Tay-Yong.*' He repeated it as it sounded to him then tapped his chest. '*Veniamin* Polites.'

The man's eyes popped, and he gazed around his group. Said something. People shook their heads.

Tae-yong pointed at the boy. 'Jac.'

Ben nodded. 'Jac.'

Discussion erupted, and Ben leaned towards Jac. 'You all right?' He raised his voice just a little over the foreign language. 'Did you find out if anyone else survived?'

Jac nodded then shook his head. 'Only us. No Englishmen.' He was pleased no end by that.

Voices died away again. Everyone stared at the two of them. In the silence Ben bowed his head in deference to the members of the group then pointed at Jac, at himself, made two fingers. Then he made three fingers, four and five, then spread his hands, a question.

Tae-yong held up two fingers, shrugged.

'Only two, only two,' Ben muttered. Then he tried to describe Zephinia: a beard, pockmarks on his face, missing teeth, and big hooked nose, bushy brows. Mean. A word was uttered here and there. They knew who he meant.

Tae-yong shook his head, sliced his hand across his middle

and indicated only the top half of his body. '*Sang-eo.*' He bared his teeth. '*Sang-eo.*'

He nodded he understood. Shark.

'He's dead, isn't he?' Jac said, and cracked a grin when Ben nodded.

'Aye, lad.'

The woman who brought the shirt, spoke up, tapping her chest. 'Lee Seo-yeon.'

Ben stood, awkwardly, and gained his feet. He bowed a little. 'Lee *Suh-Yoon*,' he tried.

She leaned back, surprised by that, and nodded at him. 'Seo-yeon.'

He tapped his chest. '*Veniamin.*' When she blinked, he offered the English phonation, tapping his chest again. 'Benjamin.' He had to sit quickly.

She tried it. 'Ben Cha-min.'

He nodded at her, offered a small smile. That was well and good. Further introductions were made to those who seemed to be the leaders of this little group. Some didn't appear happy. Arm waving and short, angry words were exchanged. The group dispersed.

Jac huddled close to Ben. 'Before you woke up, there was lots of talk and pointin' and such.'

Ben leaned against Jac's shoulder. 'Pointing where?'

'Out there somewhere, in the water. Marado, it sounded like.'

'Marado.' Ben could only wonder what that was. He hobbled back to the hut, the need for sleep a siren's song.

There were few people on Cheju, and of those, the women were held in high regard. It was they who went out to sea and dived to great depths to bring home the catch. They were *haenyeo*, sea diving women. Ben wasn't invited to go out on the raft, so he had to wait for Jac's return to hear the excited delivery of the day's activities.

Every word tumbled over the other as Jac told how this one and that one had dived. How Seo-yeon could stay down under the water for the longest time, only to burst back to the surface, holding her catch high.

There were cattle on the island. Soft-looking calm beasts, healthy and sturdy. There were native black pigs with long faces and smooth coats. Vegetables were plentiful although he barely recognised anything. His meal, once a day, was tasty, and his strength, a small tide that had ebbed and flowed a while, returned.

Most folk kept their distance. Jac had other boys his age to play with, but at a certain time, they were withdrawn to their huts. When darkness fell, they could hear family life, but were not invited to be participants.

It was after dark, when the whole village slept, that sometimes Jac's nightmares would interrupt the peaceful surface of their existence. The boy would wake screaming from his fitful sleep, incoherent and cowering until Ben could calm him.

Not even the village medicine people wanted to come near him.

Ben thought he must've been dreaming. He could hear whispers and soft laughter. Two or three people maybe, but he couldn't understand the words. He drifted in and out, resisting the tug to waken. Finally prying open his eyes, he focussed across the room where Jac slept. There, all around Jac were boys on their haunches. Ben came up on his elbows as one of them reached out and prodded Jac. A burst of low laughter erupted then Jac thrashed to his feet, yelling in a sudden fierce rage. The boys leapt back. Ben sprang off his mat, promptly fell in a dizzy heap, groaning.

Nervous titters as Jac eyed the boys then tense silence fell. He puffed out a few breaths. 'I forgot we were going off to watch the cattle.' He hitched on his trousers. 'They were just having fun. I forgot. Don't worry, Ben.'

The boys, some lanky, some stocky, dressed in their tunic shirts and pants, stared guiltily at Ben, back at Jac. Ben waved, sank back onto his mat as they filed past him. *Watch the cattle.* So the boy was making friends, picking up the language. *Good news, good news …* They might even help Jac forget his nightmares.

Sleep claimed him again, but it was restless, filled with the need to escape paradise.

# CHAPTER FIVE

Seo-yeon knelt at the tea table, its smooth surface familiar under her hands, and poured their favourite brew, a mix of seaweed and herbs, gently steeped. Then she pushed a well-used wooden cup towards her husband who'd waited for the offer. It was her turn to serve, after all. Tae-yong took it up and slurped, nodding approval that Seo-yeon didn't need.

The afternoon was humid, the warm, damp air cloying. A change in season coming.

'Song-chol said the boy had a screaming fit when the boys began to play.'

'His name is Jac, husband.'

'They say he cried and got fierce, pushing and shoving the others away, throwing out his fists and kicking.'

Seo-yeon frowned. 'What were they doing, those foolish boys?'

'Just what boys do. Rough play. Song-chol says the boy became violent when one of the others grabbed him from behind and threw him down to the ground. They couldn't understand a word of his gibberish, but the anger was obvious.'

'Fear, more likely. But what of?'

Tae-yong shrugged. 'Who would know? These people are strange. Thankfully, he didn't hurt anyone.'

Seo-yeon was quiet a moment, her cup of tea held comfortably in her hands. She put her lips to it and withdrew. Still too hot. 'What happened after?'

'Everyone settled down. Song-chol sat with him until his snivelling stopped but the boy wouldn't allow anyone to touch him. The others left, embarrassed by the sounds of things. Jin-soo, of course, thought it was very funny.'

Seo-yeon pulled a face. 'I would box his ears, that Jin-soo. Lazy good for nothing lump of a peasant. I'll speak to his mother.' She put her teacup down harder than she should have. Tea was not to be disrespected. Setting her table to rights, and under Tae-yong's glance, Seo-yeon bristled. 'It must be fear,' she said.

'Then that will not do in one of our boys,' her husband answered.

Seo-yeon's eyes widened. 'One of our boys?' she repeated, staring at the frown on Tae-yong's face. 'So, we've taken him in as family?'

'I see you have, and why not?' he said gently. 'Our loss will always be our loss, dear wife, and our two dead children will never be replaced. But our home is big, and our hearts have room to love more children, do they not?'

Seo-yeon felt her heart thud and recognised the grief. Their children, a boy and a girl had died years apart from two separate epidemics of the *hongyeok*, a scourge, a terrible illness that spread a red rash all over their bodies. She was now too old to conceive again and had welcomed the boy, Jac, who had the strange language and the round blue eyes, and who'd come to them from the sea. Despite his being outlandish, and a foreigner of the sort that invoked immediate suspicion in others, she and Tae-yong had been drawn to him.

'And Song-chol?' she asked her husband.

Song-chol, orphaned as a child, was only a few years older than Jac. He too had long been in Seo-yeon's heart, but the boy had not come into the shelter of her arms.

'He's a lonely boy,' Tae-yong said. 'He has rejected us before, from fear, too, I believe. Of what, I don't know, and we might never know. But in Jac, he has a friend. A brother. If he's to stay here, if they're both to stay, they cannot carry fear. It's a torment.'

She nodded and took up her tea once more, said nothing as the thought turned around and around. To have a child to nurture once more ... To have children under her roof again.

'We will bring Song-chol to us, again. He will come, I think, now there is Jac.' Tae-yong tapped the floor beside him, making his point. 'They have to learn to find peace in themselves.'

Seo-yeon nodded again. That would be the hardest thing to learn.

\*

Ben thought to teach Jac a few letters and numbers in English—to teach him Greek would make no sense at all—and although painstaking with a knife on timber, or drawn in the sand, it occupied both of them for a time and kept alive the memory of another life. He snorted a laugh; it was more for his own sake than anyone else's. Jac seemed happy enough here.

He sat in the doorway of their hut and studied Jac's cut marks on a stout stick. It recorded a month or so since the shipwreck. He'd had just finished notching day thirty-one when Tae-yong beckoned him to where a circle of young men congregated. He also called for Jac.

They sat, cross-legged, with others and waited. Another man appeared, a younger man, and he entered the circle. He gave a small bow to Tae-yong. This was Song-chol, whose eyes darted to Jac. He was friendly enough, still a little distant towards Ben, but today he gave a small bow to him and then to Jac who grinned at him.

Song-chol had a solid build and a little extra height on Jac. He demonstrated a gleeful character, and though Ben knew Jac couldn't understand too much of the language, he could tell that the boy enjoyed Song-chol's company over that of any of the others.

Tae-yong entered the circle. Song-chol waited, it seemed, with respectful anticipation. At the first of the fluid moves, graceful arms, and legs, Jac sat up attentively. Tae-yong's foot came up and Song-chol hit the dust only to roll back to his feet with a spring in his step. A cheer erupted from the circle.

Springing to his feet, Song-chol met the master, and down he went again.

Ben glanced at Jac. The boy was engrossed, his gaze locked onto the willowy arms of the opponents, moving in a body language he couldn't speak. The motion of feet and legs was dynamic.

Tae-yong indicated a halt to Song-chol. He turned to Jac, bowed a little and said, '*Taekkyeon*,' and beckoned him onto the sparring pad.

Jac was in their hut, kicking out his leg here and there. Ben dodged him a couple of times and then took to his pallet to rest again. *Still the damnable drowsiness.*

'Did you see that one, like this, Ben?' And up would come a foot. Clumsy, Jac would fall on his backside only to bounce to his feet again. His sinewy arms waved about, his hands flapping in imitation.

'They say it takes a long time to learn this takyon.' Ben closed his eyes. He could hear Jac's feet landing and swishing on the earthen floor.

'I've got a long time, Ben, don't I?'

More thumping of nimble feet on the floor, and Ben grunted. 'You do, boy.'

# Chapter Six

The anger, the arms thrown in the air in frustration, the stomping away from the meeting circle had at first bewildered Jac. Now he believed it was the way things were negotiated in Cheju.

They'd been here many months already, and lately things had become more worrying. The village folk were agitated.

Jac went to find his *eomeoni*, his mother, Seo-yeon. '*Eomma*, why is there trouble again? Ben thinks it's because of us.'

Her calm dark eyes met his. Smooth, serene features set in the sun-browned face lit for a moment. 'Mainland men don't like your kind being here with us.'

Jac's gut squeezed. 'Why not?'

Seo-yeon gave a small shake of her head. Her dry, curly mop of hair was a black cap, cut short for her diving. The tight ringlets bounced a little. 'Some in our village don't want you here either. They say we have to give you to the mainland men, to save trouble for ourselves.'

'I don't want to go.' Jac knew it wouldn't be good. 'I'll run away.'
He reached for the talisman that hung around his neck.

Her eyes crinkled in a smile. *Run away.* What did that mean?
There was nowhere for him to run. 'You will not. No one so far has
told the mainlanders that you're here, but it won't be long before
someone does. It's why your *appa* teaches you *taekkyeon*. You'll
learn to protect yourself, and your uncle Ben.'

'I don't want to leave you.'

She looked at him. 'Don't be afraid.'

Jac studied his hands, then his feet. He whispered, 'I left my
ma, I left my da. I left my sister. I had a sister.' He looked up, his
face bleak, and he withdrew the spoon from his shirt and clutched
it in his hand. 'Sometimes I hear her in my head. I see her when I
dream.'

'She is still with you, your sister.' Seo-yeon waited, hoping
he would tell her more. Instead, he heaved in a couple of ragged
breaths, as if to stop from crying.

'Teach me everything,' he said. 'Teach me to tend the cattle,
and to grow the seeds, teach me to...' he faltered. His fear of the
sea after the shipwreck was great. 'Teach me to dive,' he demanded
boldly.

Seo-yeon bent a little to gaze into the eyes of her foundling,
the weedy little white boy. His red and peeling skin had healed,
was already sun-browned a little, a boy who would soon outgrow
her. His eyes would always give him away as a stranger here, their
shape, and their colour, that of the sea on a sunny day. There was
nothing she could do about that.

'Diving is women's work. Besides, you don't like the sea.'
Despite his aversion, the trips out on the raft boats with the women
had bolstered his confidence a little. She had hand-picked the crew
who would look out for him.

'I am brave,' he blurted.

76

'I know,' she answered. The time would come soon enough when he'd want to leave these shores in search of his own people.

*

Ben reckoned they'd been here at the village for five months, so it was now November 1841. The autumn, and the coming winter months in this area would be calm. On the beach, he'd stared south. Sooner or later a ship would pass by this island. He just needed one to be close enough to check its colours. No point trying to take passage on a hostile ship.

A dry light breeze accompanied him from the beach to his hut.

They were going to get off this island somehow although when he looked across at Jac, who squatted in the sand with Song-chol, he wondered. The boy had taken to life here like he was born to it. Ben was happy to see Jac become settled.

For a long time, the boy's nightmares would bring back the brutal horror of Rigg Manor, Sir Hugh's house, dark and terrifying shapes and tearing pain. Those memories had been scorched into the boy's mind and were buried deep in his head.

Sometimes the nightmares were of the shipwreck and Jac would relate terrible dreams about the angry whirling sea.

Ben would face whatever resistance Jac had to leaving, if any, when the time came. In his bones, that time was close.

He was dreaming. His father, angry, his dark eyebrows twisted, waved his hands in Ben's face. *Eleni's gone*, he was shouting. *Eleni's gone.* The dream hadn't visited for years. Eleni was long gone, had run off over twenty years ago, the day before she was to marry Ben.

He tossed. There were better dreams to have, like of his mother's cooking, always a comfort. *Keftedes*, her meatballs with herbs and onions, or her *spanakopita*, spinach and feta pie, and plump *eliés*, olives—how he missed olives. Dishes were piled high in front of him. Baklava tantalised. His mouth watered and—

'Be quick.' A rough hand was at his shoulder, a guttural whisper rasped in his ear. 'The mainlanders are coming. We have to go.'

Ben darted up, shaking off sleep, and shrugged on his tunic. 'Where—?'

'To the beach,' Song-chol said, 'to the place where you stare out to sea.'

Voices in the late night were loud, urgent. The raiders were being diverted.

Tae-yong shot inside the hut, clamped a hand over Jac's mouth and gathered him under his arm. Outside, setting Jac on his feet, he gave silent, stern instructions for quiet and pushed him alongside Song-chol. Following them, he hitched a water barrel onto his back.

Ben collided with Seo-yeon outside. 'Come,' she said, one strong hand gripping his arm. 'And be quiet.'

He didn't have the stealth at night like these island folk, but he kept his breathing low and his footfalls light. Seo-yeon, deft and agile, led him through the tangle of bushes that lined the southern shore near the village. When they reached the beach, Song-chol and the others were waiting.

They crept along the scrub line in single file. Ben could hear Jac sniffing. He tapped his shoulder from behind and reached around to wipe the tears from Jac's face. 'Be strong, lad, we're all here.'

Seo-yeon chopped the air in front of them and Jac stopped snivelling. He gulped soundlessly.

Creeping to the water's edge they found Seo-yeon's raft boats. Ben, Jac and Seo-yeon took one vessel, and Tae-yong and Song-chol took the other, the water barrel strapped on. They waded the rafts out and clambered on board. Jac paddled with his hands, copying the others and gradually the low waves took them out to sea.

Under the light of a half moon, when land was barely visible behind them and the twinkling of fire-lit torches on Cheju had disappeared, Ben muttered to Seo-yeon, 'Where are we going?'

'Mara-do,' she answered in a whispered snap, paddling strongly.
'Marado.' It was an uninhabited island south of Cheju.
'Mara-*do*,' she corrected, again impatient at having to speak.
'But nothing is there,' he said, aware Jac was listening.
'Nothing,' she agreed.

Ben, still catching his breath after the paddle, crawled alongside Jac on the pebbly sand. 'Lad, Seo-yeon says we stay here a few days until those mainlanders are gone from Cheju.'

Jac nodded, huddled as far back against the rocky cliff face as he could, away from the lapping sea water. He whispered, 'Why do they want to take us?' Glad to be safe on land once again, he watched as the dark shapes of the elders moved the rafts to safer ground.

Ben clamped a hand on his shoulder, felt the thin bones shaking underneath. 'They don't like our sort.'

'*Eomma* says there's nothing here. What will we do?'

'I'm sure she will find everything we need. She's a strong woman. But for now, we need to find a place to sleep.'

Song-chol slid in alongside them. 'There is a way to the top of the hill, then at daylight we'll be able to see all around us.' He took Jac's hand and hauled him to his feet. Ben followed.

They slept in a hollow on top of the cliff, five bodies pressed together. No one moved except to go a little distance away to relieve themselves and then return to tuck back into the sleeping space. All except Jac took turns at being the look-out. When first light crept over them, Song-chol crawled to the edge of the clifftop. He checked left and right, then bellied backwards to where the others waited. 'Nothing on this side, either. We would've heard if we'd been followed.'

In the vast distance, across the water, Mount Hallasan rose in the middle of Cheju. Ben wondered how they'd ever be found on *this* speck of an island. But Tae-yong and Seo-yeon must have been here before so others would know of it. He turned, facing south, and stood, cautiously. The ocean spanned a never-ending arc. He might sight passing ships from here but slim chance, if any, he'd be able to get on one.

Song-chol spoke to Ben. 'We will wait one day. If it's safe to return, Do-Jung will come for us.' Do-Jung was another young villager.

Ben wiped salty strings of his hair from his face. The tie that kept it drawn back had dropped to the water somewhere between Cheju and Mara-do. 'Do the great ships sail past here?' he asked as Jac crouched out of the hollow and scampered over.

Song-chol chanced a look at the elders who were surveying Cheju and the strait between, their discussion animated. 'Barbarians sail past Cheju, and go south-west again to Shanghai, or to Formosa. Some to Nagasaki in the other direction.'

Ben felt something shift inside. There was a chance. 'I need to get on a ship.'

Song-chol grunted. Ben saw something furtive in his eyes before the younger man looked back to Tae-yong. 'Sometimes we trade when the time is right.'

So there really was a chance. The season had changed, and the trade for opium would be high. *There was a chance.*

The day was spent on watch. The water Tae-yong had loaded onto the raft was taken sparingly, each mouthful watched carefully. Seo-yeon would not venture into the ocean to dive for food in case they had to depart quickly. 'Chew grass,' she said testily when hunger pangs gnawed.

All the long day, no activity was seen on the strait between the two islands but Tae-yong was not convinced of their security. 'If the dolts venture this way, all we have to throw at them are rocks.'

'If they come,' Seo-yeon said, 'we have time on our side. We will be able to see them and leave quickly.'

'And go where?' Tae-yong said, but no one answered.

It was a restless night, huddled together, taking turns—except for Jac—to keep watch. Jac did try to stay awake with Ben and thought he was good at it until a warm hand clamped over his mouth. Terrified out of what had been a solid sleep, he was rolled against Song-chol. It was just before dawn.

'Quiet, little brother. I can even hear your heartbeat,' Song-chol whispered in his ear. 'There is someone coming up the hill from the shore. Don't talk.'

Jac nodded. Then he heard a yelp. A voice called out. 'Did someone just throw a rock? I can't see a thing up here. It's me, Do-Jung. The mainlanders have gone.'

They returned to Cheju soon after dawn, arms aching, bellies empty. Seo-yeon's neighbours had food waiting for them and the youngsters wolfed down all they were given. The word was that a half-hearted search had been conducted, lots of threats and yells about what would happen to those harbouring the barbarians. No one admitted a thing. The mainland men had been keen to depart; they'd no desire to be on the island, no matter what job they had to do.

Someone was advising the mainlanders. Tae-yong glared at everyone. When he found out who, he said to Seo-yeon later, he would deal with them himself. As a master of *taekyyeon*, he would fight to protect his family.

Seo-yeon had nodded. He was sure she'd been impressed.

They had to scurry away to Mara-do twice more before it seemed the mainlanders gave up. Those disgruntled locals must have forgotten their gripes, too. So far, Tae-yong hadn't found out who'd been stirring the pot; he hadn't had to use his martial art in combat, he told Seo-yeon. For that, she lifted her gaze to the sky.

*

Jac's language skills were honed on the children and the elders alike. Suspicion of him dropped away. Suspicion of Ben lingered but he was treated politely. He worked as hard as any of the men, kept to himself, and only offered a word of his new language here and there. It usually got a laugh, and a correction.

There were fewer sightings of the great ships and Ben wondered if the Opium War had finally ended. He asked for news of it, but when it carried from the mainland to the Cheju islanders, it was already months old, and most times unclear. He despaired, then laughed a little at himself. He remembered encouraging Jac to trust in something bigger at a time when hope looked lost; he should take his own advice. He began to pray in the Cheju way, and asked for guidance off this island.

The days flew by. He doggedly tracked the weeks, and the months. They shivered through the biting cold of winter, sighed with relief when the temperate climes of spring arrived. Now it was monsoon season. Storms boomed thunder and dumped torrents of rain. It was 1842 Ben calculated, so he and Jac had been here for over fifteen months.

He'd long given up his belief that *today was the day* he'd get off this island but kept a keen eye on the ocean when the weather cleared. On the top of the hill, shielding his eyes from the sun high overhead, he looked south. He watched the dot on the horizon for a while, but as with other sightings, when he saw the tempest behind it, the ship would only be another that, if it survived, would pass him by.

A wild storm rushed the island that night, and the villagers bunkered down while the coast was battered. Trees bent in the roaring winds, and some stone huts lost their thatched roofs. Fences of pitted volcanic rock withstood most of the pounding. Many possessions were lost but it wasn't as bad as others they'd experienced.

In the morning, Ben helped haul loose rocks back into place, drag away debris, and retrieve far flung possessions.

Jac was now a strapping lad with an intermittent squeak in his voice that the islanders thought extremely funny. He helped Song-chol pull a table from a tangle of trees. His chest had widened, his shoulders squared off and the rangy line of his limbs showed sinew and muscle. His hips were narrow, and large bony knees joined lean shins and sturdy thighs. A downy patch of dark hair blurred his cheeks and chin, and hair had sprouted under his arms and between his legs.

Seo-yeon muttered darkly as she swept leaf litter and broken pots from her kitchen area. It still rained, but it didn't hamper their clean-up. Tae-yong was fixing a post, readying it for the attachment of the repaired straw roof.

A boy ran in from the direction of the southern beach, and his alarm rang out. 'Ship off the coast. Barbarians,' he yelled.

Ben took a moment. Then he dropped the rocks and ran for the beach. He didn't wait to hear Tae-yong's command to seek shelter. He did hear the older man's shout for Jac to stay where he was, but Ben knew it'd be ignored.

When he got to the shoreline, he stared. Not half a mile out, the ship was listing to starboard but afloat, and safe. He squinted, shielded his eyes, and scanned. No flotsam and no bodies on the beach. It seemed the ship was unscathed.

Jac slid in alongside. 'Is it …?'

'Aye. A real ship. A real ship, Jac.' He gripped the boy's arm hard and shook it. He stared back out to sea. The ship wasn't going anywhere soon. It looked as if it had anchored or was maybe stuck on a sandbar waiting for the tide.

Not even half a mile … maybe only a couple of cables. Was that wishful thinking? A flag waved high on the mast. Red and white stripes. *American?*

'Ben?'

He turned to stare at Jac. The boy had asked him something. 'I have to try and get on it, Jac.'

Jac, wide-eyed, stared back, pleading with him. 'Don't—'

'I have to, lad. But you don't. You'll be safe here. These are your people now.'

'No.'

'Ye've got ye spoon, ye talisman?'

'Aye.' Jac closed his fist over the spoon dangling under his tunic.

'It'll keep yer till I come for ye.'

'No—'

'I'm going, lad. And you can't come. Not this time. If it's safe, I'll find you. I'll find you. Grow up to be a strong man, look after your *eomma* and your *appa*. Don't forget who y'are.' Ben squeezed both Jac's shoulders then pulled him in, held him tight. Just as abruptly, he let him go and pushed out of the scrub. He pounded up the beach to where a small fishing raft was secured, and dragged it out, running with it into the surf.

He looked back. Song-chol had Jac in a bear hug from behind and Jac thrashed to be released. Seo-yeon rushed out from the scrub-line and leapt over the storm debris to reach her boy. Tae-yong charged out of the trees and joined them on the beach. He stopped and lifted a hand in a farewell.

Ben paddled out. Jac would be safest on the island—who knew what was on that boat? The closer Ben got, the better he felt. Then he heard the lumbering roll of a chain being wound up, and the yells on board as the anchor cleared the waterline. The ship buoyed upright.

He paddled harder and it wasn't until he saw the flag and knew it to be American that he yelled as loud as he could. '*Wait!*'

He didn't stop paddling. His arms ached, the heat of the sun burned through his thin *garot* tunic and pants. A huge harpoon was over the bow of the ship and he smelled rancid fat as it clung in great swathes to the sides, staining the timbers a brackish brown.

He stopped paddling only when a rope ladder was dropped from the side, splashing into the water just ahead of his raft. A voice called down to him, 'Friend or foe, man?'

# CHAPTER SEVEN

## *1844 Rigg Manor, Wales*

A bird fluttered past the window, hovered a little and fluttered back to glance at itself in the reflection. It clearly wasn't a robin, and it wasn't a swallow or a wagtail. Lilpah didn't know what it was, and there was no one to tell her either. No one here was interested in birds or in any other living creatures.

Truth to tell, it didn't matter what it was. It could fly. Fly *away*. Many times over the days, the months and now years she had thought of flying away, being that little bird who might live to escape this life.

But there was no flight from this place. So, she'd stopped thinking about it. Besides, it was just a bird, not a grand carriage with a gentleman inside.

The bird pecked tentatively. Lilpah only raised her eyes to watch him fend off his perceived rival. At that slight movement, he darted off, quick as anything. Gone into the gloom of the noonday in winter.

Sitting by the window on the hard timber ledge, she stared down into the garden. Rain spots hit the window and the sight of Maguire, the head gardener, tending the hedgerow below, dimmed before her eyes. Her stare remained. A boy, ragged and panting, pushed a barrow full of clod, but his lean frame blurred, too, as rain began to pelt. In less than a minute, both the man and the boy were drenched, and still they worked on. And why not? There was work to be done.

There was work to be done everywhere. What did Sir Hugh do with all the money collected from his tenants if he never put it to upkeep of the house and grounds? He was a miser who squirrelled it away, out of reach.

She wondered if the workmen would catch their death of cold. *Would be a blessing.* She scoffed. Who then would the master have to tend the garden? Her gaze slid to the boy, still panting, still shoving the barrow. He slipped in the shallow garden trench and righted himself awkwardly with a dogged resolve.

He reminded her of another boy, her brother Jac. Was he even alive? Gone with that ship's mate or whoever he was. *Left me.* She thought of the carved spoon attached to its plait of fine strips of leather, secreted under a stone in the wall of her dingy closet. It was the only link she had, and it had to stay hidden. If Sir Hugh knew the value she placed on such a talisman …

Jac had left, escaped. He'd got away from this place but what fate had he met? They'd had news of that ship, the *Revival.*

She shuddered recalling the day, Foswick, Sir Hugh's valet had crept to her sleeping space. 'What do you want?' she'd shrieked, scrambling back, alarmed at the odd look on his normally stony features. Fear crowded every corner of this place, and nowhere more than in the depths of her being.

'There has been some news delivered that must be relayed to the master.' His gaze hadn't met hers, instead his eyes had shifted, slid around her.

Unease marched up her spine. 'Yes?'

'Mistress,' he started.

He never *ever* called her anything in deference. Chills scampered across her scalp.

'Someone must alert the master to the apparent demise of the ship captained by his, ah, friend, Pero Zephinia. All cargo is lost, and ah, all hands perished.'

*All hands perished.* Too canny to give way to grief, Lil said nothing. Foswick expected something of her.

Sure enough, he said, 'You tell him.'

'He'll kill me in a rage,' she seethed.

Foswick shrugged. 'It might not be that way.'

'Then you do it,' she'd snarled at him.

Rounding on her, Foswick caught her shoulder with a bony hand and squeezed it, a bruising grip. 'You who warm his bed, will do it. Tell him you heard it said when someone returned from the village. Take the sting now, mistress, he'll take it better from you. If he learns the rest of us knew his fortune is lost and said nothing, he'll mete out torture on the rest of us.'

'And what of the torture for me?' she cried, incredulous, her breath short, her face hot.

Foswick almost turned his back but she didn't miss the curl of his lip. 'As you already seek it, you are the best candidate.'

Lil lost her breath then. 'I won't do it.'

'You will.' He made a calculation. 'And you'll be remembered for it by those you save.'

She'd recoiled. 'What use is that to me?'

'You get to remain here with the master,' he said and walked out as quietly as he'd entered.

She hadn't known who she feared more in that moment.

Jac might still be alive—but how could that possibly be? How would she ever know? There'd never been word until this news of the ship. And even so, nothing from Jac himself. He might truly be dead.

*All hands perished.*

Lilpah had dashed that thought away as she still did, even now. She couldn't let herself believe it. But a hollow ache lingered.

From even further back, a memory of someone's laughter bubbled through the timeless fog. A low delighted chuckle, a ghostly tinkle on the frayed edge of her mind. It could only be her mother, but the more she tried to bring it forward, the further it slipped away. Why did it come—to torment? To give hope?

Oh, what use now is hope? None; a vague and fleeting wisp of dead space. Hope was just to be fed, clothed. Just to be sent for; to be the favourite once more.

As she predicted, Sir Hugh met the demise of the ship with a blinding fury. His heavy blows had smashed her, he spat his financial losses in her face. Then he'd snarled his hand in her hair, her scalp pulling as he hissed, 'You lost your filthy brat of a brother with that pig Zephinia, too.' The punch flattened her and she stayed down. A swift last kick to her head, and she'd played dead. He'd gone raging into the night.

Tippy came for her and dragged her to her tiny room. Lil's back teeth had been loosened but had settled, her swollen eyes and fractured cheek had taken some time to heal. Bruises had faded, and the broken bones in her ribs and her arm had mended slowly. But the last of her soul had died.

She blinked. The rain had eased. Maguire was kicking the boy who lay sprawled face first in the mud. He'd fallen. Lilpah hadn't noticed earlier. Now disinterested, she watched as the boy staggered to his feet, his sodden thigh the target of one last kick.

He leaned over the barrow and heaved up whatever he'd last eaten. It looked like the dirt of the furrow into which he'd lurched.

Lilpah's lip twitched. She couldn't allow a curl of her upper lip, or a disapproving twist of her mouth for fear the master would see and scold her with a quick backhand. Her tongue found the last place his knuckle had struck, a gap on the left side of her mouth where a good tooth had been. So no frowning, no moue of disapproval. Nothing.

Her existence was bewildering. What a difference a few months could make. Not worthy of the master's bed any longer, or of the floor by his hearth, or indeed even of a pallet by Tippy's sleeping mat. She'd been cast off to warm the beds of the old men who came and paid the master gold for the privilege.

Tippy told Lil that she was too old for the master now. How old was she—sixteen, seventeen? She had to use her fingers. She'd learned to read and write a little. Her few letters and numbers were courtesy of Tippy, but neither could afford to be discovered educating themselves. She'd tried to keep count of days and months passing, but it was too hard. Paper, pen, and ink were luxuries here, and so they were scarce.

Her master's new charge for her was to keep those raucous old men happy until they fell asleep on her, flaccid, and snoring. They deemed themselves conquering heroes.

'They can't even conquer the chamber pot and piss themselves while they sleep,' she told Tippy.

There'd be a way to creep back into the master's favour, and back into his bed—she knew it. She'd promise never to displease him … *Never to leave.* Not like others had left her. Not like her parents, dead in a skirmish that had barely made a difference. Not like her brother who got carried off and out of this place. She would find a way to survive in the manner she'd become—

The bird fluttered back, attacking the window. The interloper enemy would be terrified and flee. Yet, he didn't flee—the interloper kept pecking right back, until in frustration, the bird swooped up to the ledge, landing daintily. It shook itself, skipped about-face then took off.

Lil's gaze fell onto the boy with the barrow once more. He

appeared resigned to his fate. He hefted the barrow handles and trudged on. At the end of the thick muddy row he would turn and push it back all the other way as well.

She'd never seen him before. Then, there were plenty of people who worked hereabouts that she'd never laid eyes on.

A door creaked, the big heavy door that opened from the hall-way into the room where she sat. Lil didn't move.

'Lil.' It was Tippy.

She inhaled, disappointed, and continued to stare down at Maguire and the boy. The older man cuffed the lad, who waited half a beat before savagely slamming an elbow to the man's face.

Lilpah's eyes widened.

Maguire went down on one knee, holding his face. The boy swung a fist at the man's cheek, and then swung the other to connect with a nose. Maguire slumped into the garden trench, and like the bird, the boy took off across the field.

*Fly!*

They'd catch him, but Lil felt a smile—the first in weeks—stretch over the newly healed gap in her mouth. A fleeting taste of anyone's freedom was better than nothing. Or was it? Her smile faded. She felt safe here. What would she do with freedom?

'Lil,' Tippy insisted. 'Guests are waitin'.'

Old Tippy, twenty-three or so, would be wringing her hands on a faded worn-out pinafore. *Guests are waitin'*.

The final vestige of a life barely remembered, the last remnant of her past slipped out of her like a wraith. As it spirited away, a small boulder settled on her heart.

Lilpah Owen straightened then rose—like a lady—from her seat by the window. She thought only of survival and dreamed no more of freedom.

# Chapter Eight

*1847 Cheju*

Song-chol leaned towards him as if to nudge. 'I think she likes you.'

Jac couldn't look across to the happy, smiling face of Min-jee. She'd be laughing and talking with the other girls from his village, preparing to take her diving lessons with the older sea women.

He couldn't talk to her. Apart from his voice sticking in his throat, he'd be reprimanded if he made any overture whatsoever. Besides all that, no one, not even Song-chol, knew why he wouldn't go near a girl. Jac shied away, had long refused to explore any of that. He deliberately touched no one, male or female, and no one touched him. The only time he made body contact was at *taek-kyeon*, or by accident. Or when Song-chol felt it necessary to shove, slap, punch, or elbow him—ignoring completely that Jac would abruptly pull away and snarl.

He was better off left out of all that staring or touching business, whatever it meant. Most mornings, the urge to stroke himself to the point of release was so intense it nearly drove him mad. He'd try to outwait the urgent stiffness until it subsided and he could ignore it. Difficult, *impossible* most times. He was weak when it beckoned.

After he'd given in and relieved it, he'd roll onto his side, curled up. He was always bewildered by how good it felt when it happened, when he could push back the darkness in his head.

Yet he knew that his *thing*—other men had the same *thing*—could do the most terrible damage when it was shoved into someone else. He had not forgotten the abuse on him by the gaolers; he had not forgotten seeing Hugh Rigg's own stout pole force entry into female children.

No one could help him with his peculiar affliction and the memories of the past that were associated with it; it would have to remain his secret. Waves of revulsion for his body's reaction came with flashes of a terrifying man in that dungeon, with screams of others, the whimpering afterwards, the drained look of horror on the boys' faces. He squeezed his eyes shut and felt the pain clutch in his chest. *Let the screams leave me alone.* At night amid the terror, visions of a figure he knew to be his sister would float, an ethereal presence that sometimes calmed his racing pulse.

Song-chol pushed him with a shoulder. 'I said, she likes you.'

Jac turned his back on where the girl was standing. 'I don't care. I'm an outsider, so her parents are not going to take to me anyway.'

'Min-jee has always liked you.'

'Stop.' Jac rolled his shoulders now thick with muscle and sinew that broadened and deepened his chest. His waist tapered beneath a flat stomach. The past six years' training had hardened his body.

'And I can see that you like Min-jee,' Song-chol pointed at Jac's groin, his eyes closed in a snort of laughter. 'You could use that thing to slay many enemies. A great sword.'

Jac stalked off. Each time a glance or a stare from Min-jee caught his eye, he needed to get away, find release. He shoved down the tent in his pants and felt the anger and shame burble up from his gut. He didn't know what to do about it.

Song-chol caught up with him. 'You know, after all this time, her family might accept you.' He danced alongside, air-sparring as Jac continued to wave him off.

'I've never felt acceptance here, just tolerance.'

'That's true. We tolerate you like a little brother who is a brainless half-wit.' Song-chol had joined the family. He'd been living in their hut for as long as Jac had, no longer needing to find shelter in the fields or by the sea. He called Seo-yeon his mother, and Taeyong his father, Jac was his brother. Song-chol kept up the jibes. 'Of course, Seo-yeon,' he said, 'wouldn't allow her foundling to be drowned all those years ago, so we had to keep you. Had to try and knock some sense into that square head of yours.' He jousted with his shadow. 'Not even the mainlanders are interested in you these days.'

'That's a good thing.'

'But no change in that woman over there. Seems Min-jee doesn't mind the look of a half-fried *mandu*.'

Jac scowled at him. 'You'll be the one looking like a dumpling in an hour.' He dodged a cleverly aimed foot. 'You're in need of a good practice match.'

'Oh ho, that I am, Slow-Witted One.' Song-chol snapped a high kick across Jac's path, and bounced back, his feet agile, his movements graceful and swift.

'Come on, then, Breath of Dead Fish,' Jac said, his arms and hands moving in front of his opponent. 'To the sparring pad.'

Song-chol straightened, gave Jac the perfunctory bow, a curt movement of his head. 'I'll beat you there, Sea Slug,' he said and took off at a run.

'I'll beat you when I arrive, Flower Petal,' Jac yelled in return and jogged towards the clearing where the young men gathered to spar, all thoughts of Min-jee, and other dire situations, gone.

Jac wiped down his bare torso and flipped the rag across to Song-chol who lay stretched out on the ground. 'Good match,' he said as Song-chol clutched the fabric to his sweaty stomach.

'I let you win.'

'You always let me win.'

Song-chol grunted. 'Even a master of the art, such as I, has to admit he is in the presence of a greater opponent at times.' He twisted his head to look at Jac. 'You're my height, lean and you move with a different intensity, as if you were born to *taekkyeon*. You learned quickly.'

Jac lifted a shoulder. 'It suits me. It empties me of—' Min-jee and her friends floated by with glances at both Jac and Song-chol. 'Of useless energy. Fills me with something better.'

Song-chol's gaze followed the girls as they wandered past then he came up on one elbow. 'Useless energy? No such thing. I understand what ails you. I know. I keep saying so.'

'Is that right?' Jac snatched up his tunic and shrugged into it. Song-chol knew nothing. 'What ails me?'

Song-chol turned to look at the girls' backs. 'Same old thing. Hips that sway, breasts that jiggle in our direction, eyes that dare us to approach.'

Jac watched the girls as they disappeared behind the huts in the distance. 'They didn't even notice us.'

'They made sure we noticed them.' Song-chol sat up and wiped himself over. He balled up the rag and tossed it to the edge of the sparring mat, a square of thatched reeds. 'You need to be ready, my friend the virgin.' He grinned at Jac and shrugged into his tunic.

Jac wiped his face with a forearm. 'I don't want to be ready.' A prickle of heat raced over the back of his hands.

Song-chol flung an arm around his friend's shoulder. 'It's the best thing in the world. Except for sparring. Or sitting on a rock fishing. You'll see.' He pulled Jac close. 'Don't worry, we'll get some for you—'

Jac swung Song-chol off his feet by his tunic and hurled him into the dirt. He lunged at him, a grunt erupting, and a red mist dropped over his vision.

Song-chol was a dead weight but Jac's rage shook him like a dog with a rat. Song-chol hung in his grasp, mouth open, eyes wide then he scrambled for purchase, his balance skewed. He fell back, dragging Jac with him.

The mist cleared and Jac dropped Song-chol as if burned. He staggered back as ragged breaths rasped his throat. He stared at his hands, and then at Song-chol and words exploded out of him. 'It's cruel, that thing you never shut up about, that thing you say you'll *get for me*. It's barbaric. Why do you think that tearing apart another person using this—' he pointed to his groin, '—is the best thing in the world?' He stopped talking, his breath rough in his throat.

Cautious, wary, Song-chol got to his feet and slunk into a crouch. 'I don't understand.' He waited, baffled. 'Are we talking about the same thing?'

Jac slumped to the ground and clutching his forearms across his body, rocked back and forth.

'Jac?' Song-chol asked, worry in his voice.

Jac spewed it out. His own defilement, the other boys' shrieks, of watching, hidden and terrified as they were violated by gaolers and gentry alike. Thank the gods, those men hadn't had time to come often for him. He'd been brought up to the house that night Ben came, and rescue had been a relief so great he'd felt numb.

Rigg hadn't been interested in Jac or other boys; his penchant was for the screaming or whimpering girls he took. Jac's revulsion was complete long before their cries stopped, their bodies broken.

He'd run and hidden, held his ears to shut out the terrible noises. He tried to bury the anguish, the fear, and the loathing.

Jac spoke of his sister and the horror she'd endured; others had told what she'd suffered. Ugly recollections hurtled out of him in broken words, some in Welsh he hardly used any more, some in his new language. He wept so hard bile shot out of his mouth and snot out of his nose as tears poured down his face.

Exhausted by heaving up the contents in his stomach, he leaned on one elbow, panting, until he could sit upright again. 'I don't want to be ready.' His voice scraped in his throat. He wiped the back of a wrist over his nose. 'I have this thing,' he glanced at his groin again, 'that inflicts morbid cruelties.'

Bolt upright, Song-chol said, 'Brother, I have a thing, too, but it's not like that in our village. If that's what it's like in your old village, I'm never going there.' He scratched his head. 'I'm gonna go talk to the Sisters. They know about these things.'

Jac knew of the Sisters. They were women who gave themselves for payment. He had never understood why someone could do that, could endure that. (Had his own sister done that?) How worn down would they be? How abused, how physically ruined? Yet logic defied him—if it was dangerous, why would they continue happily? And clearly, when he had seen the Sisters in the village or on the beach, they certainly hadn't seemed distraught. They were laughing and productive women. He couldn't understand it.

He shook his head. 'Don't ask on my account.'

'I will. You're the only one who hasn't done it yet.' Song-chol stared at him. 'It's not gonna be the way you say it is. I don't lie.'

'It makes me sick whenever I think of it. I'll never do it. I'll never hurt someone like that, hurt them so bad that they die of it.' Nothing would bring Jac to do that.

'You won't hurt anybody, you fool.' Song-chol frowned. 'That thinking needs to be purged from your innards like a bad oyster. I'll go see the Sisters. We'll work out a plan.'

Song-chol had worked out a good plan, he'd said. *See the Sisters.* That was it, that was the plan.

They were knowing women, businesswomen who were used to fearful boys, but not ones without bravado, like Jac. At first, he was sick at their door. He sweated. He needed to run for the trees to empty his bowels. A visit to the Sisters hadn't purged like Song-chol had told him. He cried and tried to hide his fear of it, tried to banish this evil thing he had inside. He'd been awake but felt the nightmare niggle and goad him.

The Sisters waited. At first bemused by what ailed him, they were generous, coaxing, after his first few attempts had been disastrous.

Now, weeks later, he was with Ki, the oldest of the Sisters; the others deferred to her. Her face was unlined, her skin darkened by the sun and by the dye of her clothes. Her wavy dark hair was in a long plait that fell down her back.

'You will leave your darkness behind today,' she said firmly. She held out her hand and gripped Jac's.

As she turned away, the light bounce of her breasts and then the naked, plump wobble of her buttocks stirred something different in him. It wouldn't go away. It was too good to push away. For the first time, it felt like it might be all right.


Jac emerged from The Sisters hut in a daze. The late afternoon sun was bobbing over the trees lining the shore.

Song-chol found him in the bushes. 'You were gone hours.'

'I fell asleep.'

'There's something wrong with you, Square Head.'

'Yeah, but that was after she pushed me into the yard out the back. She had her next appointment waiting.' Jac had slept, long and deep tucked under leafy shrubs, and woke with a spring in his step. He hadn't inflicted cruelty. He'd made a mess of things, but he hadn't hurt anyone. When he was able to try again, it was good.

Scary but good. He looked forward to the next time. He wasn't cured, he wasn't without the sweats or the sick feeling in his guts. But he was better.

'Get a move on. Tae-yong wants to see us,' Song-chol said, shaking his head.

They kept pace together and jogged into the clearing at Seo-yeon's hut. She was stuffing a bag with charms, clothes, and her sewing kit.

His father grabbed the hat he wore for special occasions. Made of horsehair, it was said that he'd souvenired the wide-brimmed hat from an official who had left the village in full flight one night. He had bags packed also.

Seo-yeon looked up briefly. 'Be quick. White people have come to the mainland and made trouble. Mainlanders are coming and this time they will follow us to Mara-do.'

'Why?'

'We're hiding a white person, and they want to give you up, Jac, to show good will. There's a raiding party already on the plains. Hurry.'

Jac flung his few clothes into a bag. 'I should go alone, hide out somewhere.'

Only Song-chol answered as he pushed a tunic in on top of Jac's belongings. He grabbed their food utensils and slid them into the bag. 'We'll keep our No Brains alive together.'

A shout echoed from the hill and Seo-yeon took one last look around. She shrugged the bag over her shoulder and ran out behind her husband. Tae-yong hitched two great water barrels on his back and made careful haste past the huts, wary about spillage. Jac did not have a good feeling.

'*Appa*,' Jac called softly. 'Send me away, by myself. You don't have to leave, too.'

Tae-yong grunted without turning. 'And I'm to live with your mother afterwards? It's better this way.'

'There is nothing out there after Mara-do.'

'There is always hope.'

Jac knew about hope. It didn't feed you or bring cool water to drink. He ran on and Song-chol was at his side.

They headed for the beach, and for the raft hidden at the edge of the scrub. Jac and Song-chol carried it across the sand into the shallows, and they all clambered on board, paddled as if evil spirits were on the wind.

Out at sea, Jac turned to look back to the shore. No men waved sticks or launched rafts. 'Where do we go after Mara-do?' he asked, swivelling back to paddle hard again.

'Out there,' his father said, nodding into the wide blue.

Jac stared out to the great curve of the horizon, to where the ocean met the sky. There was nothing in between. Going that way was surely death. He stared back at Tae-yong. '*Appa*, we need to paddle east, not south.'

Tae-yong's oar didn't stop. 'East?'

Song-chol glared across at Jac. 'East?' Then he said, 'Ah yes, that's better. I get to keep my life.'

'We can hide along the shore,' Jac said to his father. 'They won't suspect we've gone that way. Song-chol can go back to the village and let us know when it's safe to return. Then we'll plan a future for me that won't endanger you.'

Seo-yeon grunted at him. 'We have become so fearful we don't think straight. You are right. East,' she hissed. She hadn't broken her strong rhythm with the oar. 'There are places to hide there, very deep.' She scowled at the menfolk. 'From now on we use our fear to help us, not hinder us.'

Jac, Seo-yeon and Song-chol lifted their oars and waited for Tae-yong. Only a heartbeat, the lap of a wave, and his father's oar came out of the water. As one, the raft turned from its southbound direction and started east.

# CHAPTER NINE

*1850 Rigg Manor, Wales*

il sat at her window, her back aching, and gazed down into the empty yard. Deserted. She'd heard some god-awful yells not long ago. Who could it be this time? It sounded like a woman. Could have been Lady Johanna, and her baby coming. The screams had stopped abruptly.

Sir Hugh had taken a wife a year ago. Must have been the onset of spring after he'd had some flit of the heart. That he had a heart was debatable. His young wife, Johanna Oswald was from the neighbouring manor, a horse stud providing for the stables of the king, it was said. She'd been a wayward, headstrong girl, and not given to obeying instructions, least of all from her two brothers. Her parents were long dead and her care was given to Morris, her older brother.

'Try as he might,' Tippy had rattled on to Lil, 'he can't keep his sister in tow, especially when he needs to go to London and beyond for his stud stock.' She knew a bit about the Oswalds, she'd told Lil.

Chaperones for the girl didn't last, so when Morris was away, the job fell to the younger brother, Ambrose.

'A soft heart, that one, Lil. Mark my words, she'll run rings around him. She won't be warned of the consequences, fool she is.'

Sir Hugh must have spotted Johanna somewhere in the town, for not long after, the house servants were put to cleaning the place from top to bottom, and great parties had been planned.

The district was being led to believe Rigg was leaving behind the debauchery as he chose a suitable wife. *Who'd have believed?* Tippy regaled Lil with the gossip, laughing herself silly as tales came back to the house of charitable Sir Hugh, of debonair Sir Hugh, of generous Sir Hugh. How those old nasty rumours about Sir Hugh must be rubbish.

Lil shook her head.

Tippy had seen young Johanna running through the town, hair flowing free, skirt clutched as her feet skimmed the cobblestones. Pink cheeks, pink lips, dark eyes flashing with mischief, the girl would fend off local boys with ease. How she thought she'd outwit Sir Hugh … Joanna Oswald did everything she could to put herself in front of Hugh Rigg.

It had begun to make Tippy sick. 'Dares him, she does. Wild and reckless, she is. And no good will come of it, mark my words.'

Where was Ambrose Oswald? And the older brother, Morris Oswald?

At the first of the parties, very few invitees attended; the snub was obvious but the music and dancing for the small nervous crowd went ahead. There'd been no debauchery, no leering old men, no money changing hands. Could have been in a whole other world. The dance hall was almost sparkling, scrubbed and oiled with citrus and lavender. The gardens were pristine. Word went around outside: there was a new dawn at Rigg Manor. Maybe the pall of the medieval house had finally lost its hold.

Inside the house, no one believed it for a minute.

Lil and Tippy had sat at the back of the kitchen and listened to the reports of the finery displayed, and the etiquette. Sir Hugh had suddenly become the oh-so-polite, genteel man.

By the evening of the third party, Johanna Oswald arrived at last on her older brother Morris's arm, and flanked by her younger brother, Ambrose. When Lil dared to peek, it was clear the young woman, dark haired and perky was not going to be let out of their sight. It was also clear how Sir Hugh was very attentive to the family, despite how stand-offish Morris Oswald appeared. A fine man to look at, Lil had thought, but what a fool he must be.

Sir Hugh was still handsome, and when he decided to be pleasant, she could see why a lively young girl might be attracted, even though knowing—she would *have* to know—that evil lurked within these walls. Perhaps she thought her charms would make her immune. Why had the Oswalds even consented to come? Morris Oswald should have sent her away to a convent. Lil heard that the women within were strict and frugal, and life was austerely lived. Didn't sound any different to Rigg Manor. Except for Rigg.

Did anyone *really* believe Hugh Rigg had changed? Or had the girl already been despoiled, and this was all for show, to keep face for an embarrassed Oswald family?

By the fifth party, the manor house had filled with gentry, land-owners, business folk from the district, and beautiful ladies on the arms of their gentlemen. Aggrieved by their attendance, Lil had cried to Tippy, 'Has all been forgiven and forgotten?' Her mouth soured. She'd hoped the hypocrites would rot.

Tippy only shrugged. 'Money buys off the bad memories, and he's fixin' up the place; he musta kept all his gold stashed for such times.'

Lil, watching the goings-on of this party from a gap in a side door, had been jostled out of the way as platter after platter oozing game and vegetables passed her by.

'You see them there, Lil?' Tippy said. 'There's only the young brother with her tonight.'

Lil stared. There was Johanna in her simple and elegant white gown befitting a landowner's daughter, (*not* gentry, she decided) and boyish, dapper Ambrose by her side, grinning like a fool.

'The older brother was called away, they said,' Tippy whispered. 'He's gone to buy a fancy horse in London. It's comin' in from France so he can't let it slip by him. I wonder if Sir Hugh knew that, somehow, and planned this night.' She'd learned that the younger two were attending, against Morris's express wishes. 'Mark me, Lil,' Tippy said. 'The master will pounce tonight.'

Lil remembered how right Tippy had been. While the guileless, dazzled Ambrose had been easily diverted by a feminine hand undoing the buttons of his pants, his sister, the beautiful, bewitching Miss Johanna had been roundly and soundly compromised in a room behind where the string quartet played. Ambrose found them, had carelessly stumbled upon them after a mistimed (or was that a timely) shove. His sister was under a rutting bare-arsed Sir Hugh.

The master had planned it, all right.

Ambrose was livid, *outraged. Of course* Sir Hugh agreed to marry Johanna (with his eye on what he'd hoped was a sizeable dowry).

Tippy had chortled. 'Oh aye. Ambrose didn't falter handing her over. He gave permission right there and then as soon as he was able to dress himself.'

'How could he give permission? He's the younger.'

'How could he not?'

Lil's lip quivered, her heart and mind in turmoil. Past jealousy, she said, 'We should warn her.'

'Nay, Lil. She had plenty of warning. We'll just have to try and look after her.'

Sir Hugh paid a clergyman to perform a marriage the following day; it was legal if he paid enough. Watching from peepholes in a hidden corridor, Lil could see the smirk on his face, but the smug smile on the new *Lady* Johanna left her feeling ill. The girl had got her own way, had got her title ... poor *stupid* thing.

Didn't stop him insisting, only weeks after he'd married, that Lil crawl back into his bed. She was to bring him back to life now that his simpering new bride hadn't been able to coax him after the wedding night. And where was she now, Lady Johanna? She took to her room more often than not, crying off with some illness. Black eye, no doubt. Seemed he'd chosen another woman who couldn't get him 'to work' on cue.

'World is full of useless women,' he'd bellowed, and shoved away a bruised Lil. He'd managed to force himself once, and that was all.

Tippy had the gossip. 'Morris Oswald has returned home, Lil, a month late after some delay, but he's got his prize stallion. His cheer left him pretty damn quick when he learned of Lady Joanna's fate. Knocked poor Ambrose senseless, he did, then come roaring after Sir Hugh.'

To no avail. Sir Hugh had the marriage paper, witnesses, and his bride. She'd been sullied by him so was no good to another, even if the impossible, an annulment, could be obtained. What a terrible mess. Hugh cheerfully held his hand out for the dowry. Morris's rage was palpable.

'Morris will murder the master, I'm thinking,' Tippy had said, her finger in the air.

Now, her hand still on her aching back, Lil scoffed at that. Sir Hugh was still well alive these long months past. She cupped her huge belly and straightened up. Not only Sir Hugh's wife was with child, but both she and Lil were due any day now.

Sir Hugh had performed a small miracle, Tippy would often mutter.

Lady Johanna hadn't taken to pregnancy. No one could mistake her these days for the robust and healthy girl she'd once been; the treatment doled out at the manor would cower the hardiest. Her belly was full, tight, and her spirit was dangerously low.

'I've often heard the woman pleading to be released,' Tippy once said. 'Falls on deaf ears.'

Lil sighed. *Folly.* Life was all a folly. At the rough scrape of timber on the cold stone floor, she turned from the window to see Tippy struggling inside, the door somehow proving to be heavier than usual this morning.

Lil rubbed a hand over her protruding belly button. 'There you are. I wondered when you—' She stopped at the sight of Tippy.

Leaning back against the closed door, Tippy shook her head. She stared at Lil, her face screwed up, her apron balled up in her hands, still tied at her waist. Did she have terrible news about some poor sod who'd been beaten? It might be news of Lady Johanna's baby born, which might have explained the gut-wrenching screams. As if in sympathy, gripping pain bore down as her baby moved her. Was it her own time now? She took a few short breaths to ease it.

Tippy did not look well. What on earth would she do if Tippy were to die? She was the only one in the house for whom Lil felt anything close to affection. Tippy had been the vocal one, the strange-looking little woman who guarded Lil from the worst of the master's deviances, if only at times by placing others in his way.

Tippy often said the master had a soft spot for Lil, which made Lil smile. *He must love me after all.* It's what she told herself daily, even as her third baby grew, even as her master ordered her be 'put away from his sight' while in her flagrant, fat, and lumbering condition.

Lil pointed a tentative finger at Tippy's apron that had been let drop from her hands. 'And that is because?' she asked in Welsh, keeping their language alive. Tippy's apron, never crisp-white or even clean by any stretch, was never as pooled with that shade of dark red, heavy with clots and spatters.

Tippy waved her off abruptly and spoke in English. 'The blood is from the mistress. I had to cut her to pull the babe out and I didn't know how to stop the bleedin'.' She crept across the room until she collapsed onto a footstool by Lil's side. 'It's been delivered safe, but she's dead.'

Lil hung her head briefly. *Dead.* She felt … sorrow. *Yes*—for the terrible death, and for the waste. That she could still feel anything came as a surprise to her. And yet, a child. A new life. But what sort of life would it have?

'What is the child?' she asked.

'A boy,' Tippy said. She was agitated, twitchy, as if she herself was possessed by an affliction of the mind.

Lil sat, neither reaching for Tippy nor withdrawing. This would not be good, Lady Johanna's death. The master would go into a rage—if he were not already in his madness again. She strained to hear the roaring, but nothing reached her ears.

'Is the master—'

'The doctor came but too long after for poor Lady Johanna and gave him a potion to sleep. His madness was severe. He wanted to kill me until I told him he had a living boy.' Tippy squeezed her eyes closed and dragged in a sob. 'But he was the one who ordered me cut her,' she wailed, and covered her mouth sobbing soundlessly into her hand, terror, and distress on her brow. 'Have I murdered her?'

Lil shook her head. 'It wasn't murder.' But Tippy could be blamed for murder, and Lil had never seen her so distraught. It was on the master, his wife's death, but she wouldn't say it aloud, not if she expected to live.

Lady Johanna's baby. The master had wanted a son, of course he had, but legitimate progeny. Not by Lilpah, who besides had only birthed him two daughters. Both had been removed from her. Both dead, or rather, 'had died', as she'd been told. Tippy had consoled her; they'd been given away as orphan babies, she'd said. No, he only wanted a son who would carry his name.

'Is everything well with the baby?' Lil asked.

Tippy sniffed loudly. 'He's weak, wouldn't cry. Is chesty. If Sir Hugh thought it was a weakling boy, he wouldna keep him.' She swiped a hand over her nose. 'I had to hide the babe quick after showing the master his little pecker. He might yet die on his own.' Her glance skittered away. 'I hope he does, little mite, and before the master wakes.'

'Tippy, is there something else?'

Tippy waved her off. 'He has a clubfoot. The master didn't see but he will kill him then me surely if the babe shows a clubfoot.' She gulped loudly.

'It might straighten.' Lil's throat quivered and she pressed her hand to her swollen belly.

'It's too bent around. He'll never walk on it without it being worked on.'

'So, the baby.' Lil spoke softly. 'If Sir Hugh finds out, are you to kill—'

'I would take a sword to the master's heart,' Tippy snarled, glaring through her gulping. 'For what he has ordered before, for what murder he has committed on others, for what I had to do on Lady Johanna. But *I* will not kill a babe, ever, certainly not just because he has a *crooked foot*.' She wiped snivel from her nose and rubbed it off her cheeks. 'I can no longer take the madness that governs all of us in this house.'

Lil, chastened to silence, could barely catch her thoughts they moved so quickly. But one thought tracked through the tumult. They had to get her baby out.

The master's doctor. 'How much sleeping draught is left for Sir Hugh?' she asked.

Tippy frowned. 'Who would know? A vial, perhaps enough for a few nights for this episode of madness to pass. It's by the bed for Foswick to administer.'

Foswick, Hugh Rigg's valet. Lil hated him. They both did.

Lilpah thought about that. She reached across and tapped a finger on Tippy's knee. 'I am only days past my delivery time, Tippy. We need to hurry my baby out.'

Tippy slowly shook her head. 'Too much risk.'

'You know he will give it away if it's another girl.'

Now Tippy dropped her gaze but her head wouldn't stop shaking. 'Too risky for you.'

'I have survived worse than a baby brought on before it's ready to come.'

'At your time now, these herbs are too dangerous.' Tippy lowered her voice. 'You would be killed by them.'

'Childbirth could kill me,' Lil cried. 'Oh, Tippy, there are worse things than being dead, I'm sure of it.'

Tippy hissed a breath. 'You haven't died so far,' she snapped hoarsely.

'But I've wished for it.' Lilpah caught a glimpse of herself in the scratchy old mirror, patchy around the edges, but good enough to clearly see her reflection. Apart from a couple of teeth missing, and a scar across one eyebrow, she didn't look much different to how she'd looked when she first arrived. But her eyes were dull, as though their own light had been snuffed. 'If I can get this baby out, and if it's a boy, he'll be saved.' She paused, her thoughts whirling. 'We'll exchange him. The master will never know it is not Lady Johanna's child.'

Tippy struggled to her feet. 'I will not administer those herbs to you.'

Ignoring her, Lil said, 'Make sure Foswick has enough of that potion so the master continues to sleep.'

Tippy huffed. 'The man's a dolt, likely to kill him, besides.'

Lil turned. 'Then let it be on his head.'

Tippy's mouth dropped open. 'And who will keep us then? Lady Johanna is dead, the monster has no issue because he won't abide a deformed child—' She stopped, narrowed her eyes and then took a long look at Lil's big belly. 'He'll not marry you, Lil.'

'I know that, but he will keep a healthy boy. Who else knows about the clubfoot baby?'

'No one. I told them that he needs rest and sleep and a special poultice for his chest to help his breathing. I have found a wet nurse and sworn her to feeding only. I will change his swaddling.'

Lil winced as a deep pain gauged within. 'What about Foswick?'

Tippy continued. 'The babe is safe for now. No one but me knows where he is.' She straightened up, adjusting her dress at the shoulders. Looking down at the blood-soaked pinafore she said, 'I will burn this.'

'Where is Lady Johanna?'

'In the chapel. Shrouded.'

The chapel. Lilpah nearly gagged her disgust. It had been locked up for years now. The only time she had ventured inside was after her first child had been born. She had gone there to plead with that god to take her baby's little soul and care for it, dead or alive.

When she'd entered the room, the dank was bad enough, but the putrefying stink of dead rodents was too much. Cobwebs assailed her and she'd collapsed through the rotten pew to the floor, weeping tears of loss, and sorrow, and horror.

Tippy had found her and helped her back to safety, to a room, and to a place in her mind where she would find strength. She didn't venture to that chapel again, especially after her second child was born, and had subsequently 'died'. Lil had given them names, but told no one, not even Tippy. As for Lady Johanna being in that chapel …

'You will have to see to her, Tippy, see that she is properly dressed to be buried.'

Tippy swallowed and her gaze went to the ceiling, then to the walls, and the floor, as if she could not believe where she was. 'Her family has been notified. I sent that letter we contrived. I paid a running boy a penny for his silence, fear of his death if he told a soul. The Oswalds will come and take her.'

Lil hadn't wanted the letter sent, and fear churned in her belly. Perhaps it was for the best. Surely Lady Johanna's brothers would demand her body be released to them, even though it wasn't their right to have it. Too late now for regrets, she tried to reason, but her heart raced and she wanted to run.

'I hope they come before he wakes up.' Tippy was rolling her hands over and over. 'He won't let her go to their family crypt.'

Lil chewed her lip. 'If her brothers are brave enough, they will come today.'

Tippy raised her blotchy face. 'If your child is a boy, will you really take the sickly one in his place?'

'I will. Of course, I will.' She wiped her mouth. 'There has been enough death here.'

Tippy squinted darkly. 'He must live, Johanna's poor babe. His lungs will grow strong with care. I'll not see him die at the hands of the monster because of his foot.'

Lilpah's eyes turned bleak, and she felt her own pain. Heartbreak as raw and intense as it ever had been. 'I must have a child to nurture. I've had two ripped away from me, and now a third is likely.' She hesitated, her voice strained, her throat aching. 'I will care for this clubfoot baby and raise him as my own, if ...'

'If?'

Lilpah cupped a hand low under the bulge of the unborn child in her belly. 'If this babe within me is a boy and spared the fate of the others. I know he's killed my daughters.'

Tippy's low moan scraped in her throat. 'Lil.'

'No need to hide it from me as a kindness any longer.' Lil closed her eyes to the pain of that. 'But what if this is another girl?' she sagged in the chair, unable to face the fate of her baby. 'How much more can I endure?'

Pressing close to Lilpah, Tippy said, 'We will deal with whatever comes our way, as we've always done before.'

A powerful clench gripped Lil from within and breath stuck in her throat. She grabbed Tippy's forearm and clung until the contraction eased. She spoke in Welsh. 'We'll not need your herbs after all.'

*

Foswick should have come into the chapel through the side door, the entrance from inside the house, but it was too risky—someone might've seen him. He was uncomfortable. The torn body of his late mistress lay not yet stiff on the rough stone slab that had once been the altar; her shroud carried the stains of her bloodied corpse.

He should've had her clothes removed and burned, her innards thrust back inside the cavity, her flesh stitched, had her bathed and re-dressed. She should have been taken with ceremony to a crypt.

Hesitating by the altar, he handled the rough woven blanket over his arm; it was the only thing he had to hide the shroud. He damned the Rigg house, damned the maniacal tyrant whose penchant for the monstrous was without equal. He damned him in front of God, in what had once been a place of worship.

They were all damned in Rigg's house.

What would the Oswald brothers make of him? He was nervous for his life; he'd think hard about his excuses. He hoped that by notifying the Oswalds they'd see him in good light.

Earlier that day, Foswick had stopped a running boy who'd already seemed on his way somewhere. The perplexed lad tried to wrench out of his grip until he stared at the penny Foswick had pressed into his open hand. The boy's other hand had been clenched tight. Panting, a sudden grin on his face, the lad was told to run to Lady Johanna's brothers ordering them to 'come quick to retrieve their sister's body', nothing else. The boy had said that he 'wouldn't tell a soul for fear of death', enunciating clearly. Before Foswick could ponder it, the boy had closed his fingers over the penny and had taken off for Oswald Hall, both fists swinging as he ran.

When he returned, his lip split, the boy only reported that the mistress's brother would come at the hour before the evening meal.

The main door creaked open at the back of this so-called chapel. He made a determined flourish and the blanket billowed over the body. After a few rushed tucks, it covered Lady Johanna well, and the stained and mucky sheet over her was hidden from view.

Somebody sobbed behind him. Lady Johanna's younger brother, Ambrose, had stumbled inside.

Morris Oswald, his features rigid, stepped in behind, a firm grip on Ambrose's arm. Sorrow and rage were tangible. 'Stay upright, lad,' he growled, his voice hard.

Foswick stood aside as the brothers approached the altar. 'Sirs.'

Ambrose, a dark-haired, well-built lad, dashed aside the tears on his face. He snivelled, wiped the back of his free hand over his nose and yanked his arm out of his brother's grip. He seemed without a voice. He was usually sunny by nature, but he knew he was to blame for some of this.

Morris stared unblinking at the covered body. Only a ripple in his jaw betrayed the tight rein on his emotions. He clamped a hand on his brother's shoulder for a few seconds and Ambrose's sobbing eased. He lifted a corner of the blanket, then the bloodied covers. Breath scraped in his throat, and he retched, doubled over, and strings of saliva dropped to the stone floor. Ambrose groaned, but didn't come forward to the altar.

Foswick swallowed. 'I could do nothing,' he burbled. 'The birth was … Her condition prior to the confinement …' He couldn't finish.

'I will kill him,' Morris grated, swiping spit away, his eyes red-rimmed, hands clenched at his sides. His black hair was pushed back from his face and it hung lank, dripping from the rain. His face, even in the low candlelight of the chapel, was gaunt and his stare haunted. 'I will kill Rigg for this,' he said, a hand on the altar. 'And I will remove her child from this place.'

Foswick huffed. 'Remove—'

'The messenger boy told me the babe was born alive.'

The boy was not to have said anything. Maybe the boy's split lip was Mr Oswald's persuasion.

Needing to do something, Foswick marched over to close the chapel door. He was more worried about prying eyes than the chill breeze clearing the odour of rodents.

Ambrose gulped hoarsely, a harsh choking noise at the back of his throat. 'We'll take her home,' he said, his voice jumping. 'We have a pallet outside.'

Foswick was glad of that; the master had ordered her buried without ceremony. 'You are right to take her, but Mr Oswald,' he said to Morris, and lowered his voice even further. 'Your sister died in childbirth.' He couldn't help it; too nervous, he rolled his hands over and over. 'It was in childbirth. To kill Sir Hugh because of it would be murder, and to take the child would be kidnapping.'

'She was mutilated,' Morris ground out and stabbed a finger at her body on the altar. Ambrose choked on a sob.

Foswick nodded hurriedly. 'To get the baby out. But … but if you remove the child it would only bring you harm.'

Morris shifted his gaze. 'Bring you harm, you mean.'

*Yes.* Shaking his head, Foswick said, 'Sir Hugh's cronies would hunt you down, and your wife and children.' He looked about, furtive, anxious. 'You have daughters, do you not?'

Morris leapt for him, grabbed his coat lapels, and snarled between clenched teeth. 'He has no cronies. Are *you* threatening me, Foswick?'

Foswick threw up his hands. *Good Lord, I'm not made for this stuff.* 'Removing the child would not go unchallenged, you know it. An heir is protected.' He couldn't help the shakes coming on either.

Morris shoved him away. 'You think you're safe?'

'Perhaps for the moment.' He wouldn't stutter, he would not. 'But—in case of his death, Sir Hugh has already nominated a regent, or some such thing, for his son.'

Morris scoffed. 'A regent? As for a bloody heir to the throne?'

'A Mr Dalton, recently appointed, who'll act for the child until he is of age—'

'Guardian, then' Morris corrected.

'—and manage the estate as well.'

'And an agent. I see. So, you're not safe. Dalton might not take a liking to you.' Oswald watched him squirm then eased a breath out between his teeth, shook his head. 'Rigg clearly thinks he's a lord of the realm. The only damned lord he is, is a landlord, a lowly, bloody conniving, thieving one. His whole family was the same.'

Hugh's father had wrestled the property from Morris's father over a contrived debt. There were rumours that old Rigg had died in circumstances at his son, Hugh's hand.

Silence followed. Morris wiped a hand over his mouth. His brows twisted as thoughts played across his features and he pinched his lower lip. Grunting despair, he rubbed his face hard then pressed fingers to his temples.

Ambrose gave a sudden, deep sob, his grief refreshed as he stared at his brother.

Morris steadied. 'Will you stay at Rigg Manor, Foswick?' he asked.

Surprised by that, Foswick spread his hands. 'It's up to Sir Hugh, or this Mr Dalton. Where would I go otherwise?'

Oswald took a deep couple of breaths. 'Would you look out for the child, where possible?'

*Me?* Foswick squinted in the dim light. 'Even if I would, in truth it can't be done.'

Morris held his stare. 'Accept, then we'll plan how to get it done.' At Foswick's hesitation, he said, 'You'll be paid. I don't want her only child to remain in this nest of vultures and abominations. You will advise me.'

'But why? You have no legal right to the child. He is Sir Hugh's heir.'

Morris's jaw was set, his dark eyes intense. 'We will avenge her death.'

Another mad one, Foswick thought. *Avenge her death? Bah, hot emotions grow cold with the passing of time.* Oswald would see sense when his grief subsided. But he reconsidered quickly. It could be a good thing if he worked it well: the Owen woman and the char woman would take good care of the boy. That's it; he'd hardly have to do anything for the money Morris Oswald would put in his pocket. Glancing at Lady Johanna's form, he nodded. 'I can see how it could be done, after all.'

'Good,' Morris said. 'Now, Doctor Evers has been prescribing Rigg a sleeping draught, has he not? I'm sure he'll continue to do so.'

Foswick looked at Mr Oswald. 'Are you saying the doctor is willing?'

'I'm sure. Rigg's madness derives from opium, from his once successful trade in the east.' Morris folded his arms. 'With the doctor's potions and tonics a few drops here and there, seems appropriate. Fated, perhaps.'

Nervous again, Foswick looked away. 'Sir Hugh is already well acquainted with opium. He would know treachery.'

'An extra dose here and there would be welcome, I assume. Administered out of the goodness of the doctor's heart. If Rigg craves it, which I'm sure he does …'

'But habitual administering—it could kill him.'

'I would do it myself, and happily.' Oswald said and glanced at his sister's form. 'But I'd rather not swing for it if there's another way.'

Foswick stared, felt the breath in his chest grow thin. 'I'm not sure—'

'Morris, for God's sake. We should hurry,' Ambrose whispered, furtive and urgent. 'Get Johanna out of here before we are discovered.'

Foswick pressed Morris Oswald. 'And if *I* am discovered for my collusion?'

'If there's trouble, come to us and we'll rethink the plan for the boy. He's our flesh and blood, not to be brought up the way of this monster.'

'The master's—proclivity is for females. He wouldn't let anyone touch his son.'

Morris's spit hit the granite stones. 'For that we should be grateful.'

Foswick sputtered. 'I meant—'

'I don't want the boy to grow up believing that his father's *proclivities* are anything but debauched and depraved.' Morris Oswald's eyes were bloodshot and glowed eerily in the low light. 'What say you, Mr Foswick? Will you also be our eyes and ears, so we might protect our nephew?'

A scrape, or a gasp of breath sounded. Foswick froze. Ambrose dropped to his haunches. Morris swung around, glaring into every dark place beyond the candlelight. No one dared raise his voice to call out. Then a well-fed rat shot across the windowpane, dropped to the floor, and scurried out of sight.

Spooked, Ambrose leapt upright and tried to thrust his arms under his sister's body. 'Help me,' he croaked, trying to lift the body. 'Help me get her out of this godforsaken hovel before the rats start on her in front of us.' He tried to lift his sister.

'Foswick?' Morris demanded.

The valet nodded again. 'I'll help. The law won't stop Sir Hugh, so until he is dead, I will help.'

'I'll speak with Doctor Evers, leave a purse for you with him. If you need to reach me, he'll be your conduit.'

Foswick nerves tripped again. 'You've planned this?'

'Since the day I learned my sister had married him, I knew I'd carry her out dead,' he said. Ambrose began to sob softly. Morris ignored him. 'Despite all, her laying with evil, her hasty marriage, she will go to hallowed ground, and not be left here to rot in this dirt. But I *will not* carry her boy out dead. If you fail, I'll come for him.'

*If I fail, you'll come for me.* Foswick was under no illusions, and Oswald knew it. *I shouldn't have agreed.* His pulse hammered.

'Morris,' Ambrose whispered harshly. 'Help me.'

Morris pushed him out of the way, scooped up his sister's body. Ambrose dashed for the door and opened it. He looked out cautiously, stepped outside, then beckoned his brother.

The icy blast of air from the doorway shook Foswick into action. He didn't wait to see them load the body onto the pallet and pressed the creaking door shut behind them. Swirls of dirt and twigs and leaves had followed inside, and he swished them about to make it look as if nothing had been disturbed. He carried the candle and checked around his feet for the boot prints and saw nothing that couldn't be explained away by the shoes of those who'd placed Lady Johanna here.

He stood for a moment and stared at the empty altar. On it, a patch of blood had left a dark smear, a stain for all time.

The praises of God would never be sung here again—if they ever had been. He turned then stiffened in shock.

*

Tippy stepped in front of the valet and braced herself. The stones under her feet were cold through her worn slippers.

'You,' Foswick snapped, covering his fright. 'What are you doing here?'

'I come to bathe the lady before her interment.' Tippy carried a bowl of water and a long cloth was draped over her shoulder.

Foswick stabbed a finger at her. 'How long have you been hiding?'

'Not hiding. I come in just now, and seen you close the outside door. Did you not know there was a door from inside?' If she sounded stupid now, he'd believe she hadn't overheard a thing. 'And what are you doing here?' she asked, enjoying his discomfort.

'I came to see if she'd been prepared already.'

They both stared at the bloodied stone altar.

'Well, there ain't no one here to prepare,' Tippy said, her face expressionless.

'No, there isn't.' Foswick's head high as if there were something unsavoury under his nose. 'Perhaps the undertaker has already come.'

'Oh, aye. Undertaker.' She made her scorn clear.

He blustered. 'Then get on with it, back to the nursery. I'll remember what you did, so you get on and look after that child.'

The threat wasn't lost, no matter that Sir Hugh had ordered the cutting. Striding to the inner door, he didn't wait to see if she followed. Water slopped over the edge of the bowl as he brushed past her.

Tippy mopped her arm with the clean cloth. So, the brave valet was to look after Lady Johanna's baby, was he, and he warns me? *Foswick would only be lookin' after himself, that's for sure.*

Standing quietly, she let the thoughts crowd her brain. She'd overheard enough to know that the Oswalds now had Foswick in their pay. He was to look out for the tiny boy, to ensure that he came to no harm, check that Mr Dalton, the manager, would do the right thing; that the rightful heir of Sir Hugh's estate, Lady Johanna's son, was safe.

*All well and good.* Now to make sure Mr Foswick also knew that keeping *both* babies safe would be in his best interest.

*

Days later, Sir Hugh Rigg sat propped up in his bed, his head lolling to one side. 'Too many people fawning about. Go 'way.' He slurred his words but the feeble flourish of his hand was direction enough.

Foswick held a jug of wine and hovered it over his master's cup, adroitly pouring in a splash. 'We're ensuring your good health, sir.' He indicated two men packing a surgical bag. 'Doctor Evers and his assistant. And Turner the footman has a tray for you. Mr Cooper, our under-butler keeping an eye, of course. And Mistress Tippy.'

'Useless lot.' Rigg's eyes opened and closed, one at odds with the other as if stuck by some glue. 'Damn fine son, eh, Foswick?'

Foswick, his large head askew on his skinny shoulders, nodded over towards Tippy who was holding the stoutly swaddled baby.

'Very fine, sir. Finest baby I ever saw.'

'Damn fine,' Sir Hugh repeated, and waved his over-spilling cup toward the woman. 'Damn fine. It's a son, Foswick.'

'Very good, sir. Excellent work. But we must try and get some more of this wine into you. Doctor Evers says it's necessary for your good health.' Foswick once again hovered over the wavering cup and guided it towards Rigg's mouth.

'Love the stuff,' Sir Hugh said, bringing the cup towards him, and slurped a little. 'He says I've had an apoplexy, Foswick. The old apoplexy, eh? Well, I survived it, damn him.'

'We must not let it take you again, Sir Hugh,' Foswick said, and tried again with the cup.

'I've beaten it. My damn face will straighten up soon, and I'll be good as new.' The crooked features were a grimace, and drool began to hang in a string from his mouth. 'I've a fine son to teach.'

'Take another sip, sir.' Foswick dabbed at the dribble, his lip curling. 'Your fine son needs a strong father.'

Sir Hugh put his mouth to the cup and drank a long draught, swallowing noisily. 'There, you dolt. It's done.' He shoved the cup away.

Foswick dutifully filled it up and set it on the bedside table. 'Splendid, sir. A good night's sleep again for you. But in case you need it for the night, it's refilled.'

Sir Hugh waved an arm about again then he sank, as quickly as a penny dropped, into a stupor. Foswick rested the jug on the table beside the bed and peered closely at Sir Hugh's face.

Doctor Evers approached. 'He'll not wake until late tomorrow morning,' he declared. With a curt nod at Foswick, and his voice low, he said, 'A drop from now on. Two drops only when his nerves get excited.' He leaned closer. 'This will also help curtail any—ah, conjugal activity. It's a cause of these types of problems if the heart is not strong.'

No one met his furtive glance.

He frowned. 'Not enough to harm, though,' the doctor said clearly and straightened up, tugging his waistcoat. 'We'll do another bleeding soon and monitor his heart rate after that. You know to call me for anything.' Then he and his assistant left.

A collective sigh rose as those in the room drooped. A moment passed. A serving maid entered and cleared the small tables of empty wine vessels and picked-over platters of food. All but Foswick and Tippy left the chamber.

Tippy swayed rhythmically with the bundle in her arms. It was a bright-eyed boy child, swaddled neck to toe.

All the staff had said how the baby had much the look of Sir

Hugh about him, so handsome, so healthy. In truth the resemblance was not too much of the master at all, but of his mother, as Tippy could well see. If anyone else had thought as much, they were clearly not brave enough to mention. Sir Hugh had called the boy Lester.

Foswick stared at the unconscious master and lowered his head to listen to the snore. 'He is well asleep.'

Tippy wished Sir Hugh the sleep of the dead so she and Lil and the babies could take their chances.

The valet turned away from his master, pointing a pale knobby finger as he glared at Tippy. 'Get that infant to the nurse before he wakes and squawks the place down.'

Tippy headed for the door, her precious cargo cradled, asleep, in her arms. 'We will go and feed our young master,' she said, a smile in her voice. 'His nurse will be most pleased to receive him.'

# CHAPTER TEN

## *1852 Rigg Manor, Wales*

Lilpah watched as the two toddlers played on the mat in the nursery. 'They could be brothers,' she remarked, her expressionless eyes following Lester. Her drawing pens lay idle on the small table at which she sat. The paper under her hand had sketches of carved spoons above a series of scrawls as she attempted to sign her name to them.

Foswick has disapproved of her penmanship, but she'd insisted on the practice.

Tippy sighed. She dropped her needlepoint in her lap. 'They *are* brothers. Half-brothers, and only hours between them. I swear at times, Lilpah Owen, you are losing your wits.'

'If I haven't already lost them.' Lilpah's gaze wandered to the chubby boy whose right foot was bandaged. 'I meant that in another world they would be brothers, together. *Hapus, chwerthin.* Happy, laughing.' Her voice trailed off.

'They are already. What does that look like?' Tippy pointed

at the boys and squinted at her. 'What's the matter with you? Is it some soft nonsense you've found in motherhood somewhere?' She sucked in a breath. 'Oh no. Are you feeling poorly for another reason?'

Lilpah turned her empty stare to Tippy. 'I woke today and felt as dead as I've ever felt. The potions you're giving me must be working—I've not been with child again, and now, I don't think ever likely to be.' She glanced at her drawings, at one of the signatures she was attempting that was not hers. She rested a hand over it. 'There's probably no need for potions any longer. It seems he is—it seems Sir Hugh has lacked the power in his cock for many months, longer, if truth be known.' She rubbed her face vigorously. 'His anger has been subdued a little, but still his face bursts with tiny red veins when he lashes out. He's feeble, but I stay beyond his reach.'

'You have survived him, Lilpah.'

'If that's what it's called.'

'And survived a number of years, now.' Tippy knew where this low mood of Lil's would take them if she let it. 'Lester is happy and strong. And look how well our other lad Daniel is doing.' Tippy went to the boy and straightened the bandage on his foot. Her hands gave it a gentle working for a moment or two and brushed off a scuff of dirt. 'Soon, when he walks, he might only have a limp.' She looked back at Lilpah.

At last, some expression. Lil's eyes widened only slightly. 'You've tended him so carefully, Tippy. The bandages have done him well.'

'Aye. An ancient doctor tended these sorts of feet this way. Exercising the limb and moving it all the time. It were a sensible notion when I heard about it, I tried it, knowing what feet are for.' She took the little foot in her hands and rubbed it again. The boy dribbled a smile at her. 'It worked. I dinna like that terrible Scarpa contraption, that brace whatnot. It's an ugly thing, and bulky. It woulda been seen.' Both women looked at the happy child play-ing with his nursery mate, Lester. Tippy drew in a breath. 'Never thought I'd love a little one, but he has such a way about him. He never lets that foot trouble him. He watches my every move when I—'

'Yes, yes. You've done great work, Tippy, I know. And it's been the best thing that the foot improves. Too many deaths already haunt this house. You were right; if Sir Hugh had suspected any-thing there'd have been another death.'

Tippy scoffed. '*If* he had his wits about him and was not so addled by the potions for his afflictions.'

'He's not always so addled,' Lil stated. He would manage to fumble his way on her until he slapped her aside in frustration, unable to finish the job. 'But *if* he thought we had a cripple here now, even he wouldn't dare kill this child who is so well-known and loved. He'd turn him out, give him away before he'd dare kill. Turn us out, too.'

Tippy shook her head. She'd extracted a promise from Foswick. It could be called a *flacmel,* a blackmail, after she'd overheard his deal with Morris Oswald. Both boys would be protected from harm, here, as long as Foswick lived. 'It won't happen. We've had this con-versation many times. Daniel is no cripple, and a limp might be all he has once he is grown. Anybody could get themselves a limp. Sir Hugh will not bother you about Daniel, but neither will he acknowledge him.' She chuckled at the joke on Rigg. She saw Lilpah eye Daniel. 'Now you see here, Lilpah Owen. But for us exchanging Lady Johanna's poor sickly babe Daniel for Lester, your son would not have his place in Sir Hugh's—his father's—affections,' she said.

Lifting a pale hand in Tippy's direction, Lilpah said, 'I have an affection for her boy, Daniel, there is no doubt.' Her chin puckered, a rare display of emotion that belied her statement. 'He is a con-stant companion for my son Lester, and for that I am more than grateful. But I know that every living thing a person loves is torn away.' She checked both boys again and her eyes followed Lester as he crawled to Daniel. 'Sir Hugh watches Lester's progress. I swear he'd have him in the saddle next week if he could.'

Tippy's shrewd gaze settled on the youngsters. 'And Daniel would be there too, learning to be his squire. As long as you care for Daniel as his mother, and for Lester pretending he's Lady Johanna's son, both boys will be safe. Don't forget that is our plan.'

Lilpah's gaze hadn't left Lester. 'I don't forget that. He can't take Lester from me.' She looked at Tippy now. 'Or either of them from us.'

Tippy sat back and worried at this strange mood of Lilpah's. Rarely did the woman drop her stony guard. Perhaps Lil was right; it was time to stop the dose of those potions she was taking to prevent a chance pregnancy. Maybe they were making her morose, weakening her hard shell. Or perhaps Lil was just weary of being used, discarded, and used again.

Sir Hugh kept demanding Lil's presence, just a convenience, at his beck and call. For Lilpah, it was more than that. For the last two years, keeping the master happy meant that she remained in favour. At least until he'd decided once again that she must be the cause of his impotence. He'd lash out with a backhand, order her to try harder until, disgusted with her lack of persuasion, would shove her away. Sir Hugh's temper was always worse when the drops were due, or late to be administered. Lil was the only one willing to return to his bed, and often gave him the opiate dose herself, carefully administered. She'd then up the dose of medicine by a drop for a day or so. It allowed her to remain close to her child, Lester.

But what a life for a woman. It was desperately lonely for Lilpah because everyone, but Tippy, despised her as much as they despised Sir Hugh. A woman who allows a monster to tear her babies from her arms, yet who returned time and again to his bed must indeed be a person to despise.

Tippy watched Lil glance at Daniel who gurgled at his half-brother. What was in her head? She sighed. One day it would all be over, and she had no idea what that day would look like.

# CHAPTER ELEVEN

*1853 Cheju*

Jac's eyes were trained on a line of men creeping over the terrain at the bottom of the hill. 'Is that them?'

Song-chol nodded. 'Mainlanders. Something about a bounty for all foreigners.' He was crouched alongside Jac, their shoulders touching. 'They might've outwitted us this time. Villagers are hungrier for payment than before.'

'Everyone knows?'

'There was always the chance the villagers would give you up but so far they've been more frightened of Seo-yeon. She's talked of your escape for a while now. Maybe this is the time.'

Jac felt the sweat pop on his forehead. The days were getting longer, and the build-up of humidity was dense. The heat of the sun was just beginning to bite. 'Even if we get to Mara-do, they'll come.' Jac looked at Song-chol. 'You don't have to run. Not at all.'

'I'm your brother; enough said. Let's get down to our hideout. We'll be able to raft out to Mara-do later.'

They crawled backwards from their vantage point and when the hilltop was high above them, they loped towards the huts where Tae-yong and Seo-yeon would be. The bracken and leaves drying off after the spring rains rustled underfoot.

Jac kept pace with Song-chol. 'What would happen if I went across the water to the mainland with them, to save all this trouble for everyone? I've thought of it many times. I could make a better escape from there.'

'Apart from killing Seo-yeon, I'd say your life would be worth less than a flea's. Forget that idea. Half the fun in my life is outwitting those idiots they send looking for you.' A few more paces and he said, 'I've often wondered if they send these fools here to get rid of them, not you.'

A clearing opened as they rounded the scrub. The village, huts tucked in behind the stone fences to keep out the roaming horses and the cattle, appeared serene.

From there, as they got to the family's hut, the serenity evaporated. Their father must have sounded the alarm. Villagers ran from Tae-yong's thatched home each carrying bamboo-lidded boxes, emptying the place. Many ran down the stone pathway, others leapt off the terraced verandah and onto the grassy slope to disappear into the afternoon.

Seo-yeon raced towards their house, pushing past the scurrying villagers. She and the other women had come from the beach, baskets under their arms filled with the latest catch of octopus, squid, and abalone. She pushed her fishing basket at a woman as she ran past. The catch would be hidden. It risked being spoiled, but better that than the mainlanders staying longer than necessary, demanding to be fed.

'Come along, come along,' she said to them, her black curly hair dripping saltwater onto her bony shoulders. Inside the hut, her eyes narrowed, and she pinned Jac under her gaze. 'There's a great ship sailing from the east. It's beyond Mara-do.' The sea women would have gone south on rafts before diving for their catches. Someone would've seen it. She shrugged into her tunic and it fell over the sleeveless diving shirt.

Breath grunted out of Song-chol and he turned and ran from the hut.

Jac swallowed. 'We've seen big ships before,' he said to Seo-yeon. Did she mean that he should abandon them, and leave by himself on one of these foreign vessels?

'Your father and I have discussed it. You are a blade in that fool neighbour, Mye-Sung's side. Always he thinks you're looking at his wife, Min-jee. He always thinks that his wife looks at you, too.'

Jac had kept clear of Min-jee all these years. Kept clear of any of the village women, except for the ones he could freely visit without upsetting people. Those women wanted nothing from him except payment. There he'd learned what he needed to learn; there he'd faced his demons and found a world without horror, only pleasure and release. He had the memories, but the demons had been tamed.

She threw an arm in the air. 'He thinks you curse him and that's why he's without sons.'

'I don't believe in curses, you know that.' He didn't carry the same superstitions as his fellow villagers. Bad things happened; that was life. No one was cursed by an unseen presence; it was all down to accident or to other humans.

'If he thinks so, it must be true, the lame-headed dolt. He is the one to betray us, I am sure.'

Jac fell to his knees, his head bowed. '*Eomma*, don't send me away. I can't leave you here. I can't go and never see you again.' The fleeting glimpse of his sister's face, and the faces of the parents he'd lost a lifetime ago gave him a moment of torment.

Tae-yong came into the hut. His voice was hoarse after barking orders for men to set up the cooking fires. He had a large bag on his back. 'Off your knees, son.'

Seo-yeon squeezed a hand on Jac's shoulder. 'Jac, we'll all go. *Appa* has my sewing kit and our prayer plates in the bag on his back. We'll all find that great ship, we'll all leave this place.'

Jac shook his head. 'This is your home.'

'Spirits roam here, and I'm not happy. Tae-yong is not happy. The spirits of our children are not happy. They're restless. Come on, up. *Up.*' She beckoned him to stand.

There had been another breakout of the red rash disease, *hongyeok*, and again, many children, as well as many older people, had died. Memories of the older wave of the scourge were still clear.

'We've slipped by the mainlanders for many years,' she said, 'and now we have no more chances. This time we know we'll leave and not return.'

Song-chol burst back into the hut. 'They'll be here soon. Let's go.'

Jac spun around as he got to his feet. 'You're coming, Song?'

'I wouldn't miss this adventure for anything. Besides, you'd trip over your big feet, or you'd put them in your mouth sideways if it wasn't for me.' He grinned and ran for the room where they slept. 'Hurry, pack your things.' He threw a bag to Jac who'd followed him.

Tae-yong stood watching them and barked a laugh. 'I have two sons I haven't fathered, and a wife who wears the trousers. I will live a long and healthy life in blessed confusion, somewhere. Come on.'

Seo-yeon stopped, took a quick look around the hut and then stepped over to a small shrine in the corner. She swept away the candles and moved the small stone figurines with reverence. She drew out a wrap of cloth from a box behind them—her treasures box, Jac had called it long ago. It held bits of dainty, unusual shell, small stones for her lost children—he'd once touched them with reverence—and a stick of dried seaweed, a memento of her first dive. She tucked the parcel under her tunic and flattened her palm on his chest. 'It's as like to me as your talisman.'

Tae-yong waved Song-chol and Seo-yeon ahead of him. He spoke urgently to Jac who stared after his mother. 'Hurry yourself, Jac.'

Jac dipped a hand under his shirt to hold the spoon that hung from a horsehair string. He'd clung to it, had cherished it, had even prayed to it for guidance. *His* only memento, a stick carving. *His* treasure. He hadn't forgotten it, ever, and Seo-Yon had always understood.

His father echoed his thoughts aloud. 'Your mother. She knows everything.'

The raft was laden. They'd kept it prepared and loaded it with the packs they carried. The water supply was intact, the fishing line and basket had not perished, and the oars were sturdy.

An insistent swell of waves and a stiff breeze swiftly took them south. They rounded the eastern coast of Mara-do and Jac thought he could see a dot on the horizon. Maybe it was the ship Seo-yeon had mentioned. Each time he glanced ahead, he saw the set of her jaw, her mouth a grim line. He couldn't tell if she had her eyes on the same dot. His heart thundered with every beat of his oar hitting the water.

Glancing at Song-chol beside him on the raft, he saw a wide grin. 'What's there to laugh at?' Jac said. He tasted the salt spray on his mouth as the searing sun tried to burn through the tanned layer of his skin. His head was protected; they all wore bamboo hats tied under their chins.

'Adventuring, my duck-faced friend.' Song-chol was enjoying himself. His muscles bunched and stretched with each pull of the oar.

'This duck-faced friend is sick of adventures,' Jac muttered.

'Better get used to it. It's not one great ship, but two.'

Jac squinted. Sure enough, two black dots appeared and disappeared as the waves rolled about, hiding, and then revealing the horizon. He wondered which way they were heading—to Chinese waters or to the port of Nagasaki where many foreigners had travelled?

'Bah.' Seo-yeon spat. 'Our luck to be picked up by a great ship only to be returned to Cheju.'

Tae-yong had been studying the dots while paddling strongly. 'They come from the east and are going south. If what some say is true, they have visited Nagasaki and the Dutch trading station there. Others have heard that the *baeg-in*, the white man, comes for war with Japan and comes from a great land far away. It is those ships we must intersect.'

Song-chol grinned again at Jac. 'Intersect, Jac. We are going to intersect.'

Good weather prevailed, though as they reached more open water the swell increased. Now that the danger of the mainlanders raiding party was well behind them, Seo-yeon and Tae-yong rested while Jac and Song-chol kept at the oars.

'We will lose them come dark anyway,' Jac said as the sun seemed to bob lower towards the curve of the ocean.

'Then we will find others,' Tae-yong murmured from under his hat. He and Seo-yeon were also under the cover of a straw mat, protection from the sun. 'Word from the villagers is that eight great ships sailed to Japan.'

'How would villagers know that?' Jac asked.

Tae-yong lifted a shoulder. 'Some speak to the mainlanders to glean information. So, if eight ships sailed to Japan, it seems to me that eight ships must return.'

'But by what route, *Abeoji*? How are we to know?' Song-chol asked his father.

'There's no knowing. There's just faith that we will find the one.'

Jac knew little about faith, only that his parents had it. He had reasoned long ago that it was only good luck that had saved him, had brought him to their village. Each time he thought that he also thought of Ben Polites. Had Ben not looked out for him, he might not have survived the shipwreck.

Song-chol nudged him. 'Time to change sides.'

His brother must have felt as he did. Jac's shoulder had moved beyond aching and into a certain rhythmic numbness. Changing sides eased one shoulder and sent his other to the same fate. Better he and Song-chol than his older parents.

As he rowed, he thought back. Tried to catch hold of some fleeting memories that these days seemed more elusive than ever. The last time he'd been on the open seas it was in a much bigger vessel than this one. Those memories weren't fleeting, they'd been constant for years—nightmares. That time had been terrifying, and he vividly remembered wondering if he'd die thrashing and heaving to a watery grave. When the ship had broken apart, when a mast had snapped overhead, and other strained timbers had screeched, when the wailing of panicked sailors reached his ears over that monster storm, Ben had been there. Ben had grabbed him before being flung into the black and roiling waves. And Ben had been with him as they were hurled towards the shore. How, he'd never know.

Sweat broke out on his forehead. Looking skywards, he squinted into the afternoon sun, and checked the horizon for any rolling, rumbling clouds. He found none.

When he concentrated again, he saw that Tae-yong had been watching him.

'It's no use. We are paddling, and these great ships are under sail, with many men to row if necessary.' Song-chol threw his oar onto the raft bed and fell back to ease his shoulders. 'We lost sight of them hours and hours ago.'

Their second day at sea was creeping towards night. Song-chol was right. What hope could they hold for a ship to see them? They'd been chasing two ships and had been far outrun. It was a desperate act. Jac kicked at his oar. 'I should have stayed and taken my chances on the island. Now we'll die of thirst, or worse be flung into the ocean to be eaten alive by sea monsters,' he said.

Tae-yong shaded the water barrel with his hat and peered in. 'We will not die of thirst for many days. And in many days, we might even drift onto China.'

'Where they'll kill us.'

'Where they might put us on a ship to sail away,' Tae-yong said as if Song-chol had not spoken. He closed the water barrel and put his hat back on his head.

'Or take us as slaves.' Song-chol spat into the sea water.

Seo-yeon glared over at Song-chol and loosened her shoulders under the pack she had strapped across her back. 'Then we will swim to meet a better fate.'

Song-chol dropped his hat lower and punched Jac lightly on the shoulder. 'If you can swim.' All Cheju children could swim, and some were stronger than others. Jac and Song-chol looked out over the water. It would take a lot of swimming.

Tae-yong settled back. 'We have an ocean filled with fish, and we have good weather. Don't spend your energy worrying.'

There was no point staying awake. Tae-yong was on watch, though how he'd stay awake Jac didn't know. Jac would try not to sleep too deep, hoping he'd spring awake at the first alarm.

It was the creaking that haunted what sleep he'd been able to snatch; he hadn't dreamed of it for years. Now on a raft bobbing softly on the water, a little higher, a little lower, he was lulled deeper into his dreams. The creaking. The *whoosh* of a bow wave. A sudden jolt instead of a bob—

Tae-yong let out a scream and Jac snapped awake, grabbing his paddle. Seo-yeon sprang to a crouch. In fright, Song-chol flipped halfway overboard before clambering back, upsetting everyone. They yelled at him and they yelled at the enormous shadow of the ship against the star-lit night sky as it glided alongside.

Jac tried to balance on his haunches. He looked up and spied a light waving high overhead. He'd yell at whoever it was … What would he yell? He'd mostly forgotten the language of his birth.

Song-chol let out a rip-roaring ululation and only moments later they heard the hollow thudding of feet on deck. Another light was held high and out over the water. On the madly bobbing raft, yelling for their lives, they heard a voice yell back.

All four on the raft listened.

'Jac, is it your language?' his father called across.

'It doesn't matter,' Jac answered. 'Just yell back.'

They kept yelling. More lights appeared but the ship was gliding past them. Jac heard more feet thudding on the deck and suddenly, a voice yelled a warning, and something was tossed over the side to them. Something heavy banged against the timbers of the ship.

Song-chol reached out, his arm a silhouette. He snatched the rope ladder. 'I've got it,' he shouted, swinging wildly, and was nearly swept off the raft. Seo-yeon grabbed his leg, and Tae-yong wrapped his arms around her waist.

Screaming, floating above the raft one minute, and dropping onto it the next, the family clung to the ladder, not daring to let it go.

Another rope ladder dropped from the deck and two men clambered down, and swung towards the first rope, shouting and beckoning with arms waving. 'You're safe. You're safe.'

It wasn't Ben Polites' raspy, salt-water strained voice he heard yelling the words above the creaking of the ship, above the waves slurping alongside the sleek hull and above the yells of his parents. But in the echo of memory, he remembered what it meant.

Jac leapt to the lowest rung, grabbing Tae-yong, and pushing him up over his shoulders, and scrambling to the next rungs above. Jac gripped his mother about her waist and hauled her onto his ladder. Free of Seo-yeon's grip on his leg, Song-chol clambered up the other rope and disappeared on deck. The ladders began to ascend.

When they hit the timbers of the deck, sailors gathered around. Their soft boat shoes and pale trousers were aglow under hand-held lanterns, in stark contrast to Jac, his parents and Song-chol. They murmured low, a laugh here and there, and one man dropped his hand to clamp Jac's shoulder.

He said something. Jac stood, gave a small bow showing his thanks though he hadn't understood. His mouth worked in anticipation of his voice, but his native tongue did not emerge.

# PART II

# Chapter Twelve

## *1855 Rigg Manor, Wales*

The boys were now five years old. There hadn't been a new wife for Hugh Rigg. It wasn't required—he had a healthy heir, didn't he? Besides that, no self-respecting family had come near him with a daughter to be wed.

'Nothing will happen to Lester,' Rigg would say, so why should he be bothered taking another wife when all his natural needs were being met by one—or another—already in his house? But 'none are good enough to bring me satisfaction', he'd been heard to say. Those who fell afoul of him were never seen again, removed from the house by stealth. Only Lil had been spared expulsion.

Gone too was the extravagance of the parties that had prepared the house for Lady Johanna's arrival. Well-to-do families in the district kept their distance; Rigg Manor was once again shunned by everyone.

This day, outside, a little way from the house and in light, airy sunshine, Tippy sat beside the picnic basket, doling out tiny cakes for the boys. In turn they demanded another. Playfully, gleefully one would snatch it, and they'd take off together, little legs pumping. They romped close by. Lilpah rested her back against a tree, and when each boy approached to tease her with a small cake, only to stuff it into their own mouths, there was a glimmer of a smile.

'They are in such fine spirits,' she remarked. She watched Lester stop to pull Daniel to his feet after he'd tripped. Not a minute later, Lester lay sprawled in the dirt, bawling, and Daniel was there to help him up.

The boys studied the scrape on Lester's knee. Daniel tapped Lester on his arm, like he had seen Lilpah do, to comfort. She smiled at that, and a memory of her brother surfaced. It lingered only a moment. Clearly not life or death, the youngsters decided, for the next moment the chortling renewed. They raced each other to the old yew and tried to scramble up the gnarly branches. 'They are the best of friends at this young age. They look out for each other.'

Tippy kept her eyes on them, a hand clamped on her bonnet in case she had to run for them. 'There are days when I swear no one would be surprised to learn they are brothers, but no one says a word.'

Lester had dark blond hair, with a touch of ginger sometimes if the sun caught it. His features were that of a younger, healthier Hugh Rigg—lips that held a curve, a brow line that was fair, a strong jaw and chin, blue eyes. His cheeks were high and nose aquiline, like Lilpah's. Daniel's hair was dark brown, like his mother Lady Johanna's, but his wide blue eyes were Hugh Rigg's. His face was handsome, intense, not unlike Lady Johanna's, which had been beautiful. There was little else in his face of Sir Hugh so far, but as he grew, he might come to more resemble his father.

'Do ye think, even this young, they know they are real brothers?' she said to Lil.

'It wouldn't matter if they do or don't. They will grow up with each other, and be like true family, if allowed. I hope for it,' Lil said. 'It's a pleasure to see them together. They are the only joy in this place.'

In the whole of the house, the boys were everyone's joy. The murky oppression of Sir Hugh seemed not to affect them and when each met other members of the household, it was a happy experience.

*

Foswick struggled with the youthful exuberance of two young boys. He'd admonish when he thought he could get away with it. But when the withering glares from Lilpah had finally got his attention, he had ceased to admonish further. She was, as he well knew, the heir's trusted nanny. She wielded a little more power than he did now, though he was perplexed at how he found himself allowing it.

Even though he appeared stern, he felt no ill-will towards the boys. In fact, he had been overheard to say that the youngsters brought life to the house. These days he'd taken the responsibility of the house on himself and with that had come a benevolence towards the children, and the two women, especially Lil. The extra purse from the Oswalds helped.

As for the boy, Daniel, his perpetual limp didn't seem to hinder him, and these days hardly anyone took any notice. He was the young master's best friend, and not even Sir Hugh saw fit to interfere. Much had changed since the tincture drops, in varying measures, had been administered nightly to Sir Hugh.

Mr Dalton, the manager, would come and go on a regular monthly basis and was only interested in pounds, shillings, and pence. He wasn't interested in the personalities of the household. Why would he be as long as the work was done?

Foswick ensured the master retained his equilibrium.

*

Lilpah watched the valet as he left the bedchamber. 'Foswick is looking weary.' They were sitting by the far window.

Tippy nodded, chortling. 'All that administering the sleeping draught. Perhaps he's taking some himself.' She frowned. 'But the Rigg monster seems to be leashed.'

'Dr Evers is looking old, too. Who should administer to Sir Hugh if they both die?' Lil asked.

'I'd be the first in a long line,' Tippy said. 'Might even slip in an extra dose, a large one, here and there.' She stretched her legs, her thin dress just reaching her ankles. The hem had frayed, been mended, and had frayed again. She took it in her hands to study it. 'Foswick grumbles all day about the lack of money and yet he looks all right. Look at this,' she said, holding the hem to show Lil. 'No new clothes for anybody except the master and Lester. The purse-strings is still pulled tight and the only money spent is on his medicine. It might be best to let go of it, let him die.'

A shadow, only the slightest raising of a brow, barely discernible, marked Lilpah's features. 'I heard a conversation between Sir Hugh and Mr Dalton not long ago about huge goldfields in one of the queen's colonies.' She smoothed her pinafore over a pale blue dress that had seen many a day.

'Didja now? And why might that interest you?' Tippy adjusted her backside on the seat.

The boys' laughter, the little squeals of delight reached them from outside, and both women watched their game of chasey around the huge tree trunk.

'Sir Hugh remarked that he might invest,' Lilpah said. 'That he might have to visit there. If it happened, it would change our circumstances here.'

'And which colony would that be?'

'Somewhere in Australia.'

Tippy's eyes popped. 'Where all them convicts went? Well, good riddance to him, then.'

'I can only find scraps of newspaper, and then I struggle to read the words, but there's a raging goldrush apparently.' Lilpah had laboured to read, and her comprehension was poor. She tried to make out the words, but because she had to do it surreptitiously— no one was allowed to read in Sir Hugh's house—she couldn't inform herself properly.

'Australia?' Tippy shuddered. 'Well, not for all the gold in the world would I go there. I heard there was a creature that bounds around on two great feet with hooks on the end and rips yer heart out with 'em. That there's birds as big as trees that don't fly and can run you down and stomp the life out of you. Or natives that will spear you while you sleep and then eat yer.'

'Ah yes. Terrible place. Why would we want to leave here?'

Tippy scowled. '*Donial iawn, am fy ngwraig, Lil.* Very funny, o my lady Lil.'

'Not only the goldfields were mentioned. He was talking one other time to that Crawford man. You remember him; he left the night my brother—' Lil stopped.

Tippy gaped. 'You remember the man's name from that night?'

'I remember a number of the men.' She drew in a deep breath then continued with a frown. 'And with this Crawford, there was a lot of talk about trade and boats on a river. That took more of Sir Hugh's interest than the goldfields, by far. There's been a big company set up by English merchants years ago and it looks after one of the colonies that is free of convicts.'

'Bah. Australia is all a wild man's country, full of misery and murderers.'

Lilpah arched a brow now.

'All right, all right,' Tippy said. 'But this here is a place we know. What interests you about the other side of the world, anyway? Why, if I didn't believe what they say about the earth being round, you'd fall right off going over there.' Tippy shifted her weight again and jiggled her shoulders.

'You're afraid.'

'Me? Of what?' Tippy snipped. 'I won't be goin', and yer think he'd take you, his little doxie, his child mistress?'

'No longer a child. And I am the only one who saves face for him in the outside world. The only one he has to brag about, to show he can still be a man.'

'Bah—we all know his pillock don't stand up no more now. He can't hurt no one.'

'As long as he's alive and holding the purse-strings, I'll be able to have Lester close to me.'

'That's true, you have to look after his boy. But would he risk going to the other side of the world with Lester?'

'Would he risk leaving his son and heir anywhere but under his own nose?' Lilpah parried.

'Who knows what the man thinks,' Tippy said. 'All I know is, since that potion, we've had peace in this house. If he goes off to the other side of the world, good.'

'He craves it, he'd still need it.'

Tippy snorted. 'We all know it's only opium, and only a drop or two of oil.'

'It's not only the potion that's dulled him. It's the stroke he had, and he's not recovered. They say he won't. He's feeble in body compared to what he was, it's true, but still he lives, on and on.' Lilpah shut her mind to the memories that crowded her. 'He can still be sharp at times.'

'Rubbish. They say the opium attacks yer innards and yer brains.'

'The doctor has made mention of removing the potion, only giving him the wine.'

Tippy was aghast. 'Can he risk that the monster might return?'

Lilpah lifted a shoulder in a small shrug. 'He might die of his affliction before that happens.'

Tippy stared at Lil. 'Die of his stroke affliction, is it? You've thought of this before.'

'I have. But Sir Hugh hasn't yet,' Lil said. 'And so now the gold-fields and the rivers of distant colonies seem attractive. He might die on the journey over there.' She smiled at that and finally Tippy smiled in return.

They watched the youngsters again. The boys shrieked with laughter as they tumbled on the grass, only to bounce up, run and tumble again.

Lilpah had heard Sir Hugh talk about the goldfields and the river trade incessantly. He'd insisted that Foswick read him the articles in the newspaper about it. Sir Hugh would notice her sitting by the window, stitching, and dismiss her. Listening at the door had been no help, either. Low voices didn't carry, only the odd shout for more wine had ever reached her ears.

Tippy leaned forward, into Lil's line of sight. 'And why would the other side of the world interest you when yer can't even get out of bed to walk to the town here?'

'Because it is the other side of the world,' Lilpah said.

Tippy shook her head. 'It would make no difference where you were if you went anywhere with Rigg.'

Lilpah muttered, 'True,' and her gaze fell back on the two five-year-old boys playing on the grassy field. She remembered another boy, the one who carried a talisman to match her own.

# CHAPTER THIRTEEN

*1854 South China Sea*

'M r Clark, can you make head or tail of it all?' Captain Walker, commander of the *USS Saratoga* stood staring at the rescued passengers. 'Who are these people?'

'Captain.' Midshipman Clark straightened. In the dim light, he'd been peering at Jac, fascinated by the round pale eyes on a man who could barely speak English, and knew an oriental lingo fluently. The man stared serenely back at him. 'Don't know, sir. Lots of hand-waving and foreign language. I've called for Mr Hirago. He might know where they are from.'

'You think these three are Japanese, Mr Clark?' The captain waved to the white man. 'This one's clearly not.'

'Hard for me to say, sir. He speaks their language, whatever it is.'

The captain made a noise in his throat. 'Poor beggars. Food and water for them, Mr Clark. After Mr Hirago has studied them, find a place they can sleep.'

'We hauled up the raft, sir. I'll find somewhere to tie it down on the deck.'

'Anything of value?'

'To them, I would say. Not to us, sir. A sturdy craft, and well made. No match for a longboat, but it did the job for them.'

'Doubt they'll have need of it again. Dispense with it later.' The captain turned towards the east and the faint light of dawn creeping over the horizon. 'Mr Goldsborough,' he called to his lieutenant. 'Good morning.'

The man finished buttoning his coat and strode over the deck to his captain, plainly interested in the four people clustered on the deck. 'Captain, good morning.'

'We've just plucked these folk out of the water. Nearly ploughed right over the top of them. What do the charts say about the land masses hereabouts?'

Mr Goldsborough craned his neck to check the rising sun, swivelled back and stared at his boot clad feet in thought. 'We've left Edo Bay, and the prevailing—' He stopped, startled by a yell.

Leaping to his feet, the older rescued man was speaking urgently, and bowed to Mr Hirago who'd appeared on deck. Startled, Mr Hirago bowed stiffly, and said something in Japanese.

'Bah,' the old man grunted and slumped to the deck again. The others crowded around him.

The woman leaned over and said something, resting her hand on his arm. The blue-eyed man murmured, and the other young man simply stared around him, then flung himself backwards and appeared to be instantly asleep.

'These people are from Korea, Captain Walker,' Mr Hirago said, his English carefully enunciated. 'Not Japanese, not Chinese.'

'Ah, yes, Korea. You don't speak their language, Mr Hirago?'

'No, Captain. It is very distinct from my language. We recognise it, but I haven't learned any of it.'

Captain Walker wondered if he heard contempt in the man's voice, but his features were as placid as always. He turned away. 'Mr Goldsborough. How far are we from Korea?'

'From mainland Korea, a little distance. The land mass we sighted yesterday is a large island known as Quelpaert Island. There are older maps that list it as Cheychudo and—'

'Cheju-do,' the older man on the deck corrected. 'Cheju-do.' He waved an arm back towards the east, then tapped his chest and waved at his compatriots.

'Quelpaert. Yes, I know of it,' the captain said, eying the older man. 'Seems they could be from this island.'

'Sir, if so, I believe they are sea-fishing people, although they don't normally venture far from home. Yet here they are.' Goldsborough nodded in their direction.

'Indeed.' The captain met the old Korean man's gaze. He tapped his own chest. 'Walker.' He tapped again.

The old man stood once again. Bowed, a movement of his head, his eyes alert. 'Tae-yong.' And tapped his chest. He reached out but didn't touch the captain. 'Wo-Ka,' he said.

The captain imitated the bow. 'Very good. Now, Mr Goldsborough. Tell me what I should do?'

'Not quite sure, sir. At least they are friendly.'

'Give them your name,' the captain said.

Mr Goldsborough also bowed to the old man. 'Goldsborough.' The lieutenant tapped his chest.

'Tae-yong.'

'Seo-yeon,' the woman piped up and slapped her chest with a flat palm.

'Song-chol.' The young man, not asleep at all, stood and bowed stiffly.

All eyes turned to the blue-eyed man. He got to his feet. 'Goldsboro,' he said, rolling his tongue around the syllables. He pressed a palm on his chest. 'I am Jac Owen,' he said, faltering as he tested his tongue.

The captain barked a laugh. 'Jac Owen, sir? I am pleased to make your acquaintance.' But at the man's blank stare, he held up his hands. 'We have a mystery, here, gentleman. Perhaps he can be coaxed to speak more English.'

The blue-eyed man bent and clamped a hand on the woman's shoulder. '*Eomma.*' And on the man's shoulder, he said, '*Appa.*'

Mr Clark spoke up. 'That sounds Dutchy to me, Cap'n. He's sayin' that's his father and his mother.'

Then the captain pointed to the other Korean man and raised his brows at Jac Owen, who said, '*Hyeong.*' He tapped both the other man's chest and his own, then clasped his hands together.

'Brothers, perhaps, Mr Goldsborough?'

'Yes, Captain.'

'Interesting family.' The captain nodded. 'We might have a problem, sirs,' he said, and his glance shifted between Goldsborough, Mr Hirago and Mr Clark. 'Custom does not allow me to put them back out to sea, but if I take them onto Shanghai it might mean death for them, anyway.'

Mr Goldsborough nodded, agreeing and Mr Hirago barely inclined his head. Mr Clark said, 'They made it this far on the open water, Cap'n. A little landing in the Chinese mainland shouldn't worry them at all.' He lifted a hand to catch the attention of a barefoot, bareheaded sailor, who, on Mr Clark's nod, bellowed, 'Hoist them sheets, boyos. We know where we're goin'.'

The hands already on deck began the business of sailing the sloop-of-war, *Saratoga*, to the Chinese port of Shanghai. The sails on the three masts unfurled, and the square rigger sailed gracefully towards the west.

*

'What did he say?' Tae-yong asked Jac. He and Seo-yeon sat side by side, and the pitch and roll of the boat had them swaying. Song-chol wasn't at ease.

They were on the deck, under some sort of bridge. Walker frequented it from time to time. The other man, Goldsborough, would meet him there and consult the charts, and wave an arm about, speaking with strange nuances.

Jac craned a look skywards. A flag, red and white striped, with a patch of white stars on a deep blue square in the corner flew high overhead. 'I don't know what they said. I'm trying to remember words. I recognise some, but the meaning ...'

'They look like the barbarians the mainlanders hate.'

Jac nodded at his father. 'They're all alike except for the different clothes they wear. But they sound different to what I remember.' He scratched his head and eyed the bridge. Walker had his head bent close to Goldsborough as they studied the great charts.

Their language, the tone, then the burring sounds of some words ... He saw a picture, suddenly, of green fields, then dank stone walls, and many voices from dark days came rushing back to him. He shot to his feet, a hand gripping the rail of the steps. As his head bobbed into their sight, the men on the bridge looked at him. Jac said, 'Wales,' and tapped his chest. 'I am from Wales.'

'Wales, you say?' Walker boomed. He beckoned Jac up the steps to the deck and said something to Goldsborough.

Jac watched him shuffle the great papers and came up with one that he flattened, a press of hands on it as if he felt some reverence. He traced a finger across the pictures. 'Wales,' Goldsborough said, and tapped.

Jac stared at the tiny picture. He shook his head. It meant nothing to him.

Goldsborough said something else and drew his finger down the page, along many strange shapes, up into an empty area of the chart, then wove it around other smaller shapes until he tapped a small dot. 'Cheychudo.'

Jac could barely see any marks where the man's finger was placed. He shook his head again. The man then drew his finger into blank space on the chart and tapped. Waved his arm about.

Jac remembered the vast voyage, long ago, when he was locked in a cabin on his back, looking out a porthole. A fierce storm, churning, angry seas. Squeezing his eyes shut a moment, he said, 'Cheju. Ship ...' He tapped his chest again and cut the air with the edge of his hand. Rolled his hands over one another in a bid to show how the storm rolled the vessel, then his hands fell apart. 'Broken.'

Both men stared at him. Walker pointed at Jac. Levelled his hand at waist height. Then at Jac again at shoulder height, then at the top of Jac's head. Jac responded with his hand at waist level. He had been a young boy at the time of the shipwreck.

'The name of your ship?'

Jac shook his head. He understood but had no memory of a name.

'Jac.' Walker spoke. 'Home. Do you want to go home?'

Jac turned the word around in his head. *Home.* Home was an island where he was hunted because he was different, because he had round blue eyes, where his presence had put the people he loved in danger. Home was where the spirits of his parent's children roamed, those who had died from the red rash sickness. It made him uneasy, and haunted. He didn't belong. *Home.* They'd escaped from home, from Cheju, not likely to return for fear of imprisonment or death. He looked over the rail and down at his parents, and Song-chol who watched him.

'Not home,' he said to Walker.

'Not to Wales?' The man looked surprised.

Jac frowned. His sister was there, and he hesitated. But Wales was not home, either. He shook his head. 'No.'

Walker fired off rapid strings of words to Goldsborough who consulted the charts once again, shuffling the great swathes of paper. Walker tapped a place on a new chart. 'Shanghai.' He tapped and repeated, 'Shanghai.'

Jac nodded. Walker indicated he should tell his friends. Jac leaned over the rail and called down to Song-chol. 'Shanghai,' he said.

Song-chol shrugged but Tae-yong threw his hands in the air. 'Bah. China.'

Seo-yeon slapped her hands to her head. 'We should have stayed on the raft,' she wailed at Tae-yong, and clutched at his shirt. 'They'll imprison us in Shanghai. We cannot go there.'

Tae-yong looked up at a worried Jac and back to Seo-yeon. 'But where else do we go? We are in the hands of these men.'

Jac said to a startled Goldsborough, 'Not Shanghai.'

The captain grunted and turned to the lieutenant. 'Mr Goldsborough. I am not in the business of pandering to folk we pull from the sea, despite our nearly running right over the top of them. We will be sailing into Shanghai.'

'Understood, sir. I think Mr Owen means they wouldn't call Shanghai home for reasons of their own, and not that they aren't grateful for our assistance.'

Captain Walker glared at him. 'You've managed to ascertain that, have you?'

Mr Goldsborough had nothing to answer but held his ground. 'We're bound for Hong Kong according to Commodore Perry.' Perry was the commanding officer of the eight ships that sailed into Edo Bay demanding trade with the Japanese. 'Perhaps he'd know of a ship needing crew, or passengers, sailing out of Shanghai, acquitting our responsibility.'

Walker's glare remained, then eased. 'Might be right. A good plan. There are ships taking Chinamen to the goldfields somewhere south. Australia, I believe.'

'Yes sir, Australia.'

'Goldfields. Lot of rabble if you ask me.'

'The passage from China to the Southern Ocean, sir, is a lucrative market. Many American ships carry men from here looking to make their fortune.'

The captain stared down at the charts, shuffling the rolled sheets until he found what he was looking for. 'Australia.' He beckoned Jac. 'We will go from Shanghai,' he began, pointing with his finger. 'To Hong Kong and will put you on a ship,' he pointed at Jac and down over the bridge to the family, 'that will take you here.' He went back to the map and traced a finger from Hong Kong, down the middle of the Philippine Sea, over the Melanesian group of islands and the Coral Sea. Lastly, down the east coast of the island continent of Australia. He stopped at Van Diemen's Land. 'Australia,' he said to Jac.

'Australia,' Jac repeated. He nodded to the men and called down to his family. 'He says we should go to Australia.'

'Never heard of it,' Tae-yong shouted back.

'Is it near China?' Seo-yeon called up.

Jac looked back to the charts. He looked over to Wales, across to Cheju and then onto Shanghai, Hong Kong and then finally on Van Diemen's land. 'Very far from China.' He stared at the map. The hollow in his chest was the vast emptiness of the ocean over which the captain had just slid his finger.

'Good,' Seo-yeon said, pushing her husband off. 'We'll go there.'

'What is there in that place, Australia?' Song-chol asked, getting to his feet, and standing as if bowlegged to balance himself. The ship was on calm waters but Song-chol wasn't taking any chances.

Jac shrugged. 'I don't know.' He glanced at Goldsborough then at Walker. Maybe there would be more conversation.

Walker nodded abruptly. 'Good day.' To his lieutenant, he said, 'Mr Goldsborough, ensure they are fed. They will sleep on deck here.' As he looked over the rail to the family peering expectantly at him from below, he turned to go and stopped. 'The younger men can be put to work.'

Mr Goldsborough turned to Mr Clark. 'Some biscuits and some beef if you please for the folk.'

Jac bowed as he watched the captain leave, and Mr Clark disappear below deck. He checked Goldsborough for anything further and the man indicated with a hand to his mouth that food was coming.

When a short timber board carrying a small stack of something was put before the family, Mr Clark had to indicate what to do. He picked up a flat, hard square and bit into it. Chewed.

Seo-yeon followed suit. Unimpressed with it, she put it on the deck and picked up a lump of something else. She sniffed and asked a silent question of Mr Clark. Again, he indicated that it was to be eaten. Again, she put it on the deck, a frown on her face.

Jac tried the flat square. He understood why Seo-yeon left it on the deck. However, they had to eat something. He chewed and swallowed, said to Song-chol, 'You better eat it. We must be grateful.'

Song-chol snatched up a square and wolfed it down.

Seo-yeon looked up at both the younger men. 'We might have to fish to keep ourselves alive.'

Tae-yong carefully took himself over to the ship's rail, dodging around busy sailors who took only momentary interest in him. Looking down into the ocean, at the rise and fall of the ship over calm water, he said over his shoulder, 'You couldn't dive here. Too deep.'

'Perhaps we just fill our bellies for now and wait until we get to land. Near the coast will be better,' Jac said.

'Agreed,' said Song-chol as he reached for another biscuit.

Seo-yeon took up a piece of biscuit and handed it to her husband as he returned to their corner. 'Eat. And hope all your teeth don't fall out.'

The three-masted ship sailed smoothly on flat water, ahead of cooler breezes, and under clear skies. Summer season, and although hot by day, it was comfortable. The sails filled, the sailors worked day and night, and the ship seemed a hive of industry that never ended.

Jac was to clean rust from the anchor chains. Song-chol and Tae-yong were put with a team on watch to oil the masts. Seo-yeon had complained that she hadn't been given work to do and was ignored. She told Jac she wanted something from their raft, and he had to make the request understood by Mr Clark. Once allowed on the raft, which had been slung and strapped to a stanchion, she dug around in her bag until she came up with her needle and thread. She proceeded to demonstrate that she could also work. Mr Clark still resisted.

It wasn't until she approached Mr Walker, talking fast, and waving her hands, demonstrating to him what she could do, that Mr Clark was asked to provide her with the necessary equipment to help mend the sails. Satisfied, she worked studiously, preferring to be on her own. One barefoot man wearing neat trousers and a clean shirt inspected her work. The patches on his clothes were stitched neatly and evenly and he clearly approved of what she'd done. He nodded, impressed. She nodded back. He flattened a palm on his chest. 'Carter.'

'Seo-yeon.'

'Good morning, So Yon.'

Then he brought her a stack of used cloth cut into various shapes. He showed her what he required. Seo-yeon began to sew clothes for the crew men. Carter would come to inspect the work each day, and leave with an armful, satisfied with his apprentice.

The family stayed together at night and were provided with cover in the form of an old and patched mizzen sail and sleeping mats. Their sail to mainland China flew past. Under the captaincy of Commodore Walker, the crew was calm and orderly but when a faint line appeared on the horizon ahead to the west, a buzz of expectation flew around the sloop.

The thriving port of Shanghai rose out of the curve of the horizon. Jostling for position before taking her place on the docks, the *Saratoga* sat smug in the haze of humidity. A flurry of men secured her within the ramshackle port area. Many boats with sails furled, and anchored on the banks of the channel, awaited service or passengers.

Jac studied the boats on either side of the *Saratoga*, a keen eye on the flags that rose over each of them.

Song-chol stood alongside, his eyes agog. 'I've never seen as many boats, or people.'

Seo-yeon leaned over the rail, watching with them. 'I think I see a fishmonger.'

Song-chol squinted. 'Your eyesight is better than mine.'

She pointed. 'There, between those big carts loaded high with bales. Jac, do you see?'

Jac did see what looked to be a trading table. 'But we have nothing to barter, *Eomma*,' he said, long ago ignoring his empty stomach as it groaned with each ship biscuit he'd eaten. He was slowly becoming used to the lumps of meat, dry and hard, that were served up each day.

Seo-yeon fell silent. She gazed over the space that sprawled before her. Banks of the channel were lined with Chinese river craft all jammed together and crawling with men. Some were toting wares or striding to sampans. Others directed traffic with arms waving and voices shouting. In the distance, a great hulk listed, once a huge vessel. It seemed no one went near it, but it was too far distant to tell for sure.

She leaned a bit further over. 'The water here is filthy. If we could get to somewhere not so busy, I could dive. Find oysters or abalone.'

Tae-yong joined them, shading his eyes, and squinting at the banks. 'We need to find out what Wo-Ka has planned for us, and not travel too far away from this friendly ship.'

Seo-yeon was planning for herself. 'Jac must stay here on the boat because he looks like them. He would be unusual walking with us, but we wouldn't raise suspicion in a Chinese place.'

Tae-yong grunted. 'I don't have a Chinaman's plait, nor his hat. You have short hair, like a boy. We have only our peasant tunics. They smell different to us. We would be found out, taken in and imprisoned as spies or some such thing.'

'I think your mind has many stories in it.'

'It does.'

'Foolish ones,' Seo-yeon qualified.

'You were the fearful one days ago,' he said to his wife.

Song-chol leaned over the rail alongside Jac. 'I say let Wo-Ka direct us. He's a friend for now.'

Tae-yong lifted his chin. 'I wonder why that is. He has many men, many ships. He's a powerful leader yet he's kind to us.'

Jac remembered, from long ago, that his own countrymen were barbarians—not just the strange types his Cheju family called all foreigners—but barbaric in practice. He shut out the memory of cruel men and women who beat children, of those who did not defend the defenceless, of bitter cold, of sleeping in the dirt hollow with his sister. He could only reason that Walker had grown up in a different environment. So far, his favour had been beneficial.

'I say we remain,' Song-chol said. 'Eat the dirt cake they've given us, after all, they eat it too. Be thankful. Wait for a new ship.' He'd lost weight but seemed healthy enough. He and Jac had begun to swing up the masts and had learned to unfurl the sails, at first causing no end of good-natured bantering amongst the crew. Now, they hardly rated a glance.

Jac didn't want to leave Mr Walker's ship. He understood enough to know that it belonged to a great government far away. He and his family had been shown kindness and that had eased their fears. Nobody had openly derided them, in fact, ordinary seamen befriended them. There was no cruel punishment on board. No one wanted to beat them. The ship was clean, and the men were not so decimated by illness.

He kept his eye on the ships in the distance, a couple of them had a red and white striped flag hoisted high. He'd wait to see if one of those ships was favoured by Mr Walker.

'I agree with Song,' Jac said. He looked at his mother, whose gaze flicked away. '*Eomma*, let's wait a while longer.'

'While we wait, our bowels turn out stone logs from the dirt cakes,' she said, her lip curling.

'Just a little while longer,' he murmured as Goldsborough approached.

The lieutenant beckoned him to follow as he strode past. Jac and Song-chol met him on the starboard bow, their feet braced at the slight roll of the ship. Timbers creaked, sails flapped in the teasing breeze, and the stench of waste floated aboard.

Goldsborough, a rolled chart tucked under his arm, stood Jac in front of him. Then with his hands over Jac's shoulder he framed one of the two ships Jac had identified. 'That ship, a clipper, the *Good Mary*, will take you to Hong Kong.'

Jac barely understood him. He shook his head.

Goldsborough pointed at him and Song-chol and waved back at Jac's parents. Then he pointed at the ship again. He made a motion with his hand as if on a wave, and said, 'To Hong Kong. And then to Australia.'

'Ah.' Jac understood. He nodded.

Goldsborough unrolled the map and spread it on the rail of the deck. 'Shanghai,' he said, and pointed in an arc around them.

'Shanghai,' Jac acknowledged.

Goldsborough pointed to the ship in the distance. 'Hong Kong.' He drew a short line with his finger on the chart between

Shanghai and Hong Kong.

Jac nodded. Song-chol shifted his weight uneasily.

Then Goldsborough drew his finger from Hong Kong along an arc close to the bottom of the chart. 'Australia.'

Jac nodded again.

'How long would that take?' Song-chol asked. He pointed at the sun and started to count on his fingers.

Goldsborough tilted his head, lifted a shoulder. He looked about the sky and found a full moon. He pointed at that, held up one finger, spread his hands and held up three fingers.

Jac looked over at the ship. Song-chol stared hard at it.

'What does that mean?' Seo-yeon asked, behind the young men.

Tae-yong stood by her side. 'It means we will turn out stone logs for a while yet.'

Later that day, Goldsborough handed Jac two folded and sealed papers, along with a small pouch of coins that tinkled. Jac didn't remember ever seeing coin before, and asked Goldsborough what they were.

'It is currency, lad,' Goldsborough said. 'To purchase goods.' Jac tucked the bag inside his shirt, as bidden. 'The *Good Mary*,' Goldsborough went on. He tapped one of the papers. Then he tapped the other and said, 'The ship, *Louisa Baillie*, to Australia.'

'*Louisa Baillie*,' Jac repeated.

Then Goldsborough pointed to the gangway.

Seo-yeon knew what that meant. She got to her feet, folding a single piece of fabric yet to be cut to shirt size pieces. She tucked it inside her bag and shrugged into her backpack, which had never been far from her side. She stood in front of the lieutenant. 'Wo-Ka?' she requested.

Tae-yong stood with her and waited patiently as the captain was summoned from his bridge. They bowed at the captain, who bowed back.

Captain Walker nodded at them. He pressed a hand to Tae-yong's shoulder. 'Safe journey to you and your family, sir,' he said and walked away.

Tae-yong looked at Jac. 'What did he say?'

Jac lifted a shoulder. 'He blessed us.'

Tae-yong nodded. 'A good thing.'

It was a bright clear day when they arrived in Hong Kong's harbor. A warm, insistent mid-morning breeze had cleared the haze. The *Good Mary* moored in the bay, and row boats had taken the crew, and Jac and his family, ashore.

Without ceremony, they were given a short, sharp wave in the direction of the ships moored some distance away, one of which would be the *Louisa Baillie* to take them far to the south.

Jac turned a full circle on the landing where the rowboat had been tied. His family clustered around him as the crew disappeared into the crowds. The noise of the chattering, bustling fishermen, the traders, and other sailors, seemed suddenly loud. The size of the buildings lining the waterfront seemed to dwarf him, and the rolling, bulbous mountain range of the island closed in on him. He took a deep breath and turned around again, staring into the bay.

Song-chol swayed on his feet. 'I'd just got used to being on a ship,' he complained, his insides believing he was still out to sea. 'I don't feel good.'

Maybe that's what Jac felt. On land again, the world seemed to spin the other way. He tried to stem the swirl of dizziness and had to drop to one knee to prevent pitching forward.

Seo-yeon, unaffected, surveyed the landing. 'There,' she said, and pointed. 'A fishmonger. Food.' And she marched resolutely towards the trading table stacked high with glistening catch, some of which still wriggled and flapped, or waved claws in the air. She pulled a small wad of fabric from her backpack.

The men weaved after her. As they got closer, a row of steaming pots caught their attention. The aroma from one pot wafted with an elixir sent by the gods. It had been months since they'd had any *momguk*, pork and seaweed soup, and Jac's stomach cried out for whatever simmered at the trader's table.

Song-chol wiped his mouth. Tae-yong swallowed and stood taller over the table as he took a quick look in the pot. He nodded a greeting at the trader who murmured back, taking a quick glance over their clothes.

As his eyes flicked suspiciously, he said something, moved a hand back and forth over his wares. Seo-yeon replied, believing he'd told her a price, so the bargaining began. 'I can only pay with this,' she said in her own language, knowing he wouldn't understand her. She held up a drawstring bag, sewn with her sturdy stitches. She could sew many more of these with what cloth Mr Clark had allowed her to take. She showed the trader the embroidered ship, painstakingly intricate, detailed the front of it, even opened the strings to show him the inside. 'A gift for your wife or daughters,' she offered, but again, knew he wouldn't understand what she'd said.

The trader stared at her as he reached for the bag. She held it fast and indicated what she wanted. The bargaining continued with hand signals. Seo-yeon decided she needed to offer more and reached into her bag to pull out a newly stitched tunic, held it up to show the man its fine crafting. The trader's head nodded. He gathered four small wooden bowls and handed them over. Then he indicated they should ladle some of his soup.

Seo-yeon stood steadfast yet again and pointed at a lobster that still clawed the air. The trader shrugged, but the shirt was shaken under his nose along with the little bag. He spread his hands as if to say he was defeated, took the lobster, and plunged it into a pot of boiling water. He indicated, along with a wide grin devoid of teeth, that they should dip the ladle while they waited for the lobster to cook.

The shirt was handed over and the little bag was taken. Seo-yeon waited for the men to fill their bowls and then she stepped up to the pot. 'The gods only know what this is, but it smells good enough. Be careful you don't spew it all back up again. Take small mouthfuls.'

Song-chol took no notice and belched numerous times to keep it in his stomach. At first, Jac did as instructed, but the flavours were irresistible. He slurped and swallowed it down. Tae-yong muttered between noisy intakes that he didn't care what it was as long as it wasn't any more of those dirt cakes. Seo-yeon dipped the ladle, poured it into her bowl, and sipped.

Once the lobster was taken from the boiling pot and plunged into cold water, Seo-yeon took it. The family bowed before the trader in gratitude. He returned in kind.

They found clear space further along the landing. There, they dropped to their haunches and picked over the lobster until all that remained was the empty shell of the body and legs. Tae-yong lay down, stretching limbs and stomach. He groaned how good he felt.

Drowsy, lay on their backs, replete.

Jac's limbs ached. His mouth still held the flavours of the soup, and his skin, after weeks of being parched by wind and saltwater, now itched as it dried even more under the blaze of sunshine. Restless, he rolled to his side, and rose to a squat. His head no longer spun when he moved, and he took that as a good sign. He looked over at Song-chol sprawled on the dirt. 'Song, we need to spar.'

'You need to empty your head of nonsense.' Song-chol had an arm flung over his face.

Standing, Jac stretched his arms, rolled his shoulders. 'I need to practice before I get on another ship. I think my guts have softened. I feel weak like a half-dead fish.'

Song-chol clambered to his feet. 'Can't have that, a half-dead fish.' He shook himself down then raised his arms, readying for the spar.

Tae-yong remained where he was, but sat up, an arm resting on his raised knee. 'Don't go hurting yourselves,' he said through a yawn.

Jac forced his sluggish limbs to work. Song-chol followed his moves, stretching and regaining his agility as they warmed up. 'Maybe we shouldn't have eaten,' he said.

They bowed to each other. The spar would begin. Dance-like, it started with soft falls of their feet, the firm, confident steps of the *pumbalbki*. In the earliest of training moves, the *hwalgatjit*, hands and arms moved like the wings of a bird across their chest to a shoulder, and with knees bent, their limbs worked in a soft flowing concurrence. Fluid and graceful, the rhythmic pace was hypnotic.

Soon, the jostlers, the seamen and the traders in the nearby areas of the harbor wandered by to watch as Jac and Song-chol sized up. When Song-chol delivered his first kick and Jac theatrically rolled to the ground a small cheer went up.

A coin was tossed onto the dusty floor of the landing and Seo-yeon, surprised, scurried to pick it up.

A collective howl hummed in the air as Jac caught Song-chol's next kick behind his knee and Song-chol lost his footing. Jac danced around him until, back on his feet, Song-chol spun with a kick high in the air, and Jac defended, blocking with his forearm. Song-chol neatly sidestepped, lashed out at Jac's ankle.

A shout of glee rose from the growing crowd, and Seo-yeon was kept busy as coins and vegetables and basketry was thrown her way as payment for the entertainment.

On his feet again, Jac saw a gleam in Song's eyes, and he nodded—there were rewards for a display such as this. They faced each other, footwork measured, arms free, and movement fluid. A step, a high kick and repeat. They worked in quick tempo, executed a series of fast and calculated sequences of feet and hands. Limbs in elegant motion, tight with skill and strength. They circled, neutralizing the other's threat. Gentle in appearance but sturdy, an arm blocked a kick, a foot hooked an ankle, a body hit the ground then bounced up, unhurt. A spin and a lengthy kick from the hip lashed an unsuspecting sparring partner. Theirs was the only martial art that need not cause physical damage, but if necessary, they knew an opponent could be dead after a lethal move before hitting the ground. But that was not the philosophy of *taekkyeon*.

Song-chol caught Jac's leg high in the air and behind his knee. He turned, grabbed Jac's neck and put him face down on the dirt. Jac conceded the match to Song-chol. A roar went up and coins rained down. Seo-yeon moved swiftly to pluck them up.

Tae-yong nodded happily. He had explained some moves, mimicking his sons', and encouraging onlookers to have a go as he helped correct, or applaud. 'It's still in my blood, Seo-yeon,' he said, pleased with himself.

'Don't spill any of your blood,' she muttered.

The crowd dispersed. The mutterings of language the family couldn't understand were cheerful noises as heads bobbed and grins split broad faces, and arms waved in friendly mimicry.

The last of the onlookers, a young man with a long glossy plait, lingered for a time, as if wanting to approach. He backed up when beckoned and headed off.

Jac looked back over to Seo-yeon with a wide smile. '*Eomma*, I thought it's not our way to take payment for others to watch our practice.'

'It is now,' she grumbled, peering into her bag, testing its weight.

'It means we get to eat more of that soup and the lobster,' Song-chol said, dusting off.

'It means we get much more for our passage to that country far away in the south,' Tae-yong said.

He bent to pick up a single shining piece still stuck in the dirt but Seo-yeon scooped it up and tossed it in her bag. Jac had told her of its value as currency. She studied what else had been thrown in as payment for the show. There were small woven baskets that she tossed off as useless. She inspected the vegetables, some she knew, some she didn't, and tucked them all deep into the backpack. The coins she gathered in her palms, tossing them a little to hear the jingling and peering at the odd assortment with some consternation. 'This is a strange thing to barter with.'

'It seems to have high value,' her husband commented.

Song-chol turned to Jac. 'I note you let me win again, brother.' He feigned his disappointment.

Jac barked a laugh. 'I don't think so, and better you win than a foreigner like me. And we have earned from the exercise.' He nodded towards Seo-yeon's haul.

'Long may it last.'

'It must last until at least we find passage on that ship Golds-boro told me to find.' Jac touched the letters tucked inside his tunic. One was an introduction to the captain, he was sure, of the *Louisa Baillie*.

The *Good Mary* had moored in a central location in the bay, but the ship to take them south had docked around to the east. So they trudged along the ragged shore lined with buildings and shacks and boats. There were familiar smells—stenches of rotting animal and fish carcasses. There were broken timbers, flotsam, human waste, and other rubbish—the detritus of a busy port.

Jac stepped up to the gangway of the *Louisa Baillie*, his family watching from the wharf. Seamen on board stared at him before one of them turned away and brought another man, stocky, red-haired, bearded and in uniform, back to the rail.

'From Golds-boro,' Jac said, before thrusting the letter forward, embarrassed now that he hadn't better practised his old language while on the *Saratoga*.

The naval man raised his brows as he read the letter. 'Lieutenant Goldsborough. Well, I'll be. Heard they did good work with the Japanese.' Bright blue eyes stared at Jac, and a large scaly hand rubbed at his wiry beard.

Jac tried not to look blank. He nodded.

The man flapped the letter. 'Says here, you got family wanting passage to Australia.' He peered around Jac. 'Where are they?'

Jac pointed to the huddle on the wharf. His mother and father and brother all stared up at them.

'Your *family*, boy,' the man enunciated.

Jac nodded and pointed again. 'They are my family.' He tapped the letter. 'It says so.'

The brows rose again, and the man read a little more. 'So it does.' He closed his mouth and pressed his lips into a line before he said, 'Wait here.'

Startled that the letter had disappeared with the red-haired man, Jac looked over his shoulder again at the three on the wharf. Tae-yong shifted his weight from foot to foot, but it was the only indication that he was worried.

Jac looked back in the direction the man had gone. He waited a good deal of time. Sailors jostled him; he stepped aside. Others spoke to him and he answered, distracted. When the man returned with another man, Jac straightened up.

In front of him stood a clean-shaven, lean man who wore his shirt open at the collar under a waistcoat.

'Thank you, Mr Wilson. Wait with me, would you?'

'Aye, cap'n.'

'I'm Martin, Ship's Master, captain of *Louisa Baillie*,' he said, standing feet apart and clasping his hands behind his back. 'Jac Owen, is it?'

'Yes.'

'This letter says these folks are Korean.' He nodded over the side of the ship.

'From the island of Cheju,' Jac said.

The captain blew out his cheeks. 'Never heard of it.' He turned. 'Mr Wilson?'

'That be Quelpaert Island, Mr Martin, sir, off mainland Korea. Some call it Cheychu, some Cheychudo.'

'Ah yes. So, Mr Owen. Passage to Australia. And I believe you can pay.' Mr Martin tapped Goldsborough's letter. His was a bland face and his tone solemn, but not unfriendly.

Jac turned back to his family before answering. 'Yes,' he said facing the captain once more. 'We can also work.'

Martin looked down at Jac's family. 'We have over sixty passengers already on this vessel bound for Victoria, Australia, lad. We'll take you on board now and you three men can work and sleep on the deck. Register the woman as a passenger, Mr Wilson.'

'Aye, Mr Martin.'

Martin inclined his head at Jac. 'Good day to you,' he said before walking off.

Jac stared at Mr Wilson as he comprehended. They were allowed passage.

'That went well,' Mr Wilson said. 'But we don't sail for five days. Much as I want to do what the master tells me, we can't sleep you lot nowhere on board till we sail. As it is, when we set off, your missus there will have to bunk below deck.'

Jac nodded, still catching up. Seo-yeon wouldn't want to sleep anywhere except on the deck, and more importantly, not far from Tae-yong. But five days—where would they stay until then? *A mere detail.*

He ran down the gangway and related the good news to his parents, and Song-chol.

For the five days until sailing, they would sleep close to where the *Louisa Baillie* was docked; the ship wouldn't be out of their sight. They camped on a flat nearby, an area disused for some years it seemed: the timbers of an old dock had rotted, and the water, murky, was choked with thick patches of reeds that stretched along the dirt bank.

On the first evening, Seo-yeon returned to the campsite with the makings of a simple meal. Song-chol was on his haunches speaking quietly to Tae-yong who sat on his knees guarding his wife's backpack.

'I've seen him lurking before,' Song-chol said, indicating a young man standing a way off. 'I wonder if he is after our coin.'

Tae-yong looked over at the short man who appeared to be studying the water lapping the dock. He was far enough away not to hear them, but close enough to catch their glances. He shied away if he was caught staring. His long plait was well oiled, his cheeks swarthy and his hands thick as if used to hard work. Was he a thief? Who could they trust in this land?

There were any number of characters here, from all over the world, it seemed. There were people who looked like Jac and Ben. There were some people whose hair was the colour of the golden winter sunrise, or red like the hair of Mr Wilson. There were men whose high cheekbones resembled theirs, but their flaring nostrils and the sounds of their language were foreign. There were men dressed like Golds-boro here, other men with skin the colour of polished wood, whose sing-song language was strange to the ear. There were men whose high foreheads, fierce stares, glowing black skin on sinewy limbs gave them the look of mighty warriors.

*Who could be trusted?* Jac and his family kept to themselves.

Seo-yeon dumped her basket close to the charred pit. Soon she would re-light the fire and roast the fish. 'Where is Jac?' Her glance was furtive.

'Latrine.'

As Jac loped back to the clearing, the man by the water spun about and intercepted him. It was the young man who'd lingered after the first sparring session days ago. As Jac stood there with him, other people began to appear alongside. Gangly youth, and hard muscled men.

Song-chol sprang to his feet to join Jac.

The young man held up his hands, as if to say he was no threat. Then he pointed at Jac and at Song-chol and waved his arms and shuffled his feet. He said something in his language, waving a hand at both and then mimicking the hand-and-arm waving again. After this, he tapped his chest and stood still, his eyes on Jac.

The milling crowd was silent, waiting. Another youth put up his hand and tapped his chest, too. An older man did the same and his face split into a grin.

Song-chol spoke to Jac. 'It seems we have pupils.'

'We are not masters to have pupils.'

'We are now,' Song-chol replied and beckoned the man to copy him.

Seo-yeon strode across. 'You pay,' she said to the Chinese man, and held out her hand.

He understood and immediately reefed under his tunic and produced a coin. Seo-yeon studied it but thrust it back. The man offered another to add to it and then showed her his empty pockets. Again Seo-yeon glared at the coins he offered—a couple of sterling pieces, and a Spanish coin. This time she nodded, accepting the payment. The others followed suit, and with bits of different currencies in her hand, she declared training could now begin.

By the second day, Jac and Song-chol had many more pupils.

'I have never seen such a motley group for training.' Song-chol looked over the mixed band of men.

Seo-yeon took a payment from each man. She and Tae-yong settled back to watch the opening spar after Jac and Song-chol had exercised. When onlookers appeared, she also insisted on payment. She won some and shooed away any recalcitrant misers.

Jac and Song-chol sparred with the joy they remembered. Each time one or the other gained a winning point, his opponent retreating, cheers and calls arose, the crowd clamouring for more. Song-chol beckoned some young men to step forward, to learn simple moves. He lined them up and demonstrated technique, corrected stance, delivered controlled blows. Some new students tried their hand with Jac, all eager to begin, all laughing when they failed.

'It's not easy, boys,' Tae-yong would say to them, nodding sagely, not understood at all. But he was an elder imparting knowledge and exhibiting moves of his own. His long-practised discipline was much admired.

By nightfall, the sessions were over, and Seo-yeon's bag of coin was heavy. She was happy. Happier still when the third day, a crowd arrived with more money, and Jac and Song-chol began their sparring to entice eager students. The day was filled with training, sore backsides, and later after the bouts, hoots of laughter. There were few bruised egos but most were happy for the entertainment.

The family ate well. Seo-yeon bartered the vegetables and baskets for fish and savoury cakes. She wasn't always happy with the quality of produce but that meant she wouldn't return to favour the merchant with her trade. As for the coins they'd been tossed, she hoarded them with fervour.

On the morning of the fifth day, when they were to board the *Louisa Baillie*, a crowd arrived as usual, and the taunts and friendly jeers began when training partners were sought. Jostling for position had started on the sparring ground. Jac and Song-chol would demonstrate a move, adjust a stance, correct a delivery. Seo-yeon was busy, and her basket of coins grew heavier.

The laughter was easy, the camaraderie natural now. Jac and Song-chol had taken their places, and the usual hush descended. The spar was fast, fluid, swift and the crowd shouted appreciation.

Set to resume after midday when the sun had lowered a little, Jac noticed new men arriving. Song-chol looked up from his mat. The drop in the tone around them was tangible as the newcomers wove through the pupils. Partners were separated, shoved as the men pushed forward. They stood and stared at Jac as one, hands loose by their sides.

Song-chol got to his feet.

Seo-yeon faltered, hung back, narrowed her gaze at each stranger. Chatter in the crowd dropped away and some of the original pupils backed off. She glanced at Tae-yong who watched from his mat by the cooking fire. Beckoning her, he slowly began to gather their belongings. She tucked her coin basket by her side and shuffled behind the retreating crowd, gathered her utensils as her husband snatched their backpacks.

The interlopers, densely built men, had dark stares and grim faces. The crowd edged further back until only the six sturdy Chinese faced Jac and Song-chol on the sparring pad.

'Maybe they don't want to pay,' Song-chol said conversationally. Anyone could hear him.

'Maybe we're on their territory,' Jac said in the same tone. Chinese gangs, *tongs*, were known to be in the area. Most were headed for America as workers on the railroads. 'There's six of them, did you count?'

'Ah yes, my brother, but two of us.'

'Three,' Tae-yong piped up and stood.

Jac heard Seo-yeon snap, 'Two. There are *two* of them.'

The six circled Jac and Song-chol.

'Take a deep breath, brother,' Song-chol said. 'No flat foot strikes for this lot.' Flat foot *Taekkyeon* strikes were deliberately non-violent.

'Here they come,' Jac muttered, and unhurriedly turned to stand back-to-back with Song-chol.

All six Chinese lunged with fierce battle cries, lumbering great solid battering rams. Jac lashed out, and a thick head snapped back. Song-chol leapt, his hard foot connecting with a jaw. The two men had dropped to the dirt. The remaining men re-grouped.

'Then there were four,' Song-chol said, eager, and smiled at the attackers. The crowd whooped and waved fists, surged forward, watching. Some men dragged off the two unconscious bodies. Yells went up, coins were thrown.

Seo-yeon dared not dart forward. Tae-yong had shouldered their packs and was in a crouch next to his wife.

The four came on, belligerent but less confident. Jac's foot slammed a solid chest, and the body hit the ground with a grunt. Song-chol kicked and connected with a forehead and down went his attacker, out cold. A knife skittered.

The crowd threw up a low growl and someone darted in to kick away the knife. Another body was dragged away. Whoops and yells continued.

Two Chinese men came flailing, and the man Jac had dropped charged for his legs.

'Not a good enough foot, brother,' Song-chol said and whipped around to slam his heel onto the man's cheek and down he went. The last two had gone for Jac and as men from the crowd dragged away the fourth man, Song-chol leapt.

Back-to-back again, they danced and kicked. Feet hit soft targets, backs of knees, ankles, and the Chinese were tiring.

'Stop playing,' Tae-yong yelled shooting upright. He disappeared when Seo-yeon grabbed his tunic and tugged him out of sight.

Another knife whipped out and jumped nervously in a grimy Chinese hand. The crowd hissed, booed. The man waved it at Jac then at Song-chol and lunged.

Jac turned, kicked a kneecap, thrust an elbow under the man's jaw missing the soft tissue of his throat. The knife flew, the crowd rushed in grabbed the fallen man and his weapon, dragging him away by his feet.

Song-chol danced, his arms and hands hypnotic, his stare flat, dark. One to go. And this one took a stand. He would do battle; he had training; it was clear. They edged around each other.

The crowd hummed.

The man danced high, and the kick missed Song's head by inches. Song-chol struck with a foot as he swung past, pirouetted, and slammed a forearm onto his opponent's shoulder at the neck. A heavy grunt as the man dropped to his knees. The mob crowed. Song-chol waited. The man staggered to his feet, and ready to resume, danced, feigned. When he parried with a kick, Song-chol leapt high, scissoring in the air, and delivered two sharp blows that connected one after the other to chest and head.

The crowd yowled; fists waved in triumph. More coins flew. The sixth man was down, dragged from the ring as money changed hands and wagers were paid up.

Jac and Song-chol bowed to each other, then to the gleeful crowd.

Jac said, 'That last move. Not strictly in the spirit of *Taekkyeon*.'

'Not strictly,' Song-chol replied. 'But he's not dead either.'

As the men in the crowd slapped their shoulders, congratulated in languages they still couldn't understand, Seo-yeon and Tae-yong pushed closer.

'We get to that boat quick, Jac,' Seo-yeon said, juggling her basket of coins.

Tae-yong was loaded up with their backpacks and the rest of the gear. 'Our time is finished in this camp, that is in no doubt. No one will bother us if we're with the Americans.'

Jac approached the gangway of the *Louisa Baillie*.

Mr Wilson waved them on. 'Now, it's ten-pound passage for the woman, lad.' He held a writing instrument over an open book.

Jac blinked hard.

At his hesitation, Wilson said, 'Could've been ten pound each but you men will be working on board.'

Seo-yeon, standing close to her husband and to Song-chol,

said to Jac, 'He wants payment? Of course he would. Give him the coins.' She rattled her bag, the chink of coin sounding from within. 'How much does he want?'

'Bring out a handful,' Tae-yong said. 'Let him choose.'

Seo-yeon squatted on the deck and pulled her bag to the front, scooping out a handful of coins. Song-chol sat with her.

Jac beckoned Mr Wilson. 'We need you to tell us how much for passage.'

Mr Wilson bent to Seo-yeon as she carefully placed the coins in front of her. Mr Wilson squinted. With a finger, he dragged two coins out from the rest and indicated Seo-yeon needed some more. He pulled another seven of the same type of coin and asked for one more. Seo-yeon shook the bag. *Empty.*

Jac held his breath. She had loads of money somewhere. He watched Mr Wilson survey the rest of the coins. The man straightened as Mr Martin strode towards them.

Wilson frowned. 'Not got quite enough, Mr Martin.'

Jac's gut squeezed. Seo-yeon's gaze narrowed on her son then her look shot to Mr Martin. She ignored Wilson.

'Come now, Mr Wilson,' Martin said. 'There's plenty of coin here. Looks like they've accepted all the sterling coin they've been given, God knows no one else wants it. Take four Spanish dollars as well and call the transaction settled.' He nodded at Jac and walked off.

Seo-yeon refused to stay below deck. She tucked herself into a stairwell and took up her sewing kit again. Mr Wilson protested only once and, after the tirade she aimed at him, found it wasn't worth the trouble again. He grumbled about her being in the way, but they knew she was not. Jac heard mutterings from some deckhands, but her presence on deck through the day was hardly noticed. As the master of the ship said nothing, Seo-yeon remained where she was.

They'd been at sea for weeks. Sometimes the land mass to the west seemed never-ending. Other times, it was a broken ridge on the horizon in the hazy blur of humidity.

The weather was changing. One day, the mugginess sucked out their breath, the next, a wisp of cool breeze teased their drying skin. The ocean changed, waves grew choppy and short. The ship sailed on; sails opened to harness the wind, the wheel turning to command a tack to the coastline or to set a course further from the tug of land.

Jac bent his back to the tasks on board as required. He, Tae-yong and Song-chol worked alongside the others on the boat, their strange sounding English improving as the jibes and the jokes were traded back and forth.

Seo-yeon kept her counsel in the stairwell, her sinewy fingers at work with her needles and her sharp eyes never without her family in their sight. So, she was the first to see Song-chol drop off a boom clutching his abdomen. As he hit the deck, his face was white, and his mouth was stretched in agony.

Jac swung to the deck to clutch at him, but Song-chol yowled in pain, rolling onto his side with his knees bent. Sweat had popped on his face, and when he finally focused on Jac with blinking eyes that were more owlish than hooded, he called him by another name, spoke about things Jac had never heard before.

Someone shouted a name, 'Cranwell!' and an older sailor dropped down from the rigging to kneel beside the writhing Song-chol in Jac's arms. It only took one finger's light pressure on Song's abdomen, the right side near his groin, and Song-chol let out a wail of agony.

Cranwell snatched his hand away and shook his head at Jac. 'It might subside, lad, but it don't look like it. If his gut ruptures, I canna do nothin' for it but hope it takes him quick.' He pressed a rough hand on Jac's shoulder and went back to his work, scaling the ropes and riggings.

Jac stood, stunned. He stared down at Song-chol, who was shaking and hot with fever, clutching his tunic shirt tight and muttering of being cold. Tae-yong beckoned Jac and together lifted him, got him onto the floor of Seo-yeon's stairwell. Song-chol cried out, doubled over to vomit. Seo-yeon waved her husband away, tended Song, rested his head in her lap. She dripped water into his slack mouth and crooned motherly things to him as he spasmed weakly in and out of consciousness.

Jac took over when Seo-yeon fell asleep. He settled Song, his brother, hot and clammy, and rocked him like a mother soothing a babe.

In Song's ear he whispered the memories of days on a Cheju beach, fighting imaginary foes, and of high adventures on the raft, escaping the mainlanders. He talked of their Appa and Eomma, of food, and *Taekkyeon*. While he murmured, Song-chol would squeeze his hand. Jac's pain welled up. 'We sparred with the best of them, my brother, but we were better.' Memories flooded in, and soft murmurs didn't stop. Wave after wave of boyhood adventures crowded to be heard, so many adventures filled the night air. 'We were the best, my brother.'

Song's grip on Jac's hand became weaker.

Tae-yong sat with them long after dark, long after the night watch had changed. Sometime before the next bells, their father beseeched the ancestors to call Song-chol into the afterlife.

In the dark just before dawn, Song-chol slipped away to join the spirits. Jac gathered him in his arms and wept.

The ship was holding fast, waiting for the signal to enter the port. Jac braced on the deck and took his time scanning the flat line of the coast.

Sand dunes broke the horizon, stark against an unremitting blue sky. The country hardly looked what they'd been hoping for, and from what they'd been told it was as good as it was going to get.

Talk was that they would sail west, far along the south coast to a port not far from the mouth of a mighty river. Maybe that would be where they'd begin their passage inland. No one seemed to know.

The midday sun beat down. Jac rolled his shoulders under a worn cotton shirt and hitched his trousers. He straightened the cap on his head, made by Seo-yeon from the fabric that had been salvaged from an old shirt. It was some protection against the fierce, dry southern heat.

Earlier today, they learned that they would be landing at the southern city port of Melbourne. There'd been some worrying talk of each 'alien' having to pay taxes if they disembarked here for the goldfields, but they'd learned from Mr Martin that it wasn't law yet and not enforceable. That was a weight off Jac's shoulders.

Somebody yelled, and men scuttled here and there. Jac felt the ship lean and he took a step to brace. They were underway again.

It had been weeks since Song-chol was committed to the sea.

Jac hung his head. *I miss you, my brother.*

It was a twist of fate that Song-chol succumbed to the gods just as they were about to embark on their next adventure. He wasn't sure he believed in the afterlife for himself, but for Song-chol he hoped so. He flattened a hand over his heart and closed his eyes. Song-chol's spirit would wander, lost, far from Cheju, and might cause mischief or harm. Jac wished him peace. He was sorely bereaved of his brother, and sometimes the pain of it was hard to bear.

Shouted orders barked but Jac understood little more than when they'd first boarded. His old Welsh language was almost gone, and the alternative, English, was just as hard to comprehend. So many accents and dialects to train his ear, and only if spoken slowly was it easier to comprehend.

He swore to learn English properly and, at the same time, learn more about sailing the ship. A few sailors tried with hand signals and some crude verbals, but mostly they gave up, impatient when a job had to be done in a hurry. Determined, he picked up what he could. If he was to return to Wales, he would need to work on the ship and be useful. His language skills grew every day.

Many diverse groups of people gathered from all over the world on the goldfields in this country. From there, when he'd mastered the language of his birth, he would find his way back to Wales.

Jac held out his hand for Seo-yeon. She gripped it, climbed out of the rowboat and stood in the shallow water, tilting her head up, sniffing the seaweed laden breeze. 'It feels good to be in the sea, not just on it.'

Tae-yong clambered over the side. Flanking Seo-yeon, they waded ashore towards people who had milled on the beach waiting for them to disembark. A few were white-skinned folk in longish robes and trousers, with heavy-looking crosses that dangled from their necks. Jac touched his own talisman, hidden under his shirt. Others were dark-skinned, even black-skinned, men in trousers and shirts, the women in baggy dresses. All round eyed. Mostly staring back at them.

Seo-yeon stumbled in the water, but Jac and his father held her steady.

'Not long now, *Eomma*,' Jac said. 'We're nearly on land again.'

'I feel it already under my feet,' she said. 'It's a good land.'

'Any land is good,' his father grumbled. 'But better is food in our stomachs. When we get there, we will be growing real food, catching the best fish, eating clean again, not this garbage they call food.' His father hadn't stopped grumbling since leaving the shores of Cheju all those many, many months ago.

'Perhaps it is a place where I can dive once more.' Seo-yeon gazed back out to sea.

Jac was sure that she wouldn't be diving where they were going, nor would they be catching fish any time soon. They'd heard from others on the ship that it took many days walking to get to those goldfields from here, and then only if they had good weather and found water along the way. Jac knew many people had already trudged the path before them, so perhaps the gods of his parents would be kind.

He glanced at Seo-yeon. She already missed her diving, her life in the sea. He doubted she'd ever see the ocean again.

# Chapter Fourteen

*1854 Ballarat diggings*

Jac straightened. He'd just begun to hammer in a tent peg when he heard the voice call to him in abrupt English. It was the second time in a week.

'You not Chinese. You not camp here.'

Seo-yeon came to the opening from inside the half erect tent. 'What does he say?' she asked and glared at the man with the long plait down his back.

Jac didn't answer her. Instead, he looked around and sighed. They had chosen a spot on the edge of the Chinese camp, closer to the Ballarat township itself, but far enough away from other sites to blend in with the men who'd rushed here in their thousands from China.

They'd had to move camp the first time when the miner he worked for got married and needed the space. Once Jac moved, he no longer had a job. Tae-yong worked alongside Jac and together they'd managed to find only enough gold to pay the licence fees, and to eat. All who lived and worked on the goldfields had to have their own licence whether they mined or not, all except wives and the indigenous people.

Seo-yeon had taken to weaving baskets for miner's wives. She traded with Aboriginal people for skins and for grasses to make shoes for children and did a roaring trade at times. That, too, helped the family's coffers. Refused to learn anything but the basics of English, she'd managed well, often bemoaning that she was far from an ocean in which to dive for decent food.

Tae-yong had just come back from hunting with his friend, a Koori man. The chortling and hand waving signalled camaraderie, and Jac had long believed they understood each other. The kill, a kangaroo, had been welcome.

Tae-yong's gifts of horsehair hats had been a source of great amusement in the Koori man's family, and they were worn proudly. Tae-yong always found plenty of horsehair here. It seemed the round-eyes wasted good resources.

He came to stand alongside Jac and scowled. 'Chinaman still thinks he owns the world,' he said in *Cheju-eo*.

The Chinese man's cool gaze slid from him to Jac. Maybe he picked up Tae-yong's derision. In English, he said to Jac, 'Backward peasants not welcome.'

Jac decided not to translate either of their spoken words to the other. He addressed the Chinese man. 'We are here to dig for gold. No harm, no trouble.' He didn't want to fight with another Chinese group.

'You,' the man said pointing at Jac. 'You not welcome here, English. You go, too.'

Jac sighed. There it was again, the reference to his home country. According to the Chinese, looking western and sounding different made him English and so came the orders to move on. He guessed it was the same everywhere. If you looked Asian, you were all Chinese. If you were white, you were all English. There were so many nationalities here, it was hard to tell who was from where unless you asked.

As he stood determining his next move, Jac heard Seo-yeon mutter behind him. 'Better we go again. I don't want to keep risking conflict in this place. It has bad spirits.' The tent flap dropped and then he heard the sounds of her packing their few belongings.

Tae-yong lifted his chin towards the Chinaman. 'The feral herds of Cheju horses are held in higher regard than you are.'

*Good insult.* Jac kept his face blank of expression.

The Chinese man lofted an insult of his own. 'Man from Korea, your country weak. We are unhappy you here.'

Jac had learned a little of the politics of mainland Korea and China while on Cheju, but the conflict had hardly touched the island. Cheju could easily have been overrun by any number of foreign and antagonistic usurpers greedy for free trade in the area, but it had remained stoically unencumbered.

Mainland Korea refused to trade with the British or the Americans, and shut its doors, vulnerable to unsavoury treaties. Everyone seemed to be aware of it, even on Cheju, but there they chose to ignore most of what they heard.

'What did he say?' Tae-yong demanded.

'He said it was too hot in the sun to argue and that we should be going.' Jac scratched his head. His mother was already packing up. His father was puffing out his chest, but Jac knew he didn't want conflict either.

'You're right, this is not the place for us,' Jac said to the Chinese man. 'Instead, we will look for happier people to live beside.' He turned without a customary polite nod at the man and addressed his father. '*Eomma* is packing. We will find a better campsite.'

As he yanked out the tent pegs he'd just sunk, he caught sight of a lone white man on a horse, watching him. The man lifted a hand in a wave and then he dismounted, adjusting his black hat. He brushed aside long sidelocks from his face.

Tae-yong, still muttering, stalked into the tent. A moment later the only pole erected for the tent came down and Jac heard his mother squawk and rush outside. A grumbling Tae-yong began to fold the canvas.

'Pardon my intrusion, sir,' the man said approaching Jac. 'I thought you might've needed assistance, so I waited in case an altercation ensued. It appears you didn't need help after all.'

The man had spoken quickly, and Jac concentrated to unravel the language. 'We did not need assistance but thank you.' Jac gathered up tent ropes and wound them into skeins on his hand.

The man sounded much like the men on the *Saratoga* and was maybe from America. 'Chinese fellows hardly cause a problem, especially amongst themselves.'

Jac inclined his head, didn't correct his assumption.

'Hope you'll be all right,' the man said, his longish head of hair and the shadow on his jaw typical of many men hereabouts. The dark hair was unkempt and the longer sideburns on the man's cheeks were curly but sparse.

Jac heard his mother quite clearly decrying the sad life of the Chinese man and what nefarious things she wished would happen to his chickens.

'We will. We'll move on, find another place to camp.' Jac nodded, offered a grateful smile.

The man would not be discouraged. 'I know somewhere that's recently been abandoned if you're interested. It's close to where my people have our site and we don't mind who camps nearby, as long as they are law-abiding quiet folk.' He waited for Jac to reply, misinterpreting the slow response for reluctance. "Course, it's just a suggestion. I had not meant to suppose that—'

'We have need of suggestions,' Jac interrupted and looked apologetic for it. He glanced at his father who shouldered the bag he'd brought from Cheju. His mother also loaded her bag. Their possessions were meagre, but they had all they needed. Almost nothing had been lost between them on their boat journeys. So they guarded what they had—the prayer plates, Seo-yeon's sewing packet and seaweed stick, Tae-yong's horse hat, Jac's spoon carved by his Welsh father. Now they had a tent, and some old blankets and mats that they'd found abandoned along the way from Melbourne.

Jac said to his parents, 'This man can show us a new site. He says we are welcome.'

'He has a good hat,' Tae-yong said.

Seo-yeon turned her gaze to the white man. 'We thank you.'

The man nodded in return as Jac interpreted.

Seo-yeon said, 'Then get on with it, boy.'

Jac kept that to himself. 'I am Jac Owen, from Wales. My parents here are from Cheju Island off the coast of Korea.'

Unsure what to say to that, the man nodded at both the older people. 'Forgive me that I've never heard of it. I am Elias Barkin from America.' He didn't remount but waited until Jac finished packing their tent and set it on a pallet. He and his father would share carrying it.

'This way,' Barkin said. He walked east. When Jac drew alongside, he said, 'My curiosity is not bounded by my manners, I'm sorry. You must tell me how you came to be the son of people from that land.'

The site was a much better one. A communal well was not far away, and a line of latrines lay in the other direction. The space Elias showed them was next to other tents that had been erected, and the attributes of camp living were all around. Rough-hewn logs served as seats. Pans and picks, shovels and sieves were piled in neat stacks. Other implements, broken and discarded or in need of repair, had been thrown to the ground in abandon, as if those inanimate tools were at fault for the lack of gold finds.

Jac and his father re-erected their tent and Seo-yeon was busy getting it in order.

'You provide for them?' Elias asked, when Jac stood back and stretched.

'My mother has a sewing trade, and my father hunts for kangaroo meat, so we eat well enough.'

Elias's people were camped differently to that of others in the surrounds. 'The men with families live over there,' he said, and pointed. 'The single men here, which is where I am.' He gave a rueful smile. 'We wait for women of our own faith to arrive so we can marry.' Then, 'We are trades people, or some of us are miners. I'm of business folk. We all must have licences and every so often I dig, too. You do have a licence?'

Jac nodded and patted a deep pocket in his trousers. 'I had to work for another miner to buy my own licence, and my father's,' he said.

His licence wasn't the only thing in his pocket. The carved spoon was in there, too. When digging for gold it was better there than dangling from his neck on a piece of horsehair twine. He would soon have to find a safer place for it.

'Good. A friendly reminder to keep your licence on you always,' Elias said. 'The police have organised hunts for them, and they're getting nasty now. There's trouble afoot, I can feel it.'

# CHAPTER FIFTEEN

## *1855 Rigg Manor, Wales*

Lilpah sat by the window in the room adjoining Sir Hugh's bedchamber and could hear him bellowing, even above the teeming downpour outside. The last stroke he'd had hadn't lessened his temper by much. It only served to slur his words and make the noise incoherent, which frustrated Rigg more.

Tippy, sitting beside her, gripped Lil's forearm. The two boys were sprawled asleep at their feet, motionless under layers of tattered coverlets, appearing immune to the shouting.

Lil glanced at Foswick who hovered near the doorway. Doctor Evers pulled open the door. The dank, moist air of Sir Hugh's private room floated behind him as if attached to his coattails. He turned and quickly pulled the door closed, the back of his hand to his mouth as he spoke. 'He does not cope with a reduction of the dose, Foswick,' he said through his teeth.

'No, Doctor.'

'But we must keep the dose of his medicine stable.'

Foswick sighed. 'It was only that we came close to running out before I could send for more and—'

'He's addicted to it, man. You cannot run out of it.' The doctor looked more perturbed than he sounded.

'I understand.'

The room was cool, yet the sheen of perspiration on the doctor's face, and the damp stain at his collar betrayed his controlled fury. 'I don't think you do understand. If his body is let crave, you will have a monster on your hands, the likes of which you have never seen. Quite different to the monster that he was. He will be a bedridden, soiled, nervous tyrant who will scream for his wine. We're only just beginning to comprehend the far-reaching effects of this so-called calmative.'

Foswick nodded grimly.

Vehement, the doctor continued. 'Not to mention he will have the most horrible night terrors that will keep you awake for as long as you live.'

Sir Hugh had been a nightmare long before the threat of opium withdrawal.

Lilpah got to her feet, carefully stepped around Lester, and approached. 'So should he be weaned off it like a child is weaned?' She dreaded the answer. If it were so, would the monster that had been Sir Hugh return? There'd been years of relative peace; no one wanted a return of the man he used to be. No one.

'I'm unsure of that. All I know is that I've seen people die from deprivation of it after they have developed this dependency.' The doctor swallowed. 'I have given him a little extra to stave off this affliction. But too much now and he will die, and he must not be allowed to die, Foswick. How much less did you give him?'

'Perhaps half, a dribble only, perhaps less than half, just to get through until—'

'Less—? Good God, man.' Doctor Evers mopped his brow. 'In that case, have you sent someone for it?'

Foswick dropped his gaze and flattened his palms to placate the situation. He huffed a little, but no words came.

Doctor Evers stared at him, incredulous. 'Your credit can't have dried up.' He leaned in. 'You know what this means for you,' he hissed. 'Perhaps I need to report this,' he said between his teeth.

Reporting it to whom? Lil assumed he meant to Sir Hugh but that seemed odd. Foswick had flushed a deep red.

The doctor recovered. 'I can leave you a vial now, but you better *find* the funds to purchase it. The dose must be administered carefully to bring him back to a manageable state. Have I made myself clear?'

Foswick nodded and held out a shaky hand for the tiny glass bottle the doctor pulled from his bag.

'You know the correct dose, but do not administer the full amount immediately. A scant added drop, no more, each day. Am I clear?'

'Yes, Doctor.'

'If you need me, send someone advising me of his exact symptoms.' His dark frown wasn't lost as he pulled his hat from Foswick and tamped it hard on his head. 'Good day.' He marched away.

The door shut behind him. Foswick, rebuked, stood at a loss for a moment longer before he closed his hand over the vial. 'I'll put this away.'

Tippy shot to her feet. 'You've endangered the lot of us with your penny-pinching,' she seethed. 'Miss Lil should administer the dose.'

Foswick stood firm. 'Sir Hugh will not trust her, not after the years I've been giving him his wine.' He faced Lilpah. 'And you know it, too.'

She looked at the tiny bottle. 'I know it. I also fear I would be charged with his murder if something went wrong.' The chill that entered her bones at that moment also seemed to affect Tippy.

Foswick also.

In the silence following, Lester stirred behind them and called out in his sleep. Daniel shifted, avoiding a restless foot aimed at him, but both remained in their dreams.

A sudden, lashing shower of rain pelted the windows, and then stopped as abruptly. The wind had picked up and Lil drew her shawl more tightly about her shoulders. The thin threads of it give way, and in dismay, she removed it to stare at the rent in the fabric dividing the flimsy garment in two.

Tippy sighed. 'Give it here. There's an old one I got hid that belonged to Miss Emily.' She tut-tutted at the anguished look Lilpah shot her. 'Girl's dead, Lil. Her spirit's long gone out of it. And we need warm clothes,' she said to Foswick, removing her shawl and handed it to a shivering Lil.

Foswick, his mouth downturned and chin jammed against his chest, walked back towards the master's bedchamber, muttering all the while.

Tippy called the valet. 'Mr Foswick.'

'What is it?' Gruff and dismissive, Foswick flicked a glance in her direction.

Tippy stepped in front of him, barring him from shoving open the master's door. 'You know the Oswalds would visit here, make themselves acquainted with their kin more often.' She glanced back at the sleeping boys. 'If the master was kept sleepin'.'

Foswick pushed past her, twisting the iron ring handle on the bedchamber door, and pushing it open. Foul air from inside rushed to envelop them and the stench of fresh vomit hung low. On the bed, Sir Hugh, twisted in the greying linens, lay with his mouth open, his glassy eyes half hooded by thick lids.

'Dear God,' Foswick whispered, disgust in his voice. 'Would that he'd die anyway.'

'Then where would we be—livin' on the banks of the river?'

Foswick kept his voice low. 'What about the Oswalds?'

'You'll be in trouble now, for sure, spending their money and not deliverin' on a promise.' She tut-tutted. 'What if they learned what you've done?'

The valet glared at her, leaned in. 'They won't,' he said, his breath on her face.

She smiled. 'Or what if Sir Hugh learns that you denied him his medicine?'

He reared back. 'No one would heed his ramblings, no one would believe it, and he'd have no one to care for him if I was gone,' he snapped hoarsely. 'Even addled, he'd know that.' Foswick rolled his shoulders uneasily. 'I know you have a suggestion.'

'I've seen him, the older one, Morris Oswald, sometimes watching from a distance when we're in the field with the boys.'

Foswick frowned. 'You think he might snatch his nephew?' He nodded across at the sleeping boys. 'Has he ever approached the house without my knowledge?' The Oswalds had been fobbed off time and again; Foswick too scared for his life to risk them coming to the house. The payments had kept coming, but after the doctor had just discovered Foswick's transgression, there might be hell to pay. He swallowed. He'd misjudged.

'Only from a distance.' Tippy checked that Lilpah couldn't hear. 'Never when a soul was around. Never close enough to grab the lad, but I wonder what he's thinkin'. He never looks happy about it. Then there's what the doctor learned just now.'

She wasn't even sure Morris could distinguish which child was which from afar. The Oswalds were not aware of the baby swap and nor was Foswick. But Daniel's growing resemblance to his mother, Lady Johanna, and therefore to his kin, his uncles Morris and Ambrose Oswald, was unmistakable. That none of the servants had yet noticed was a miracle—or if they had noticed, no one said. That too was a miracle.

Foswick peered at the sleeping children at Lilpah's feet. 'They are at the age when they would chatter,' he said, making excuses.

'That's why it hasn't been a good idea for Morris Oswald to visit in person, they would innocently tattletale.'

'Then perhaps the better idea would be to increase the dose of that medicine and let Sir Hugh meet his maker, sooner than later,' Tippy rasped, her hands on her hips.

'I wish I could, and get away with my life and my future,. Be safe. But while he is master here ...'

Tippy waved a finger. 'He's master in name only.' She pointed to the children at Lilpah's feet. 'It's that child who'll inherit and be the master. After the pox killed old Dalton there's been no manager since. I reckon the Oswalds are getting keen, they're the boy's blood kin, his uncles. And you've not kept your bargain with them.'

'I—I haven't been able to, not yet.'

'They might not see it like that, and ye took their money willingly enough. Maybe now is the time to make things right.' She nodded towards the unconscious body in the bed. 'He won't know.'

Foswick squinted at her, silent a moment. His eyes brightened. 'It would do us well to be accommodating to Mr Oswald now.'

'It would.'

'Yes, yes. Let me think on that some more.' Sir Hugh retched up again in his sleep. Foswick stalked over and rolled him onto his side. 'Get someone to clean this up,' he said to Tippy and stood well back as another shot of bile purged itself.

'I'm sure there'll be someone along soon to clean him up,' Tippy said, and turned and walked back to Lil with no intention of calling anyone to attend the monster in that bed. There was something more important to do: Lil had a note to write.

*

The torrents of rain ushered in a storm. Thunder boomed overhead, windows rattled, and the sky darkened as if night approached. A crisp whistle of freezing air sliced its way through the room adjoining Sir Hugh's bedchamber where Lilpah, Tippy and the boys sat huddled by the meagre fire.

'I shouldn't wonder it weren't be better living down by the river,' Tippy grumbled, remembering what she'd said earlier to Foswick. She shrugged deeper into one of the small blankets she'd rescued from the downstairs store, which was now flooded after a drain had blocked and overflowed.

Lilpah fed each boy a biscuit from the kitchen. 'A word now,' she said to both children. 'There's no more tonight so you must chew slowly.'

Sombre, and wincing with each boom cracking the skies, the boys scoffed the biscuit. Lilpah did have more tucked into her pinafore pocket, but she'd keep those for when the hunger pangs became too much to bear. She and Tippy would have some jerky and the wine they'd siphoned from the master's jug before the tincture had been dropped in. Their cups were warming on the mantel above the fire.

She tucked the threadbare blankets around the boys and settled back in her chair, its seat stacked with cushions lumpy with straw. 'This hardly looks like a wealthy man's abode, Tippy. How has it come to this? He must have a cache of funds somewhere.'

'I heard Foswick say that since old Mr Dalton died, Sir Hugh wouldn't nominate another agent to look after his affairs.'

'Surely that's rubbish. He would've had his lawyer do something.'

Tippy shrugged. 'He'll have to loosen the purse-strings, otherwise how is he going to get to those goldfields in the colonies? Perhaps there are no funds to pay his lawyer.'

Lilpah thought about that. 'Has Foswick done anything about sending for Mr Oswald?'

'I doubt it. Foswick has his head stuck up his own arse. We'll bring Mr Oswald here, ourselves.'

Lil frowned, thoughtful. 'Morris and Ambrose are uncles to the heir here.'

'Yes?' Tippy said and waited.

'Could Mr Morris Oswald—because he is so worried for his nephew—appeal to Sir Hugh's lawyer to visit, to see for himself the state into which the place has fallen?'

'I see. *Yes*. To witness how neglected the child might be—'

'And be persuaded to appoint an administrator on behalf of the ill incumbent.' Lilpah stared at Tippy.

'What's incumbent?'

'The present owner.'

Tippy stood to reach for the two cups of wine. 'Who'd ye learn that word from, Lil? Watch yourself. I seen you making your sign with that quill over and over, an' I seen you making Sir Hugh's sign too, on your drawing papers, the ones with all those fancy spoons on 'em.' She watched Lilpah flame red.

'Don't mention a word about any of that to anyone.'

'Aw, don't worry 'bout me,' Tippy said. 'They're a good like-ness. You're clever at it but be careful. I know you draw the spoon you got from your ma, the one you keep hid.' She sighed, paused a moment. 'I wish I had the love spoons me da had made for ma.' She handed Lil a cup. 'Perhaps Sir Hugh will appoint you, Lil, now you're so learned with reading an' writing an' all.'

Lil took her wine in one gulp. 'Perhaps I will grow two heads.'

*

Morris Oswald arrived at the house within a few days. When ushered in to speak to Foswick, the valet was shocked, caught off guard, unaware that Sir Hugh had requested his visit.

Foswick, shaken, said, 'I had no knowledge, sir—'

'I didn't think to bring my invitation to prove it, Foswick.'

Leaning in, Foswick whispered, 'Of course not, sir.' Looking about, he raised his voice. 'Sir Hugh is very unwell now, you see, it

196

came on quickly. He won't even know you're here. Perhaps he just forgot to tell me earlier that he'd sent you a note.'

'If Sir Hugh is unwell, it might serve us all if I stay a while.' Morris's words were carefully measured.

Foswick recovered. 'It has been some years since we've seen you, Mr Oswald—'

'Who'd have thought so long?'

'—and now you are here, of course, you are welcome,' he said, and swallowed down the warning inside to hold his tongue. 'Would you come to the drawing room? As Lady Johanna's kin, you might be able to assist with a vexing problem here at the house.' He checked over both shoulders.

The faded room's tawdry past was decaying under mould, and the moth-eaten fabrics and threadbare carpets were mere glimpses of their former flamboyance. Morris settled into a chair, high-backed but creaking. He rested his hat on the floor; no servant had emerged from the gloom to relieve him of it. Foswick seemed not to have noticed.

'Explain yourself, Foswick, before I cry foul and have you arrested. I know about your parsimony with my money, my orders,' he grated. 'My patience is thin.'

Foswick didn't protest the accusation. 'You see, since the manager, Mr Dalton died and now with Sir Hugh fallen further into this affliction, there's been no one else appointed to administer the property. So if you were found to be here, uninvited, it could very well implicate you if something untoward were to happen ...' His excuses were lame. Foswick leaned a hand on the back of another chair to steady himself. He could well lose his life over all of this. Oswald or Sir Hugh could kill him.

'But I was invited, and by Sir Hugh's own hand.'

Foswick clamped his mouth shut. *Those two bloody women.*

'Why don't you sit down?' Morris said. 'You seem poorly.'

'Thank you, sir, but I should rather stand.'

The other chair might not even hold the valet's weight. Unsure of his own seat, Morris remained alert. 'So, to your knowledge, there has been no correspondence, no visitor attesting to his right to administer the property?'

'To my knowledge, nothing.'

'No kin of Sir Hugh?'

Foswick shook his head.

Morris Oswald was the eldest son of his family. He had inherited the house and lands after his father died. How then would it work for this house if Sir Hugh became permanently incapacitated with no administrator appointed?

'Do you know whose services Sir Hugh uses for his legal matters?' he asked the valet. 'As his son's uncle, I should consult with that office.'

Foswick spread his hands. 'I have not been able to discover any paper authorising a firm of solicitors.'

Morris's frown deepened. Lacing his fingers, he dropped his hands to his lap. He had no clear understanding of the law in these matters. 'I'll consult my own advisors to determine if there is anything I can do.'

'Sir, surely as the boy's uncle—'

'It's a large estate, Foswick. And it seems almost derelict. I'd need to know if the taxes and such have been paid. Perhaps it is beyond redemption. At best, I might be awarded ownership if I appeal.' He looked around, a curl on his lip. 'At worst, it reverts to the crown.'

Foswick flinched.

'Your pay will be cut until I am recompensed for what can only be called thievery.'

'I had only hoped to buy a little more food.' Trying to look desperately uncomfortable, he flinched under Oswald's intense scrutiny.

'If you further dissatisfy our arrangement, I will ensure you are removed. Understood?'

Foswick nodded as if he couldn't stop.

Morris stood and walked to the window, peering through the grime. 'I have no way of knowing if the rights to administer would fall to me without a challenge. However, I *could* claim guardianship of the boy, which might allow ...' Lost in thought and with his back to the valet for a moment longer, he continued to stare out the window. Abruptly, he turned. 'No one would contest that, as it's a fact.' Dark hair fell across his eyebrows and, impatiently, he flicked it away. The frown was still as deep as before.

Foswick's eyes, alight, met his. 'It is a fact, sir.'

Morris's gaze narrowed. 'I have been lenient today, Foswick; it serves my purpose. But if my access doesn't improve—'

'It will, of course.'

'If the financial burden of this estate is too great, I will take only my sister's son with me, make no mistake. All I can do to avenge her now, is to leave Rigg perish in his own muck.' He took a deep breath. Five years it had taken to let the rage cool. It was better, his blood had run hot for too long. His own family had suffered because of the hatred for Hugh Rigg. The only important thing now was the boy's welfare. 'I would consider a way forward for this house, but as I said, it might already be beyond my capabilities. And you have benefitted all these years.'

Foswick started, his hands rolling. 'I would be grateful if— I had to wait for the right time—'

'How incapacitated is Sir Hugh?'

The valet hesitated. 'He is, in truth, Mr Oswald, mostly sedated by the tincture.'

Morris stared at him. 'Laudanum has had prolonged use on the man.'

'It still keeps his demons at bay,' Foswick said, quickly, 'which indeed it has for the years after the apoplexy. If he doesn't have it, it brings another madness. I'm fearful that if ...'

'Yes?'

'… that if he recovers, he will be worse than the man he was.'

Morris barked a laugh. 'No one recovers from this drug, Foswick. Not anyone I've known. Survive apoplexy *and* an addiction? In fact, many of us are greatly surprised that he has survived this long.'

Foswick was taken aback. 'His condition is widely known?'

'Not all house servants hold their tongues, no matter what threats. They've related much, far more worthy of my notice than you have been.' Morris inclined his head. 'But back to the immediate problem.'

The valet cleared his throat. 'Mr Oswald, it was never the right time. And now if Sir Hugh dies without a successor—'

'He is not dead yet and he has a son who will inherit when he comes of age, who until then needs a guardian. You might not be around to benefit further, so no need to be fearful.'

Foswick gaped. Swallowed.

Morris stooped to retrieve his hat from the floor. 'Where is the boy? I might see him now. The time has come for you to do as bid, Foswick.'

'I'll call for his nanny.' He hurried to the door.

Morris followed; the room was suffocating. He emerged behind the valet. Lilpah Owen was already walking through the great hall, the boys on each side of her, holding her hands. Tufts of their hair lifted and dropped in the draughty rushes of cold air. Both were dressed in layers to ward off the seeping cold that permeated the hall.

One boy limped. Morris knew that was his nephew; there was no mistaking him as family. He must've had a small accident and was dragging his foot as a result. The other boy chattered without a care.

'Mistress Owen,' Foswick called. 'If you will.' He beckoned her to bring the boys. 'This is Mr Oswald,' he said to Lilpah. 'He wishes to see his nephew.' He indicated that Lester should step forward.

*

Lilpah's glance darted to Mr Oswald. She saw, at first, the man's joy when he looked past Lester to Daniel, his true nephew. Then saw his confusion when Foswick beckoned Lester.

The valet waved an open hand indicating the young boy. 'He is well and happy, as you can see,' he said. 'Master Lester, this is your uncle, Mr Oswald.'

'Good morning, Uncle Mr Oswald,' Lester said cheerily and came forward to bow formally.

'Good morning, Uncle Mr Oswald,' Daniel repeated, and stepped beside Lester, oblivious to Foswick's sudden frown. The boy stared at Oswald, his gaze searching the face, as if in some recognition.

Mr Oswald's gaze darted between the two boys. He finally settled on Daniel. Then he looked at Lil and she returned a steadfast stony glare. 'I see he is indeed a well and happy boy.' His mouth a grim line. Then he spoke to her. 'This lad's foot,' he said, grimly and pointed at Daniel. 'Something's amiss?'

Foswick opened his mouth, but Lil cut in. 'A small defect which has righted itself with a little assistance. It doesn't bother the boy.'

'That is Daniel Owen, Mr Oswald,' Foswick blustered. 'Your nephew's nursery-mate. Mistress Owen is his mother.'

Morris Oswald eyed both boys again. He rubbed his chin and once more, spoke to Lilpah. 'Mistress Owen. Were you present when my nephew was born?'

'No, Mr Oswald.'

Foswick gave a start. 'If I might say, the midwife was ordered to deliver the babe by—'

'You forget who you're talking to, Foswick.' Morris Oswald's glance was ice. 'I doubt midwifery was involved. It looked to be nothing short of butchery, as I recall. Who was there?'

Foswick was mortified. 'The master declared Mistress Bowman bring the child out.'

'And where might she be, this Mistress Bowman?' Oswald demanded. Foswick still gaped. He turned to Lil. 'Not dead, I hope?'

'Tippy assists me in the nursery with the two boys.'

'I would speak with her.'

Lester piped up. 'I know where she is right now,' he announced and rushed out of the room before Foswick's half-hearted shout could stop him.

Lilpah's hand tightened on Daniel's as he tried to follow. 'We will wait here for Tippy, Daniel,' she said, watching Morris Oswald who studied the boy.

'He seems a fine lad, this Master Daniel,' he said.

'He is. Mistress Bowman saved him at his birth.' Unflinching, Lil met his stare.

'Is that right?'

'She did, against her life, she did.'

He stared back. His chest rose and fell as he struggled with the implication of it, not lost.

'You have no understanding of what goes on in this house,' Lil said fiercely. 'Only an inkling, nothing compared to what is really dealt here.'

Tippy bustled into the hallway. 'Master Lester,' she grumbled behind an insistent Lester. 'I canna keep up with you—' Taking in the visitor, the horrified valet, and the glowering Lilpah, she stopped, took a breath, and patted down her pinafore. 'Ah, there you are, Mr Foswick. I heard a footman yellin' from the grounds for ye. I came directly to say there might be terrible trouble some-where.'

Foswick excused himself in a blinding hurry.

Oswald watched him go, then turned his attention to Tippy. 'I am Morris Oswald,' he said. 'I believe you attended my sister, Lady Johanna.' His teeth were clenched, his chin puckered with rage.

'Tippy Bowman, sir.' She dipped a curtsy, her face studiously bland. 'I did, sir.' She licked her lips. A brief look at Lil and she said to the boys, 'Now, there's a sweet treat later if you go and play by the hearth over there, and don't come back 'til I say.' Lester and Daniel took off and soon soot erupted from the cold fireplace. 'Mr Oswald,' Tippy began. 'My sorries to you, sir, on the passing of your wife.'

Taken aback, he faltered. 'Some six months ago now.'

Tippy blathered on. 'I heard she were a good wife and a good mam to your three daughters.'

Oswald went rigid. He cleared his throat. 'I had a note delivered from this household, said it was from Sir Hugh. Mr Foswick has no notion how that could be.'

Lilpah was tight-lipped. Tippy had sent a running boy with the letter despite Lil wanting it destroyed.

He looked from one to the other. 'It's a mystery, but no matter. I will visit again if Sir Hugh is still incapacitated. Perhaps my household can assist until his well-being is restored.' At their silence, he said, 'What do you think of that?'

Lilpah sucked in a breath. 'Nothing to concern the likes of us,' she said, her voice taut. Tippy gave her a dark scowl when she said, 'We have no say here.'

'I see there is much to concern the likes of *me*,' he said. 'The thing is, whenever I ventured to the hill where I could see the boys at play, in all those years I was never able to discern which of them was my nephew.' His smile was false and Lilpah felt the chill run through her. 'But seeing them up close here ...' His gaze was on Lil.

Tippy flapped her pinafore. 'Of course, Mr Oswald. Your family would certainly be interested in young Master Lester.'

Mr Oswald shot her a look. 'I assure you I'm not simple, Mistress Bowman,' he said, the venom paralysing Lil. 'Not about my nephew nor his delivery into this world. Do you hear me?' Tippy gave him a tight nod. 'Master Lester bears no resemblance to my family like Master Daniel does.'

Another flap of apron. 'A strange turn of nature, sir.'

His temper was barely held. 'I think not. Don't let me have cause to call you a murderer, mistress.'

Tippy's mouth fell open, terror etched painfully on her face.

Lilpah's cry was desperate. 'Sir Hugh has no knowledge of the swap. We were fearful he'd kill both boys—'

'Why?' Oswald cut in.

'He's mad, he's mad.' Lil shook her head. 'Daniel was born the true heir, but he was sickly, deformed. His foot. My son Lester was strong and healthy,' she breathed, and checked if there was anyone hovering close by. 'Sir Hugh's rage knew no bounds. If he found out he'd been dealt a cripple in Daniel ... We couldn't let either boy die. They are half-brothers.'

Tippy wrung her pinafore. 'Nobody knows but us that the bairns were swapped.'

He pointed at the Daniel. 'The stamp of Oswald is all over that boy. Not even an idiot could miss it,' he said hoarsely, keeping his voice and temper in check.

'Idiots who speak up in this house lose their lives,' Lilpah cried.

'All right, all right.' Morris rubbed his eyes hard, paced a few strides. 'This place is an abomination,' he burst. At his raised voice, the two boys lifted their heads, their gleeful chatter interrupted. A moment later, they resumed their play. Morris glared at Tippy. 'You. Tell me what happened.'

Tippy vehemently shook her head.

'My sister's body was destroyed. We had to sew her together to bury her.'

Every part of Tippy shook. She looked at Lil, for the first time unable to speak.

Lil took a deep, ragged breath. 'It was five years ago,' she said. 'Let your sister rest.'

'You will tell me.' His hands slowly fisted.

Tippy shrank by Lil's side.

'Lady Johanna's labour was much too prolonged, she was too far gone to be saved,' Lil said, relaying what Tippy had told her in the hours before Lester was safely delivered. Oswald's eyes were bright. 'The babe couldn't birth properly; his head was stuck in—'

'The master ordered I cut her,' Tippy sobbed, her eyes wide. 'But Mr Oswald, her babe, we saved him. He were poorly, was mucky on his chest and his foot was twisted, but otherwise he was all right. Yet the master would have dashed him to the cobblestones as sure as anything.' She'd twisted her apron into a thick rope. 'Lilpah birthed a healthy boy. We swapped Lady Johanna's sickly bairn for Lilpah's strong one, so that they both would live.' She unrolled her apron, brushed at the tight wrinkles. Her breath was short, her voice jagged. 'There had already been too many deaths.'

Lilpah's heartbeat was wild, her breath shallow. She glanced at the boys, glanced at Tippy, blinking rapidly, her apron twisting once more.

Oswald's fury leached out in a breath. 'Aye,' he said. 'Too many deaths.'

Lilpah closed her eyes a moment, let out a quiet sigh. Tippy still shook like a terrier at a rabbit hole.

'This Lester will inherit.' Oswald eyed Lilpah, squinting. 'But he is your child. The bastard. I see treachery—'

'It wasn't done for one to *inherit* over the other,' Tippy cut in vehemently, her ire returned. 'Was to ensure their little lives was saved. The clubfoot was never discovered but had it been, sure as I stand here, the boy would have been killed.'

'Bah, killed for a clubfoot.' Oswald was still unconvinced.

'Or killed if they were female babes,' Lil burst, and with a hand she slapped her mouth shut for fear of saying more. Sudden pain welled in her chest and surged up. Hot tears spilled onto her face, and she turned away, no control over it.

'What?'

'That's right, sir,' Tippy said, her face fierce. 'Wrenched from between her legs, barely born, both Lil's daughters, one year after the other, as God is my witness. He defiles someone else's daughters, murders his own.' Tippy went to Lil. 'And for Daniel, don't doubt that the master woulda done him in.'

Brushing Tippy away, Lilpah wiped her nose on her hand and straightened to glare at Oswald. 'All before the good doctor availed us of the medicine to keep the monster subdued.'

'Sweet Christ.' Morris Oswald swiped a trembling hand through his hair. Squeezed his red-rimmed eyes shut.

Tinkly laughter availed them and all three glanced across at the boys, soot-covered and happy in their play.

'If he was in his right mind, he could still decide to kill Daniel,' Lilpah said, her hard gaze on Lester. 'If I was in my right mind, I'd kill Rigg myself.'

Oswald held up his hands. 'That you must not do.' He hesitated. 'None of us. He must live out his pitiful life and die in front of others as he is,' he said roughly. 'Not with a knife in his heart, or a dagger in his eye. If the true heir is to inherit, it must be without the taint of Rigg's murder in this house.' His voice caught in his throat. 'God knows, though, others have got away with that.' Shaking the thought away, he took a slow breath, waited a moment. Steadier, he asked. 'Is there anyone who's been here, anyone who might have put themselves forward as Sir Hugh's agent?'

'How would we know such a person?'

Morris Oswald snorted at Lilpah. 'You two would have the best eyes and ears in this household. I have no doubt of that.'

'And you trust the judgement of the likes of us, do you?' she snipped.

He looked across at the two boys. 'Aye. I do. And there's my proof.' The children played cheerfully in the soot. 'And it's the likes of you women who'll fix this unholy, fiendish mess.' The blood-shot whites of his eyes were stark.

Lil shook her head. 'There's been no one.'

'Could anyone you know do the job?'

Tippy rubbed a hand over her mouth and followed Oswald's gaze to the boys. 'Perhaps I know of someone if the pay is right. A Mr Crawford,' she said. She glanced at Lil.

Morris Oswald thought a moment. 'Ah, yes. I know him. I know his circumstances well enough—'

'I'll not agree to him.' Lilpah shook her head. *Mr Crawford.* How could he be trusted? He'd been there on the night Jac had left with Mr Polites.

'You were right earlier, Mistress Owen, you have no say,' Morris said sadly. 'Resist me,' he continued when she glared, 'and there is a terrible tale for me to tell, not only of the wrongful death of my sister, but of two boys swapped at birth. I'll make sure I get the one I want and the other be damned in this house with all its evil occupants.'

Tippy grabbed Lil's hand. 'We're pleased with Mr Crawford.'

Lil snatched away her hand, swallowed the bitter pill.

Oswald placed his hat on his head, took one long look at the boys. 'Good day.' He marched out of the house.

Tilly's slumped, bent double. 'I saw me life and death flash before me. My gizzards are like jelly. Never have I been so scared in all me days. Never.'

Lil grunted. Her life would still be controlled by another.

# Chapter Sixteen

*1854 Ballarat, 4th December*

B eside the cart, Jac snatched off his hat and bowed his head as the white trimmed coffin passed, heading to the burial grounds. It was the procession for a woman who'd begged for her husband's life before a trooper on horseback butchered her.

Hard to watch the cortege for her, but not the hardest for him.

These rich fields, plump with gold, were now stained bloody. The stockade had fallen to the government cowards who attacked only hours after midnight, a time when most decent folk slept, supposedly safe in their beds. But not here.

Jac squinted as the sun climbed high. The ache behind his eyes drew a taut band inside his head. *Grief.*

Thousands of boots had disturbed fine dust and it danced and eddied on the warm northerly. The breeze feathered his hair and dried the sweat before it could trickle down his back. Wiping a hand over his mouth he glanced at the line of mounted troopers sent to keep order along the funeral march. They were nervous; any look at them, any grimace directed their way would be dealt hard. The night hadn't gone well for the miners. Men were wounded, some women too they'd said, and one man was shot to death in his own shop, in front of his wife. How many had they gunned down in the onslaught before the clouds covered the bright moon and the muskets had finally fallen silent?

Jac shook his head, tried to stem the rage. A barrage of demon memories from Wales and beyond had surfaced more and more in this place. *Let go of the fury*, a voice whispered.

He drew in a deep breath; he needed to face the day in peace. *Taekkyeon* had always helped. His family had helped. But today, his family was gone, and there was no room in his heart for forgiveness. *His family was gone. Slain.* Anger simmered under the heavy sorrow. Gripping the side of the cart carrying his parents' bodies, he bowed his head again, and quelled the turbulence within.

In the cart, under a sheet sewn with intricate depictions of their beloved gods, Seo-yeon and Tae-yong lay peaceful in death, innocent victims of the panic last night. They hadn't been anywhere near the stockade. Now, they were on their next journey in the afterlife.

He took another deep breath and looked around. He saw skittish troopers; they were scared. Some of their own had been lost last night. Since more had been injured, maybe there would be more deaths, too.

There were many wounded miners as well. Some had hidden in the bush or in the tents avoiding capture, and some of those would, no doubt, die of unattended injuries.

Cartloads of bodies rattled past him to where grave diggers hacked away at the baked earth. Some, like this woman of the white trim, had coffins, others only shrouds of second-hand sailcloth.

Further up the ragged line, Elias Barkin, married earlier in the year, was helping his wife Esther tend some of the bereaved families. Esther had emigrated from England on the *Caroline Chisholm*, a newly built ship that carried nineteen other ladies of the Jewish faith. On arrival in Melbourne, they travelled to the goldfields. Some of the people Esther now tended had been friends of her new husband. Some had been injured in the melee.

In his head, Jac heard the cries in the bright night, the deafening musket shots, the shrieks of fearful horses, and of men and women ambushed. Of children, whose screams had forced his hands to his ears.

There were whispers on the fields already: *Mr Lalor will lose his arm to gunshot.* Peter Lalor, an Irishman, had led the fight. *The flag is torn down and stolen, or worse, burned and gone.* The flag, once so proudly unfurled. It had five stars shining on a white cross against the deep blue of the skies, modelled on the Southern Cross constellation. For a brief time under its brilliance, he'd been at home here. But no longer. Not after the murder and the blood spilled at his feet.

*My family is gone.* They'd settled happily on the site next to Elias's people. Along with the Jewish folk on the diggings, they were outcasts of a sort. Except for his Aboriginal friends, Tae-yong had found it difficult mixing with other folk. Seo-yeon seemed content so far, and they'd managed to eke out a good living. They kept to themselves.

Despite the world's nationalities represented here, Jac stood out in this area. How could it be that a white-skinned man—albeit one with the dark golden tinge of the sun—black haired and blue eyed, was the son of these two crones with brown skin and hooded eyes?

Jac had been able to speak for his folk if the troopers made an unannounced visit. His English had improved. That was, in part, due to the help of the Barkins. Learning the language was one thing; loathing Englishmen was another, and he hid his burning hatred most of the time.

Now, without his family, he would move on, go wherever the wind took him. Cash the family's gold and maybe buy land down by the sea. He'd heard that in the south-west of the colony the soil was rich and fertile. Work was plentiful, labour was scarce. Men had abandoned their families and homes, their farms hoping for riches on the diggings.

Following the white coffin, he was one in a line of mourners that stretched for a mile. Jac planted on his hat. An anxious trooper nudged his horse past Jac who stared at the uneasy man. Simmering rage soured his gut.

He watched the trooper, upright and stiff on his horse, amble past the bereaved. Someone waved his fist, crying. They couldn't arrest a person for expressing sorrow; there'd be too many arrests. Too much grief at the horror of last night.

*To knock that Englishman off his horse—*

Jac turned away.

The mourners' ranks swelled as the day wore on, but no trouble sparked the tinderbox; the government men were still hunting dissidents. He tugged his hat low. It was time to move with the cart, as it took its turn to lumber behind the others. Nodding his thanks to the driver, he walked alongside, his hand still on the dray.

He would not avenge his parents, but the need for it was like a boulder in his gut. So, as he trudged, he prayed that the weight of their deaths would ease, and that his heart would become light again. He hoped his prayers were enough, but he feared they were not.

Jac leaned on the long-handled shovel, watching another man with a mattock slave over the big pit fifty yards away. The earth was like granite in that section.

Instead, he'd made a space for his parents a little further back. From the cart, he laid them beside the hole he'd dug. He turned away, fell to his knees on the ground. His eyes streamed. He let go the bile. Pulse pounding in his temples, he panted, waited out the spinning in his head. He eased onto one knee wiping his face with the back of his hand.

Moments passed. Ready to say his final goodbye, he eased into the hole and reached for his mother's body. *Steady. Steady.*

Light as a swag of her favourite herbs, she fitted snugly in his arms. The dried stick of seaweed, her keepsake, was tucked in her hands. He lowered her body, covered her with part of the bedsheet. Grief lumped in his throat and he staggered.

*Eomma, Eomma.*

Red mist dropped over him. He wept. He would avenge. He would *kill.* Shoulders bunched, ready to spring at the closest troopers, he lifted his head—

'Let me help, mate.'

The fury cleared. Through the fog in his brain came a familiar voice.

'Let me get your old da and hand him down to yer.' Another Welshman, Joe Mole, with his wild, dark hair, onyx eyes and the sinewy muscle of a lean man, was standing on the edge of the grave. He bent and scooped up Tae-yong's body and edged towards Jac. 'I'm sorry, mate. I'm sorry you lost them.'

Jac wiped the strings of snot and saliva from his face. He cradled his father. He stood a moment, stuck in the hole not able to move, the unbearably light weight of Tae-yong disabling him. This stoic, loving man would no more walk the earth. He would rest in this hole in the ground, in this foreign place leaden with hatred. Jac shuffled, crouched, and laid his *abeoji*, his father, Tae-yong, on top of his *eomeoni*, his mother, Seo-yeon. He gathered the rest of the sheet and covered his father.

Then, with a hand from Joe, he clambered up to level ground.

Joe grabbed off his hat. 'I dunno what words you say in their language, but if you do, I'll say 'em with you.'

'I can't say any words, I can't perform the right ritual. I am supposed to wait three days ...'

'Same for us, mate, but we can't this time.'

'We are far from Cheju-do, and far from the land where my mother's spirit would go.' He looked at Joe without seeing him. 'She was a diving woman.'

'Where would your father go?' Joe asked.

'He would follow her.'

'Ah. Well. I don't know where that land is, but I reckon it'd be as far as hell from 'ere.' Joe looked around. 'You could say Chinaman's words, couldn't ye?'

'We are not Chinese.' How often had Jac repeated those words over the years?

'No, that's right. Sorry. You're not.'

A while ago, he and Joe Mole had met staring down a couple of belligerent troopers who'd been just a little too enthusiastic in their licence hunt. Joe had kept Jac from having his head beaten in with a truncheon. He hadn't known then that Jac would've been able to look after them both without blinking. Then again, Joe, holding him back, had saved him from going to prison, or worse.

'Lots of people are away from their church here,' Joe said, and clamped a hand on Jac's shoulder. 'I'd reckon if gods were so good, they'd find their folk anywhere. So, say any good words and their gods will hear 'em.'

Jac looked at Joe anew. He could say good words. He and his parents had talked of dying in a foreign land, and what should happen. They'd agreed that Jac would speak words to calm their spirits and send them to their ancestral home. They would find a way there.

Joe stood respectfully, his hat still in his hands. Faltering at first, Jac whispered the prayers he knew. Then there was nothing else to do except bury them. So, Jac pushed the earth back into the hole over his parents. Joe slapped his hat on and worked with him, the only sound was the soft thud of soil as it fell. Sand trickled into the hole as they worked, so too did pebbles, twigs, and dried grass.

Jac would build a high mound over the site, and surround it with a *sandam*, a low stone wall. Then he would make *donjaseok*, child stones, so the deceased children of his parents would provide company, and he would place them inside the stone enclosure. He should have had herbs for his mother.

There was an eerie hush. At times, snippets, words, and cries suspended in the haze high up, and drifted across the burial site. Jac saw others walking the length of the big hole, then falling to their knees close to where they knew their loved ones lay. He closed his heart to the crying of the women, to the wailing of frightened children. He closed his heart to the guttural sobs of some men, and to the others who stood in stoic silence, heads bowed.

He and Joe finished as best they could. The mound was not as high as it would have been on Cheju, but it was good enough for now. Jac dusted off his hands and glanced about him for rocks to make a wall to signify that folk were buried here. The stones were the basalt from the island. It wasn't a job he could finish today.

'I could make you a cross, Jac.'

'No cross. But I thank you for the offer, and for the help.'

Joe stood alongside, staring over the mound they'd made. 'He was a good bloke, your pa. He and your ma were good people. Great shame. Do ye know who did it?'

Jac shook his head, didn't trust himself to speak as he stared at the police. *One of those men fired point blank at my parents.* He scanned the troopers' faces streaked with soot and sweat as they scanned the crowds at the gravesite. Anxious horses skittered.

Jac would never know who killed his parents. He hadn't been at his tent. He'd gone down to see what was happening at the rough stockade, believing his parents, and others, were safe. Believing that another night would pass with nothing more than the raucous drunken miners doing what they'd always done. Most others had been sleeping when he ventured down to Eureka Lead. The night had been hot and still.

Sudden gunfire had started. He heard the yells and the battle screams, and horses' hooves had pounded down from Government House and in from the surrounds. Someone had grabbed him, swung him back under their protective arms, prevented him from going into the fracas. Older men were holding back the struggling younger. Then they'd stood helpless, in abject horror and watched the skirmish evolve into slaughter before the clouds dulled the moonlight.

Jac hadn't known until later. While he was being held back at the Lead, other troopers had rampaged through the lines of tents, and his parents, peaceful hardworking people, had perished at the hands of a maniac, driven by musket shot and then bayonets. His parents had been slain. It had been madness. *Murder*. It could only have been an Englishman who'd killed his parents. He didn't need proof.

He breathed deep into his lungs. Centered. Exhaled. Inhaled again. The simmer dropped away as if the pot had been lifted from the fire.

He rolled his shoulders. 'Time I was gone from this place.'

'Gone where?' Joe looked concerned. 'Ye've still got a licence, laddie, isn't it bringing ye return?'

Jac looked down at his hands gritty with soil. 'I just buried my folk, the people who grew me up. I got no reason to stay where they were murdered.' He remembered they'd told him their spirits would not cause him illness or distress if they died a violent death here. But all the same … He glanced up and saw a mounted trooper watching. He looked away again. 'There'll never be any right come out of this.'

Joe leaned in. 'There will. Things are changin'. *We* made it change. *They* made it change.' He pointed to his parents' grave.

A horse clopped slowly towards them. A snort, a puff of hot breath, the creak of leather. The fetlocks close, a little dance. Neither Jac nor Joe looked up. If Jac stepped back, he'd stand on his parents' grave. He would not retreat.

'Thought I heard ye say ye was movin' on.' The voice from the trooper was stark, devoid of fear and emotion.

Jac nodded. Joe squared his shoulders.

'Nobody moves on until the Commissioner says so.'

'Free country,' Joe said, squinting into the sun.

The trooper ducked down to their eye level, his whisky breath and stringy hair too close. 'No, it ain't. Yer under martial law. We'll be coming for the others, roundin' yer up as we see fit. And there's still licence fees to pay despite all the nonsense of last night. We'll be collectin'.'

Joe stepped forward, his nose right by the horse's muzzle but Jac gripped his forearm.

The rider wheeled the horse. 'So, arseholes,' he said over his shoulder, 'we're still watchin' you.' He rode off.

Jac dropped Joe's arm and said, 'They won't be taking one more penny from me. I'll be leaving.' He took a long look back at the grave. Then he headed off against the flow of mourners making their way to the mass burial site.

'Where ye goin'?' Joe lengthened his stride to keep up.

Heads turned in their direction, then hollow eyes glanced away.

'Whichever way is forward.'

Joe picked up his stride and fell in alongside Jac. 'Forward is good. I've been meaning to tell ye something, just an idea I had in mind for later, maybe.'

'What's that?'

'It's all gone to shite here, so my plan would be to head for South Australia. I don't intend being a digger all me life, and I've heard there's solid opportunity over there.' He stopped a minute, and Jac stopped with him. 'You might think about goin' there too, one day. If you do, look me up. Flinders Ranges, that's where I'll be.'

'You sound like you'll be going soon.'

Joe Mole shook his head. 'No way of knowing when, martial law and all. Meantime, there's still nuggets to find.' He slapped Jac on the shoulder and they walked on together until Joe veered off for his own site.

Back at his camp, Jac stood over the flattened tents. Their rickety cots were nothing now but splinters. He looked across the few yards that separated his camp site from the Barkin family's. There, not a twig was out of place. Not a log overturned, not a cooking pot upended. It looked as if Elias would march out of his tent and beckon him to share tea as he'd often done before.

Ironically, it had been Elias who'd warned Jac of the unrest. They'd both attended the huge meeting with over ten thousand others weeks before at Bakery Hill. The Ballarat Reform League had drafted a charter for free and fair representation in Parliament.

Jac wanted distance from the trouble. Even though much had happened in his life since, he vividly remembered another huge riot in Wales when he was a young boy, the night of his Welsh mother's murder.

So he'd been in no hurry to align himself with others who might become part of a deadly crowd. Elias Barkin would be horrified that it had come to this, despite his foreboding. Neither had imagined it would be this bad.

Troopers patrolled in the distance.

He saw his Seo-yeon's carefully tended cooking fire no longer smouldered. The remains of her prayer books, their bark scorched, and her painstakingly etched symbols twisted and flaked, were there. Someone had dumped them; they'd never been out of his mother's work bag before.

Everything had been trampled under hoof and foot. The fire's tripod lay mangled, their one cooking pot was half buried in the soft dirt alongside.

Jac checked how far away the troopers were. Two hundred yards—they were harassing people on the other side of the small gully. No one else was around. He had enough time to do what he needed to do.

At what had been his own tent, he held up a ragged piece of canvas, its once sturdy rope ripped away. Straightening the centre pole, he secured it into position, shelter only on one side but it was enough.

He went to the firepit, knelt, and scraped away the soft dirt under the dead coals. Digging deeper, he withdrew a tin box, weighty and noisy in his hands as the nuggets rolled inside. Tucking it into his body he retreated to the sheltered side of canvas.

Opening the tin, he fed the nuggets into every seam of his shirt and trousers. The one high up on his arm was reserved for his carved spoon. The seams had been secured at each end by buttons his industrious mother had sewn on all their clothes. This way, they secreted their small finds until they could get to the assayer's office.

Once done, he tucked the tin back into a corner of the tent. Hefting the rest of the salvageable canvas off the ground, he set about repairing it.

Slowly the filthy and trampled tent took shape again, not as it had once been, but a shelter, nonetheless. Drawing in a long draught of air, he went to the remains of his parents' tent, retrieving utensils, a little stool miraculously intact, and his father's tiny table that was now minus one leg.

He dragged out the rest and dumped it onto the fire pit. After laying new fixings, he scratched a match and waited until smoke wafted from the dry leaves. Fanning it until the flames licked high, he watched as the last of the ravaged possessions fled the earth.

The damaged canvas he balled up. Someone would use what

they could of it. He jumped when he heard the man behind him.

'Hope that weren't yer licence goin' up in flames as well, mate.' A smoke hung from the trooper's thin lips. He slouched on his mount and leaned over his saddle.

A tremor started in Jac's feet. 'It wasn't.'

The government man cocked his head. "Course, if it was, I could be asked to keep me mouth shut.' The droopy smoke bobbed up and down as he spoke, stuck on his bottom lip.

Jac met the man's stare. 'It wasn't,' he said again. 'It's here.' He patted the top pocket of his loose cotton shirt. 'I just came back from the burials. There was naught to burn but the bloodied clothes of my murdered family.'

The trooper narrowed his gaze. 'Murdered, is it? Who ye callin' murderers?'

Jac stood his ground, the buzz of battle in his veins. Maybe the man would dismount—or maybe fear would propel him away. The horse fidgeted, shuddered, and threw his head. The rider stared a moment, then looked left and right.

*So, he'll dismount.*

Jac moved his feet, centered. Breathed. *This stinking Englishman would feel the mullock dirt on his face today.* He looked about. *No one would see.*

The trooper slid off his horse and dropped the reins. 'You makin' an accusation, man?' His bowlegs steadied under him.

Jac moved a shoulder, barely noticeable. Then his foot came up, a swift kick landing on the trooper's neck and the man collapsed in a heap, the only sound a grunt as his breath escaped.

The horse stepped aside a little, looked down at his rider then nodded. Not bothered by Jac's presence, it dropped its head to pull at tufts of trampled grass. Jac checked the saddle and its meagre trappings, determined it had no elaborate tell-tale markings. He left everything in the saddlebags except the flask. He emptied its rotgut, would clean and refill it with water. He took the reins—

'At the risk of being kicked in the neck by one of your *taekkyeon* moves I have to say that taking that there horse would amount to theft and could be a hanging offense in these unsettled times.'

Ice scaled down Jac's otherwise hot and sweaty back but a faint note in the voice tickled his memory. He frowned.

'Told you I'd find you. And here you are in this godforsaken shithole of a place.'

Jac spun. Incredulous, he barked a laugh at the man before him. Grey haired now and bearded unlike long ago, his skin weathered, it was still clearly Ben Polites. The intense dark eyes could not be mistaken, the crinkle at their corners more pronounced. The man looked well, and strong, if leaner. They gripped hands, hard, Jac's only concession to touching another man. He squeezed his eyes shut, but tears scalded through. 'Ben,' he said, and memories rushed back.

'Benjamin Polites, the one and same, lad.' He clapped his other hand over Jac's.

Jac hung on. The man had been hurled with him by the angry ocean and flung onto the shore at Seo-yeon's coastal village. Ben had stayed until the longing for other shores had called him to sea again. 'How can this be?' Jac asked. 'How can you be here?'

'Stranger things have happened.' Ben stepped back at arm's length. 'Why, I was camped over the way not a week back, and two fellas I met there had been transported as convicts after the Rising, back in thirty-nine.'

'From Newport?' Jac had heard that talk.

'Aye, many of those who escaped the gallows got seven years' transportation, and more. Stayed on in the colonies, some comin' here, hoping for riches on these fields.'

Jac's Welsh father hadn't been so lucky.

'Bound to come across someone you know in these parts—we're

from all over the world.' Ben grinned and clapped Jac's shoulders again. 'Look at you, boyo, a grown man, now. How long has it been?'

Jac palmed off wet eyes. 'By that old stick of yours, if it was 1842 when you got on that ship, it's been over twelve years.'

'Aye, and I see I left you in good hands.' Ben Polites looked him over again. 'You're a great solid man, Jac Owen.' He looked around. 'But, ah, it might not be the time to revisit the hospitality of your fine parents.'

'Killed last night.'

Ben stared. 'You were buryin' *them*? So sorry, lad. That's shockin' news.' Ben shook Jac a little, waiting a beat taking it in. 'But where might you have been going with the trooper's horse?' He lifted his chin towards the crumpled officer.

'Just away.'

Ben slapped him on the back. 'Let's have ourselves a little fun. Let's tie this arsefly onto his fine steed and let him wander the fields while he sleeps.'

Together they lugged the trooper atop his patient horse, tied him upright using the reins strapped around his hands. Useless bits of rope from Jac's tents secured him from back to front in the saddle. When done, Ben slapped the animal's rump. It wandered off, headed down the diggings gully where they could see other startled diggers jump out of its way. The trooper lolled in his seat, subject to much mirth as the horse plodded along. Finally, Jac allowed himself a laugh.

'Wouldn't expect him back,' Ben said.

They crouched outside the lean-to tent. Jac wiped his face on his sleeve. He poked at the coals and then dropped twigs and logs on it. He righted the tripod and set the billy boiling. He'd find the tea leaves. Back to his parents' tent site, he kicked over the dirt, and soon his boot hit a buried tin. He scooped it up and pried open the lid with his fingers.

'The ship you boarded, it must have sailed you home,' he said to Ben as he came back to the firepit. He threw a handful of tea into the billy.

'Not directly. That was a ship of Americans sailing down the east Australian seas, hunting whales and seals. Come all the way down to the Southern Ocean, we did,' Polites said, his gnarled hands around a tin cup. 'Rough going even in the good season. Not my sort of riches, whale meat. But I needed to keep going.' He dipped his cup into the billy. 'Got off that one once we got back to the Cape. I wanted to get onto a decent ship and get home.' He snorted. 'No such thing.'

Jac filled his pannikin. 'So, you came here why? How?'

'Same as anyone else. For the chance of fast money, big money. The whole world knows about these diggings.' He blew on his tea and slurped. 'Jumped aboard the *Augustus* bound for South Australia in 'forty-four, worked farms there, ever since.' He swallowed a mouthful of tea. 'Then thought to try my hand at making my fortune, so I walked across from Adelaide with the Chinamen. Many others were getting off the ships at Robe down the south of South Australia and walking to the goldfields that way. People streamin' in from everywhere.'

'We walked that way. Was busy.' Jac sat in the dirt across from his old friend. 'How the hell did you find me?'

'Weren't lookin'. But there you were, large as life. I'm at the big gravesite, taking care that my dead mate's wife doesn't fall in the hole after him, and looked across. Looked like you were digging the hole with your bare hands.' Ben shook his head. 'I couldna get to you quick enough; you'd gone. I had to ask someone if they knew you. I asked him, who's that fella, black hair and blue eyes yonder.'

Jac grunted. 'Lots of us Welsh folk are here.'

'And he said you were a Brit with Chinese parents. Close enough for me, I thought. Even though the years have grown you up, I knew it had to be you. Saw you walkin' off with that other fella who helped you at the graves.'

'He's a Welshman too. Joe Mole. He's going to South Australia if he ever gets shot of this place.'

'An old captain of mine is there. Could be all right.'

'So you followed me to my campsite here?'

'Just to be sure it was you and yep, saw you deck that trooper with one of your old da's moves and that just proved it.' He laughed. His wide smile now had a couple of gaps, his teeth either fallen out or been knocked out. 'Was always a smooth move. Still smooth. Tae-yong taught you well.'

'Trooper will have a bloody headache when he wakes up.'

'He will, and better that he does wake up, lad.' Polites looked at him from under raised eyebrows.

Jac shook his head. 'I wouldn'a killed him.' He was sure of that now. With a hard fist, he rubbed the madness at his chest that gripped him at the gravesite. A remnant swirl in his guts reminded him of its menace.

'But you could if you chose. We both know it.' Ben saluted him with the pannikin. He shifted to sit in the dirt. 'And young Song-chol. What of him?' His smile was expecting good news.

'Died on the ship that brought us south.'

Ben hung his head. 'He was a good boy.' A moment later, he looked up. 'I hear the troopers have got martial law or some such bollocks. That'll make it hard to escape.'

'I'll leave by night. Don't need to carry much. A bag maybe.' He thought of the spoon and rubbed a hand over his sleeve where it had been stitched. 'Besides, they're too scared of the dark to try and stop anyone leaving.'

'We saw last night what scared men can do.'

Jac was silent. Fear had panicked both sides. Rum ingested by the miners on the night before the ambush had added fuel to the fire. He looked down the gully to where the horse and his unconscious trooper meandered in the distance. Heard the jeers and laughter of miners erupt as they watched it pass. It brought some light into a dark day. Jac would be long gone before the trooper decided to come looking for him.

He took a long draught from his pannikin and smacked his lips against the sharp tang of bitter tea. 'Still. I might go back the way I came. Get on board a ship to Wales.'

Ben snorted. 'Naught there, Jac.'

Jac shrugged. 'Maybe my sister.'

Frowning at him, Ben said, 'After all this time you want to go back there, into hell itself, into that rotten, stinkin' place?' He reached over, wrapped his sleeve around the handle of the billy and dipped his cup. 'Best to get yourself set up in this country. A man could get ahead here.'

'You went back.'

Polites looked off into the distance. 'Listen, Jac. Even if your sister's still alive—'

'Did you go back to Hugh Rigg?' Jac asked.

'Nay, lad. I went back to Newport only because I jumped on a ship headed there, hoping to get on another one going out.' His mouth twisted. 'I heard some things when I got back, but nothing about your sister.'

'I just want to know she's alive.'

Ben Polites nodded. 'Write a letter to her care of Rigg. See if you get an answer.'

Jac studied his hands. 'Maybe I might when I get somewhere a return letter will find me.'

'You haven't written already?'

'Forgot most of what you taught me once you left the island, the few learnings that I had. I'm not much good at writing.'

'Well, maybe I can help you with that again.' Ben set his pannikin on the ground. 'But I'm thinking that this is no place to be if you're not going to fill your pockets with gold and keep out of the troopers' way.' His tone was wry. 'I mentioned an old cap'n. Mr Hart, the one off the *Augustus*, is a landholder in South Australia now. I was thinking to go there and maybe see if he has work for me. You could come, too.' Ben's face was creased in sun-weathered wrinkles, his kind, dark eyes widened under his brows. He shrugged. 'You might find work. There's land opened up to the north of Adelaide.' He glanced up and down the diggings gully. 'Not so crowded as here. And there's a mighty big river there too, waitin' for clever merchants to ply their trade.'

Jac remembered Joe Mole's words. He looked at the remnant pieces of his parents' possessions burning under the billy, the ragged useless tent, the destruction of the campsite where a living had been eked out of the dirt. He stared down the gully at children panning where diggers had been.

*I'm ready to leave now.*

The nuggets in the seams of his clothes seemed to answer. They rattled gently as he moved, a chatter. He rubbed his face, felt the squeeze in his chest, around his ribs again. *Grief.*

He'd start his life over. He could do it. He'd done it before even though he'd had Seo-yeon and Tae-yong.

'I'm guessing you know we have an audience.'

Jac glanced at Ben who nodded a little way up the hill. The black man crouched, his hair matted with leaves and twigs, his eyes wide, his long straggly beard tinged with grey. His dusty feet were bare under ragged trousers. A shirt, no sleeves, hung open over his scarred chest.

'He works with us. Was my father's friend. *Koori Wadawurrong.*'

'That's his name?'

Jac shrugged. 'That's all he says of himself. Decent man. He's the one person my father didn't seem to mind being with here.' Jac lifted his chin in the man's direction.

Rising in an easy movement the black man steadily made his

way down the hill, carrying two sticks in one hand, each about a foot long. He squatted again some distance away, his gaze darting to Ben and back to Jac.

Jac stood and went to Ben, gripped his shoulder, and said, 'Uncle.' He beckoned the man come further, to sit by the fire. Handing him a pannikin, he filled it with tea.

Koori sat and placed his sticks at his side, drank. He nodded at Ben. Then he stroked his beard and pointed at Ben's beard. He said something in his own language.

Ben did the same and nodded in return. 'It seems he and I are the elders here.'

'Would seem.' Jac looked between the pair. Though he couldn't tell, he'd wager Ben was the older of the two men. Koori had never tried to explain his age.

Then the black man stretched his lips and pointed to his missing tooth in the top row. Ben did the same and Koori said something.

Ben glanced at Jac. 'What did he say?'

Jac tilted his head. '"You old fella." He agreed with you. You're the elders here.'

Ben nodded at the black man and looked at Jac. 'Where's he from?'

Koori lifted his chin and flung a hand behind him and up over the hill. *This place.*

Jac poked a stick into the fire, stirring up the coals, and smoke wafted over him. Flies buzzed away. 'They say we're taking their lands, digging it all up, leaving nothing of theirs behind.'

Ben nodded. 'I agree. But they're successful traders here on the goldfields. I see a lot of them doing good business.'

'Aye. We should learn from them.'

Ben studied the fire. Koori studied the fire. Jac kept prodding it with sticks.

*

Days passed. The Christian festival of Christmas came and went with an English celebration in December. Elias and his family, too, had a festival for their Dedication, *Chanukah*, starting mid-December. Ben would wait until early January before he found a Greek family, if any, to celebrate. Koori took no interest; he celebrated his dreaming gods every day. It was a solemn time, a quiet time to reflect this year.

The goldfields were hushed, but business resumed quickly, and the rank-and-file of government men was not so cocky now. Scores of men had deserted. Unrest rumbled, but no one wanted a return of the terrible events of the third of December.

By the campfire for billy tea, Elias sat with Jac and Ben. Koori was trading further up the creek.

'Merchants and bankers hear of a lot of opportunity,' Elias was saying, his hands around his pannikin. 'These fields are the most lucrative ever seen, but too many have flocked here, all nations of the world. It's crowded.' He looked across at Jac and Ben. 'A man might be wise to find an opportunity beyond here and quickly establish himself. Before the gold runs out. Before all these men need to look elsewhere, too.'

'Will the gold ever run out?' Jac asked.

'Nothing surer.'

'And where will you go when it does?' Ben asked. 'Your family is here. Will you move on?'

Elias smiled and shook his head. 'We'll stay. Even when the landscape changes again, we're good at what we do. And now that my wife is here, too, it makes sense for us to build on what we have.' His smile grew wider. 'And for who we are expecting.'

Jac and Ben nodded at the sage comment. Then, both stared at him.

'Yes,' Elias said, and laughed. 'The next generation of Barkin is on his way.'

Ben whooped and tossed the contents of his cup in the air. They landed with a sizzling splash on the coals of the fire. 'Well done, laddie, the promise of the future.' He reached across the fire and pumped Elias' hand, the fervour dislodging the Jewish man's *kippah*. Elias clutched the skullcap to his head, still laughing.

Jac grinned at him and reached across to shake his hand. A fleeting thought struck him. Elias's wife had come out on a boat with other Jewish women not long before. That such happiness for a man could happen so fast. It was indeed the promise of a future.

Settling themselves again, with the billy tea topped up, Elias spoke earnestly. 'If you do intend to venture out of here, there's good opportunity in South Australia.'

Jac looked at Ben who lifted a shoulder as if to say, 'I told you.' Joe Mole had said the same.

Elias checked to his left and right; no one was in earshot. His intense dark brown eyes narrowed. 'A river, the Murray, has been hailed as a trading route. It's said it goes for fifteen hundred miles or more, and the country along its course is opening up, all the way through three colonies.'

'We know of it,' Jac said.

'You already know my thoughts for you on this subject,' Elias said, and sat forward. 'Go to South Australia and make good on the river.' He grinned. 'If you do, remember your friend here when you need advice, or investment. None of us knows what's ahead of us, but we should take all opportunity to secure the future.'

Jac gave a laugh. 'We only have the rags on our backs. I know nothing about river work, or boats.'

'You have brains and you have wisdom. Between the two of you, you have gold. And a reasonable amount of it.'

An ear-piercing whistle gave them a start. Koori approached, carrying a haunch of kangaroo over his shoulder, one hand gripping it firmly. His wide grin showed off the gap-toothed mouth. He tossed gold nuggets in his free hand. Clearly, he'd sold the rest of it.

'And if you take him with you, you'll never go hungry,' Elias said.

Night descended, and the four disparate men sat around a fire. Above, the serene Milky Way united them under the southern sky.

*

The searing summer had retreated, the change in seasons had arrived, and the massacre at Eureka was four months behind them. They'd left the goldfields weeks ago and gone south looking as if they'd been taking a Sunday stroll. The walk was long, and against the rising human tide of Chinese people still coming off the great ships.

Jac stretched out on the dune, salt and kelp scenting the air. The light, cool breeze missed him as he lay in the hollow, and the gentle heat of early morning tingled along his limbs. Glancing across at the lump under another great fur cloak, he heard the soft rumbling snores of Ben Polites. He looked as if a strange creature had collapsed in the sand.

He couldn't see Koori. He'd be off hunting with his spear and his *nulla-nulla*. That meant more meat for breakfast, though Jac would be happier if the carcass was skinned before it was thrown in the campfire. But he wasn't complaining. The fur cloaks, compliments of Koori, had come with them from the fields. The garments had been much in demand there, especially through the freezing Ballarat winters. It had been with great aplomb that he'd presented Jac and Ben with their own cloaks. Expecting to pay, both white men had presented Koori with tobacco, tea, and sugar. A little gold had also crossed hands, but Koori had asked for it to be exchanged for coin. It was an easier currency for him and his trade.

Jac sat up and let the sun warm his back. From the Ballarat goldfields they'd journeyed to the sea, the southwestern-most reaches of Koori's language group. They walked through the rich alluvial plains and over the ancient volcanic fields of the *Gunditj-*

*mara*, trudged over the cold, windy limestone coast of the *Buandig* people and on to the Murray mouth over the 'neck', the long stretch of land known as the *Kurangh*, or Coorong, as white locals pronounced it.

The ocean was calm today, and light and wispy clouds sailed high in the cerulean sky.

More than once on their long walk from the goldfields to South Australia, Ben mentioned he would one day visit his old captain, Mr Hart. First, he was keen to check the new wharf at Goolwa, not far from where they were now, and near the mouth of the River Murray. He mused aloud that, as he was a sea-faring man, it shouldn't be too hard a leap to take a few runs on a river. Maybe there was even boat building to be done.

Jac rolled the gold nuggets that were still stitched safely into his shirt. Soon he'd relinquish some for cash; up until now he hadn't needed to—Koori provided good hunting and he taught the white men to forage for wild food. Ben reckoned they'd probably never eaten so well since the days on Cheju. It took Jac back to a time at Seo-yeon's cooking pot, to the fragrant soups, and to her dumplings. To her triumphant shout as she broke the surface of the sea, a big crayfish in her hands and her fishing basket full. How long ago now were those days?

He leapt at the sudden tap on his shoulder, and with that, Koori jumped back laughing. He threw a dead wallaby onto last night's coals, still chuckling, and rattled off what seemed to be a great joke at Jac's expense, pointing his finger and miming Jac's fright with a beaming grin.

Easy camaraderie. Good friends. Jac believed he might have found a home in this vast country, after all. He just had to pick a place to settle but hadn't seen enough of it yet; maybe there was something more interesting just over the next hill.

He hunkered down near Koori's freshening fire as fur singed, and a dark smoky plume rose from the fire. Jac turned his thoughts to Wales, and his sister. He counted on his fingers to calculate the years gone by—sixteen years since he saw her last?

His memory of her was strong; her voice had faded but not her face. Not her features, nor her intense protection. He remembered screaming when he'd left that house under Ben's arm, a solid band around him. Ben had tried to hush the boy as he'd grieved, leaving Lilpah. It was a child Ben had carried under darkness to the cabin on Zephinia's ship. It had been a child that the wild ocean threw onto Seo-yeon's beach, and it had been a young man Ben left three years later.

In his mind, Lilpah remained that young girl, a lean lass, barefoot, and her wild reddy-gold hair so different to his. She'd had a cold blue-eyed stare that could impale, and a wary darting glance if she thought danger circled. She'd protected her brother with her life at the time. Throughout the years, she'd come to him while he thrashed in his dreams and nightmares.

What had happened to her over the lost years? Had she married? Had she died? He felt the burble of unrest start in his belly. Even after all this time, he still felt a twinge of something he couldn't name.

'What's that you said?' Ben asked and threw off the fur cape. He sat up, yawned, stretched, and stood to unbutton his fly. He walked a little way over, took a piss, and returned to the fire.

He peered into the billy. 'You were wondering about your sister again.' He grabbed the three pannikins close by and dipped each one. Koori took his with a nod of thanks and prodded the wallaby with a stick. He flipped the body to singe the other side, talking all the while.

Jac took his cup from Ben. 'Hadn't realised I'd spoken aloud.' He sipped, made a face. Stewed gum leaves were not for the fainthearted. 'I'll take me a wash in the ocean before I go to the town, get us some proper tea leaves.' He threw the contents of his cup into the soft scrubby bushes of the dunes.

'Good idea, and rum, while you're at it.' Ben yawned again. 'I'll follow you into the water, give my clothes a salt bath as well.'

They all waded in, even Koori, though he didn't like the idea too much. It only took a few minutes before he'd had enough, and he headed back, waving his arms, beckoning Jac to come back with him. Jac stripped off his shirt, dunking it carefully, aware of the nuggets, before heading back towards the shore.

After more arm waving and shouting from the Koori, Ben followed, and shrugged out of his shirt to thrash it clean. As the saltwater rolled over his body, the old ropey scars of the lash glistened in the sunlight.

Jac lifted his chin towards Ben. 'Free of the lash on dry land.'

'Maybe.' Waves buffeted him, and he was pushed gently to the shore. 'Let's go. Koori could be right, there might be hunters of the deep around here.' He dunked his shirt, thrashed it around again and wrung it out. 'I like the sea, mostly,' he said. 'Saltwater can save your life. Cleans wound like this.' He thumbed to the scars on his back. 'It can deliver you to the land, like it did us all those years ago. But I don't trust it, or what's in it. You swallow it, you're dead. Sink in it, you're dead. Something in it takes a bite out of you, you're dead.' He shrugged back into the wet shirt. 'All this land-lubbin' and I'm out of the way of it. Not sure I'll be taking a sailor's job again.' He waded towards the shore; the shirt thrown over his shoulder. 'Not on the ocean, anyway.'

Jac followed him. 'Do they still even have the cat o' nine on the ships?'

'Not the good ships.' Ben stopped at the water's edge. 'But as long as there's men, there'll be the lash.'

Jac had thought about boarding a ship for the old country, but after the tempestuous journey south from Cheju to the colonies of Australia, he struggled with desire. Added disincentive, he could die at sea, like Song, and never get back.

*Or am I a coward?*

He swung his shirt viciously at the diminishing waves.

Ben shouted at him. 'The nuggets, lad. Take care.'

*Shit, the nuggets.* Frenzied, Jac groped at the shirt for the hard pebbles he'd diligently sewn into the seams so many weeks ago now. *Shit. Shit. Shit.*

A long, hard exhale. He fell to his knees in the shallow water. Hung his head as his fingers traced every one of the nuggets. He breathed easily again. Each one was still secured, still safe in the fabric of his shirt, and secured by the keenly woven thread of his mother's cottons. Jac found the hard turn of the carved wooden spoon, his talisman, and swore that from now on, he'd wear it secured around his neck.

He faced the dunes, staring at the shoreline. Waves lapped his feet and dragged the sand out from under him. Lifting his nose in the air, he breathed in the fresh scent of the sea, felt the salt itch on his face. A soft breeze hinted warmth. He inhaled and exhaled, concentrating. He still had too much anger. *Too much.*

Ben approached him at a run, worry on his face. 'If I had a donkey, lad, he'd have more brains.'

'I'm sure of that.'

Ben clapped a hand on Jac's shoulder. 'Nuggets all there?'

Jac nodded. Looking up, he squinted against the sun and turned to Ben. 'How old would I be now?'

Ben thought a moment. 'Twenty-five, give or take.'

Jac nodded again. 'Lilpah was older. I'm not sure by how much.'

Ben scuffed the sand, and said, 'Aye, older by maybe four years. Hard to say exactly,' he continued as Jac stood silent. 'Could be dead too, lad. You have to face that.'

Jac gave him a bleak stare. 'Can't. Not while she's still so strong inside my head.' Awake or sleeping, from time to time Jac would feel her presence.

'But we'll still write that letter, eh?' Ben said. 'See what happens from there. Hugh Rigg can't get you now.' He turned away. 'Let's keep walking,' he said over his shoulder. 'We're still a ways out of Goolwa.'

It would be a good day when they got to the town and its new wharf. Folk said the river was a hive of industry, opened for trade after competing captains Cadell and Randell had raced in paddle steamers for prize money a few of years back.

He thought again about writing Lilpah that letter. As soon as he put roots down somewhere, he'd do it. He felt for the spoon again. He wanted peace. He wanted to live without the demons.

*

The Goolwa wharf, a narrow timber platform, stretched along the river's edge before them. Koori headed upstream, checking the water.

'Looks a fine sight, Jac. Grand it is, compared to the Ballarat camp,' Ben said, standing with Jac.

The sun had dropped low, and dusk wouldn't be far off. There was still a small group of men nearby. They milled around where a paddle steamer was tied, the *Amy*, a squat and grubby looking vessel.

'Nothing grand about those fellas, though.' Ben gave a lift of his chin in their direction as he spoke to Jac.

'Aye.' Jac had glance over, enough to gauge an undercurrent. His blood hummed.

'*Oi.*' One of the men called out.

'Jac, let's go.' Ben started back the way they'd come. 'We'll find a place to camp and come back tomorrow.'

'*Oi,* you lot. What do y'think you're lookin' at?' Cantankerous. *English. A man should turn his back and walk away.*

Koori, some distance away by now, stopped, listened. He casually made his way back, using his nulla to poke and scrape the river sand here and there as if he were looking for something.

'Jac, come on,' Ben urged.

Jac nodded, grunted. He tried—he was *trying* to cap the funnelling heat that rose in his chest. Head bent, he followed Ben.

'I *said*, what do y'think you're lookin' at?' The man and his three mates had taken a few steps closer. All wore hats that had seen better days, loose shirts over singlets, everything smudged with dirt and soot including their trousers and boots. A couple were younger, brasher.

Ben answered ignoring the belligerence. 'Admiring the grand view. We heard about the new wharf, came to see it for ourselves.'

'There's been some who've stolen stuff off our boat.'

'Not us,' Ben said, genially.

'What about 'im?' One of the younger men, his large Adam's apple bobbing in a scrawny throat, pointed at Koori.

Jac turned. 'What about him?'

'Jac, let's go.'

Koori came to stand beside Ben. He eyed each of the other group in turn.

The men had spread out. The younger one tapped his thigh with rigid fingers and thrust out his chest. His mate slouched beside him. The two older men approached.

Koori let the nulla jump in his hands, and the younger men edged away, uncertain now.

Ben sighed aloud, disappointed in the men, and stood between Jac and Koori. 'Was none of us,' he said, holding his ground, his voice level and calm. 'We just wanted a look at the wharf.'

'Well, now ye've looked.'

'And now we'll go,' Ben said.

'Me and the mates will see you off.'

'Ye'd be a fool, man,' Ben muttered.

The pungent stink of fresh sweat, sharp on the cool air reached Jac, and a growing patch could be seen in the armpits on one of the men's shirt.

236

'See about that,' the man said and all four of them lunged.

Koori sidestepped and with the nulla swept aside the two younger men and toppled them over the water's edge.

'Can't swim,' one of them squealed, splashing.

Ben walloped the third man with a bunched fist dropping him on his arse like a stone. The man scrabbled to gain traction, and wobbly on his feet stumbled away, fleeing his stricken mates.

The man with the mouth came at Jac with fists high in front of his face, dancing like some mad puppet. Jac threw a sharp a kick and buckled both the man's legs. Down he went, fists still high, his mouth open in surprise. Jac kept coming.

*English.*

Rage hurled through a tunnel. Jac slammed his elbow under the man's nose. The body lifted before it fell with a thud onto the dirt, his head bouncing. Blood streamed from his shattered face.

Ben stared at the prone body. He grabbed Jac's arm. 'Shit, Jac, that's a killer crack, stove the bones into his brain. We have to leave, quick.'

Jac froze; the rage had cooled fast. His head spun. 'I haven't killed him.'

'Reckon you have, lad.'

'I can't have.' Jac dropped to his knees by the man.

Koori had been waving the nulla, censuring the sputtering men in the water at his feet. When he saw Jac's handiwork, he marched over, knelt beside Jac, and put his head to the unconscious man's chest.

A shout. Running troopers were sprinting towards them, rifles across their chests, with the man Ben had clobbered.

'He lives,' Koori said, and pushed Jac. 'You go.'

'We all go,' Ben said and darted back towards the cover of the scrub not far off, and the dunes beyond, a hard run ahead of him.

Koori muscled Jac to his feet and tugged him after Ben.

Bunkered down in a sandy hollow, the voices of the troopers could no longer be heard.

'You just snapped, Jac,' Ben said, not happy. He peered over the ridge of the incline.

'Not my finest move,' Jac agreed, slumped by his side. It wasn't the *Taekkyeon* way. Taught mainly for self-defence, a lethal blow should rarely be used. He hung his head; he hadn't controlled the maelstrom that hit his brain and erupted through him. His heart pounded, and he had the shakes.

Ben ducked back and looked at him. 'We can't stay here, now.'

Jac rubbed his face. Ben was right; they'd risk arrest. *Dammit.* He'd let go of the leash—*I let it go*—and the demon had run rough-shod.

Jac reached for the nuggets still stitched in his shirt hem. It was so good by the river; opportunity was ripe. He'd have been able to make something of himself here, he could feel it. The water, serene, flowing downriver to the sea.

He'd messed it up, messed up his own plans. Clasping his hands, he squeezed hard, willed the shakes to stop. He felt sick in his guts as well as in his head; he hadn't controlled it. He couldn't. He'd have to start over.

'You stay, Ben. There's plenty here. I'll go.'

'You're talking shite, lad, feelin' all sorry for yeself,' Ben rumbled. 'We'll go north of Adelaide somewhere, find Mr Hart. He's got land there, he'll have work. We'll give this place wide berth for a while.'

'Hot as hell further north, I've heard,' Jac said, his thoughts drifting. Joe Mole had also said he'd be in that area of the colony.

Koori was looking to the sea, his face inscrutable.

'Then just the place to burn that devil out of your soul,' Ben said, his mouth a grim line.

Just before dawn, Koori woke them. He'd hunted early, had caught and butchered a kangaroo and was roasting a skinned haunch on the low coals of their fire. He wouldn't bother skinning it for himself, so this was for Jac and Ben. Koori had other ideas about where he was going. '*Wadawurrong.*' He tapped his chest and lifted his hand towards the east.

'He's going home,' Jac said to Ben.

Koori slapped each of them loosely on the shoulder, pointed at the spitting meat and said, 'Good tucker.' Then he hitched his trousers, picked up the other hindquarter of the 'roo and slung it over his shoulder. He nodded at them, turned, and didn't look back as he headed into the coastal bush.

'We know where to find him again, lad,' Ben said, as the vegetation closed around Koori. 'We know his country.'

Jac nodded, said nothing. Koori's leaving weighed heavily on him, and he would keenly miss his friend.

He and Ben walked in the other direction, northwest, away from the river, and headed through hard terrain of low hills, at times scrubby flats dotted with tall timbers. There were creeks and wells on the worn tracks they found, and Koori's roasted meat sustained them. They arrived at the young city of Adelaide after three days easy walking, fifty miles away from Goolwa.

'Far enough away,' Ben reckoned.

Captain Hart owned a flour mill company in Port Adelaide, and being the important man he was, had been elected to the Legislative Council the year prior.

He hadn't recognised Ben, which was a disappointment. Ben rattled off the names of ranking officers and some crew members to prove he'd been on the *Augustus*. The old captain had been impressed then directed him to the mill manager with a nod. 'Happy to help an old seaman of mine,' he'd said, largely dismissive.

Working the mill wasn't what Ben had in mind. 'So much for that,' he said. 'I carried a picture of him in my head for years as a person who'd do right by an old hand.'

'Maybe he has—we don't want to work a flour mill,' Jac said. 'It's not for the likes of you or me. We should look further afield.'

On the wide streets of Adelaide, steadily making their way to the port, Jac had met men who talked of outstations, of small towns on the edge of the world. Country named the Flinders Ranges, Joe Mole country, where vast tracks of land were to be had, to be worked. Fortunes could be made, they said, though Jac never met anybody who'd made their fortune.

'Further north, you mean?' Ben asked.

'Aye. Away from the city. The place is full of Englishmen.'

Ben scoffed, gave a grim smile. 'Time to realise you can't outrun 'em, lad. Englishmen are everywhere, not all as bad as you reckon. You have to cut the demon out of you.'

Jac let out a breath, looked to the sky. The humming deep down had begun again, and a low heat spread in his gut. 'I can't outrun them, you're right, but every time I see a threat, it's like pulling a scab off a sore. It can't heal.'

'Then we find a place to let heal,' Ben said, his mouth taut.

'I don't know it can be.'

Dropping his chin, Ben frowned, a hard twist of his brows, and sucked in a breath. 'Lad, I've been with you through thick and thin, and I know your mettle. I've been silent.' His voice shook, his gaunt stare locked on Jac. 'But this thing is a poison in ye,' he ground, jaw clamped. 'It boils through ye, destroyin' ye. Get rid of it, Jac. It's an abscess in ye, you gotta lance it deep, let it drain away.' Ben caught Jac's eye. 'It's been eatin' you inside since Rogerstone, more lethal now you're grown, and with *Taekkyeon* as your weapon, ye'll finally kill someone. I saw it on the river.' He grabbed Jac by the shirt, pulled him face to face. 'So I've *had enough* of being silent,' he said, 'watching you make truce with it. It's no good, I'm tellin' ye.' He thrust Jac away, rubbing his head hard, his temper up.

Passers-by took a wide berth around them. Jac rocked back from Ben. He'd heard him, his friend. He listened. A spark of light flickered behind his eyes.

A crowd of young folk on the footpath jostled him, laughing among themselves as they walked past the mill. Jac barely noticed. He blinked, hearing the echo of hope, deep within, a sound through a fissure.

*Lance it deep.*

Ben blew out a breath, craned his head at the huge brick building and listened as the grinding stones inside crushed tons of wheat. 'Let's go. I was never one for towns anyway.' He stalked off.

Jac traipsed after him. He would purge the demon and he'd do it in a land beyond civilisation. It was 1855.

# PART III

# Chapter Seventeen

## *1856 Rigg Manor, Wales*

Lilpah didn't like leaving the house.

It had nothing to do with stone and mortar, and neither with feeble sentimentality. Nothing to do with the protection the house afforded against the elements—it barely did that; it was too neglected over the years. The money from his tenants was piling up somewhere, certainly not spent on his house and grounds.

It was that if she left the house, she'd have to return; there was nowhere else for her to go.

This house was a place she knew, and it knew her. Sir Hugh had saved her, even though he'd used her. If she left, she would have less than ever: freedom and nothing. So, it was easier not to leave the house at all, not to chase freedom, or hope; that would only be folly. If she never left the house, she'd never feel the dread of returning.

Tippy was insisting that Lil accompany her to the meeting with the Oswald brothers, unusual as it was.

The two young boys had been run ragged in the late morning in the hope they would sleep in the afternoon. But Lilpah found them awake, chortling in her tiny enclave, rifling through her measly possessions. Lester was gleefully clutching the carved spoon she'd kept hidden all these years and waved it in front of Daniel before plunging it into a mound of discarded clothes—now rags—and shouting, 'I'm digging for gold.' Finding it less than adequate as a shovel, he started poking it at an equally gleeful Daniel who tried to snatch it.

'I want to dig for gold in Ostria,' Daniel cried.

'Ostr-*alia*,' Lester yelled.

Lilpah dived to grab the spoon from Lester, hissing at him to give it up. Emboldened, Lester shot away from her, only to be snatched off his feet and shaken in her hands until he was screaming incoherently in her face, still waving the carving out of her reach.

She sat him on the floor and, astride his wriggling body, clawed at the spoon in his fist. She wrenched it, felt it snap and let out an outraged scream. The boy panicked and his bellows rose in terror as Lil's hand came up ready to soundly slap his ruddy cheeks.

Tippy flapped into the room and charged Lilpah at speed, grabbing her wrist. 'Not a finger on him, Lil,' she rasped. 'He is the master's son. Not a finger laid in anger.'

Lil strained against Tippy but was no match for the stout woman. Lilpah sagged to the floor. Tippy clutched at Lester who scampered from under his mother, snivelling, bewildered, rubbing his wrist, pouting. Daniel, also pouting, walked over and patted Lester's arm, a gentle mimic of Lil's own signal of reassurance.

Tippy rumbled, 'Off to the corner, you two boys. I will deal with you later.'

They were terrified of Tippy, of her withholding rare treats; she was not one to be messed with. They slunk off, arms around each other.

'You're losin' your mind, Lil,' Tippy chided, tight-lipped.

Lil opened her hand to find the spoon in two pieces. 'Yes. Finally, that could be so.' She stared at the little keepsake and sighed in despair. 'A blessing.'

The spoon was the one thing of her old life that she hadn't destroyed, although it was a remnant of a life she'd just about forgotten. She glanced at her only friend, waited while Tippy tended the children and then hid the broken pieces of the spoon.

Mid-afternoon and Tippy insisted that the boys be left in the nursery room, bedded together, warm and snoring, the earlier adventures forgotten. She herded Lil outside.

Lil looked over her shoulder at the house. Always the same. Smug, squat, and ugly atop a small hill, its trees decimated by the weather, the new grass green and sloshy underfoot as the early summer rains soaked the grounds without spare. Overgrown weeds lined the scarred driveway, and some had the audacity to rise out of the old wheel ruts.

Tippy rushed ahead, her dark cloak whipping about her skirt, her shoes sodden. 'Watch yer don't slip, Lil,' she said breathlessly, but kept up a pace belying her own advice.

'Where are we?' Lil wiped the dew misting on her face.

'You never been here before? We're on the edge of the Oswald's place. There's an old shepherd's hut up yonder.'

'I never had any need to be here before,' Lilpah said, and glanced about. They were in a deeply wooded patch, and the path they took was only a foot-track. The big house had disappeared behind her; the trees and shrubs had closed it off from view. She felt a bit strange, and her heartbeat had started to race.

Tippy tut-tutted at the dry snipe. 'A body needs some distance from that house.'

'You've been here before? To do what—tend the sheep or the shepherd?'

Snorting good-naturedly, Tippy kept her pace. 'As if there'd been a shepherd good enough for me.'

'I don't understand why I need to be here.' Her booming pulse was making her ears ache.

'You'll see. Mr Oswald needs us to bear witness.'

'What for?'

'Do hurry along, Mistress Holier-Than-Thou. You have to sign your life away.'

Lilpah stopped. 'Wait.'

Tippy stopped, huffed and puffed, and turned. 'What is it? It's still too soddin' breezy to be standing here gabbin'.'

'What is it he really wants? I know you know.'

'*Pfft*. You will see. You will *see*.' Tippy beckoned Lil, her hand waving her forward. 'I've never had you put a foot wrong, I'm not about to start now. We must show some guts here, Lil. Come along with you.'

Lilpah swished her cloak and pushed ahead of Tippy. 'Hurry up then, show me. I'm feeling sick about it, God knows, but what's the worst can happen?' She could think of a hundred things worse than meeting Morris Oswald. In fact at times, she'd forcefully turned her thoughts away from him.

The shepherd's hut appeared under the darkening gloom of threatening rain. A tendril of smoke from its short chimney wandered into the densely clouded sky above. The walls looked solid enough, the one window was battened shut and the frayed timber door was closed. It would be a single room dwelling, sometimes where man and beast sheltered together when necessary. Two horses were tethered outside at the rotting hitching rail, their reins loose and dragging in the damp soil underfoot. Dank, mouldy air wafted around them.

'Come along,' Tippy said and pushed past Lil. 'I don't want to be missed at the house. We must get back directly.'

Exactly how Lilpah felt; she didn't like being away—she didn't want to get used to it. But if the boys awoke and their nannies were not there to see to them, suspicion would be aroused. She hurried to catch Tippy who pounded twice on the door.

It scraped open to the outside. Ambrose Oswald stood aside in the entrance. The fire behind him sputtered happily, its smoke floating up the chimney. Warmth permeated the room as did the odour of sheep dung. Urea clung to the air.

Tippy rushed towards the fireplace and thrust her chafed hands towards the heat. Lilpah stood just inside the door as Ambrose closed it behind her.

Morris Oswald stood at the far wall with his hands behind his back. A crude table sat close by, and loose papers were stacked atop it. 'Good afternoon, ladies.' He indicated that the women should each take a seat on two stools, which were no more than cut logs.

In the silence following, Tippy said, 'Oh aye, good afternoon,' and rubbed her hands together. 'Might be summer but it don't feel like it out there.'

No one commented. Lilpah hadn't moved. She glanced from Morris to his younger brother and back again.

Morris Oswald began. 'Let's get straight to it, Mistress Owen, and I note your reluctance. I have here on the table a paper stating that Daniel Owen is the legal heir to Sir Hugh Rigg, his rightful son by his lawful wife, Johanna Oswald. I beg that you sign it.'

Tippy continued to warm her hands as if she hadn't heard Oswald's request.

Oswald wanted Lilpah to openly admit Lester's illegitimacy. That would endanger her. She and Tippy had swapped the babies. She glanced at Tippy who still faced the fire, rolling her hands over and over. 'You know that Daniel is your kin, Sir Hugh's legal heir, and that it's obvious.'

Oswald inclined his head. 'You need to attest to it.'

'Why would anyone believe a paper I sign?'

Oswald tapped the paper that authenticated Daniel's rightful birth. 'It's an oath you have declared, and it will have a witness's mark.' He shuffled the other page to the top and said, 'And you will sign this one which states that Rigg has accepted Mr Percy Crawford to act as his agent on all legal matters.'

*Mr Crawford, of that horrible night.* Lilpah barely glanced at the table. 'I could scarcely sign any such document for Sir Hugh. I am a woman, a servant.'

'Ah yes, and you are also an excellent copyist. The note to summon me late last year, for instance, which I still have. So, not your own signature on this one, Mistress, but Sir Hugh's.' Oswald set the papers side by side.

Lil narrowed her gaze. 'And what of Lester Rigg?'

'He's your kin, your son. I would see he is well cared for, as you would be.' Tippy gave him a look. Morris Oswald added, 'It would also mean no harm to your kith, Mistress Bowman. She, too, would be safeguarded.'

Lilpah turned it all over in her mind. Yes, yes, she could sign a passable forgery of Sir Hugh's signature, shaky and illegible as it was now, on the contract of employment for Crawford but how could she trust that the Oswalds would not betray her with the paper she would sign in her own name?

She glanced at Ambrose who leaned against the door, and with head down. He gave nothing more away as his older brother continued.

'When Mr Crawford is in situ, we will visit often, as if to see Lester. All we ask is that Daniel is brought to us as well. We have a right—'

'You have no right,' Lilpah seethed and then glared at Tippy's back.

Morris spoke quietly. 'Mistress, it is you who has no right.'

Tippy turned sharply. 'Think carefully, Lil. If Rigg finds out, Lester is likely to be imprisoned, or worse, and we are likely to follow. And who knows what they'd do to Daniel—'

'No harm will come to Daniel,' Morris cut in, his voice hard. 'No matter what the circumstances. And if we are careful, clever, and we are all strong, no harm to Lester, either.'

Lil hadn't survived this long by trusting anyone other than Tippy, but even that seemed compromised. Her heart banged. 'And when Daniel comes to inherit? It will hurt. They are brothers,' she burst.

Morris Oswald met her glare benignly. 'That they are.'

He couldn't understand. 'It would tear them apart,' she cried.

'That presumes Sir Hugh will die when they're much older. But now, as youngsters, it wouldn't mean anything to them who inherited what.'

Lil blinked. 'Sir Hugh has lasted this long through unimaginable trials. He could go on for years.' Met with silence, she stood taller. 'Where is the guarantee that Lester will live a good life if ever this comes to be?'

'You have my word.'

'Words don't mean—'

'This Mr Crawford,' Tippy said, holding up her hand and stepping closer to Lil. 'I know him a little of old. His spine sometimes bends in the wind.'

'It's true,' Morris replied. 'But he's a man who has to provide for his family. I've discussed many things with him on this very subject, including his ... motivation. I am satisfied of him.'

Tippy narrowed her gaze and stared directly at Morris Oswald. 'You have *flacmel,* blackmail on your side, it seems, over all of us.'

His eyes glittered in the low light. 'Blackmail serves me well. This will also relieve you and Foswick of the same.'

Tippy's mouth firmed in a hard line, but she didn't look at Lil.

Lil gaped at Tippy. 'What?'

'Tippy has come to me, worried for her charges, and for you, of course,' Morris said, dismissively. 'Foswick has also been in my employ.' Then he caught Lil's eye, reached across to tap the papers on the table.

Drawn to the witness's mark, Lil recognised Tippy's written name underneath. *Tippy has betrayed me? No, no—*

'Mistress Owen, sign the documents, and then I'll have both Foswick and Mr Crawford in my employ. Neither of those men will learn that the infants were swapped at birth. On my word. I can give no greater guarantee.'

Lil knew that hers and her son's fate was in his hands. She turned her flat stare on Morris. 'You want Sir Hugh's holdings for yourself. That's it, isn't it?'

Ambrose pushed off the wall, his fists at his side, his face twisted. About to speak, he was waved down by his older brother.

'Years ago,' Morris said, 'the holdings were to be mine before they were stolen from my father by Edward Rigg.' He gave a laugh. 'Who in turn had them stolen by his own son, Hugh Rigg.' His face held a smile, not a friendly one, nor a happy one. 'You are a very smart woman, and I admire you for it but truth to tell, it'd take a much richer man than I am to rebuild the estate. As for that house, and the bastard who's inflicted great harm inside it, it should be burned into the damned ground.'

Emboldened, Tippy tut-tutted. 'Waste of a good house,' she said, slyly. 'All it needs is some care and a few funds from the coffers.'

'Would have to be a deep coffer,' Ambrose muttered. 'Rigg's coffer can't be empty with what he's stolen from his tenants, the poor souls.'

'Aye, his coffer is well hid,' Tippy agreed. 'I can see the land would be worth something to ye. Why not save the house?'

'It gives sanctuary to evil,' Ambrose said and turned his fierce gaze on Lilpah and she flinched.

'Mistress,' Morris said patiently to Lilpah, indicating the papers on the table. 'If you please, your own signature on this document.' He pushed a paper to her. Then he tapped the paper underneath. 'And Sir Hugh's signature needs to go on this one.'

'You think a wrong like this, the likes of which was done to your family, will bring you satisfaction?' Lil knew she was signing away her life.

'I do. Indeed I do.' His gaze roved over her face, as if he really did admire her. 'It's merely a correction. And if it doesn't work, I will simply take back what is rightfully mine, by force. Then there will be more deaths, rest assured.'

Tippy rested a hand on Lil's forearm. As if reading her mind, she said softly, 'If you don't sign it, Lil, your life is damned anyway.'

# CHAPTER EIGHTEEN

Lilpah watched as Doctor Evers stared at the crumpled form, the clothing ragged, dirty, and streaked with human excreta. He'd arrived for his usual weekly visit only minutes earlier. 'What happened?' he snapped and bent over Sir Hugh who was unconscious in the garden bed.

Foswick spread shaking hands. 'I came up to see— I heard glass breaking and for pity's sake, I know we can't have any more windows lost. They have to be boarded up; we can't replace the glass.' He wiped a hand over his mouth. 'I went to his room and found the window open, broken, and there he was down in the garden. Mistress Lilpah came in after me. She can attest to it.'

Lilpah nodded. Her hands shook and she hoped no one would notice.

'It's true, Doctor,' Tippy piped up. 'I was comin' in from collecting herbs.' She held out what looked like a thick bunch of weeds. 'I seen him dive out that window, yelling about summat as he hit the ground.'

'Get him up to a bed,' Evers demanded. 'And quickly.'

Two burly yard workers had run for a timber pallet and lifted the master onto it.

Sir Hugh looked to be dead. When he belched a guttural moan, Lilpah grimaced, disappointed. *Not dead. The creature can still feel pain.* He was her jailer, her abuser, and the end of his life was near. She felt nothing ... That was wrong. She was anxious, then bewildered at that. She hadn't thought further ahead. Only *if* he were to die.

'Go easy,' the doctor ordered as the yard men lumbered up the granite steps into the house.

Their great thick hands hefted the pallet and, as they hurried, Sir Hugh's body bounced all the way up the stairs. In the bedchamber, they rolled him onto the bed covers and plodded out of the room.

'Foswick, the dose?'

'Not changed, Doctor.'

Evers grunted as he bent over the rank body. He pried opened Sir Hugh's eyelids, and put his ear to the man's heart. He slapped Sir Hugh's face. 'Wake up, Sir Hugh.'

'I'll get the wine for him—'

'No. We need to know what his injuries are.' A sweat had broken out on the doctor's face. He stared, worried, pinching his lips. 'How in God's name did he drag himself up onto the sill?'

Everyone turned to look at the broken window. Furtive glances passed to and fro.

'Could he have found reserves of his former strength?' Foswick asked, filling the silence. He was nervous and his glance went to Lil who stared back.

Doctor Evers lifted a shoulder, in thought. 'Normally the drug keeps a patient passive.'

'This is not a normal patient,' Tippy muttered.

The doctor said, 'He needs to be weaned off the medicine. I don't know what it's doing to him.'

Lilpah hovered. *So now* we *wean him off the medicine.* She'd already been careful about that. She looked at the pitiful form in the bed. What horror would they await then? But if he were to die, Mr Oswald and his new agent would surely step in and administer the estate. Uneasy, and as if perhaps her thoughts might have been heard, Lil glanced around. Tippy caught her gaze and shrugged.

Days later, Sir Hugh still lay prone in his bed. The linens had been changed, the room aired but then closed again, and a servant woman had been assigned to his needs.

Lilpah and Tippy returned to the nursery. Inside, closing the door, Lilpah leaned on it. 'The doctor says it's a "stupor", that his brain is rattled, and he might not live,' she said.

Tippy raised her brows. 'I heard. I wonder if it came before the fall or because of it. Just how did he manage to get up onto the sill?'

Lilpah shrugged. 'His madness drives it. You've seen it, power comes from somewhere. Maybe rage. God only knows how he manages it after the onset of the apoplexy.' She shot Tippy a glance. 'Why is it you're so concerned?'

'I value my neck. And yours.'

'There's no need to worry. I was already back in our chamber when Foswick thumped up the stairs. You might remember he said he got into the room before me.' Lilpah took a seat by the window. The cold from the glass seeped towards her and she drew the shawl closer about her shoulders. The boys played quietly with simple unadorned blocks of wood that masqueraded as horses and carts. 'What will it mean, this agreement with the Oswalds?'

Tippy huffed and took a seat with her on the bench. 'It means that as long as Daniel is alive and well, so will we be. And long may that continue, would to God.'

Lilpah nodded, rolled her eyes. 'Yes, would to God.' Any mention of God made her nervous. Her stoic resistance to any formal worship rarely brought attention to her these days. She had forborne it for so long that no one took any notice. Some had earlier damned her soul to hell for it. Others wondered if she'd had a soul to damn so in the light of that, she did enough kneeling in the sorry excuse for a chapel (scrubbed by God-fearing staff), to forestall any talk of witchcraft, or worshipping the devil. That would be the last thing she needed. Though, she admitted, the devil certainly had a hold on her in the form of Sir Hugh.

His death was certainly on her mind.

Tippy rubbed her rough, reddened hands. Nothing much had changed for Tippy in all these years, and she seemed unaffected. As far as Lil was aware, Tippy had never caught the eye of the master, nor of his cronies but she'd never said, and Lilpah never asked.

Lil's heart gave a little jump, as if it missed a beat. Without Tippy, she would most likely have been dead long ago. She went to touch Tippy's arm, but pulled back. Where had this daftness come from? Wasn't it Tippy who'd told Morris Oswald of Lil's skill with the pen and ink? What else had the woman imparted?

Tippy noticed Lilpah's withdrawal. 'Something amiss?' Her tone was wry.

'Have you sent a message to your Oswald man?'

A gleeful smile changed Tippy's features. 'A boy fair flew across the field not a day gone by, a paper in his hand.'

'A paper?' Lil inclined her head. 'And who wrote on that paper, Tippy, for I certainly did not?'

'Foswick, of course. Though his hand is not as good as yours. I expect we'll see our new administration man very soon.'

They both turned to stare out the window, misted with their warm breath. The weather was bleak; thin sunshine peeped through the scattered thick clouds, and rain threatened. Summer was not its usual this year, and any warmth had been sporadic. Autumn approached and the cool weather would continue.

'If he dies, I wonder what will happen,' Lil said.

Tippy smiled, her hands chafing together once again. 'We've no way of knowin',' she said. 'But I'm sure of this.' She ducked her head and stared at Lil from under a frown. 'When he dies, I'll put on me best slippers, and dance on Hugh Rigg's maggoty grave.'

# Chapter Nineteen

Mr Percy Crawford alighted the coach at Rigg Manor and set down his overnight bag. The chill of late autumn air rose from the ground and pierced the soles of his boots, sending a shiver coursing through his veins. He hadn't been back to this place for many years. The last time was at the onset of the Opium War when Sir Hugh had invited him, and other gentlemen and reprobates alike, to offer them the opportunity to invest.

Crawford hadn't lasted until the dinner. Once the drunken talk had turned to the ravaging of children, of slavery, and to opium smuggling, he'd left the house as quickly as he could. *Scurried* from the place, *fearful*, some had said. So be it. One's life was hard enough without the taint of debauchery clinging to it like shit on bedlinen.

Yet here he was.

Morris Oswald didn't think him a coward. Oswald regarded him as useful, he'd said, especially as Crawford's circumstances had become more difficult in these last years. Crawford's management of great estates was widely known. He himself thought he'd achieved more than reasonable results in his work although Rigg Manor was another challenge entirely.

Mr Oswald knew of an indiscretion, a child fathered by Crawford, born to the daughter of one of his own tenants. Hardly anything to turn heads, but the father of the girl had died in mysterious circumstances after a confrontation; murder it was rumoured. Crawford maintained his innocence but lost everything. The rumour hung around; Percy was nearly destitute, his family threatened with eviction. Then Morris Oswald offered him employment—*in the Rigg household; a double agent if you will*—and went on to explain the task.

Percy Crawford had taken a deep breath and agreed.

The great oak doors opened, creaking and groaning as the hinges complained. The valet, or whatever he called himself, stood there as if he presided over a grand castle rather than the crumbling hulk of a house. Fosdyke, or Fishwyck or something.

Crawford felt his gut crawl. Having to revisit this house, to meet its vile occupant once again, made his innards gripe. But Mr Oswald was paying well. Percy would have to make the best of it and hope for the short fifteen-year tenure Mr Oswald had indicated.

'Ah, Fosdyke, good morning,' Crawford said, and adjusted his coat against the brisk breeze that seemed to come out of the rotting house. He nodded at the man on the top step.

'Foswick, Mr Crawford. Welcome.' He glanced over Crawford's shoulder to the coach. 'I can arrange for your bags to be—'

'No need. I carry only an overnight bag. I trust staff will attend to any laundry for a few days if need be. I won't reside here.' He couldn't yet stomach the idea of having to live in this house.

If Foswick thought anything of those arrangements, he showed nothing. A good valet, then, it seemed. Foswick hadn't been in Sir Hugh's employ when Crawford had first visited, so he didn't know much about him, but the valet had been a stalwart here for many years. Rumours and strife had not been reported for a long time, so perhaps this attested to his good character.

Foswick scooped up the bag and indicated Crawford go ahead of him up the steps and into the house. Inside, no one met them there. No servant man or woman to take his hat and coat, though he was happy to keep his coat. The chill inside was as bracing as outside.

The valet and the two nannies ran the place, according to Mr Oswald, though none of them had any estate managing skills. Neither should they, Percy thought.

'Might I say that we are happy to have you administer for Sir Hugh. His health is certainly concerning for all of us—'

'No doubt.' Crawford cut him off.

The cleverly constructed letter to Sir Hugh from the 'Queen's Exchequer' via a firm of solicitor's was compelling. It demanded that Rigg accept Mr Crawford as administrator of the property or Sir Hugh risked losing it. It was enough to keep the reprobate quiet, and he'd signed an agreement accepting Crawford.

Morris Oswald was indeed a man to keep onside.

Turning this way and that in the hall, Crawford sized up the state of the place. Admirably, the place had not totally disintegrated. However, the place smelled and was rotting away here and there; maintenance and repair work was necessary. The wider grounds, the fields, and the tenancies were another matter requiring urgent attention.

It was much as he remembered. A huge doorway was at the far end of the room, another door was off to his right, and opposite, on his left. A staircase hugged the right-hand wall. Its steps, disintegrating in places, led up to a darkened space. A floor, which in the gloom, gave him no clue as to its occupants. Crawford hoped his eyes would adjust quickly if he had to stay up there. He could almost feel the rats peering at him.

'I will need to see the estate ledgers,' he said. The more imperious he was, the more likely staff would pander to his demands. 'I trust you know the banker contracted?'

'I do, sir.' Foswick was quick to be conciliatory. 'Mr Crawford, if I can explain, it will—'

'I've heard there are dungeons in use here, great gaol-like cells below that lead to the kitchen.' The rumours from long ago had not been dispelled.

'Not in use for many years, sir.'

'I will inspect for myself, then they will be sealed, never to be used again.' Crawford removed his gloves, but promptly replaced them. The place was freezing. 'Why aren't the fires alight, man? Isn't there firewood?'

'Ample, but I have instructed that we must be frugal, for there might come a time when—'

'Nonsense. Have someone attend to setting and lighting fires at every hearth in every room immediately. Every safe fireplace, that is.' Crawford turned again, sweeping his gaze over what was before him. 'Is Sir Hugh up to visitors?'

Foswick cleared his throat. 'He is in and out of a conscious state, Mr Crawford. The doctor believes he might've had another small turn after his fall from the window. When he's awake, his eyes follow everything, but his speech can be slurred.'

*In that case, the man might not be long for this earth.* Crawford would have to make haste to secure Mr Oswald's objective: he needed to be confirmed as his nephew's guardian. The document was in his bag and for some reason, Percy was to give it to the Owen woman. Apparently, she would be a witness as would the charwoman, her companion. Unusual, but he wasn't going to argue the point.

'And now, Foswick. Show me to my office so that I might begin to save this ungodly hulk, and everyone in it, from complete ruin.'

*

Tippy and Lilpah took turns lighting the fires after the few remaining servants had set the makings in each room. For half the day, choking smoke covered the lower floor. Without a chimney-sweep child handy to push up and clear the flues, much was made of shoving sturdy tree limbs into the stacks to dislodge accumulated debris. One by one, the rooms cleared of smoke, but soot covered everything in fine oily dust.

The only room that was clear of smoke was the kitchen. Its chimney had always been cleaned and cleared as it was the only fully functioning room in the house. It was there that Lilpah and Tippy sat with the boys.

'It begins well,' Tippy said.

'With the chimneys, who'd have thought?' An old memory of a chimney fire and a little child's death came to mind, but Lil pushed it away. There would never be many good memories in this place. She held onto the happy times with the two boys as though they were her only lifeline to sanity. 'He'll need to employ more people if this grand notion of a warm house is to come to pass.' Lil huddled closer to the fireplace. The blackened kettle, sitting on a grate over the coals, boiled its contents, and steam puffed into the air.

'Naught too soon. Another winter biting at our heels might be one too much. At least one thing—Foswick has opened the stores and there is plenty of wood to burn in the fireplaces. I'm beginning to feel my bones fair jumping for joy.'

Tippy poured water from the kettle into the pot for tea. The boys would drink it milky, and the women would spike theirs with a tot of wine pilfered from the master's store. That was the one thing for which the purse-strings were always loosened—grog.

'If I was Mr Crawford,' Tippy started. 'I wouldn't know where to start. I'm trying to look around with fresh eyes. Why, even the very clothes on our backs are rags, not to mention the bed linens, and even the beds.'

Lilpah shook her head. 'He will attend the fine house and grounds, if that is his purpose, before anything as lowly as clothes for the servants. But first he must report if it's worth the effort. If Mr Oswald thinks not, then we must prepare for another blow.'

Tippy murmured, agreeing. She took a glance at Lil. 'Ye're still feeling bad over his Daniel and your Lester, aren't ye?'

Snorting, Lil took the pannikin of tea Tippy had pushed towards her. 'What good would that be? If it happens, I'm sure Daniel would look kindly on us.'

''Course he would. Have we not been like mothers to him?' Tippy lifted her eyebrows.

Lil didn't wonder about that. What she wondered about was whether there would be lawful retribution for swapping babies at birth. She held up her cup for a splash of wine from the bottle Tippy wielded. Hopefully, any reckoning would be a long way off.

Lester snatched a toy from Daniel's hands. As Daniel let it go without a fight, only smiling, she jumped up and corrected Lester. He would *not* become a bully like his father. But when Daniel reached across and easily snatched the toy back, maintaining his smile in Lester's shocked silence, Lil settled in her seat.

Lester protested and Lil wagged a finger in his face. 'Uh, uh,' she rebuked, then took the toy away from Daniel, who immediately put on a pout. 'Nor you, either Daniel. You'll both go without supper unless you apologise to each other, right this minute.'

They complied and set about finding another game to play. She had been wise, as Daniel's 'mother', and as 'nanny' to Lester, to treat them as equals. No one had stopped her, and nor did she expect it. Daniel had always maintained a respectful distance when in Sir Hugh's company, and that had been sufficient to keep the status quo.

Whatever came to be, due to her efforts, Lester would not, by nurture, resemble the monster who had fathered him. By nature it was a different thing, but so far, she'd seen nothing of the debauched spirit of Sir Hugh in either boy.

# CHAPTER TWENTY

*1859 Flinders Ranges, South Australia*

Angorichina Station was a vast, unholy land filled with flies, dust and a striking landscape of blues and purples and reds that took Jac's breath away. The searing heat of summer also scorched it dry in his throat.

What madness was it to toil on this land? (The thought often crept up on him. The River Murray beckoned at times: all that water.) But toil it he had, along with Ben, on horseback or on foot tending flocks of sheep or herds of cattle.

Jac was on his back in the swag. By habit, his fingers curled around the amulet he wore, worn smooth by years of such contact. He watched as the sun threatened to rise, its red glow burning on the hills; it bobbed above the horizon auguring another day of intense heat. Over the years, his skin had cooked to leather; in Ballarat he'd rarely known how quickly a man's sweat dried before it got the chance to drip from his brow.

Yet, as much as the land was unforgiving, the sunsets were

among the most exquisite he'd seen in all the world. Dawn would break free of the evening's heat and either unleash the summer's day, or weakly warm the morning after a freezing winter's night.

He sat up, reached over, and shook Ben, who lately had been harder to rouse from sleep. This land here, and the six years they'd been on it, had taken its toll on him.

'Come on, old man. Time we were up. Robert over yonder needs a stir.'

'Who you callin' old?' Ben muttered and rolled onto his back. After a moment, he pushed himself up on his ragged swag, a thin couple of blankets, his eyes owlish.

Jac stood and stretched. From under their humpy, a shelter of boughs from the stunted vegetation around, he saw the sheep staring at him, almost as one, willing him to drop feed from his hands. He left the shelter and stirred the cooking fire for the billy, then walked to Robert's swag and nudged him with a foot.

Robert Blinman, nicknamed Peg-Leg because of his wooden right leg, was a man whose eyes drooped, whose nose was large and long over firm lips. He'd been a shepherd on Angorichina for some time. Last night by the campfire, he told Jac and Ben that he'd staked a mining claim a few miles from where they were camped.

Instantly intrigued, Jac asked, 'Mining claim for what?'

Blinman's sunken cheeks had creased in an enigmatic grin. 'Copper. I seen an outcrop and knew what it was straight away.'

'Copper,' Ben repeated. He glanced at Jac.

'Aye. And I'll need investors. Can't do much with it—I spent me last ten quid buying the claim.'

Jac had heard the faint rattle of those gold nuggets, his cache carefully intact since they'd run from Goolwa all those years ago. He noticed Ben had also reached for his own much sewn-over shirt hem and knew he was thinking the same. *Could they buy in?*

'How much d'you need?' Ben asked.

'Another eighty pound for the first year's rent. I got Alford and

Frost to invest, and there's one other. Joe Mole.'

'Joe Mole, you said?' Jac asked.

'Aye. Real tycoon waitin' to happen, that one. Lookin' for anything and anywhere to make a quid.' Blinman squinted. 'You lookin' for big money work? It's here in the copper seam, for sure.'

Ben shook his head but Jac said, 'Count me in.'

Later that night, Jac and Ben had talked.

'Jac, it'd be work underground to mine for copper. You're doing all right lately. No nightmares, or rages, not for a couple of years now. No elbows to the face for anyone. It might be a backward step to take to a mine, and a copper mine at that, like in Wales.'

'This place is nothing like Wales.'

It was true; Jac had found some peace. Englishmen were few out this way, and those he came across, he turned away from. He practised *Taekkyeon* daily, early in the morning. It kept at bay the demons that rose to shriek in his head. At night he would lay bare his soul and sometimes, run into the pitch dark until the rage petered out, his throat raw, his head aching, the soles of his feet bruised and bleeding. Then would come relief, like a dawn after the desert's night, with light creeping over the horizon. He began to sleep without fear of closing his eyes. No terrors lately ravaged his mind and body, but vigilance was everything.

'How would you go in a dark tunnel again,' Ben rumbled. 'Nothing but a wick and a tiny flame for light?' He wasn't convinced. 'You've done what needed to be done. Let's walk out of here now, forget about workin' a copper mine. It's time to go back to civilisation.' He was tired and worn down by the harsh climate.

'Let's just see where this is going. Keep your gold safe. I'll put in the work for Joe, and hope for the best.' When Ben gave him an unhappy glance, he said, 'I've wrangled the beast, old friend. I have to test that I can keep winning.'

Now this early morning, Jac hoped he hadn't talked Ben into something that would kill him.

*

Robert Blinman, Joe Mole, Alfred Frost and Henry Alford had been granted a lease to mine in early 1861. The work would be back-breaking if they undertook it, the gouging and the tunnelling, and done in the crackling heat of central Flinders Ranges. It showed great promise; there was plenty of copper to extract.

Joe Mole had greeted Jac with the greatest affection at the site, and promised a bonus—from his own pocket for Jac and Ben's work—would be forthcoming after a deal was struck to sell the lease. There were, at that time, a number of lucrative leases in the area.

In February 1862, the Wheal Blinman copper mines sold for twelve thousand pounds to the *Yudnamutana* Mining Company.

Jac—his demons behind him, he thought—was glad of it too. He and Ben took their leave before the real mining began in the September; Ben needed to repair his health after those long years in an unforgiving climate. It was decided to head back to the mighty river that Ben had oft lamented leaving.

With good money in their pockets they waved Joe Mole goodbye. Jac was finally on his feet.

# Chapter Twenty-one

*1863, River Murray, South Australia*

Jac stood on the deck of the *Song-chol* and turned to Ben. 'Fresh air in our lungs, clear skies, fish ready for catching, and the chug of a paddle-steamer going upriver. What more could a man want?' Idly, he rubbed the carved spoon that hung from his neck and rested on his chest. He'd refashioned what Koori had done a long time ago—a tightly woven horsehair plait to keep secured. He stopped rubbing, fearful that eventually the carving itself would be worn too far and break.

Ben, on the deck alongside him, aimed his fishing spear at shapes darting in the water. 'Just tell the fish they're ready for catching.'

'I'm glad we're on the river itself,' Jac said. 'Lake Alexandrina was a trial. I don't want to cross it again.' They'd taken their first solo journey on the new purchase, the *Song-chol*, from the mouth of the river at Goolwa. The small boat, a shallow draught side-wheeler, had made it easily to Point McLeay mission but had tossed dangerously while crossing the vast lake. They hugged its eastern reaches before arriving at Wellington. 'Once we landed off the *Louisa Baillie* all those years ago, we went overland after leaving the mission.' He told Ben of the landing with *Appa* and *Eomma*. 'A lifetime ago.'

Leaving there, with luck and with good business management, they hadn't needed to return to Goolwa. Trade from Wellington upriver and inland, was the plan.

They'd only spent a short time at Port McLeay but it gave Jac pause to think of Koori. Jac missed him but knew the Aboriginal man had been uncomfortable in the homelands of others and had been increasingly wary. Language could've been a problem, but it appeared that hand signals were universal. Also universal, it seemed, were the drawings they etched in the dirt or in the sand. If verbal language was used, English was the most understood by any of the nationalities they'd encountered, black or white.

From the goldfields so long ago, they'd passed through the lands of the Ngarrindjeri people and Koori had sought permission to do so, seeking out the clansmen where he could, keeping his distance from the white settlers. As far as Jac knew, the indigenous people they'd encountered always allowed safe passage but that hadn't stopped Koori feeling unsettled. He was *Wadawurrung*, of the Kulin nation, and he had been, at that time, far from home. Jac hoped he'd returned safely to his country.

The goldfields were a memory of necessary hardship and hard-won fortune, same as Joe Mole's copper mine.

Jac had no longing to return to the dirt and the noise of the diggings in either place. He imagined Wheal Blinman would be at furious pace now. Here, on the river, was peaceful.

At Milang on the shores of Lake Alexandrina, they found a Mr Albert Landseer had made a prosperous life for himself and so Jac and Ben decided to follow suit; river trade was the lucrative market they sought. Mr Landseer had done well on the goldfields, too, and now his company carried wool and grain, timber, iron and bricks up and down the Murray. There was room enough for more than one good operator.

Only two things Jac and Ben had needed at the time: a boat and a contract. They soon stumbled across both.

By the time they'd trudged into the small and now industrious port of Goolwa, thirsty, hot and dirty, the long arduous trek from the Flinders Ranges became worthwhile.

They saw it almost immediately: the half-finished shell of a boat on a simple slip by the river. It had taken their eye. Raw red-gum timbers sat stacked beside the cured lengths of russet red wood. Painstakingly fashioned into a sturdy frame, it housed a small engine and a boiler.

A stocky man stood on the short wharf staring at it, hands on his hips. Close by was a rough looking cart with an old, tired horse harnessed to it. The man wore a pale shirt with sleeves rolled tight to his elbows, and braces to hold up his dirty pants that hung loose as if he'd recently lost condition. The hat clamped low on his head seemed ill-fitting. He turned. A smoke was glued between his lips.

He pushed back the hat and nodded at them, taking in their ragged clothes, their worn footwear, and the heavy fur coats of wallaby pelt. 'Got no work, boys,' he said dismissively. 'Findin' m'self in some bother without trying to help someone else.'

'That so?' Ben said as he came to stand alongside the man. 'Sad to hear. Looks like a fine operation to me.'

The skeleton of the boat waited patiently for more work to be done. Clearly unfinished, but there were no cranes about, no smithys, no carpenters. A fully finished barge was tied up only a little way down.

A shout went up behind them. 'When are you gonna get yourself out of the way, Driscoll? We need the space.'

Jac turned to find a team of men and horses pulling heavily

laden carts, tying up over yonder. No one approached them but unloading began as soon as the horses were secured.

Driscoll didn't budge. He called back without looking, his voice hoarse. 'I'll leave when I'm good and ready. You can't force me out. I paid my fee.'

'At last you paid,' the shout returned. 'You shoulda been moved along afore now.'

Driscoll coughed into his forearm, spat into the water. 'Two years fighting with the banks. And finally, finally they agreed. Two years, and now she's not far off done.' Driscoll was still gazing out over the unfinished boat.

He hadn't been talking to them in particular. Jac looked past Ben and addressed the man. 'That's to be commended. Well done, Mr Driscoll. This looks to be the makings of a fine boat.'

The bleary-eyed, slump-shouldered man cast a glance over them. 'But I'm given a death sentence. Just this mornin'.' His eyes vacant, distant.

Ben folded his arms. 'Sorry to hear that, Mr Driscoll. We're strangers here, my friend and me—'

'Can tell by yer speech,' Driscoll said, nodding. 'Watch ye don't get into trouble. They guard their territory good around here.'

'Who?' Jac wondered at that. They'd had no trouble so far.

'Those people. Those vultures.' He thumbed at the team of men waiting, who'd started shouting orders, and jostling their cart's unloaded stock. 'Steal your heart and soul for a place at the docks, they would.'

Jac recognised the mob's accents. An echo in his blood stirred him, nothing like it used to be. Nevertheless he breathed deep. He had to cap it. Opportunity was here, and his hatred of Englishmen would no longer force him out of the way. He met Ben's quick glance. He, too, had felt it.

'You don't want to blow, Jac,' Ben warned, quietly.

Jac nodded, and the niggling spark inside fell away.

'So, Mr Driscoll,' Ben said, filling the void. 'What death sentence are you talking about? If it's to do with the banks again, word has it this is still a lucrative area of business. My friend and I are interested in investment here. If you're local, your advice would be welcome, particularly where money-lending is concerned.'

Driscoll coughed again, spat, and what floated on top of the water was thick with blood. 'Investment?' He looked over at them. 'I'm no fool. You look like two ruffians, with nary a penny 'atween yer. I don't need more empty talk from ruffians, the likes o' them.' As he thumbed over his shoulder, his face flushing, his cheeks puffed. Then a coughing fit spluttering blood and snot, erupted. He grabbed a rag from his pocket but sagged to his knees.

Ben grabbed at him, stopped him toppling into the water. Yells and guffaws burst from the team of men behind them. Jac got to the man's other side and, with Ben, dragged him back from the edge.

Mr Driscoll was right, he had a death sentence; consumption. Jac met Ben's glance. 'We have to get him to a doctor somewhere. Use his own cart.'

The man pulled up his kerchief to cover his mouth. 'Doctor's orders if I'm near to folk,' he said, voice muffled, breathy.

Hands under the fallen man's armpits, Ben said quietly, 'Help me get him into it and I'll go with him.' He dropped his voice. 'Don't worry, I'll keep me distance from him.' Tuberculosis was rife. 'He's sick; he might be interested in doing some business. You agree?' Jac nodded as they got Driscoll into the back of his cart. 'You're better here with those smooth moves of yours,' Ben said, 'if that lot gets any stupid ideas.'

'I appreciate your help,' Driscoll said then fell back into a faint.

Ben alighted the cart, took the reins and gee-upped the horse. He called across to the teamsters, standing agog. 'We're Mr Driscoll's investors. I don't recommend you approach this boat if you know what's good for you.'

One of the men milling about the unloaded stock by the cart, laughed. 'That so? One man against all of us.' He waved a hand at the others.

'Aye, that's so,' Ben said as the old horse clip-clopped past them. He glanced at Jac whose head was bent as he studied the dirt underfoot. 'You good, Jac?'

'I'm good.'

Jac's rage against Englishmen hadn't miraculously evaporated in the scorching heat of the Flinders Ranges. It had taken hard, dogged work to dissipate, drop away to a low, manageable level. There were days when Jac walked like a half-dead man, not really in his own head. Finally, he'd had some peace; the rage had abated over time, hadn't reared for years.

Ben hoped it wouldn't today.

When he returned an hour later, on foot, Ben found Jac sitting on the dock, his legs dangling over the edge. He was admiring the boat and barge. The other men were nowhere to be seen, but their stock had been unloaded and was now stacked and tidy.

'You right?' he asked Jac. He didn't see anything that worried him. Not yet anyway.

'I am.'

That was a good thing. 'Poor bastard, that Driscoll,' Ben said, and held out a paper for Jac. 'I might've seemed a bit keen, but the man jumped at the chance to sell up. Said he'd put the funds to a stipend for his wife and daughters. Poor bastard,' he repeated. 'Got him to his doctor who put his signature as witness to this, then I took him to his house. He hadn't told his wife about the consumption, so I left him to it.'

Jac took the paper. It was a bill of sale to Mr Jac Owen and Mr Benjamin Polites for both the unfinished boat, 'Unnamed', and the finished barge, 'Unnamed'. A sum of one thousand five hundred pounds had been witnessed as transferred and receipted by the doctor. Jac could barely read the signature.

'It'll hold up, laddie.' Ben correctly read the question on Jac's face. 'He's printed his name underneath, means anyone can check with him. So,' he said, hands on hips as he surveyed the half-finished boat and the barge moored behind it. 'Time to get this new venture of ours fully in the water.'

Jac got to his feet. 'And take on our first cargo.' He pointed at the tumble of bales and boxes the other team of men had left.

'No bloody ruffians in sight. Did you demonstrate a few moves, lad?' Ben asked as he jogged towards the cargo.

'Could say one or two of them had a lesson and decided to sell up as payment.'

Ben stopped. 'How hard a lesson?'

Jac shrugged. 'Not real hard.'

Ben and Jac finished their boat. Took their time to get it right. They learned as they went along, gleaned information from their peers on the wharf, from some old timers who'd stopped by to offer expertise. They employed a boiler maker's team, and when the boat was finally ready, they unveiled the name of it, painted grandly over the wheelhouse. They pushed the boat off the slip into the water.

The *Song-chol* and its barge *Seamaid* had been launched.

# CHAPTER
# TWENTY-TWO

*1868 Adelaide, South Australia*

How long had it been now, twelve, fourteen years in Australia?

A hard but rewarding time on the Ballarat goldfields before lucrative years in the Flinders Ranges. Hot, back-breaking work in some of the harshest of country on earth, beautiful in hue, deadly in climate.

Joe Mole had written to Jac, reported that Mr Harris, who'd bought a part share in the mine had also bought a share in a clipper, the *City of Adelaide*. Soon Blinman copper would sail to market in England. Joe talked of visiting on the river soon.

Now in an Adelaide hotel and a couple of days easy ride from where they called home, Jac was in new clothes—underwear, shirt, trousers, socks, and boots. It always felt foreign. He glanced to the back of the door where Koori's gift of long ago, the ragged fur cape, still hung, reminding him of a life gone by, and in some ways, better days.

He reached for his amulet, the treasured Welsh spoon that dangled from the same hook. He looked at it anew; laughing a little, he used to think it was elegantly carved. After dunking in the ocean, then being hidden safely on Cheju only to have more dunkings, freezing with him in Ballarat, soaking up his sweat at Blinman, and recently many years drying in the hot sun on the River Murray, it didn't look as elegant as he previously thought. His repeated repairs on the twine were less artful than practical.

Worn, too. Perhaps not so sturdy any longer, the consequence of persistent handling over many years. His carving's design was clever, a key—the bittings now long gone—and delicate 'twine' wrapped around its shank. The bowl of the spoon was smooth, and deep. He figured it was carved from oak. He knew that the love spoons had meant something when passed between lovers who'd become husband and wife. His Welsh father and mother. He couldn't remember what the other spoon was, nor if he had his mother's or his father's spoon. Memory faded.

He slipped it from the hook and dropped it over his neck.

And Lilpah? No word of her or from her. Jac might well be the only surviving member of his family now. He put that thought away as he'd done every other time.

Adjusting his shirt, he reached for the waistcoat slung over the chair in his room. He touched the love spoon again and stood a moment.

Jac Owen, once gold- and copper miner, now businessman, landholder, riverboat captain, esquire. Ben had chuckled at that. 'Jac Owen, Esquire. Benjamin Polites, Esquire. Successful partners we are,' he'd said. 'We've well earned 'esquire', lad.'

The gold nuggets sewn into their clothes had long ago been put to good use. As they'd trudged from the Murray to Blinman, had eyed the copper of Robert's discovery, worked hard for their pay in Joe Mole's employ, things had now taken a turn for the better back on the Murray. Life would change forever, once again.

He sorely missed Koori. Jac envied his freedom and his staunch refusal to compromise. Koori hadn't enjoyed the prospect of the Flinders Ranges, and decided he was going home. And that had been that.

Jac refocused on the carving. Yes, he'd come a long way from Wales, from that child who stood snivelling in the great room of that dank and sinister house. From Cheju where, as a youth, he learned kindness and love and self-sufficiency. From the goldfields, where he met anguish and sorrow once again, learning that his demons had always been close to the surface. From Blinman where he'd grown lean and hardened and healed with the back-breaking work. And back to the river for a good life that sometimes seemed soft by comparison.

He buttoned his waistcoat. Today, he and Ben would meet with representatives of certain English gentry who were keen to invest in their colonial holdings. He was prepared; he would not fail himself.

A knock, a light tap-tap of knuckles, and the door swung open. Ben Polites entered the room they shared, took off his hat and threw it across the untidy room strewn with discarded clothes, papers, satchels, to drop on a bed.

'I've brought the cart around,' he said. 'It's only a short drive to the bank's merchant rooms, but better to arrive like gentlemen than not. And you look the part, Jac.' He looked him up and down. 'Slap a top hat on you and you're born and bred.'

Jac stood aside for Ben to get past him. 'A new cabbage-palm hat will have to do.'

'As fine as any top hat,' Ben said and held up his own wide, flat-brimmed hat made from fronds of the popular palm.

'We won't be mistaken for servants, then,' Jac said, and grinned. He bent and picked up a leather satchel filled with references, letters, and legal papers.

'Had we a rabbit felt hat, perhaps.' Ben pulled at his own waistcoat. 'Let us depart for our meeting, Mr Owen, Esquire.'

Top hats, indeed.

In the banker's meeting room, Jac stood on one side of the long hardwood table as the three gentlemen filed in. Ben stiffened alongside him. He was staring at one man who took no notice of him, or of Jac. The man was studying his fingernails and seemed annoyed at one in particular. He looked up as he was introduced. This was Mr Crawford.

Jac turned his attention to a younger man but was distracted when a stooped clerk entered the room. He carried a tray of nib pens and an inkpot and set the tray at the top of the table. Then he turned to place three top hats one by one on the narrow cupboard against the wall. He left the room without a word and closed the door with a soft click.

Ben swiped up their own hats from the floor and stacked them on the narrow table behind their chosen chairs. He adjusted his waistcoat once more, shifted his weight, cleared his throat. He was uneasy.

High-backed chairs, leather upholstered, scraped heavily on the floor as each delegate took up his seat.

Regaining his feet, one of the older men stalked to the only window, unlatched it, and pushed open both panes. 'Unbearably hot in this room, sirs. Damnable country. Adelaide city has turned up the temperature.' Barely a breeze found its way in. Returning to his seat, he pulled a handkerchief from his inside coat pocket and mopped his brow. 'Gentlemen, thank you for coming today. As you know, I'm Hamish Wood and I'm here to broker a deal between your two companies. I'm looking forward to arriving at a suitable outcome.' He patted a small stack of papers in front of him, his black-eyed glance darting across the table.

Jac recognised his own letters, stamped as received and dated, written in reply to Mr Crawford, the pale fingered older gentleman. He represented the English company, Lordacres Investments that had a London address. That gentleman now sat across from him. Jac had a similar stack of letters in his satchel, along with those from Mr Wood. He wondered why nobody had introduced the younger man.

Ben's chair edged closer to the table. Tension seared off him as he stared at the man opposite. Crawford was past middle age, slight build, receding hairline, thin lips, slim hands. Typical gentry of the old country ...

Jac took a breath, distracted himself by glancing at the young man sitting beside Crawford. There was something familiar—

'We'd already arrived at a suitable outcome.' Ben's voice was clipped.

Mr Wood only nodded and carried on. 'My client is interested in a greater percentage share in the partnership.'

Jac showed no surprise. 'That wasn't the original arrangement.'

The broker gave him a tight smile. 'Nevertheless.'

'A greater share for your client was never on the table, Mr Wood.' Ben sat forward, ignoring the others. 'Your client came to us to invest a small sum for agreed return to enter the marketplace. Five per cent, affording him little or no risk.'

Mr Wood's gaze turned obsidian. 'As you've just learned, my client wants much more, Mr Polites.' He turned his flat stare to Jac. 'So, I beg you both name a figure in his favour higher than fifty-one percent.'

Ben couldn't stop a derisive snort.

Mr Wood sighed, a theatrical noise that accompanied a tut-

tut. It drew an embarrassed cough, an unguarded response from the third representative. He was the younger man, whose colouring and demeanour suggested that he too, was from the old country and gentry. At a sharp look from Mr Crawford, he withdrew to silence, dropping his stare from Jac.

Ben addressed the young man. 'And who, sir, might you be?'

Mr Crawford sat forward. 'A witness only, Mr Polites, who's learning the business. Remiss of me not to introduce him. I beg your pardon. This is, uh, Mr Lester,' he said, dismissively. His gaze shifted to Jac and a slight frown appeared on his pale features.

Ben acknowledged the younger man with a perfunctory nod, and although Mr Lester had bowed his head as if to avoid further scrutiny, his glance returned to Jac. He couldn't keep from staring.

Mr Wood cleared his throat and continued. 'My client requires a greater stake-holding as just indicated. We're thinking in the vicinity of eighty-twenty, or higher.'

Jac sat forward, hands splayed on the table. 'We're not in the market to be bought out.'

'As they say, everything is for sale, Mr Owen. Everything has a price. We could negotiate. My client would abide a lesser share as long as he held the majority.'

Jac was stony-faced. Even at seventy-thirty or sixty-forty he would lose every gain he and Ben had striven for. He looked around the table, first at Mr Wood, a black-eyed dark-haired Scot, then at Mr Crawford, and then at Mr Lester. They all stared back at him. Jac took a moment before he answered. 'Then no, sirs. There is no deal to be brokered.'

All three nodded to each other as if they fully expected the answer.

'In that case, my client—'

'Who amongst us here is your client, Mr Wood?' Ben Polites asked.

# CHAPTER TWENTY-TWO

'He's not here, Mr Polites.'

Mr Crawford sat forward. 'Gentlemen, I represent the company. I'm a financial advisor for the principal of Lordacres Investments. I can assure you we are serious in our endeavours to secure a sound investment.'

Ben stared at him. 'A sound investment comes with a fair and reasonable price. We were not here to be bought out.' Then he glanced at Jac. 'Excuse us while we discuss a way forward.'

Jac took Ben's cue and stood with him. 'Five minutes of your time.'

'Of course.' Mr Wood waved them towards the door.

Across the hallway, Ben spun around to Jac. 'A definite no.'

'A rough beginning, ambushed by hostiles,' Jac said, arms folded as he leaned back on the balustrading over the atrium. 'Why the sudden interest in more than five per cent? There might be a lot more to Lordacres Investments than we're aware of. Maybe the river has somehow been appraised of flowing with gold.'

Ben paced the short balcony area. 'I know that Crawford from somewhere,' he grated. 'A long time ago. I never forget a face.'

Jac rubbed a hand over his forehead. 'I say we abandon these talks. Abandon negotiations. Five per cent was all we offered, no more.'

'Agreed. No sense taking things further. It was never about selling out.'

'No sense in that,' Jac said.

# CHAPTER
# TWENTY-THREE

Percy Crawford trudged back to his hotel, made heavy work of it up the wide staircase and onto the landing. He paused a moment to catch his breath, but also to choose his words carefully. He would relate to Sir Hugh that the first attempt at railroading the principals of Southern River Enterprises, Mr Owen, and Mr Polites, had not been successful.

It was to be expected, but who knew how Sir Hugh would really react?

His knuckles tight, Crawford knocked on the hardwood door. Lilpah, Rigg's 'companion', answered in silence. Her stare was cold, her faded blue eyes disinterested.

'Ma'am,' he said as she stepped aside to let him in. Closing the door, she indicated with a flick of her wrist the hook where his hat and coat should be hung. Without speaking, she turned and walked away into another room, and swung the door shut.

Crawford shrugged out of his coat and draped it over the hook, hung his hat on top of it. Smoothing his hair and taking a breath he turned for the main room. Sir Hugh was slumped in a bulky chair and Lester stood alongside.

The long journey from Wales to Australia had taken a further toll on the man's physical health, but his mind was still working, and at times, his recall sharp. However, he hadn't personally attended meetings over the last year or two, due to the threat of unpredictable bowel incontinence. *Damnably messy business.* Rigg had enough pride left that he hadn't tempted fate again—one episode of involuntary purges was enough.

The sea journey had been bad for him and, no doubt, for his troupe. How the man had survived for all those years opium addicted and apoplectic, was beyond comprehension. At least Rigg's perverted urges had been suppressed.

'Lester tells me you didn't have a long meeting,' Sir Hugh said, the words slurred, his voice low.

'Just as you expected, sir,' Crawford said. 'I assume the proceedings have already been related to you?'

Sir Hugh gave an almost imperceptible nod. His glassy eyes remained steadfast on Crawford.

'I'll continue, shall I, Father?' Lester said with an impatient glance at Crawford's interruption. 'And then, after a few moments, this Mr Polites became agitated.'

'Agitated? What say you about the whole thing, Mr Crawford?'

Ignoring the set of Lester's jaw, Crawford said, 'There was a definite rapport between the principles of the company. Very few words, sometimes only a nod, a glance here and there. It's true, Polites became unsettled. It was he who suggested they withdraw from the talks today.'

'And the other man?'

'Jac Owen, sir.'

'Ah yes, Owen.' The flaccid mouth moved, and Sir Hugh's tongue snaked out to flick over his lips. 'Owen. Curious. Same family name as Mistress Lilpah.'

Crawford schooled his features and remained silent. The resemblance between Mistress Lilpah and Mr Lester was strong, any fool could see it and know it for what it was. But it had been a long time since Crawford had put any thought to it. Until today because Lester also had an uncannily strong look of Jac Owen. He strongly suspected the lad had seen it, too.

'Common enough name at home, Father,' Lester replied. 'Just a coincidence, eh?' He laughed it off. 'But do we, ah, know anything about Jac Owen, Mr Crawford?'

'Only that he's another of the colonial rabble to have made good,' Crawford answered. 'Mr Owen's business is registered and is a success, which is why it attracted our attention. It's well known in business circles as a solid enterprise.' He had dutifully researched as much for Rigg as for his real master, Morris Oswald, whose interest was also keen.

The subterfuge had become easier over the last twelve years. Routine had been established; Foswick deferred to him in all matters. In the latter few years the man's services had become fewer due to his advancing age. That was when the Owen woman had stepped in, changing her role from nanny to the teenage boys, to somewhat of a housekeeper. Crawford kept an eye on her; Rigg had to be controlled. At times, she'd seemed a threat but with her mother's instinct firmly wrapped around her boy, she kept her counsel.

Lester nodded. 'I intend to find out more about Jac Owen.'

That wouldn't be easy. For a lad two years shy of twenty, not yet allowed any autonomy in the house, he had a high opinion of his abilities.

Taking up a crystal goblet he swallowed fortified sweet wine from his father's favourite vineyard in Portugal. Clearly the old miser had loosened the purse-strings a little. 'In the meantime,'

Lester said, 'we'll round up his main suppliers and buy them out, won't we, Father? That'll put the squeeze on things.'

Crawford resisted making a comment.

Lester refilled his glass and yelled, 'Mistress Lilpah,' and waited until he heard the woman enter from the other room. 'We need more port,' he said without turning to look at her, waving the empty decanter in her direction.

The woman deliberately paused, her stare cool.

She'd always been known as one of Lester's nannies. Those who'd been around long enough well knew she'd been Sir Hugh's prisoner and victim. Some even said she was Lester's mother; to look at them it seemed obvious.

Did Sir Hugh know? He'd never acknowledged it. He thundered long and hard about his late wife, Johanna, leaving him Lester, a strong son. Certainly, no one had never challenged it.

Lester still had his back to Lilpah, the empty decanter thrust out in his hand. His confidence wavered a little as he waited for her tardy response. Uneasy, jittery, he took a glance.

She finally answered. 'Yes, all right. I'll fetch more port.' She turned her cold disdain towards Mr Crawford.

The flesh on his arms crawled. The woman was an empty creature, but what she was said to have endured over those earlier years could not be spoken, could not even be imagined. That Rigg was now incapacitated, a pitiful creature to look at, did not negate the trauma and the pain he had inflicted on others.

Some said that there'd been an attempt on his life before. Had that been by Mistress Owen's hand? Who would know? There were many, many other victims of those years, as Mr Crawford had learned.

He shook off the thought—he wasn't being paid to dwell on the sinister past. He'd done well enough to get this far working for two masters.

The woman's stare slid away. She took the decanter, gave Lester the eye until he shied from it, and left, unhurried.

As a youngster, Lester had his volatile moments, though thanks to the ministrations of both his nannies—Mistress Lilpah and the other woman, Tippy—he hadn't become a cruel boy. Nor was he a cruel man, just one without manners at times, such as now, trying to flex his muscle.

Daniel Owen, Lester's constant companion, was a delightful lad. These days Daniel was not privy to the conversations between Rigg and Lester but it would all be related to him afterwards. Such was the strong bond between the boys.

Daniel also bore a resemblance to Sir Hugh, and to Lester but a darker haired version. Crawford was hard pressed to find a likeness to Lilpah Owen, and more to the Oswalds, if anything. Not that he'd broached the subject, but he had observed the charming Daniel held more of the Oswald's interest than the effusive Lester.

The whole place held too many mysteries and nothing would be solved any time soon: the Oswalds had kept more distance since the boys had reached their teens. Even when the trip to Australia had first been mooted, Oswald remained aloof. Crawford agreed; Rigg might not survive the return journey, in which case, their plan would be made easier.

Rigg addressed Crawford again. 'Even if they don't accept our terms from today,' he said, his speech laboured, hollow. 'We have a contingency, do we not?'

'We do, Sir Hugh. If necessary, we have the documents to confirm that the company in which we are interested could be on the brink of bankruptcy.'

Southern River Enterprises, owned by Jac Owen and Benjamin Polites was not in any such state, but the size of its mortgage could persuade a banker to accept a takeover bid to ensure the bank's protection in case of a financial crash.

'Good.' Sir Hugh slurped at a string of saliva over his lips. 'Now, Mr Crawford, to the other man. Polites is not a common name.'

'Perhaps not here, or in England, but in Greece—'

'Yes, yes, but we're not anywhere near there. Remind me of the man's Christian name.'

'Benjamin, sir.'

Sir Hugh struggled in his seat and grumbled as his head tilted up. His speech, though slurred for many years, was clear to those who were accustomed. 'I knew such a man. Not a very tall fellow, black hair, swarthy skinned, but with excellent English.'

Crawford nodded. 'A little grey at the temples, but swarthy, and yes, excellent English, Sir Hugh.'

'Now describe Jac Owen.'

'An accent of sorts, faint, but distinct, unknown to me. He would be past his middle thirties, I should think.' Crawford frowned a little as something occurred to him. Had he also seen this Polites man somewhere before? He glanced at Lester whose stare was on his father.

Sir Hugh's brow furrowed. He squinted as he thought back. 'This Polites. He stole something I was about to trade.' He waggled a finger in the air.

The old lecher's recall never failed to astound. Mr Crawford had heard similar utterances before from Sir Hugh and it had never boded well for the 'thief'. Crawford cleared his throat. 'Mr Polites is very highly thought of in the colony. It would not be prudent to upset—'

The bleary eyes turned owlish. 'Odd you suggest such a thing.'

Mr Crawford clamped his mouth shut. What on earth could Polites have stolen, and when? A glance at Lester revealed his curiosity had been fanned.

Without a knock to herald her return, the woman returned with a dark and mottled glass bottle. The string and tag around its neck attested to its quality and the cork had already been removed.

'Thank you for your attendance today, Mr Crawford.' Lester reached for the bottle and splashed a generous amount into his goblet.

That he hadn't offered any refreshment was not lost. 'Good day, Sir Hugh. Good day, sir.' Crawford inclined his head to Lester then turned to the woman. 'Ma'am,' and dipped his head.

Sir Hugh addressed her. 'Lilpah, you had a brother I remember.'

Lester snapped to attention and stared at her, incredulous. 'A brother?'

Percy Crawford decided not to linger to hear the woman's reply.

# CHAPTER
# TWENTY-FOUR

Ben slumped at the small table in their hotel room. 'I remember that Mr Crawford.' He rubbed his hands over his face and stretched out his legs.

Jac stepped over them to get to the tall boy dresser. 'From where?' He peeled off his coat and tossed it on one of the four beds. He'd paid for the whole room, so no other occupant could share the sleeping quarters.

Ben grunted. 'At Rigg Manor, the night I took you to Zephinia's boat.' He poured two shots of rum from a dark bottle.

Jac digested that. He turned and pushed open the only window in the room. It was cooler outside now with the sun on the other side of the building. He stared out into the late afternoon, his heartbeat a hard tattoo under his ribs. 'I don't remember much about who was there on that night.'

'You were only a boy. Crawford didn't stay. Got a case of the lily-livers and left before some others when Zephinia started to carry on.'

*Zephinia. Dead.*

'You think he remembered you today?'

Ben took a swig. 'He might have.'

Jac shot him a look. 'Wouldn't matter, would it—after all this time?'

Ben was silent a moment. When he spoke, it was as if he was thinking aloud. 'After all this time,' he repeated Jac's words, 'would it be possible that the reach of the beast has found you here?'

'What?'

'Could it be that this Crawford, representing Lordacres Investments, is in Sir Hugh's employ?'

Jac took a breath. 'A coincidence. There was nothing I noticed on their papers to suggest it. Lordacres is registered as a company in England. It has a London address.'

'But we never saw the names of its owners, its directors.' Ben looked at Jac who was shaking his head. Clearly, he wasn't taking the same leap. 'Rigg and Crawford were in the same vicinity in Wales, even in the same house at one point.' Ben got to his feet and paced the small room. 'There's no way of knowing for sure any time soon, short of asking it of them. Gleaning information from England would take months to come back.' Ben eyed Jac. 'You find it hard to believe.'

Thoughts bumped in Jac's head. He tried to make sense of it. He leaned back on the open window's sill. 'It *might* be so, but a long stretch. The colony is going ahead, the river trade is lucrative, word of its fortunes has taken the eye of English businessmen. Any number of moneyed folk could be interested in us.'

'All right,' Ben capitulated. 'Perhaps as you say, a coincidence but think on this: the reputation of a good business in this colony— ours—has got back to England, to Wales. It might mean it's not such a stretch, or a coincidence. Your name as a director on the company papers might be a familiar one to them, and certainly your face might tweak a memory.'

'No one would remember my face,' Jac said. 'I was a child of Welsh miners like hundreds of others. As for my name, it's common enough.' He folded his arms as a peculiar chill crept up his spine. A gnawing moment in the past that tickled and teased but would not reveal itself. Then he remembered. It was the look of the young man's face across the room, head bent, no eye contact. *Mr Lester.* It was a familiar face, yet how could that possibly be? Annoyed at himself, he said, 'I was one of dozens of children to go through that house, abused and discarded.'

'Let me find out who those men are.' Ben's gaze was piercing. 'I can ask for a meeting with Crawford. Find out who he represents at Lordacres Investments. We'd then have more information than we do now.'

'Does it matter?' Jac hoped the tremor in his voice wasn't noticeable.

'Aye, it matters. If the director is Sir Hugh, do you want him pulling your strings once more?' Ben caught his breath. 'A monstrous coincidence but if it is him,' he began again, keeping his voice low. 'Then he can answer for your sister's whereabouts. See how he likes that turnabout.'

Jac grappled with the possibility. It would be the greatest stroke of luck, good or bad, crossing the decades and the oceans, that he'd have the answer after all these years. Had it found him, not the other way around?

*Lilpah.*

Jac might be as close to his sister as reaching across a table in a stuffy room over an ale house bar in South Australia. His sister. The little carved spoon seemed to thrum on his chest. He looked at Ben. 'If she's alive ... *If* she's alive, she might even be here.'

'And if she's not alive, chances are, he's killed her. Or she died in that great house years ago as many of them would have.'

Jac blew out a breath between taut lips as his thoughts raced ahead of an unnamed panic. 'We don't do anything yet. We don't show our hand one way or the other.'

Pushing off the sill, he swung to look out over the street. The late afternoon sunshine glared on the dusty road, and the clip-clop of horse's hooves, the squeaking of cartwheels and the chatter of people on the streets all seemed to boom in his ears. 'I wish to the gods we had Elias with us. He'd know what to do.' Elias Barkin, their advisor since the goldfield days, had taken a journey back to the United States to visit family and was not expected to return for months. 'There's nothing to suggest it is Rigg,' Jac said, trying to reason, trying to put distance between himself and the possibility. His shoulders hunched.

'Except that this Crawford is someone I remember from way back, at Hugh Rigg's house, on that night,' Ben said, flatly.

'You said he left the room, left before—' Jac felt his blood prickle, felt the memory of childhood nightmares beat under his ribcage. 'I'll go. I'll seek an appointment with Mr Crawford.'

'Jac, wait.' Ben joined him at the window. 'This stirs up terrible memories and these could be powerful men. We need to think more. Maybe it's best to walk away after all, and not take it any further. Abandon the talks, find another investor. Better a colonial—'

'If it's him, there's the question of my sister.'

Ben's gaze locked Jac's. 'Aye, but are you ready for the answer to that question?'

# CHAPTER TWENTY-FIVE

Lester wouldn't let her pass. He dodged playfully in front of Lilpah with each step that she took to get around him. Too much port, no doubt.

Lil mopped her forehead with the palm of her hand. *Damn hot, this colony.* The city of Adelaide was by the sea but it offered no respite from the cloying heat. 'I'm not interested in your meeting, Lester. And it's not seemly to bail me up as if I'm some sort of servant woman.'

'Mama,' Daniel said, his voice chiding. 'He teases you. Lester, relate your important business meeting to me, instead. I promise to be attentive.'

Lilpah glanced at Daniel. He stood near Tippy who sat at the back of the room they shared. She looked quite comfortable; not at all hot and bothered. Was Lilpah the only one who felt the heat of this place? At times she could barely catch her breath. Sweat she never knew she could generate trickled between her breasts, and her legs. *Awful.* Perhaps she would take ime to bathe again soon.

Lester grinned. 'There was a man at the meeting, the other man besides this Polites character. Said his name was Owen. I stared at him when I could get away with it. He seemed so familiar, yet how could that be?' He shook his head. 'Looked well-to-do for one of these colonial types and, as far-fetched as it seems, I felt I knew him.' He stepped aside for Lilpah, giving her an exaggerated bow as she passed. 'After all, he does have the same family name as yours, Lilpah, and Father did ask about your brother.'

'A brother, Mama?'

'Long dead, Daniel.'

*Said his name was Owen.* Emotion tightly controlled, she looked back to see Lester's keen gaze on her. There was a glitter in his eyes she hadn't noticed before. *Not possible. It wouldn't be my brother. It would not.*

Hours before, when Sir Hugh mentioned it, she'd given a dismissive answer, said that her brother couldn't possibly be alive, and that she'd long since forgotten to think about him.

*Not true, of course.*

Sir Hugh had stared vacantly at her. There was no doubt in her mind that his thoughts were anything but vacant. She shuddered. A wave of revulsion threatened to engulf her.

Heading to the only window in the room and leaning out of it, Lilpah fanned herself. As the warm air swirled, she grew increasingly queasy. Her mouth filled with saliva and she fought to swallow it, and not gag.

Lester went on. 'This Mr Owen was not impressed when Mr Crawford let forth to show the rabble how a takeover bid is launched.' He looked back at Daniel. 'Was the strangest feeling, though. It was as if I was looking in a mirror seeing a reflection me, but twenty years on.'

'You've clearly spent too much time looking at yourself,' Daniel said.

Lester gave a laugh, but he frowned, troubled. 'Me, but not me. A wiser me.'

Daniel looked at his friend. 'Don't let it spook you. Though I agree it'd be frightening to imagine wisdom in you,' he said, laughing a little to lighten the sudden downturn in mood. 'In either of us,' he finished, realising his joke had fallen flat.

'Very funny. Your wit is unsurpassed.'

*A reflection of me,* Lester had said. Lilpah wanted to let the conversation go over her head. She had to, but she couldn't. She needed time to adjust her thoughts around the tangle of words and feelings, around the strange goings-on. Did it mean anything at all, any of it?

Her pulse thudded a little harder.

At the window, she watched carts rattle on the street below, watched pedestrians stroll, or scurry. The air smelled clean, only a whiff here and there of chamber pots and horseshit. Nothing like the nausea-inducing stink of London, or like the vomit-soaked, sordid, cramped quarters of the ship they'd endured for the three months to get here.

At least the hotel's rooms allowed her some comfort without having to venture out. It was one thing for Tippy to have coaxed her from the great house at home to go and sit in the field, or to visit the shepherd's hut, but entirely another to have her explore her new surroundings halfway across the world. It had been a torment as they'd left the crumbling old house for the Newport wharf. From there, her anguish had heightened when on the ship bound for South Australia, she'd been forced to take fresh air on the deck. The ocean, wide and rolling all around as far as the eye could see ... No walls, no barriers ... She'd felt sick.

Now, here, a screaming distress—which she could barely contain—would bubble up and threaten her days and her nights. So intense was it that Tippy could barely offer any comfort. Her heartbeat would go wild even at the thought of going outside. It had been persecution for her when they'd disembarked the ship in the port of Adelaide. On the coach journey to the hotel, she had pressed herself against Tippy, her head buried in the woman's shoulder and her eyes squeezed shut.

Thankfully for Lil, moving the semi-paralysed wasted hulk that was now Sir Hugh had been left to Mr Crawford. On his insistence, two manservants who'd accompanied them from England were the ones to physically handle the chair-bound master. They were to keep Sir Hugh clean, fed, and his clothes in good order, free of his own excrement. Thank god it had been their job, not hers; Lilpah attended his medicines and ... whatever else.

Mr Crawford had been about to deny Tippy Bowman passage but Lil's strident objections had worn him down. Tippy was an essential part of the service to Sir Hugh, she insisted.

Lester was going, and he insisted on having Daniel with him, a squire for a gentleman, he said.

Crawford still thought Lil's presence on board and in the colony would be superfluous, and annoying. He'd been about to object again when Lester intervened. He'd said that the two women would make their household appear like a wealthy one, one with servants who knew their habits well. *God knows, there are no other servants*, Lester noted sardonically. Daniel raised his brows. Lilpah bristled. Tippy had been cautious. They'd left Foswick to manage Rigg Manor; he'd assured Sir Hugh he was capable.

Lil wondered what Morris Oswald had thought of Daniel going halfway around the world but he'd have had no good reason to try and stop him.

How much longer would she and Tippy be able to remain at the big house? That was her most pressing worry. She hoped that when the time came, Lester would allow both of them to stay close for the rest of their days.

Her belly hollowed, unsettling her. They were in this hostile foreign country; the relative safety of Morris Oswald's mantle was a long way away. She thought that once they were back in England, she should meet with him again and discuss her future. After all, she and Tippy had saved Daniel's life, and the boy regarded Lil as his mother.

If Lester thought to be rid of her when Sir Hugh died, Morris Oswald owed her peace in her old age. To her surprise, the thought of him gave her a spark of light in her dark cave. She tried to snuff the spark; she didn't like surprises, but its glow remained.

Gazing down at the dusty street, the heat was a tangible shimmer as it rose from the dirt. Figures that moved about were distorted in a mirage. She was reminded again how far away she was from home and the hollow in her belly yawned wider. She clenched her shaking hands as a burst of surprised laughter brought her back to the conversation.

Lester had answered the door to one of the hotel employees delivering a message. Lester turned and amazed, said, 'It seems he's here, in the foyer, demanding an appointment.'

'Who is here?' Lil asked.

'Mr Crawford has sent for me because Mr Polites says he wants to tackle this situation head on.'

*Mr Polites.*

*Said his name was Owen.*

Lilpah sensed the world opened at her feet, not opportunity but an abyss. One misstep … *Too ridiculous to be real.* A coincidence only. Memories rushed from a night so long ago. A split lip. A shaking hand with the wine jug … a small boy wriggling in the tight grip of a—

Lil's pulse hammered the truth of it home. Her head felt strange. Empty, like the hole in her guts. Vertigo threatened and sweat popped on her lip. Her skin was clammy and her throat dry, swallowing difficult.

'You look like you need to sit down, Mama.' Daniel gripped her elbow firmly. 'This way,' he said and guided her back to the window seat.

*

Crawford met Lester and Daniel in the foyer. 'Both Mr Polites and Mr Owen have gone to the private parlour room behind the bar. Be prepared for anything but follow my lead and do not say a word unless I instruct it.'

Lester frowned. 'Should not Sir Hugh be here for this?'

'His health precludes disturbing him. I'm his agent, so it's best I deal with this. It would do no one any good to have his comfort further compromised at this stage.' *Though if he were dead, it'd help everything.* Crawford smacked his lips together, licked them, and then wiped them with his fingers. 'And you're not required here, Daniel. This—'

Lester's chin was firm. 'I'd like him with me as my second, if you will.'

Crawford stared at Lester. *It's not a bloody duel, you young fool. This could all unravel.*

Lester eyed him. 'You're not confident, Mr Crawford?'

Crawford almost snorted aloud. 'I'm wary, sir. Negotiations of this sort are fraught. Sometimes the outcomes of such business manoeuvers are not quite as one would hope.' So be it. He'd have to take matters as they came and hope he could protect Mr Oswald's interest, which indeed when it came down to it, was his own interest. He straightened his coat and pulled at his collar with a finger. *Damnably hot.*

*

'If we were home,' Tippy said, sitting alongside Lil, 'we would be freezin' our arses off, an' our fingers would be so cold we wouldn't be able to strike a match to light a fire.' She patted her face, wiping away the sweat, leaving streaks of dust on her cheeks and neck. 'Hot as Hades.'

Lil sat tight by the window in their room. Her finger on the sill tap-tapped in unison with her foot on the floor.

Tippy peered out the window. 'Nothin' interestin' down there. Well, could be, if I were a mind to go down and look. We're at a loose end, you and me now, Lil. The boys, all growed up, gone along with Mr Crawford an' all.' She eyed Lil. 'Makes me wonder why we're even here. Long journey for two women who ain't exactly needed no more, wouldn't you say?' She'd never uttered the thought aloud before. Lilpah seemed not to have heard her. 'Lil,' she prodded.

'Lester said that we make the household look respectable,' Lil said, distractedly.

Tippy barked a laugh. 'Respectable? We look like low born servants. You have last decade's dress still on your back and I'm wearin' the last of the cloth from the flour sacks.'

Lil turned, and her ghost of a smile was heartening. 'Then your grand gown is far more recent than mine, you braggart.' She wiped her mouth with the back of her hand. 'I hear you, though. What better way to rid themselves of us, than to abandon us here in this god-awful colony?'

'They wouldn't do that,' Tippy cried then tilted her head. Would it be so bad, now she thought about it?

Lil nodded. 'Oh yes. They could charge us with something unlawful and leave us here in this hell hole. Or not even bother charging us with anything, just dump us. Refuse to pay our passage home.' Her voice was a shaky whisper as the words tumbled out. 'That would kill us without even lifting a finger.'

Tippy's chin puckered. A future flashed in front of her—abandoned, dumped in the antipodes, in these bright sunshiny wilds where nothing was dirty, and—

Her head cleared. 'Oh, Lil,' she said. 'We done left a hell hole, that rotten hulk of a house in Wales.'

*This is far better, at least it's a sunny place. Aye, the heat of the day would fry an egg on the dirt, but the streets are clean ... And I ain't seen none of them strange animals killin' folk with their claw-pronged feet.*

Tippy huffed. 'And people like me have work here. Paid work.' She rubbed her face with both hands.

Survival was paramount. Would returning to that horrible estate be her fate when this place could afford her so much more? Her mouth dropped open as she stared at Lil.

For the first time, she didn't see her. Instead, she saw her freedom. *A life—short, who knows how many years left, but it would be a life, nonetheless.* She'd find the bag of coin she'd scrimped and scrounged and stolen over the years and hug it tight. She had it in her ragged belongings, in the room she shared with Lilpah.

*Lilpah.* She looked at Lil anew. This tired and beaten woman who'd never given up looked back at her. 'What is it, Tippy?'

Throwing her arms in the air, she said, 'I'm thinkin' we should stay in the colony.' Her breath caught as if uttering the words might cause her to crumple into dust. But nothing happened. Just a lifeline stretched out before her. Looking beyond, she had hope. She squeezed her eyes shut. *It was a madness; surely it would pass soon, but ...* 'It wouldn't be so bad, would it, to stay?'

'Nonsense. It'd kill us.'

'Like the life at Sir Hugh's has not killed us both already.'

'You're not thinking about the boys,' Lil said. 'They wouldn't stay here with us. If I stayed ...'

'You have been thinkin' the same,' Tippy cried.

Lil shook her head. 'If I stayed, I'd be left only at the mercy of—' She stopped. In the silence, Lil reached out and gripped Tippy's hands. Then, 'The men are doing business with a person I think might be my brother.' Her eyes were bleak.

Lil's mind was working too fast for Tippy to keep up. 'Your *what*?'

'The brother who abandoned me.'

Tippy stared at her. 'What are you *saying*?' She gaped and searched for the right words. 'Your brother never *abandoned* you, Lil. Not by choice. I remember.'

'And now,' Lil sobbed a laugh, 'He's in talks with my son. If I believed in the fates, that the shackles of the past—'

'What sort of talk is this?' Tippy balked. 'We can choose to stay here. If it is your brother, it appears he must have some means. He might be generous to us. I remember a kind, loving boy.'

Desperation rasped in Lil's voice. 'We can't *choose* to stay. And if we ran, we'd be accused of something terrible—theft, or worse. Sir Hugh would ensure it. It would fall in with his plans to be rid of us.' *What plans?* Now Lil was believing her own stories.

'We could be free here,' Tippy said warily, shaken. Freedom came at a cost—it was true, if they were caught running away and accused of theft, it could be death by hanging. But going back to England could be just as deadly.

Lil dropped Tippy's hands. 'We don't even know what being free means. I can't leave this room because of the fears I have that *shackle* me here.' She pushed to her feet and paced the small room. 'Had I the courage, I'd go down the stairs and meet the man I think might be my brother.'

'You have the courage,' Tippy grumbled, thinking hard, and wondering if she herself would do it. 'But what if he isn't your brother?'

Lilpah stopped by a wall in the room and braced herself against it. 'You have to be my courage one last time, Tippy.'

Tippy watched Lil clutch at the wall as if it were the only thing between her and a great chasm. *If it is Lil's brother, so what?* What would he do, really? He might dismiss Lil as mad—easy to think she was. She had a mad-woman's hair, and her eyes were wide and darting. A gaunt face, her body emaciated, ravaged by time—and by a monster. Or he might want to shelter her with him, here in this far away colony. But what of Daniel, and Lester? What of Mr Oswald?

*What of me?*

'Tippy?'

Tippy gaped again. Was it all out of her hands now? Had the past—what, twenty years and more—come to this? She shook herself. *Stupid woman.* Most probably he was *not* the long-lost brother. What sort of joke would that be on them all? That Sir Hugh's evil should reach around the world and grasp, once again, a boy, Lilpah's young brother, who'd been whisked out of his control years ago?

Lil's breathing sounded laboured, as if her throat was closing.

*Damn it to hell.* If it is Lil's brother, well and good, and Lester needn't be any the wiser for it. And Daniel? Well, it's no matter to him. *But there is Mr Oswald.*

'Wished Mr Oswald was here,' Tippy muttered and bunched her hands in her skirt.

'Oswald?' Lil asked, her voice croaky, but she was paying attention.

'Aye. He's not some weak-kneed milksop. He'd know what to do here. He's on our side.' Tippy puffed out a few breaths as she pressed a hand on her throat, wiping away a trickle of sweat.

'He's on his own side?' Lil's voice was incredulous.

Tippy glared at her. 'What are you talkin' about?' she snapped. 'It's easy to see his word is worth more than anyone else's, and you've a mind to heed it. Not to mention the man has a soft eye for ye, Lil.' Lil looked away. Tippy paced. 'All right, I'll go to that meeting, claim I have information. I'll find out who that Mr Owen is.'

'At the meeting? But Sir Hugh—'

'*Bah.* They won't let Sir Hugh be there, he'd dirty his pants,' Tippy said, and curled her lip. 'If I'd been thinking straight all these years I shoulda done away with him m'self. Shoved in a dagger and taken for the hills.'

Dear God, she needed to get to Mr Crawford before the meeting. It might mean nothing to reveal that Mr Owen could be Lil's brother, or it might put them all in danger. Chewing her lip, she wondered why she thought to do anything.

*Would that it is Lil's brother—*

'You can't just barge in,' Lil said.

Tippy held up her hand as she voiced her thoughts. 'I'll speak wi' Mr Crawford and perhaps he'll investigate. He'll know what to do.'

Lil sagged against the wall, her hand pressed over her heart.

'Wait here, Lil. I won't be long, I hope.' Tippy flew out the door. Sir Hugh's rooms were at the end of the hall; she'd seen his chair being lifted in and out of there and the two servant men fussing about. The door was closed; she wouldn't be seen so she headed down the stairs. God willing, and if she used her best manners, the owl-eyed clerk would tell her where Mr Crawford was.

*

Lilpah sagged against the wall. *Weak. I'm a coward and been a coward for years.* She shook herself. *Yes, and survived that way.* Air scraped along her closed throat, noisy, painful. *So now the survivor must prevail.*

How, when her feet were planted as if in rock?

She looked over at the closed door to their room. She should try to follow Tippy and go outside. Down the stairs. Her heart thundered at the thought. One step at a time. *A step.* The shakes came again. Her eyesight wavered. Take another step ... Oh, the worms in her belly. Her mouth filled. Her pulse pounded in her temples. She clutched at a pain threading down her arm, rubbed over the thudding in her chest. Felt the packet she kept hidden there, the two pieces of the spoon.

*Wait.* Something Tippy said.

*Shoved in a dagger.*

# CHAPTER
# TWENTY-SIX

Jac stared at the objects on the mantelpiece behind the bar in the meeting room. It could have been the owner's private parlour, but it appeared devoid of any personal items. Two single brass candlesticks sat on the expanse of polished timber over the fireplace. A statue of some ancient god missing an arm and draped in a toga sat at the other end. The obligatory clock—he checked his pocket-watch—with good time. A framed picture of Her Majesty, the Queen, gazing off to his right—

The door burst open. Both he and Ben swung about to face the short servant woman who propelled into the room, hot and overwrought.

'Sirs,' she said and dropped a wobbly curtsy. 'I were lookin' for a Mr Crawford.' Wide-eyed, her gaze darted from Ben and then it settled on Jac. Her mouth dropped open and she blinked.

'He's coming along right behind you,' Ben said and nodded over her shoulder towards the approaching man.

Tippy stumbled, her gaze still on Jac before she swivelled. She rushed back out the door to stop Mr Crawford before he entered the room. Breathless and determined, she said, 'Mr Crawford, a word, if you please.'

'I've no time now. As you can see,' he said and nodded towards the room. 'I was about to have a meeting with those gentlemen—'

'It's about that, sir,' she whispered, urgently.

He paused, about to listen, surprised by her fierce glare and the set of her mouth then his attention was taken by something over her shoulder. 'Whatever it is, Tippy, it'll have to wait,' he grouched and pushed past her into the room she'd just left. He shut the door without looking behind him.

Turning to stare at the closed door, Tippy froze until she heard Master Lester and Master Daniel behind her. She spun around. *Dizzy.* Too many turns, too much excitement.

Lester greeted her effusively. 'And what are you doing here, Tippy? Lost your way? Where's Lilpah? You two are never far apart.' He wobbled a little, maybe he'd had a glass or two.

Daniel spoke. 'My mother ails, if you recall, Lester. But Tippy, you look as if you've seen a ghost.' He was smiling at her. 'Are you quite well?'

*Ah, lovely Daniel. Poor lovely Daniel.*

'Tippy?' Daniel pressed.

Her eyes darted back to Lester. *Oh, dear God, yes. As sure as I'm standin' on me own two feet, Lester is, without a doubt, kin of the man in the next room.*

The door behind her opened and Mr Crawford called, 'Gentlemen, if you would?'

Tippy snaked an arm out to stop Daniel and pulled him to her. 'Don't go in there, Daniel,' she pleaded, a rough whisper. 'Your mam—'

He bent and said to her, 'Someone has to look after our young

Lester, Tippy. If not me, then who?' He patted her hand and then prised her fingers from his sleeve.

Lester was now in the doorway. Impatient, he beckoned Daniel.

Tippy wrung her hands and waited, undecided what to do next. Worried, she looked back up the stairs.

\*

Lilpah sidled along the wall of the corridor, inched her way past closed doors, careful to go around plinths under porcelain busts. She crossed to the stairwell, peered down. Nearly gave in when she felt the pull of gravity. She could let go and hurtle down the steps, break her neck. *Ah, what peace.*

*Coward.* She reached the opposite balustrade without looking down, her fingers curling the rail.

Against the final expanse of wall before his door, she shuffled, step by stealthy step, sucking in air. She was sure the wheezing was so raucous that if anyone was close by, they'd be alerted to the mad woman in the corridor.

She should hurry, but she couldn't. Her nerves were already stretched, taut and keening as if a bow on a fiddle string. Still, the time was right. Use it wisely. She almost laughed then. Wisely? She could barely move, and if her heart didn't give out on her—

*Nearly there.*

Any time soon, one of the two manservants would be taking Sir Hugh's soiled garments to the laundrywoman. He would return and then the other man would fetch medicine from the chemist. It was a daily ritual while the sick and ravaged body would sleep until it was time for his dinner.

Her hand came up to knock, but the door was pulled open. She fell against the jamb.

'Mistress Owen.'

It was one of the men, Peter or Patrick or whatever his name.

He carried a bundle of rags, and the warm stench of fresh shit wafted across at her.

'All the others are in that meeting,' she said, breathless. 'I thought I'd come to sit with Sir Hugh while you both go about your errands.' Since being in the hotel, she'd sat with him from time to time while he slept, for no other reason than to hope that he would stop breathing while she was watching. It had never happened.

Neither the man in the doorway nor the other man who appeared behind him seemed surprised at her request. 'Oh good,' the man at the back said. 'Leaves me free to get medicine. He is asleep in his chair, missus.'

She nodded, and still clung to the wall. She tried a smile and knew it was weak. Her voice shook. 'You know he'll sleep for ages now. Why don't both of you sit a while in the pub before you return.'

'No need to tell me twice, missus,' the man carrying the bag said. 'There's a good rum I've found in a tavern down the street. I'm off.'

'Bless you, missus,' the other man said and followed.

The door was wide open, and Lil rested on the jamb. She watched as the two men hurried down the stairs then she stepped into the room and closed the door. As she crept close to his bedroom, hooded eyes watched her from inside.

'I always thought it would be you to come for me,' Rigg said. He wasn't asleep and had hauled himself out of the chair. He leaned on the low ledge by the open window that swung gently back and forth.

The faint stench of him reached her and she pressed a hand against the terrible thudding of her heart. Slipping her hand inside her bodice, her fingers finding the broken spoon inside the little cloth bag. *Courage, coward.* She stood taller, just a little. Then a little more.

Ignoring her, he shifted his backside onto the sill, grunting with the effort, his useless bare legs dangling beneath his nightshirt.

She stepped inside the room, pushing the door shut behind her.

# CHAPTER
# TWENTY-SEVEN

The five men were meeting inside that room. Tippy stared blankly at the wall, at the door. Surely one of them would note the likeness between Lester and the colonial Mr Owen? Would she hear yells? Perhaps there'd be a fight, or even gunshots.

Her hands flew to her head. She couldn't grasp any of the thoughts, couldn't put order to them. What to do? What to do? What would happen in that room if it was discovered that Lester was kin to Mr Owen, not Daniel? *You only had to have eyes in yer head.*

*Get out of sight.* If any of those men voiced suspicions, they'd call for Lilpah, or her— Why would they? They were only women of the household, not important ... except Lil and Tippy *had* knowledge.

*Can't think. Can't think.* She had to get away from the door, had to get back up to Lil. Sit there and wait for something to happen. *Keep your wits about you, stupid woman.*

On the stairs, Tippy gripped the rail and hauled herself up. *No longer a strong young girl.* She got to the first landing, puffing, and holding her side. She made it to the first floor and took another moment before tackling the next flight. The stairs creaked under her plodding feet as she pushed on. She reached the second floor, and waited until she caught her breath, then headed for their room. She knocked briefly and pushed the door open.

'Lil, I tried—' She looked around. No Lil. Not on the narrow bed, not huddled in the chair by the window. She stood a moment. The privy room was downstairs, but Lil wouldn't have taken herself there. There was a chamber pot that suited most occasions and if the need was greater Tippy always accompanied Lil out of the room.

She shot into the hall. Checking left and right, she headed in the direction of Sir Hugh's room, stopping at the two other doors between and listening for voices. Nothing.

Dare she knock on Sir Hugh's door?

She couldn't hear a sound as she edged closer.

# CHAPTER
# TWENTY-EIGHT

Jac indicated that the three men should take up seats in the parlour room. The hotel wasn't a big place, but it had all the accoutrements of a fine establishment. He idly wondered that if he and Ben ever decided to get out of the river trade, he might like to buy into a hotel. Or maybe build one. Adelaide seemed a fine city.

He rested his hand on the papers beside him on a small table.

Mr Crawford spoke to Jac. 'Before we sit down to business, I'd like to introduce Mr Daniel Owen, a gentleman travelling with Mr Lester. It's a curious note that you and he share the same family name.' He watched as Daniel and Jac acknowledged each other. He turned to Ben. 'Mr Polites.'

'Mr Crawford.' Ben studied Daniel Owen. 'Good afternoon, Mr Owen.'

The young man stared. 'I am delighted to meet you both.' He addressed Jac, his eyes searching. 'And yes, very curious about the name. I'm from—'

Lester interrupted with a cough, although his gaze was on Jac.

Daniel Owen, still staring, said, 'Of course, first to your business, gentlemen.'

'To what do we owe your request to meet again?' Mr Crawford asked. 'I trust because it's so soon, that it's a counteroffer on which we can negotiate further.'

'I must disappoint, sirs,' Jac said. His hackles began to stir under Lester's open scrutiny. 'We take this opportunity, in person, to formally withdraw from negotiations. We will of course, put it in writing. We seek an investor who doesn't need control of our company.' He frowned. 'We have no intention of relinquishing control.'

Mr Crawford steepled his fingers. 'Halfway around the world is a long way to come only to be told the deal has fallen through.'

'The deal,' Jac said and picked up a bundle of papers bound by string, 'was for a five per cent interest.' He slapped the bundle back to the table. 'We agreed to that in writing. That you have come around the world for anything other than that was entirely at your own risk.'

Mr Crawford seemed unfazed. 'My investor has considerable reach, Mr Owen,' he said to Jac and looked at his steepled fingers. 'In fact, he has some sway in local banking here in the colony.' He ignored Ben's frown. 'Yes, we would put a proposal to your lender here to pay out your mortgage. I believe it would be met favourably. If your business is as good as your ledgers indicate, why then do you have such a mortgage? And bankers are notoriously ...' He seemed to search for a correct word. 'Nervous, are they not?'

Jac flexed his fingers. 'Our bankers have no reason to be nervous,' he said. Ben straightened beside him.

Crawford waved that away. 'No reasons are required. Now, I have the funds with me,' he said and nodded at Lester, 'in banker's notes, to clear your debt immediately.'

Lester shot a look at Mr Crawford. 'Uh—'

'Do you have the cash to do the same, Mr Owen?' Crawford demanded of Jac. In the bullish silence, he leaned forward. 'We can settle this right here and now if you prefer. I have the papers to hand.' He turned to the two younger men. 'Mr Lester, the satchel if you please.'

'The satchel?' Lester's cheeks flushed.

Crawford took a patient breath. 'Mr Owen, er, Daniel, go upstairs, if you will, and fetch the satchel from Sir Hugh's room.'

# CHAPTER TWENTY-NINE

Lilpah answered Sir Hugh. 'I didn't come for you.' Tired, she leaned against the closed door, her hand on the doorknob.

'Not to be with me then, my loyal Lilpah?'

Said to goad her, she knew it. She felt as if earlier, fire had been in her belly, as if its heat had threaded through her, but now it was gone. She was burned out, gutted. Numb. He was obscene.

'Or did you come to try and finish me off again, hmm?' He was immobile for a moment, his ugly, pale hands hanging over the back of a chair he'd got himself out of.

Lil felt nothing, not fear, not alarm. 'You were demented at that time; you can't accuse me of attempted murder now.' She stayed where she was, taking shaky breaths, watching, anxious.

He hauled himself along the ledge. How could that be? His apoplexy had been debilitating, and ocean travel had taken its toll. But here he looked stronger. It made her more uneasy. What else was he able to do?

'What are you doing?' Her hand slid off the doorknob. Her other was in a fist pressed against her chest.

He rested on the sill. He shuffled again, grunting. Waited, then shuffled until he could slump against the window frame.

'Why are you dragging yourself around?' She edged closer. Her hand clenched over the broken piece of carved spoon. A sting niggled. She'd cut herself. She'd hardly handled the spoon since it had been broken, and the edges were still sharp. The niggle deepened, a pain now.

'To breathe some fresh air,' he said. 'You can help me.'

'I won't help you.'

'You will,' he said and turned to give her a look. 'Because I command it. Because you want to. Always have.'

That leer used to signal his depravity but he was useless now, and helpless. She felt her lip twist, her gut quiver. There was nothing to lose. 'I want to—' a breath stopped in her throat, '—kill you a thousand times over, and over again ...' She swallowed her words, tightened her fist around the edge of the spoon. 'You can go to your mortal death, forever damned.'

He pulled an expression, a mocking moue. Tilting his head, his voice curled around her, 'Ah, and stay forever in your head. You loved me a little, I know, didn't you, Lilpah? You won't kill me. I'm defenceless now—you can see it. Look at me. Come be with me. Come help me back to bed.'

Lil stood there squeezing the spoon, her hand wet and sticky. 'Not back to bed,' she said. 'I'll help you up and over that sill.'

He hitched his shoulders once more and peered out. 'Not so far down,' he said, as if disappointed. 'It wouldn't kill me. Come to me, Lil.'

'No.' Her voice jagged in her throat, a noise on the air. Yet to do as he bid was strong in her. She took a step closer, tried her voice again. 'You can't command me any longer.'

He gurgled in amusement. 'You stupid slut. You'll do whatever I say.' He frowned suddenly as if a lancing pain had struck. Regaining a breath, he said. 'You always have. You were putty from the first, so protective of that urchin brother of yours, you did anything. And then the skinny little whippet got away, didn't he, and you still did anything. For years after.' He turned to look down the street again.

Lil choked on rage that surged inside. She saw nothing. Felt nothing but the thumping heartbeat pounding in her ears. She heard nothing, not his ragged breathing, nor the door opening softly behind her.

'Ah, Lilpah,' Rigg said softly, still staring out the window. 'My only sorrow, my only regret would be leaving Lester behind, my beloved, sweet Johanna's son,' he said, his voice hoarse with effort. 'Thank God he's strong, and capable. My Johanna was a good girl— poorly though she was—to deliver him to me before she died.' He scoffed. 'You could only manage a sickly bastard, although male, I'll give you that.' He turned back, and then his lightless gaze settled over her shoulder. The leer moved, and a dart of shock appeared on his face before his eyes narrowed, crafty, shrewd. 'Did you not think I knew Daniel had a clubfoot? I could've murdered him without scarcely lifting a finger, but I let him live to watch you dangle in fear for his life.' A hand fluttered weakly. 'And here he—' He gave a cough, his eyes bulged.

'No, no, no,' she cried, worried apoplexy was about to rob her of revenge. 'Learn the truth before you die.' Lilpah burned for telling him, burned and burned. He was staring beyond again, had stopped goading. *Is he smiling? Am I too late and he's already gone mad?* 'I've beaten you,' she seethed, creeping closer. Clenched in her fist against her belly, the spoon-dagger bit down. Blood soaked her skirt. 'You, so depraved, so many atrocities and murders of girl *babies*, of *my* babies,' she cried. 'Daniel is Lady Johanna's. The clubfoot boy is *hers*, forced on her by your rape. Lester is *mine*, and everyone knows it but you,' she spat, the shock on his stinking face not lost on her.

The click of a door sounded. She froze, then twisted to look. *Nothing. A trick of my mind.* Spinning back, she advanced on Rigg. He was grunting, and panicked, muffled noises came from his throat and nose as he clawed back off the sill. His eyes rolled.

His skinny arms flailed, flopped as she scooped her good hand under his deadened legs. She shoved and the window smacked against the side of the building, glass shattering.

With all her might, Lil heaved him out the window.

# Chapter Thirty

Tippy had heard a wild yell. She burst into Sir Hugh's room. The window beyond was wide open, and Lil was there, her fists high, blood trickling down one arm. Her feet gave way and crumpling, she slid to the floor, the jagged piece of spoon clutched low over her belly.

Tippy rushed to the side of the window and peeked out. There he was, on the ground, Rigg the monster with eyes wide and mouth slack. She turned. 'Get up, Lil,' she wheezed, dragging at her arm. 'Get up. Hurry. We have to get out of here.' Panic rose as she stumbled over Lil's rocking body. She tried to get her to her feet and pulled a hank of hair. 'Lilpah, come *on*, girl, don't let me down now. *Come on.*' Nothing but the rocking. Tippy knelt and took Lil's face in her hands. 'Come with me, Lil, come on. We do this together, like everything else. Come on, girl.'

Scooting behind her, Tippy hoicked Lil under the arms, and managed to haul her to her feet. Steadying, she said. 'Let's go. Our room.' Lil grasped at Tippy with her good hand. A pause at the door and then they scrambled out of Sir Hugh's bedchamber. 'Hurry now, Lil. Lift yer feet.'

Lilpah stumbled down the hallway, her bloodied hand pressed close. At their room Tippy threw open the door and banged it shut behind them, leaned on it to catch her breath. Blood still dripped down Lil's arm and she held up the broken piece of spoon in her hand. She looked as if she was seeing it for the first time. Her palm had a deep hole in it.

Tippy charged at her. 'Give it here,' she said and snatched the carving, dropping it into the empty chamber pot. She poured water from the pitcher on the dresser into it, pulled Lil over, plunged in her hand and swished it around. Pulling it out, she wiped it with Lil's pinafore. Tippy snatched a wet flannel from the wash basin, pressed it on the open cut in Lil's hand. 'Get in the bed,' she ordered. Then she plunged her hand back into the chamber pot, pulled out the spoon carving and rubbed it with the pinafore. Once satisfied it was dried, she returned it to where Lil kept it, in the little cloth bag tied about her neck, under her chemise.

'The servant men saw me go in, Tippy,' Lil cried, compliant, snuffling, and clambered into the creaking hotel bed. 'I couldn't ... I didn't want—'

'I don't want to hear. Not another word. Get your skirt off,' Tippy ordered and helped as Lil fumbled out of her clothes. Tippy threw the skirt and the pinafore into a corner and fished in her pocket withdrawing a sachet of nerve powder, a sleeping draught. She emptied it into a cup for Lil. 'Drink this. Now, that's all we can do,' she said, as much to herself as to Lil. 'That's all we can do.' She placed the tumbler on the dresser and sat in a chair by Lil's bed.

Then she stared at the blood-smeared clothing across the room and looked down at the trail of drops that followed from the open door. Nothing to do about it now—too risky cleaning up, she might be seen. *Think, woman. Think.* She eyed the bloodied skirt again as it lay crumpled on the other side of the room. Heaving out of the chair she marched over, snatched it up and studied it. *Yes, that might work.* She took stock, went back to her chair, and waited.

Soon foot traffic thudded along the corridor. They heard the muffled grunts and shouts as a door was banged open, heard a growl, a cry, a shout and then an eerie silence.

*

Tippy checked that Lil was calm and huddled in the bed, asleep. The nerve powder had quickly done its job. The hammering on their door seemed to come after much time had passed.

It didn't startle her. Composing herself, Tippy headed for the door and with a deep, bracing breath, she cracked it open. Daniel's face was the first she saw. Behind him, a man in a dark blue uniform.

*Good God, he's brought the police.* Tippy gaped. Air was thick, suddenly difficult to suck in. Her heart was in her throat.

'Tippy,' Daniel started, his eyes, reddened under a frown, wouldn't meet hers. 'A terrible occurrence. It seems Sir Hugh has taken another fit and has thrown himself out the window.' He looked past her to peer over her shoulder. 'If my mother is still not well, should we wake her?' His eyes were wide as he looked back at her and gave a short nod.

*Strange.* Tippy turned to glance at Lil's sleeping form before she looked back at Daniel. 'She's in pain—'

'Missus, we followed a trail of blood from that room to this,' the trooper said and pushed Daniel aside.

Tippy let her face pinch. 'Blood?'

'Seems the Sir took a fit and went out the window, but blood is dripped in the room.' He glanced around. 'Look 'ere,' he said pointing, and stepped inside the room, bending low to the blood splashes, and a couple of smears that looked like they'd been walked through.

Tippy stared. The trooper's pointing finger was gnarled, the nails torn to the quick, and his hands ingrained with dirt. 'Ah, yes,' she said. 'An unfortunate experience my mistress had,' Tippy said.

'What unfortunate experience?' The policeman squinted at her. 'What happened?'

'It were women's business,' she said, cranky, but her story prepared.

Daniel winced. 'Can this not wait, Constable?'

The constable ignored him. 'And the other young gentleman said his father could barely walk much less move hisself anywhere. But there he is, layin' on the ground under the window, him all struck down with nary but his eyes movin', his head and his neck gashed, blood everywhere on him.'

*So. Not dead.* Tippy pointed a finger at the policeman. 'Are you sayin' you think me poor mistress took Sir Hugh off 'is chair and flung him out the window?'

Daniel touched Tippy lightly on the arm. 'No one is saying that,' he placated, firmly. 'But Tippy, we must explain the blood they found.' His eyes pleaded as he nodded at her.

'It were women's business,' Tippy insisted, glaring.

Daniel glanced to the policeman and back to Tippy again. 'Peter and Patrick said they left my mother in Sir Hugh's room, Tippy.'

'Mr Daniel,' Tippy said, bringing herself up to her full height, still only reaching to his shoulder. 'She was in the room. And the blood on the floor is of a woman's private nature.' She indicated with a flick of her eyes towards Lil in the bed.

The trooper took over. 'Don' care if it's Queen Victoria's private nature.'

She seethed at him. 'She went from her sick bed. She'd been Sir Hugh's nurse for years, and now because 'is two servants had to be out on chores, she stepped in when she heard him callin'. Then she took a turn.'

'So,' the policeman continued, arms folded as he sauntered

across the room to check on the sleeping woman. 'Sick, is she?' He prodded Lil's shoulder; she didn't stir.

Agitated, Daniel said, 'Constable, my mother is clearly ill.'

The policeman pointed a finger at Tippy. 'You said this woman was in Sir Hugh's room?'

'To tend him,' she sputtered.

'She coulda stabbed 'im and throwed him out the window.'

'Stabbed?' Tippy looked horrified.

He raised his eyebrows at her. 'Ye'd better answer the truth, woman.'

'Ye fool man, I only know this truth,' she said, and with hands on hips, demanded, 'Do ye have a wife?'

'Eh?'

'Oh, I'll not be surprised if ye don't,' Tippy stormed, enjoying herself. She marched across the room to the bloodied skirt and snatched it from the floor. Holding it up, the blood from Lil's injured hand was a bright stain in the middle of it, clear to all, which suited her. Shaking the skirt in front, she thundered, 'I said was of a private nature. A woman's body's workin's, this is, and it's always bad with Mistress Owen. She took sick with it, as if it's your business.' Tippy tossed the skirt back to the corner and glared at him.

The policeman blanched and stepped back.

Daniel hung his head, mortified.

'I'll check with a medical man about them gashes on the Sir,' the constable muttered.

'I would say from the broken glass,' Daniel offered calmly.

The policeman couldn't meet Tippy's glare any longer. He stalked past Daniel and headed for the door. 'I take it ye'll be with the lordships 'ere in Adelaide for a while?'

'I will,' Daniel replied.

The policeman nodded. 'Good day to ye, sir.' He ignored Tippy as he marched out of the room.

Daniel turned to Tippy. It was a moment before he spoke, his features pained, and an anguish in his voice. 'There was attempted murder in that room, Tippy.'

Tippy was stern. 'Mr Daniel, no, there was not.'

'I was there at the last moment. I saw it.' He stood his ground under her fierce glare. 'And it seemed my—mother believed she had good reason.'

Tippy struggled with a reply. He wasn't going to give up Lilpah, she knew it, but she had to be careful. 'So put murder out of your head.' Her anger bubbled close to the surface. 'There have been many good reasons to do it over the years, when you were babes, and when you and Lester were youngsters. And long before that, because of terrible things that happened. But it didn't happen.' She swallowed, looked back at Lil a moment. 'You're both young gentlemen now, safe—*because of her*—and you have lives of your own.' She stared him down. 'Hugh Rigg is a—'

'I'll go back down to Lester,' Daniel said quietly, and held up his hand as if he didn't want to hear any more. He paused at the open doorway. 'Tippy.' He looked across at the bed, at Lilpah's sleeping form. Sadly, he said, 'From now on, all our lives will change.' He shut the door behind him as he went.

Tippy stood for a moment, and then put Daniel's words to the back of her mind. He wouldn't betray Lil; she was sure of it. For the moment, all was well. She crossed to the bed. The danger the policeman had brought was foremost on her mind.

'Weak-kneed, spotty-livered, good for nothin' trooper. The master's all but dead, and the trooper's a bit squeamish about a spot o' blood on a skirt.' She sat down beside Lil and patted her shoulder. 'Wish you'd done it proper, me darlin'. Wish ye'd stuck 'im hard with that bit of wood right in his eye, no less.' She stroked Lil's hair. 'Nary but his eyes movin', so the fella says. Then he's good as dead, after all. Old Hugh Rigg is good as dead.'

# CHAPTER
# THIRTY-ONE

J ac had stared at the bloodied mess being carried to the ambulance cart. Police were still around, keeping the onlookers away while the hospital men lifted the stretcher and slid it onto the back of the cart. They secured it and placed a thick blanket over it.

'Was that him?' Jac asked.

'I'd say so,' Ben said.

*Sir Hugh Rigg.* It hadn't looked like the creature Jac remembered. There were only shadows housed in his mind of that long-ago time. A snarly grin, or the key of a raucous laugh that sometimes echoed, would bring it back sometimes wherever there were crowds of Englishmen. He hardly recalled Rigg; he had never been one of the monsters in the dungeon, but the shrivelled, bony, bloodied form in the ambulance cart did not resemble anyone he knew.

On the other side of the road, Mr Lester, ashen faced, had mounted his horse. Crawford stood by with young Daniel Owen. All three men kept their gaze averted from Jac and Ben.

Craning his neck, Jac looked up at the window of Rigg's room. Second floor, a policeman had said to the ambulance men. Jac stared at it. His sister would be there, on that same floor. He was sure of it.

Ben said, 'I'm readin' your mind, Jac. They'll all be in a turmoil. Leave it a while. Plenty of time to visit later if you still want to.'

Jac let out a long breath. 'I'm not sure what I want to do. Not sure what I feel.'

Ben inclined his head. 'None of it is real yet.'

Jac looked up at the second floor again. 'She's up there. I know it.'

'That could be true, lad, but Crawford and young Lester will soon be up there as well.' He clapped Jac on the shoulder. 'They'll all be so sadly occupied they'll be a long while before thinkin' about us,' he said without any sympathy. 'We should get ourselves a drink in that fancy hotel of theirs. It's as good as any.'

The saloon bar was abuzz with gossip about the body that had landed on the road from an upstairs room. All manner of blather was touted, but by the time Jac and Ben had their tots of rum, conversations around them had dropped the topic about a *Sir of the realm being carted away*. 'Sirs of the realm' were not highly thought of in other colonies, but here in South Australia plenty of them vied for land and for business.

Ben rested his chin in his clasped hands. 'I keep thinking about the odd circumstance of that boy's name, the Daniel boy.'

Jac took a swallow of rum and pulled a face. He never really enjoyed the stuff. 'He's Welsh, maybe, and it's a common enough name.'

'Is it? And you'd know how, you've been away so long?'

'I've been thinking only that he could be Lilpah's son, therefore my kin. My nephew.'

'Her son, with her name? Then he'd most likely be—'

'A bastard.' Jac gripped his cup with both hands. 'Matters not to me. Except if his father is Rigg. But even then, we don't visit the sins of the father, et cetera, do we?'

Ben blew out a breath. 'We don't, lad. If the boy is their son, naught to be done. And no business of yours. You're not even sure it is your sister up those stairs.'

Jac frowned into his cup. 'And then there's young Mr Lester. You see the look of him? You see he has my look, don't you, and not the Owen boy?'

Ben only lifted a shoulder, remained silent.

Jac stared at Ben. 'Aye, you see it.'

Ben sat back, checking the people around him as they caroused at their tables. 'It's a mystery.' No one could hear, but still he leaned forward. 'One of them has your name, the other has your look. I can't make sense of it. Perhaps there are many such look-alikes in the village where you're from.' Ben scratched his head.

Hunching over his hands, Jac said, 'If she's so near, I need to speak to her.'

Ben pushed closer to Jac. 'And what if she doesn't want to speak to you?'

Jac shook his head, staring at his friend. He couldn't find the words to answer. Drumming his fingers on the table, he pushed his cup away. *What if she doesn't want to speak to you?* Would that matter right now as long as he learned that it was his sister, that she was alive? That there was a possibility of building a relationship with her—letter writing, a well-timed visit later? Just as he thought he could speak his mind, Ben was bumped in his chair by a pass-er-by and the table shuddered.

Startled, Jac looked up as Ben swung around.

'Oh, I beg your pardon,' a female voice said, her tone a surprise coming from a woman working in a bar. It was a little refined and had a friendly lilt to it. The young woman carried a beer jug in each hand, but her apparel indicated she was no ordinary barmaid. 'I'm sorry, sirs. I was so intent on getting these to Binky up there,' she said, nodding towards the massive bald barman with a nose flattened so badly it spread across his putty coloured face. He leaned on the long timber counter, talking to another man behind the bar. 'I completely missed my step. I've spilled your drink,' she said to Ben, as she struggled to hold the jugs upright. 'Come with me and I'll get you another.' She smiled at him.

Jac shot to his feet and said, 'You shouldn't have to pay for another drink, it's not spilled much.' His eyes never left her face. 'Your boss won't hear about it from us, don't worry.'

She laughed then, and the sound of it cranked open a space in Jac's heart.

'I'll tell him myself,' she said. 'But he won't complain. My father owns the place, he's behind the bar with Binky.' She thumped the jugs down on their table. 'Oh, do you mind? I never get used to how heavy they are. I'm normally doing the ledgers.' She shook out the fingers of both hands. She didn't seem to have noticed Jac except for a perfunctory glance.

Ben glanced at Jac then at her, and back again.

Jac said, 'Let me take them to Binky for you.' He grabbed up the jugs and indicated he'd follow her to the bar.

One last nod to Ben and she headed off, weaving through the throng. Ben lost sight of her but soon caught a glimpse of fair hair, piled high, as the crowd parted to let her through. He could see Jac was at the bar with her. A little chit-chat—when was the last time Jac smiled, and at a woman?

Ben turned back in his seat. They had other things to do. He leaned over his cup, contemplated a visit to their bankers. Might be worthwhile. Pay out the mortgage, beat this take over business, nip it in the bud.

A new pot of rum landed in front of Ben. Jac sat back in his seat, a smile still on his face. 'True to her word.'

Ben looked at him. 'What's that in your eye, man?' he asked, squinting. Jac shook his head, bemused. 'I see a glint at a pretty face.'

Jac looked towards the bar and Ben swivelled as well. 'Miss Sedney Verrinder. Have you ever heard such a beautiful name, Ben?' Jac nodded in her direction. Miss Verrinder disappeared into the room behind the counter.

Ben turned back, shaking his head in wonder. 'I don't believe I ever have. But a girl like that might be spoken for, Jac.'

Jac shrugged. 'Maybe.' He wasn't convinced.

Ben swivelled to look towards the bar and back again. 'Well, if a pretty face has taken your mind off the other business awhile—'

'As I live and breathe,' a voice boomed over Jac's shoulders. 'Jac Owen and Ben Polites.'

Jac jumped to his feet. '*Joe.*'

'Look at the pair of you, masquerading as gentlemen, for God's sake.' He reached cross the table and shook Ben's hand, then grabbed Jac by the arms. 'Happy to see the pair of you.'

It had been years since Wheal Blinman. Jac made room, grabbed an empty chair. 'Join us, join us.' He waved at their table.

'Soon as I let my intended know I've arrived.' He gave them a wink. 'A lot of news to tell. I'll be right back with a couple extra tots. Rum, isn't it?'

Before Jac could answer, Joe was weaving through the crowds, a slap on the back for patrons here and there, familiar with people. He must have been hereabouts for some time.

Jac watched him as he approached the counter. Binky gave him a crooked grin, and Miss Verrinder's father beamed broadly and waved him out the back. Joe was well known.

*My intended.* Jac felt himself deflate. Miss Verrinder was spoken for, and Joe Mole was the man. Bloody good thing he hadn't made a fool of himself.

When Joe returned through the crowd, Miss Verrinder came

with him. She didn't seem to mind the jostle and the rowdiness. Ben laughed with her over the spilled drinks and then she'd gone again.

Finishing their second rum, they talked of Joe and Miss Verrinder's impending marriage, of Joe's role as a bailiff in Port Augusta. They chuckled over the irony of the time Joe spent as a trooper in the district despite the run-ins with troopers at the goldfields.

'And one day, I intend to buy my own hotel. My sights are set on Adelaide.'

'A grand plan,' Jac said. It was good to see Joe, real good. He could have sat there all day talking to him, but he knew he had to leave. Miss Verrinder's presence in Joe Mole's life only highlighted a gap in Jac's own.

Ben finished his rum, stood, and gripped Joe by the hand again. 'We'll keep in touch now we know where you are.'

Out of the hotel, they stood on the footpath, their eyes adjusting to the brilliant light of mid-afternoon. Jac wasn't thinking anything. His belly was warm with rum in it, and he'd reconnected with a great friend. Felt good. He had to put Miss Verrinder out of his mind.

'There'll be another girl, Jac,' Ben said. 'Not like she's been the only one.'

'No,' Jac agreed, not even surprised Ben had read his mind. 'But she would've been one for more than a night.'

'There'll be another,' Ben repeated. 'It's just a sign for ye, that you're coming into yeself after all these years, that ye can feel good things again.'

'Aye.'

Daniel Owen came out of the hotel. 'Good day, gentlemen,' he said and tipped his hat. He carried a letter and seemed reluctant to linger, but he didn't stride by either. He slowed as he approached them

Jac spoke first. 'Do you have news yet of the injured gentleman, Mr Owen?' Strange to address another man by his own name.

Daniel stopped. 'Sir, he's in a fixed state where nothing moves except his eyes. A nasty fall somehow, through the open window, it would appear. He's aware of his surroundings, and he can hear and understand a little, but cannot move or speak.' He looked then as if he had spoken too much. 'He never gives in to it.'

Ben took the young man's attention. 'And were the police able to ascertain if a crime had been committed?'

'News travels fast.'

'Indeed, it does. We were having a drink in the saloon, here,' Ben said and indicated the bar with a tilt of his head. 'It was all the talk.'

Jac was intent on scuffing a boot. He scraped it back and forth over the rubble on the side of the road.

Daniel said, 'Mr Lester is at the hospital awaiting more news.' He shifted his weight.

Ben asked, 'Are you in a hurry? Maybe you'd like to join us for a drink.'

'I must find the post office. Mr Crawford wishes to catch the mail packet sailing for England tomorrow.' Daniel held the letter aloft, spun around and headed off.

Jac let out a breath. 'If he'd come to the bar for a drink, you would've asked him about his family origins, and Mr Lester.'

'Aye, I would have. But there's a better way to find out,' Ben said. 'These new hotels with their bars and saloons by law have to have rooms for people to rent, and they have to have records. There was a clerk manning the desk before. We should go back inside and find out who is travelling with Sir Hugh. When we get that information, we can devise a plan.'

*

The clerk was nowhere to be found. They waited for a member of staff to show themselves. Soon, a young woman wearing a dark dress with a pinafore over it and a white cap on her head appeared at the top of the stairs with bundles of linen in her arms.

Ben tucked his hat under his arm. 'Miss, we're looking for Sir Hugh and his family who we believe are living here. Might you direct us?'

'He's not here,' she said abruptly as she took the stairs down. 'He got carted off by the ambulance this morning. But the two young gentlemen still hold their rooms, and so do the two manservants. They have the whole second floor, and they're filthy beggars,' she said, turning up her nose. 'I woulda thought that gentry from the old country knew how to live proper-like. The old women up there with 'em aren't much better, neither. Talk to the clerk, Mr Whiteley, before you go up. Not my place to say.' She sniffed, stepped onto the ground floor, turned smartly, and walked back behind the stairs to a door at the back.

'Devoted to the job, then,' Ben said, and with eyebrows raised, looked at Jac.

# CHAPTER THIRTY-TWO

E ven as Crawford sent Daniel to post the letter to Mr Oswald's solicitor in London, he went over his conversation with Morris Oswald, the one prior to leaving for the colony. He was assuring himself he'd covered all his tasks.

'If the sick old reprobate becomes incapacitated or dies,' Mr Oswald said, a finger stabbing the air. 'You, Crawford, will see to it that young Lester defers to you as the agent, in all matters of the estate. He should already be aware of that. If he digs in his heels thinking he's finally lord of the place, state to him that, pending probate, his affairs retract to his holdings in Wales, nothing more. Produce the paper with Sir Hugh's signature on it, fob him off, and make haste returning to Britain. I'll take over. Under no circumstances are you to go ahead with any bid for the colonial company or anything otherwise. Is that clear?'

Crawford had previously become aware of Sir Hugh's interest in Southern River Enterprises in South Australia—it had emerged most conveniently at one of his visits—and he'd reported as much to Oswald. They then sought information on the company and had it confirmed as a sound business. They orchestrated Sir Hugh's offer. By the by, a curious fact had surfaced. On the company's papers, the family name of one of the directors in the colony, Owen, was the same family name as Mistress Lilpah's.

Mr Oswald eyes had lit with interest. 'That is curious. Hardly an unusual name, though.'

Mr Crawford's memory had been tested. 'I do recall an event from years ago—it left a nasty taste in my mouth. A few us had been invited to invest in Sir Hugh's illegal trading. It was during the Opium War. Worse, young boys were on offer in the manor house that night, and one of them was Mistress Lilpah's young brother.' He remembered the surge of bile in his throat at the time, and that he had, amid the snorts of drunken derision, immediately taken his leave. 'The boy was apparently taken away. It might only be coincidence, but there's a chance he could have ended up in the colonies.'

It was some moments before Oswald spoke again. 'If there is a familial connection between her and this Mr Owen of Southern River Enterprises, I've no objection to your revealing it. In fact, if it is so, it could prove in my favour to reunite them. Mistress Lilpah is a strong woman, and I much admire her. I should like to make her more than an acquaintance.'

Crawford had kept his surprise to himself.

Once they were in the South Australian colony and at their business meeting, Mr Crawford indeed saw a resemblance between the healthy, strapping man who was Jac Owen, and the emaciated woman who was Lilpah Owen. It was there, a shadow in her face but more in the shape and intensity of their blue eyes. He could see now how Lester and Jac Owen could possibly be related. It niggled at him, but he dared not question Mr Jac Owen. He tossed it off, not wanting to think what it meant.

He sent Mr Oswald as much information as he had about Sir Hugh's teetering health and bad turn. He reported Sir Hugh's plan, and the failed takeover. Regardless, although mail could take up to twelve weeks to reach England, he was authorised to act on Mr Oswald's behalf.

He was also Sir Hugh's agent. A plan of action had already been discussed: if Sir Hugh died in the colony, which now seemed likely, then Crawford was to handle—*guide*—Lester in business matters and return with the small entourage to England.

Mr Oswald would begin his takeover of Sir Hugh's property. He'd present his case to the Queen and because he was prepared to pay the last of the back taxes owed, it might be looked on favourably. If so, he'd acquire the deeds of the land and the crumbling hulk of a manor house, hopefully before it deteriorated further.

Lester Rigg would be at the mercy of his uncle for a few years yet. Confusing set of circumstances.

God knows what Mr Oswald would do with Lilpah Owen, and her son, Daniel. If he was interested in the woman, he'd perhaps keep her close. What of the faithful, wily Tippy Whatever-her-name? (She'd been around so long she was grafted onto the woodwork.) *Rabble.* Mr Oswald should cast them all out. Then again, he didn't strike Crawford as a heartless man. He was sure there'd be a plan for those three, he just wasn't privy to it.

Nothing for him to ponder; he had his immediate future to draft. Crawford put aside his uneasy thoughts, pulled on a coat and hat and walked a couple of city blocks to the hotel where Mr Owen and Mr Polites were accommodated. He sat in the foyer to wait.

*

It was late afternoon before Lester returned. He'd taken the rented horse back to the stables and had walked the short distance to the hotel.

Daniel met him as he ascended to the second floor of the hotel. 'Any better news, my friend?'

Lester shook his head. 'It appears it was broken glass that cut him, not to mention his head had split landing in the dirt. He is unable to do anything for himself. I'm to prepare for the worst.'

'It would be a blessing if he dies.'

Lester looked to the ceiling. 'He'd laugh at that. I remember he'd say that if he'd been a believer, he'd go to hell for all his sins. Then he'd laugh as if it were a huge joke.'

Daniel said nothing. People in the village at home had long hoped that Hugh Rigg would die a terrible death. Both young men knew that on the manor grounds far from the house, the earth was humped in many places, haphazardly, as if the contents of the holes had been hastily thrown in and forgotten. There were stories that those who opposed Hugh Rigg were buried there. They both knew of worse stories. Of the nameless women who came and who never left. There were some that were not mounds at all but only hollows in the dirt. Dead babies.

So Daniel said nothing more but not out of deference to Sir Hugh—it would indeed be a blessing for everyone if he did die—but because of Lester, and of what Daniel now knew.

Lester clamped a hand on Daniel's arm. 'I know he's an abhorrent creature but he is my father.' He leaned on the balustrade, folded his arms, and gave Daniel a bleak look. 'If there is truth between us, we both know he's your father, too.'

Daniel bent his head, was careful with his words. 'We've been brought up as brothers, and you as the legitimate son.'

'So you already knew it?'

'I'd suspected, but I was never interested enough to ask it of anyone, certainly not Sir Hugh. Why would I? I'd seen what happened to those who questioned him.' Daniel looked up. 'When did you learn about me?'

'Lilpah is—was his mistress, and there was always talk of it. Often there's truth in rumour, in servants' whispers.' Lester drew in a long breath and let it out. 'And they thought I wouldn't understand if I overheard.' Lester rubbed his eyes. 'It doesn't matter, not to me.'

Daniel just nodded.

'If he dies here,' Lester went on, 'I have no idea what might befall me.'

Taking a sharp breath, Daniel said, 'Mr Crawford will have things in hand, he's the agent. I'm sure there'd have been some contingency plan before we left England. Come along. We don't need to discuss this now. There's dinner downstairs, and a good rum. We'll rub shoulders with the colonial throng and forget things for a while.'

Lester nodded, grateful for the distraction. As he moved off the landing, he said, 'And Mistress Lilpah? Is she recovered?'

'She's sleeping.'

Lester stood alongside him, his brow furrowed a little. 'Whatever happens, Daniel, we are brothers, and friends, are we not?'

'We are brothers, and good friends,' Daniel said. 'We always have been.'

*

Tippy listened at the door. The young men were planning to go to the dining room for a meal. 'I heard him say that the master is naught able to do anything for himself.'

Lilpah sat in her bed, groggy with the after-effects of the sleeping draught. 'I didn't plan to kill him, Tippy.'

'Did you not? Well, you didn't kill 'im, more's the pity. If he wakes and tells, we'll be lucky we don't hang for it.'

'He knew Daniel had a clubfoot. He said he'd let him live to watch me dangle in fear for his life.' Lil tried to laugh but it sounded like a choke instead. 'He left me that boy alive, not even *my* boy, yet he murdered his own daughters.'

'Aye, he's depraved, and where he's goin', he won't have no mercy.'

'Bah, mercy. He'll die, and his bones will rot. The end. There's no retribution.'

Tippy wiped her nose on the back of her hand. 'Well, before he dies, we'll tell him what we think of him, the old scum.'

'I wanted to stab his eyes, but that would only kill him once. I want him to die in agony over and over again.' Lilpah swiped hair away from her face. 'I told him that Lester is my son, not his precious Johanna's. He knew it was true, just like that.' She flicked her fingers. 'He knew all along about Daniel having a deformity. Who could have betrayed us?'

'Lil, it was so long ago. All that matters is that he let the boy live.'

'If only to watch my torment that he'd find out and snatch him away, too,' Lilpah cried.

Tippy nodded. 'Aye, that's the beast he is.'

# CHAPTER
# THIRTY-THREE

A s they walked back into the Duke of York hotel, Jac dug Ben in the ribs.

Mr Crawford was sitting in the foyer and stood immediately. 'I regret that this is just before your dinner, sirs, but if I might have a few minutes of your time,' he said. At Jac's frown, and Ben's consternation, he added, 'Mr Hamish Wood—you recall our business agent at the meeting—advised that this is your accommodation.'

Jac knew someone must've followed them. 'A very thorough agent for you, Mr Crawford,' he said benignly.

'He is, indeed.' Crawford waved towards the bar. 'If you please, gentlemen?'

They took up seats in the compact saloon, and the aroma of hops hung in the air. Making their choices, drinks were delivered to their table.

Nursing a cup of port wine, Crawford said, 'This unfortunate business with Sir Hugh's health has impacted a number of plans that were to be implemented.'

Jac leaned back in his chair. 'Before we continue, Mr Crawford,' he said. 'To be clear, it is Sir Hugh Rigg, and his manor house is in *Tŷ du*,' Jac said, then translated the Welsh. 'Rogerstone.'

There was a hesitation before Crawford said, 'That is he.'

Jac didn't move. Ben closed his eyes briefly.

Crawford continued. 'It's a complicated situation and, due to the turn of events, it would now not be in the best interests of my employer to press a takeover bid.' He met Jac's gaze briefly, flicked a glance at Ben and cleared his throat. When no response was forthcoming from either, he went on. 'We won't be pursuing investment in your company at this time.'

Ben checked Jac whose stoic lack of response was not lost on him. He said, 'Thank you, Mr Crawford, for informing us directly.'

Crawford shifted in his seat and took a sip of wine. He began to speak, changed his mind, then tried again. 'The outcome of Sir Hugh's so-called medical event is not yet clear, and while that is the case, I am the proxy for my employer. However, should Rigg die, his son, of course, succeeds him.'

Jac had no reason to respond.

Ben lifted a shoulder. 'As we would understand. But why is that our business?'

'I'd been instructed to return home as soon as possible should things not proceed according to plan,' Crawford said, and paused before continuing. 'However, there's another reason for my being here to meet you.' He wiped a hand on his trousers.

Ben looked at Jac again. Nothing but a fixed stare on Crawford.

'Mr Polites, my recognition of you, sir, is sketchy, to say the least.' Crawford turned to Jac. 'But you, Mr Owen, I remember. I remember that you were a young boy at Rigg Manor, in the presence of a filthy degenerate by the name of Zephinia, and Sir Hugh, an equally degenerate individual, on an evening I wish I could forget.' He brushed a hand over his mouth. 'You never saw your sister, Lilpah Owen again. You were taken away—I presume it was under your arm, Mr Polites.'

'It was.'

'I left not long after that, sickened to my guts,' Mr Crawford said, his eyes downcast. 'I did nothing, just left.'

Jac sat rigid in his seat, clenching the arms of the chair.

Looking up at Jac, Mr Crawford said, 'My employer wishes to inform you that your sister is indeed here in Adelaide, travelling with Sir Hugh's small entourage.'

Lilpah stirred in the bed. She moaned and turned on her back. Opening her eyes, she fumbled with the bedcovers and held her sore hand aloft. Scowling, she focused on the bandage around her palm.

Tippy leaned forward '*Ydych chi'n newynog*? You hungry, Lil?' She pointed to a cup of dark liquid. 'You've slept all day and night, and now it's late mornin'. Can you get a little tea into ye? I cooled it down a bit.'

Lil struggled to push herself up with one good hand. Tippy hooked her under one arm and heaved her forward. She stuffed thin pillows behind Lil's back and handed her the tea. She unwound the ragged bandage on Lil's hand. It came off easily enough and she saw a neat scab had formed. 'Better'n I thought,' she said and sat back, throwing the rag to the floor. 'Now, I got news. Mr Crawford sent Daniel here this morning.'

Lil's brow furrowed. 'Is Sir Hugh dead?'

'Not yet. But better news than even that,' Tippy said, beaming.

*

'She won't come out of our room, Daniel,' Tippy said at the foot of the staircase near the saloon bar.

'I'll go up and get her. Is she dressed?'

Tippy nodded. 'She's had a wash, I helped her dress. She's been sat in the chair, staring at the wall ever since.'

Daniel nodded. From time to time his mother would keep herself locked away in her room. 'Maybe we should wait a while.' He looked towards the lounge room.

The room had been hired in Mr Verrinder's hotel specifically for Lilpah to meet Jac Owen. There was no doubt that they were siblings—memories had been shared, and dates validated. Daniel watched Mr Owen pace or stop every so often to say a word or two to Mr Polites. He seemed nervous.

Tippy sighed, and said, 'I'll go up and sit with her again. Perhaps she's calmed herself.' She took hold of the balustrade and climbed four or five steps before she turned. 'Where is Lester?' she asked.

'In the saloon.'

'Maybe he could more convince her to come down. You know how very fond of him she is,' Tippy said, her face alight. She turned again and made her way slowly up the stairs.

Daniel watched for a moment before he headed for the bar.

*

Tippy stood in front of her. 'You can stop that rockin' in ye chair right this minute. Naught's to happen to ye.'

Breathing in and holding it, letting it go and breathing in again, Lil gradually stopped the rocking. 'I've decided, Tippy.'

'Have ye?' Tippy asked. Waiting in the silence, she finally asked, 'And what's it to be?' She marched over and thrust the window, the hinges easily carrying the heavy frame. Air drifted in, warm and clean.

Lilpah wiped the back of her good hand over her nose and cheeks, under her chin and down her throat. 'Can you help me fix my hair? My sore hand hurts and I can't keep my arms held up for long. My heart is pounding so hard.'

Tippy tut-tutted. 'Stop whingein'. We'll get you right.'

Lilpah had time to don a clean house dress Tippy had found somewhere, and to have her hair pinned.

At the knock on the door, Lil froze. It opened, and Lester stood there. 'Can I help you down the stairs, Mistress Lilpah?'

'I can't go down the stairs,' she cried, suddenly then her face softened at the look of her boy. Oh, to feel his face in her hands again.

There was an impatience when he came to squat by her chair. 'Lilpah. You'll take my arm and we'll go down the stairs.' As if an afterthought, he said kindly, 'Daniel waits for us, also.'

# CHAPTER
# THIRTY-FOUR

J ac and Ben looked toward the open doorway. Young Lester
Rigg and Daniel Owen flanked a stooped, gaunt pale woman
with neatly pinned hair. Tippy followed along behind, hovering, until she spotted a chair. With arms waving, she directed
the boys and the woman towards it.

Ben sucked in a sharp breath. Jac stared at her, struck dumb.

Daniel stumbled back, leaving Lester alone to guide the woman
to the chair. She straightened a little and pushed away from Lester,
without taking the seat. One of her hands was bandaged and the
other was pressed to her chest, as if something pained her there.
Then she met Jac's eye, recognised him, her mouth moving. No
sound came.

Years echoed in Jac's brain. His fearful cries boomed in dark
spaces as memories funnelled back to him, down long corridors
of time. Her soothing voice, her strength, and her warmth as he'd
huddled for protection back then in the safety of her arms wrapped
around him.

There was nothing in this woman of that girl.

'No.' Jac's voice shook. 'No,' he said again, his voice hoarse. 'My sister is fierce, and brave, and—'

'She used to be, Jac.' Lilpah's mouth had twitched. She opened her good hand and flicked something at him. He looked at his feet where two pieces of twig fell. 'But now, she's broken.'

His eyes watered. This pitiful creature, this ill woman, her skin sickly pale, her once soft reddy gold hair streaked with wiry grey, was his sister. He would care for her. He wanted to say something else, but his chin shook. He looked about him, at the strangers in his midst and his gaze settled on Daniel who backed out, his feet sluggish, his eyes wide.

Mr Crawford appeared behind Daniel. 'Hold, lad,' he said quietly, a hand on his shoulder, gripping his collar. 'Mr Lester, if you would come this way,' he called, and beckoned him to the door. Lester had been gaping from Lilpah to Jac Owen, but he answered Mr Crawford's instruction and left, closing the door.

Tippy stepped beside Lilpah and gripped her forearm as she spoke to Jac with joy in her voice. 'Ye growed up strong, and brown, Jac, where the sun got ye.'

He blinked at her. Recognition dawned, and he nodded. *Tippy.* 'Aye.' He looked back at Lilpah, fumbled in his pocket, and bent to retrieve the pieces of the broken spoon.

Tippy went on. 'And I remember you, Mr Polites, though ye got white hairs on yer head now, and not so much the look of a pirate. And I seem to recall ye were taller in yer boots.'

'Ah, that was me, Mistress—Tippy? Aye, I was taller in me boots, those days.'

The words floated about Jac's head, jovial and fun, words light enough to lift the spirits. He straightened beside Ben, Lilpah's broken spoon cradled in the palm of his hand. His eyes were wet as he looked at it. He pulled his own spoon from his pocket. The horse-hair twine that Seo-yeon had plaited for him, so long ago now, was mostly gone, threaded through with other twines over the years. A living history that wove the presence of all his parents around the twig of his carving.

'You kept it all these years,' he said, noting the shadow behind her eyes. 'But Lilpah, it's only the spoon that's broken.'

'A talisman,' she said, her face contorted with emotion. She scoffed. 'I believed it would keep me safe and keep my memories alive.' She tried to stand apart from Tippy but couldn't manage it.

Jac couldn't keep his thoughts straight. 'Are you Sir Hugh's wife?'

'Never,' Lil spat. Tippy gripped her arm and held her. 'But I belong there.'

She need not belong there, Jac thought. He'd look after her here, in the colony, that she need never go back to that house. 'You don't belong—'

'You *left*,' she burst, a ragged sob escaping. 'You left me there while you went on your adventure into the damned sunshine. *Fy mrawd*,' she railed at him. '*My brother* left me. The only family I had left in the whole world and you *left* me.'

Jac blanched, faltered under the hurt and betrayal in her voice. The young child inside him cried, a wail from long ago. 'No.'

Ben stepped forward. 'Nay, lass. I took him. He didn't leave you. He was a child—'

'*I* was a child, too, but you didn't take me,' she accused.

'I couldn't take you. Yours would've been a more terrible fate.' Ben looked as if he was about to weep.

'That is not possible,' she hissed. 'We should have gone together.'

Jac's voice came. 'Stay with me here,' he urged, and held out his hand. 'I have a fine house and a good business. I can house you and Mistress Tippy—'

'And my son, what of him? My only family now.' Her gaze was cold.

Tippy sucked in a breath.

Jac stared at his sister. He waited a beat until the words in his head made sense. 'I can look after all of you.'

'Can you?' Lilpah snapped. She waved towards the door. 'Daniel and Lester? Oh, you have no idea what all this is about.' Tippy struggled to keep her upright.

Jac looked down to the carvings in his hand. 'It's about this,' he said, his shoulders heavy. 'It's about these, what our father made for our mother. It's about family, about connection, and blood.' He held hers out to her.

She drooped as energy fled her. 'I don't want it. It didn't keep me safe or rid me of evil. Childish notions. I've no use for it.' Then she closed Jac's fingers over the broken pieces. 'You keep it,' she said tiredly, then absently patted two fingers on his sleeve.

Her touch was a blow to him. Her cool hands were just as he remembered, light and firm, but he took no comfort. 'Stay, Lilpah. Be my sister. Be my family.'

She pulled back. 'We're strangers, Jac. Let it be.'

'I can't. You've always been here.' He tapped his chest, then his head. 'I always knew I'd find you.' He watched a light flicker in her eye. 'I always thought to go back to Wales.'

The light vanished. 'Wales,' she said.

'We'll find a way.'

She shook her head. 'Be on your own way. *Yr wyf yn falch o'ch gweld chi, fy mrawd,*' she said, beckoning for Tippy to help her as she walked from the room.

Jac's head pounded. He stared after them, his chin shook. He couldn't grasp the Welsh. 'What did you say?' When she didn't turn, his anger surged. 'What did you *say*?'

Ben grabbed his arm. 'Jac.'

At the door Tippy turned. Lilpah moved past her, into the hallway towards the stairs. 'She said, "I'm glad to have seen you, my brother."'

Jac took heart. 'Tippy, we'll meet again, my sister and I,' he said, and looked down at his open palm and the pieces of his sister's spoon resting in it.

'Perhaps ye will, young Jac.' Then Tippy closed the door behind them.

# CHAPTER
# THIRTY-FIVE

Daniel Owen sat in his hotel room on the end of his bed. He stared at his hands. Turned them over as if answers lay in his palms.

What should he do with the knowledge he'd had for the two days since Sir Hugh's 'accident'? And who to trust with that knowledge?

*

In his room, Crawford eyed Lester, his mouth grim. 'You, sir, are not yet of age.'

Lester shouted, 'My father is incapacitated and cannot order his house.'

'He's been like it for many years, and still, he's not dead yet,' Crawford enunciated clearly. 'And I have informed you before, sir, that I was employed to ensure that should he become so incapacitated, the responsibility of the house falls upon me until you are of age. You know that.' He waved the young man into a seat. Good

God, he needed to keep Lester in line at least until they all got back home, where he could hand it all over to Mr Oswald.

Lester fell onto a chair by the small desk. 'I say we push on with this deal. Shore up the investments—'

'Hasty and ill-advised, even if I hadn't already told Mr Owen that we would not be going ahead.'

Lester made a noise. 'Mr Owen. A colonial braggart. New money, no society. No title.'

'He needs no title here.'

*

Lester knocked on Daniel's door and walked in with a stout bottle rum, but Daniel already had a jug on the table by the window. His glass was empty.

'Here's another so we don't run out,' Lester said and grabbed two cups, pouring a generous shot into each. He pushed one in Daniel's direction, he said, 'Life of excitement here, isn't it? What a bloody mess.'

Daniel lifted his chin. 'Who'd have thought?' He grabbed the tot of rum and downed it.

Lester refilled it, a little surprised at Daniel's mild sarcasm. He said nothing and downed his own. He poured another shot for each.

'Where's Mr Crawford?' Daniel asked.

'Skulking about in his room. Why?'

'I'd like a word.'

'Probably packing his bag in case my father drops dead so he can scuttle to the first ship sailing for England.'

'And how is Sir Hugh?' Daniel asked, his gaze on the tot in his hand.

'No more news. I'm not hopeful, though. He can't last much longer, for Christ's sake, and God only knows what will happen if he dies here. Crawford says we must hold fast, not make a move on the colonial company. He takes over should my father become ... well, as he is, or if he dies. He's in charge now.' He took a swallow of rum. 'Much as I'd like to override Crawford, I can't. Even if I was of legal age, I know my experience is lacking—I'd do more harm to our ailing estate than good.' Daniel looked up at that and Lester went on. 'It's ailing, we both know it. I don't know how it's held on for this long. I can't wait to have a crack at it, find where all the money is stashed.'

Daniel nodded, nursed his next drink, his eyes still on his cup. 'My ... mother. It must've been a shock for her, to learn of her brother.'

'I imagine so. And you, to learn you have an uncle here in the colony. A rich one at that, if you don't take into account the mortgage he has. Though Mr Crawford said that your uncle could pay it out if he uses up his ready cash, which he has a lot of, apparently.' Lester was impressed.

Daniel, appearing to listen, nodded again. He was silent for some time, his gaze still downcast. 'Do you ever wonder about the Oswalds? Why we were never allowed to visit there, visit your family? Why we only saw them a few times a year when they visited at Rigg Manor?'

'What the hell made you think of that?'

'Odd times, odd thoughts,' Daniel said.

Lester shrugged. 'Only what we've both always thought over the years, that it was because of some feud. When I'm of age, I'll make sure to get to know them better. I feel I might be in need of family. Other family,' he qualified, and shifted in his seat. His friend's heavy mood was unsettling. 'After all, I intend to redress the situation at the manor. Bring it back to its glory. I'll need to know my neighbours, especially as they're family.' He leaned over and shook Daniel's shoulder. 'Things will change for the better when we get back home, good friend.'

Daniel looked up, the light in his eyes bright. 'Yes. Things will change.'

*

Tippy pulled open the door. 'Mr Daniel. Come in, come in.'

'Good afternoon, Mistress Tippy,' he said and stepped into the room the women shared. Lilpah was sitting by the window, fanning herself, encouraging the warm breeze to move about her. She smiled at him.

'Take some tea with us,' Tippy said, then winked, delighted to see him. 'Unless you'd like to share some sherry? We told the house-girl it was fer—'

'Mama.' He nodded to Lilpah. 'Though should I still call you "Mama"?' he asked of Lil, his soft brown gaze on her.

*

Crawford frowned at the knock on his door. He'd just lit a candle, preparing to write another letter to Mr Oswald. He only had to follow original instructions, but the situation appeared to be going off the rails. He'd have to be very firm with Lester and didn't like the idea overly much. He prayed for Sir Hugh to die in the night and save everyone a protracted stay in this hot-as-Hades colony, with a young man who might soon be out of his control.

He went to the door. 'Daniel.' Surprised, he stepped aside. 'Come in.'

The young man stalked past him. A faint breath of rum came with him, but Daniel seemed to be sober enough. Maybe the two lads had partaken of a bracing drink after the events of earlier in the afternoon.

'Mr Crawford,' Daniel said and stood in the middle of the room, agitated, his fingers rubbing the thumbs of each hand. 'You wrote a letter to Mr Oswald, the one I mailed two days ago.'

Crawford felt the young man's disquiet. *What on earth is this?* 'A

362

matter of business for him. He'd been interested in first-hand news of the colony.' It was a story both he and Oswald had decided would work, if questioned.

'Yet you are employed by Sir Hugh.'

Crawford took a deep silent breath. 'But as Mr Oswald is related to Lester, the man has expressed—'

'Is he related to Lester?' Daniel's eyes, usually warm and fun-filled, were stern.

'Of course. You know it.' Crawford frowned, and felt himself beginning to falter at Daniel's blunt interruption. 'Lady Johanna Oswald was Lester's mother. The poor woman—'

'Lester is Sir Hugh's son, but he's not Lady Johanna's son, Mr Crawford.'

Crawford faltered, then snorted. 'Young man, your manners.' He knew then, suddenly, that he'd been under a connivance, that maybe he'd even allowed it. Morris Oswald had employed him to protect his *nephew*. He, like others, presumed that to be Lester. Percy Crawford might be in the grip of a more powerful blackmailer than he already believed. God knows, Oswald had him over a barrel when he first employed him. It would explain everything ...

Daniel shook his head. 'Manners? Yes, I'm remiss. I've been brought up much better than that, and by two women who are baseborn, who are treated with disrespect and scorn. Yet their manners show grace in the light of what has been perpetrated on them by Sir Hugh.'

Straightening up to his own imperious best, Crawford said, 'Mr Owen, I have no knowledge of what—'

'My name is not Owen. My real mother, Lady Johanna, is Sir Hugh's legal wife. My name is Rigg.' He paused. 'Unfortunately.'

'No,' Mr Crawford breathed, trying to deflect Daniel. 'Not pos-sible.' *But it is, somehow. It is.*

Daniel went on. 'You've only to look at Lester, at Mistress Lilpah, and at Jac Owen to see a resemblance there.'

'Yes, but these sorts of things can be explained—'

'Just moments ago, I spoke to the woman who I've called "mother" all my life.' His face darkened under a frown. 'Lilpah Owen confirmed to me that Lester is her born son and that I am Lady Johanna's son.' He pointed a finger. 'You will write another letter to my true uncle, Morris Oswald.' He stepped closer, eyes flashing in anger. 'And I'll tell you exactly what needs to be said.'

# Epilogue

Standing under shelter on the deck of the *Song-chol*, Jac watched the rain pelt into its depths. The empty barge, *Sea-maid*, was at his landing on the bank of the mighty river, tied to a pike further along, and bobbed as it rode a ripple of waves.

He'd just finished loading on board the wood for the steamer. The cart, its horse waiting patiently, stood a few yards away up a gentle slope, ready to be driven back and reloaded from the stockpile under cover at the back of Jac's house.

He didn't reckon being a bullocky today would be a happy occupation. The bales of wool they stacked onto massive drays the day before were on their way to Adelaide. The journey would be fraught; the wet weather over that steep descent into the city played havoc with bullock teams. Chances were the load would be late to port.

'Ahoy the cap'n,' Ben called. He sprinted to the gangway and ran onto the boat, his gait nimble belying his age. 'Almost beat that,' he said, pointing skywards at a heavy dark cloud. 'Pouring down in the town.' He handed Jac a wrapped bundle. 'Mail. Might be a letter in that lot to interest you.'

Jac flipped open the rawhide packet and withdrew the tied envelopes. Amid the notices from his wholesale merchants, invoices for payment, and notes of invitations for him and Ben, his gaze fell on Mr Crawford's letter.

What news would it hold for him—Sir Hugh's death? Surely the old bastard wasn't still holding on. His sister's death? She hadn't answered his letter, but he'd keep trying and would write another until either she answered or someone else did. A burn of frustration bubbled in his chest.

What else would Crawford have to write to him about? Business between the companies was finished, and more than a month had passed. He and Ben decided to use all their available cash, bar a tiny sum, to pay out their mortgage. That way, their business was safe from another takeover, safe from any banker's nervous shenanigans.

He tapped Crawford's unopened letter on his thigh and slid it back into the packet. Had Lilpah—

'We still going upriver end of the week?' Ben asked. He took off the cap he wore these days to shake raindrops from it.

Before he jammed it back on, Jac noticed again that his friend's head of hair was more white streaks than dark, and his knuckles were knobby with arthritis. *Time marches resolutely, my old friend.*

'We are,' Jac said. 'Big consignment to load and take down to Renmark.' Jac looked out over the river to the other bank. The trees, tall and still had their roots at its edge. There was no breeze, and no other sound than the steady drum of rain hitting the earth, the cabin roof of the boat, the water.

He looked for one tree in particular on that side, a sturdy youngster it seemed. Jac knew from the older men around the place that these slow growing trees—river gums— looked older than they were. The tree he sought had a branch that stuck out at a ninety-degree angle. A landmark for him, so to speak. He reckoned it to be about thirty, maybe forty years old, that it would've begun to shoot in that loose soil of the bank at about the same time that he'd been born in Wales.

It hadn't seen what he'd seen in his life. He looked for the tree now, this marker of home, of a place he could trust that would be his for as long as he wanted. No one would displace him, chain him, chase him or drive him off.

He stood on a boat named for his brother who'd lost his life on the sea. He looked at the barge, named for a sea-diving woman who'd become his mother. He lived on land he owned, the block he'd named '*Appa*', where he'd planted ceremony stones to signal to the spirits that the souls of his Korean family would be safe here if they visited. He placed his hand over the small carvings of both spoons that hung around his neck, the only connection to his birth parents, long dead, and to Lilpah, his sister. He hadn't named anything for her—she wasn't dead unless that was the news in Mr Crawford's letter.

'You all right, lad?' Ben asked.

The rain was easing. Jac looked up to a break in the clouds, the last of the drizzle tapering off as the sun shone through. 'I'm all right.'

'The letter from Mr Crawford. Open it, get it out of the way. It can only mean one of two things.' He clapped a hand on Jac's shoulder.

Jac reefed it out of the packet, tore the seal carefully, and unfolded the large sheet of paper. He read aloud.

'"Dear Mr Owen, I write to inform you that, after the death late last month of Sir Hugh Rigg, in Her Majesty's Colony of South Australia—"'

Jac took a moment, searching. He felt nothing. Rigg's death didn't magically change anything, but he thought he'd have felt something. Maybe later when it all sank in.

. Ben barked a laugh. 'I note Crawford doesn't use any niceties, no *sad* or *regretful occasion*.'

'"—Mistress Lilpah Owen elected to return to Wales and at the time of writing, is one week bound on the clipper, *City of Adelaide*, due to make the dock at London some two months and two weeks hence."'

Jac gave a wry laugh. 'The *City of Adelaide*. You remember, Ben? Mr Harris, who bought a share in Wheal Blinman also bought a share in the very same clipper to haul the copper to market.' He continued to read from the letter. '"I am also bid to inform you that the Honourable Lester Rigg and Mr Daniel Owen have accompanied her, along with her companion, Mistress Bowman. Mistress Owen wished you well and congratulated you and Mr Polites in your endeavours.

'"It's not clear to me at this time that you'll be contacted in the future by any member of the aforesaid party. I take this opportunity to join Mistress Owen and congratulate you on your fine business, Southern River Enterprises, and I wish you every success. I remain yours sincerely, Percy Crawford."'

Jac took a moment more to take in what he'd read. He looked at Ben, who tilted his head and said, 'Rough on ye, Jac.'

'I partly expected it. She never answered my letter.' Jac lifted a shoulder, as if he didn't care. He folded the page and tucked it back into the envelope.

He'd follow Lilpah and go to Wales. Back in the Old Country, he'd put to rights this distance between them, get to the bottom of the mystery about Lester. He was certain the boy was Lilpah's son and knowing that his sister was still alive, and that he had more kin, he wasn't about to let—

'If you're thinkin' what I think you're thinkin', don't make a decision just yet,' Ben said, raising his voice over another sudden downpour. 'Give it more time. Things will look different in a few weeks.'

'Aye. Maybe.'

Jac had unfinished business in Wales; he didn't have to take time thinking about it. And then afterwards, he would return to the mighty river in this free country with light and warmth and much opportunity, because it was finally home.

He'd return, no question, and with luck, Ben would still be working with him. He gazed over the river to the other bank and easily found his bent tree. He and that tree would grow old together.

Might be he'd find a good woman to be by his side too, and if all the gods willed, his children would come, and he would never forsake home again.

# ACKNOWLEDGEMENTS

"Trust in Mine" is written, produced and published by San Luro, a collective based on Kangaroo Island, South Australia, partnering with independent writers and filmmakers.

San Luro wishes to acknowledge the contributions of the following individuals;

Darry Fraser, *www.darryfraser.com*

Dion Cavallaro, Paul Thomas, San Quach

Four Point Films, *www.fourpointfilms.com.au*

Susi Parslow

Priscilla Thomas, Joel Naoum, Rebecca Hamilton

Jenni Woodhead, *www.gaiadesignstudio.co.uk*

Andrew Railton, *Chip off the Ol' Block Welsh Lovespoons*

Sandra Muggleton-Mole

Rohan Muggleton-Mole

Lucy Casaretto

Todd Casaretto

www.ingramcontent.com/pod-product-compliance
Lightning Source LLC
Chambersburg PA
CBHW030511120726
47904CB00005B/1423